SUMMER FIRE

SUMMER FIRE

DOUGLAS H. THAYER

Signature Books
Salt Lake City, Utah

Cover painting by J.S. Wixom
Cover design by Philip Barlow
Cover model Jason Kimball

Printed in the United States of America
Salt Lake City, Utah
ISBN 0-941214-18-4
First edition 1983
Second edition 1987

For

Emmelyn, Paul, James, Katherine, and Michael

1

We all stood under the sodium vapor lamp by the running Greyhound bus, except for Randy, who was talking to Lana Baker in the parking lot. The bus was leaving for Las Vegas at three-fifteen. Randy and I were supposed to meet Mr. Johnson's daughter Helen in Las Vegas and take another bus as far as Silverton. One of the ranch hands would pick us up there and drive us the twenty miles out to the Johnson ranch on the Battle River.

Uncle Mark had gotten us our jobs. He wanted to get Randy away from Lana, and he wanted Randy to learn how to work. Uncle Mark had kept telling my mother that I needed to stop reading Church books and practicing the piano for at least one summer; and he said it wouldn't hurt me to be away from my grandmother for a summer either.

Above the noise of the running bus I listened to Uncle Mark talking to my mother and grandmother and Aunt Susan. Diesel exhaust nauseated me. Eight of the through-passengers to Los Angeles stood smoking cigarettes, the smoke curling into the darkness above the high lamp. I turned. Lana sat in her Thunderbird back by the fence at the edge of the light. She put her hands on the open window. Randy bent down and put his hands on top of hers, and then he leaned farther down and kissed her on the arm. Randy was dressed like a cowboy, his Stetson pushed back on his head. I was the only one watching them.

"It's too bad Owen couldn't stay for his birthday Saturday, Mark. It would only be a matter of a few more days."

I turned back to look at my grandmother. She wanted to have a special birthday supper for me Saturday, and then I would be ordained a Priest on Sunday. And she wanted me to be home to receive my Duty to God Award in sacrament meeting as soon as it came. I'd already earned it, and Bishop Matthews was just waiting until I was sixteen to send in my papers.

"He's going to be fine, Maude. Working on a hay ranch for the summer will help make men out of both of them."

My grandmother thought I wasn't strong enough for the hard ranch work and desert heat. I was thin, and I'd been sick a lot before I was fourteen. She wanted me to spend the summer practicing the piano for a new recital, reading, and taking a special algebra class BYU offered for high school students. And she wanted me to be able to see Dr. Parker, my dermatologist, about my face every two weeks until it cleared up.

Uncle Mark said something to my mother I couldn't hear because of the bus. She nodded her head, and he patted her on the shoulder. Uncle Mark was my mother's only brother. My father didn't have any brothers or sisters. I was three when he died just before he would have finished medical school at the University of Utah. My baby brother had been born dead two months earlier, and my mother was still sick from that. Grandmother Nelson came and got us and brought us back to Provo to live in her house. My Grandfather Nelson had died the year before, so she was alone. My Grandfather and Grandmother Williams had died.

Uncle Mark kept talking to my mother. She always looked pale; she had to rest every evening when she got home from work at the telephone company. My grandmother said there was no need for my mother to work if she didn't want to. Uncle Mark reached over and patted my mother on the shoulder again.

Uncle Mark was a real estate agent, and he'd sold property for Mr. Johnson to people in Utah. He'd been to the Johnson ranch twice. He found out there was a branch of the Church we could go to in Silverton, so he asked about summer jobs for Randy and me. Mr. Johnson had emphysema and lived in Las Vegas with his daughter. A foreman named Staver had run the ranch for twelve years with two permanent hands named Stan and Frank, and the housekeeper was Mrs. Cummings.

My grandmother had phoned Mrs. Cummings twice to talk to her about the ranch. Mrs. Cummings had been born in Manti and was a member of the Church, but she wasn't active anymore.

Staver was trying to buy the ranch. He and Mr. Johnson's son Brent had been friends all their lives, and had been drafted and gone to Korea together. Brent had won the Medal of Honor and been killed, and Staver had been wounded in the heart. Mr. Johnson didn't change anything on the ranch after Brent was killed. It was the last ranch at the top of the Battle River valley, and they cut three crops of hay each summer. Uncle Mark told us that they had brush fires every summer along the river, so we would probably have a chance to fight fires.

Above the sound of the bus I heard Uncle Mark explaining again how good the summer would be for Randy and me and how we would get to know each other. Randy was my only male first cousin. My mother's sister Fae, who lived in Salt Lake City, didn't have any boys.

The diesel smell was stronger, and I tried not to breathe deep. The people under the lamp still smoked. I turned to see Randy take off his Stetson, put his head half in the window and kiss Lana on the nose. She put her right hand on his shoulder. Lana was a cheerleader, but she went to seminary. So did Randy, and he planned to go on a mission for the Church. He was on the Provo High wrestling team.

I'd thought that maybe Becky Stewart would come down to see me off. I danced with her at all the ward parties, and we rode our bikes to school together sometimes and ate lunch together. She had lived in the ward a year, and I liked her a lot. I didn't tell her I was leaving, but I thought she might hear about me and Randy and come. I'd never kissed a girl. I didn't think you should until you were engaged.

The bus driver banged the baggage cart out through the metal double doors at the rear of the station.

"There's your bag, son." My grandmother touched my arm.

I nodded. I wanted to work on the Johnson Ranch, but I felt all hollow inside. It was like pain. I'd felt it all week.

Uncle Mark had promised Randy a new Volkswagen for his senior year at Provo High if he worked hard all summer and didn't get fired. Uncle Mark had built a new house in Indian Hills with a swimming pool so that Randy would stay home more and invite his friends. He said that what Randy needed was the kind of discipline they got in the Marine Corps. Uncle Mark had been in the marines, but he didn't ever fight in a war. Around school Randy had a reputation for drinking beer sometimes and playing poker with the football players, but he didn't smoke, and he wasn't immoral. He was very popular. All the girls liked him.

I took off my gold wire-rimmed glasses, polished them with my handkerchief, and put them back on. I was glad to be going to work on the Johnson ranch; I'd always wanted to work on a ranch. Every summer I cut our lawn, helped my grandmother take care of her flowers, and took care of the yards for four of my grandmother's friends in our ward who were widows. We had the biggest yard in the ward, our two-story brick house set back and all surrounded by trees. A pioneer bishop who was a polygamist built the house for one of his six wives. He built a house in Provo for each wife. He became an apostle.

I turned toward the bus station. Somewhere in the darkness somebody was laughing. I saw myself reflected in the big glass window to the right of the glass passenger door. The red neon Coca-Cola sign inside the station cast a faint glow around me.

I stopped now before mirrors, glass doors, big windows. I would ride my bicycle down Center Street at night on the sidewalk past store windows under the neon signs to see myself moving. I wanted to walk into the Academy or Paramount and see a movie of myself since I was born. My body had become different. Sitting in class at school I kept looking at my hands. I'd go in the restroom and comb my hair just to look at my face. It surprised me that I had to think about myself so much.

I'd read *A Mormon Boy's World* and *Sex and the Boy.* In seminary one morning while we were studying the Book of Mormon, Brother Anderson wrote down on the chalkboard the good words for us to think and talk about sex with. He made us say each word as he wrote it down, the boys and girls together, out loud.

"Talk about sex all you want, but don't use obscene words. Why should you be obscene about something that is sacred?"

But it wasn't just sex, puberty, the physical changes in my body, which I'd read all about. It was like I was a big house I'd never been in. I'd always kept the commandments. I had the Aaronic Priesthood and was entitled to see angels. I had been baptized and received the Holy Ghost, who would guide me, and give me knowledge.

Brother Anderson said that we all needed the atonement; he said that the Lord would suffer for our sins if we would let him and his blood wash us clean. I asked Brother Anderson after class if you needed the atonement if you kept all the commandments. He said, no, not if you kept them all, and he asked me if I kept them all.

"I think I have."

"That's good. Keep it up. But keep the Lord in mind. You may need him some day."

Brother Anderson had been a lawyer in Los Angeles for ten years before he moved to Provo and became a seminary teacher because he wanted to do something important. He'd been a sergeant in the infantry in the Second World War, and he had eight children. He invited his seminary classes up to his house in Oak Hills for parties.

The bus driver slammed the doors shut on the baggage bays and walked back into the station. My grandmother took my arm.

"Randy!" Randy turned his head to look at Uncle Mark. "Do you plan to say goodbye to your mother?"

"Sure, Dad." Randy turned back to talk to Lana.

Randy wanted to stay overnight in Las Vegas and see the strip, but Mr. Johnson's daughter Helen was going to meet us there and put us on the bus to Silverton.

The bus driver came through the baggage doors carrying a clipboard. The passengers under the lamp closed their eyes and took long pulls on their cigarettes. Sometimes I went all day in Provo without seeing a person smoke. I wanted to walk over under the lamp and tell them about the Word of Wisdom. You didn't have to smoke, drink tea or coffee or alcoholic beverages, or eat very much meat. They dropped their cigarettes and stepped on them. Smokers died fifteen years earlier than nonsmokers.

"Through-passengers to Los Angeles, please." The driver stood by the open bus door.

"Come on, Randy. You're going to get left." Uncle Mark turned back to say something to Aunt Susan.

Randy leaned in the car window and kissed Lana on the lips. She reached up and put her hand on the side of his head. He kissed her wrist and then stood up. He waved. Lana drove slowly out of the parking lot, her arm out of the window waving. Randy kept waving. Whenever I saw Lana in the hall at school she always said hello. Randy turned and walked over to us.

Uncle Mark shook hands with us both.

"Remember, Randy, if I hear any complaints from Staver or you get fired, you don't get that Volkswagen. And I mean it this time. It's not going to be like the motorcycle. You can't be a playboy all your life. You need to get away from that girl friend of yours for five minutes and learn what work is."

"Don't worry, Dad."

"I won't, but you'd better. Kiss your mother."

My grandmother kissed me. She reached up and pushed my hair back from my forehead with her hand.

"Be careful, son. If you get sick, call us, and we'll come and get you. Wash your face every day with the soap Dr. Parker told you to use."

"I'll be careful." I hugged her tight. I kept swallowing hard. I didn't want to cry. My mother stood looking at me.

"You'll be sixteen when you come back." My grandmother held both my hands. "I remember when your father turned sixteen." She shook her head and smiled. "We'll have a nice birthday supper when you get back. Your father got a beautiful new navy blue suit when he was ordained a Priest."

My grandmother always gave me new clothes for Christmas and my birthday. She'd given me a new white shirt and blue tie for my Duty to God interview with Bishop Matthews. I would be the only boy in the ward with both his Eagle Scout badge and his Duty to God Award.

My grandmother looked down at my hands. She squeezed them.

"I hope that desert sun isn't too hot for you."

"He'll get used to it, Maude." Uncle Mark nodded toward me. "That ranch is in the Battle River Valley, not in the middle of the Nevada desert. It's a beautiful place. It cools off in the evenings."

My grandmother had made an appointment with Dr. Clark for me to get a physical to see if I was strong enough to work on a ranch. After I got dressed, Dr. Clark told me to sit down. Watching him read my chart, I straightened my tie. I didn't like to undress for physicals because without my clothes on I didn't feel like an individual person. I didn't like to be naked in the gym showers.

Dr. Clark looked up.

"Well, you're almost sixteen, now, Owen. Have you got any questions about yourself?"

"No."

Dr. Clark looked down at my chart again and then at me. "What about erections, wet dreams, masturbation—no questions?"

"No. I've read all about puberty."

"Oh, you have." He kept looking at me. "Well, maybe next time. You've been a little slower than most boys developing. Your face looks better, but don't count on that dermatologist being able to help you too much. A boy has to count on a few pimples."

I watched Dr. Clark write on my chart. He'd asked me before about masturbation. A boy didn't have to do that. He could wear pajamas to bed, stay in bed only to sleep, take short showers, wear an athletic supporter, and he didn't have to read obscene stories, or look at obscene pictures, have obscene thoughts. Nocturnal emissions and dreaming about girls were nature's way of releasing sexual tensions. A boy just had to divide his life up into days and concentrate on not doing anything wrong just for one day. Brother Anderson said that some boys became preoccupied with sex and thought it was the most important thing in the world. A boy didn't have to think about girls all the time.

Dr. Clark wrote something down on my chart and looked up.

"Working on this ranch won't kill you, Owen. Your grandmother worries too much about you, but then she did that with your father, too. You're liable to gain some weight and grow an inch this summer. A boy like you can have a real growth spurt in three or four months, but it depends on the boy."

The bus driver stood at the door looking at his clipboard. Randy and I were the only passengers not loaded. A woman wearing a hat looked down at us through the tinted bus window. She was laughing.

My grandmother squeezed my hands once more and let go.

My mother hugged and kissed me. "It will be a good summer for you, son." She wiped her eyes with her handkerchief.

I swallowed hard and breathed deep. "Yes."

"Be careful, son." She hugged and kissed me again.

Uncle Mark shook my hand. "You two are on your own. Don't expect any visits. We'll see you on Labor Day right here."

"Las Vegas and return," the driver said when I handed him my ticket. He marked a column on his clipboard and handed me back part of my ticket. Keep that so you can come home.

"Thank you."

I climbed the steps into the dark bus ahead of Randy. The cooled air smelled like cigarettes, diesel fuel, and upholstery. I found two seats halfway back and slid across to the window. Randy sat down. He still wore his Stetson.

The driver walked back through the bus, and then he shut the door. The bus engine grew louder behind me, and we backed out. I waved. Randy leaned across to wave. I watched until the corner of the station blocked my view.

"It's going to be worth it to get that Volks," Randy said. He adjusted his seat to lay back as far as possible. "I'll bet I can talk Dad into a Triumph. That's what I really want. A car of my own—it'll be bitchin'." Randy tipped his Stetson hat down over his face. "Wake me when it's over."

I didn't want a car; I wanted an Avanti, a ten-speed bicycle made in Italy that cost six hundred dollars. The name meant "go." I was going to buy a new Schwinn in September with some of the money I would save. An Avanti was too expensive. Studies showed that boys who drove cars in high school didn't get grades as high as those who didn't. But girls liked boys with cars.

Through the bus window I watched the dark houses. My grandmother had wanted Uncle Mark to drive us to Silverton, but he said we'd probably get there alive on the bus. I sat up and turned. Across the aisle and back one row a man had lit a cigarette. I turned twice to see him. When the bus stopped for the Seventh East light, I stepped over Randy's feet and went up front and told the driver.

"I can't do anything about it, kid."

"But it's against the law, isn't it?"

"Everybody else is asleep. People got to smoke sometime, even in Utah. We got air-conditioning in these buses."

I stood there.

"You better go sit back down, kid. Passengers aren't allowed to talk to drivers while the bus is moving." He shifted gears. "That guy'll be going to sleep in a minute."

Randy lifted his Stetson when I climbed back over his feet.

"What was that all about, cousin?"

I told him.

He groaned. "It's going to be a long summer." He pulled his Stetson back down over his face.

Behind me in the bus somebody suddenly started laughing, and then stopped. I watched out the window. Above the houses and the trees lightning flashed in the darkness. I didn't like to be called kid. A person could stop smoking if he really tried.

The bus was passing the Provo Cemetery. The sixty-foot-high black spruces came out to the fence. In the summer evenings I would ride my bicycle out to sit by my father's grave. It was cool and dark there under the spruces where he and my Grandfather Nelson were buried.

I had my father's room. When I was little my grandmother told me that my father watched me from the spirit world and helped me. Lying in my father's bed at night in his room, which my grandmother had always kept the same, I would watch the full-length mirror on the back of the closet door. I thought that my father would appear in the mirror and step out. I wished that he would, that he would sit on the bed and talk to me. But when I woke up he wasn't there or in the mirror. I lay looking at his picture on the lamp table by my bed. In every room my grandmother had pictures of my father. When she talked to me about him she always picked up his picture. She said that she was going to redecorate my bedroom while I was gone.

I watched the cemetery out of sight and sat back. I closed my eyes but didn't try to go to sleep. I didn't take off my glasses.

I dreamed a lot now. I dreamed about flying by just waving my arms. I flew everywhere—over Provo, through the halls at

Provo High, over the mountains. I dreamed about losing my clothes and having to hide because I couldn't find them. I saved children from drowning and from burning houses and was awarded medals, and I played piano concerts, won races and football and basketball games against East High School in Salt Lake City. Dreaming was like not being asleep, so my dreams became part of my memories, and I had to think about my dreams sometimes to know if they were real or not because I'd started to dream about girls. I didn't know that I would think about girls so much.

Lying back in my seat, I kept my eyes closed. I still felt hollow inside, but it didn't hurt so much now.

Outside Nephi the bus slowed down. I opened my eyes. We were on a new section of freeway. A car was turned over. Two bodies lay covered with blankets. The flashing red lights threw a red glare inside the bus. I turned to watch the lights fade. I was going to be a doctor like my father and save lives.

I woke up outside of St. George, where we ate breakfast. I wanted to take a shower. In the restroom I rinsed out my mouth with water; I wished I'd brought a toothbrush. I checked my face. Randy bought two car magazines and a bag of candy kisses. The *Newsweek* cover said, "The Holocaust—Twenty Years Later." Brother Anderson had made us study about the Holocaust in seminary.

"You want some candy?" Randy held out the sack.

"No thanks." It wasn't good for my face. Every morning I checked to see if I had any new pimples.

"I'll be glad when we're in Nevada."

On the counter was a wire rack full of Book of Mormons. The sign said You're in Mormon Country.

South of St. George I watched the desert begin. I'd never been in a real desert before. Ravens and magpies fed on the car-killed jackrabbits, and we passed a National Guard convoy. Randy kept leaning across me watching for the Nevada border sign. When we crossed, he sat back in his seat.

"We're in Nevada now."

Passengers who hadn't been smoking before lit cigarettes now. It felt funny not to be in Utah anymore. The bus went faster. Except on the completed sections of freeway, there were no speed limit signs. I hadn't known that Nevada didn't have speed limits. Randy said that he knew it.

We stopped in Mesquite and Randy played the one-armed bandits. The sign on the wall said that you had to be twenty-one, but nobody stopped him. I asked him why he did it, and he said because it was fun. He said he wasn't hurting anybody. I'd read a book called *The Las Vegas Gambler.* When people lost all their money they sold things so they could keep gambling. They bought guns and robbed service stations. They got divorced right in Las Vegas, stayed drunk for days, committed suicide.

I bought an orangeade. All the ashtrays were bronzed curled rattlesnakes. Mesquite was hotter than St. George, and I was glad when we left.

"You boys going to Disneyland? I'm Matt Wayne. Glad to know you, son."

Mr. Wayne reached across the aisle and shook my hand. He'd gotten on in Mesquite. Randy sat by the window; he wanted to watch Nevada.

"No, sir. We're going to work for the summer on the Johnson ranch by Silverton."

He leaned toward me across the aisle. He was old and had a big fat stomach and a round red face. His cowboy hat was dirty.

"Ya, I know old Johnson. He's a good man. Staver runs that place for him now. Got all shot up in the Korean war, and carries a big scar from it they say. He's a mean man in a fight they say. Knows how to use his hands."

Mr. Wayne leaned farther out into the aisle and tapped my knee. "Son, I own the biggest ranch in Nevada, the Bonanza. Got over a million acres. I got two hundred thousand head of purebred herefords. I run a hundred thousand head of purebred suffolk sheep and over ten thousand horses. I got twenty oil wells on my ranch, and I got one gold mine and two silver mines. Son, how old do you think I am? I'm ninety-nine years old. Be a hundred in September. The governor of this state is going to come to my birthday party, maybe the president. I had to fight Indians to get that ranch."

"It sounds like a wonderful ranch."

"Son, it is. It's been a real bonanza." Mr. Wayne laughed. "Son, they make movies on my ranch. I know all the cowboy movie stars. I teach 'em how to shoot and ride. They buy their horses from me."

Mr. Wayne kept telling me stories about his ranch and fighting Indians. He laughed after every story, and he took the Lord's name in vain. He rolled a cigarette and put it in his mouth, and then he told a story about a man who wet his pants in a gunfight. He laughed. He didn't light the cigarette. I wanted to ask him what he knew about the Church, but I didn't get a chance. Every member was supposed to be a missionary.

"There's Las Vegas," Randy said. He pointed out the window.

"Go ahead. Take a look, son." Mr. Wayne reached across the aisle and pushed my arm. "That's quite a town. I've lost fifty thousand dollars in one night more than once and never gave it a thought. I've won a lot too. Take a look, son. Go ahead."

I sat forward and leaned across Randy.

Tall glaring pastel buildings rose at the center of the city. "See those buildings all in a line on the west side. That's the strip." Randy pointed. I watched the buildings, and then I watched the people on the sidewalks and in the cars. I knew that Las Vegas was the biggest gambling city in America.

"Son, it's a great town if you want to have a good time." Mr. Wayne laughed.

We drove into Las Vegas to the Greyhound bus station. Mr. Wayne got off in front of me; he shook my hand and told me goodbye. He walked off across the parking lot laughing. Nobody was there to pick him up.

"Who was that?"

"A rancher."

Mr. Wayne walked down the glaring street shaking his head and laughing. I couldn't understand why he rode the bus if he had so much money. Big ranchers had airplanes.

"Come on and get your bag, cousin."

In the cool smoky bus station I phoned Mr. Johnson's daughter. She said that she wanted to take us out to eat. Our bus to Silverton didn't leave until five-thirty. Randy phoned Lana to tell her that he was in Las Vegas. I sat by our bags. I'd never seen so many people smoking. People sat bent forward with their heads in their hands smoking and looking at the floor. I watched the front door. Mr. Johnson's daughter would be wearing a yellow dress. She told me to call her Helen.

A woman pushed open the big glass door. She stopped, looked around, and then walked out again. I watched two more women do that. They all wore tight bright blouses and pants. They carried purses on straps. I'd read that a lot of prostitutes lived in Las Vegas, and they were all registered with the police and had to have physical examinations. I couldn't understand how a woman could need money so much that she would let a man rent her body. The three women all had white blonde hair. No prostitutes lived in Provo.

Randy stood at the magazine rack eating a Power House candy bar and looking at a magazine. I stood up and walked over, but I watched our bags. Randy stood in front of a high double stack of *Playboys*, and he was looking at one.

"Want one?"

"No, I don't."

"They're interesting."

I looked at the rows of fishing, hunting, car, detective, war, girl, and cowboy magazines. I'd never seen so many cowboy magazines. The picture of the concentration camp on the front of the *Newsweek* was in black and white.

I turned to watch the door. Miss Johnson walked out of the sunlight. She stopped, the light behind her. She was tall and thin, and her brown hair gleamed around the edges, her dress pale yellow. She smiled and I walked toward her.

"You're Owen." She held out her hand. "I'm Helen Johnson."

"I'm glad to meet you, Miss Johnson."

"Please call me Helen, Owen." She didn't let my hand go. She looked at me, her smile very faint. "You remind me a little bit of my brother Brent. He wore glasses like yours, and he was fair. He was killed in Korea."

"Yes my Uncle Mark told me that. I'm sorry." She let go of my hand. Her hand was cool. "Uncle Mark said Brent won the Medal of Honor."

"Yes, he did. He was a very nice person. He loved everybody."

I wanted to ask her what her brother had done to win the Medal of Honor. I'd always wanted to be in a war and win it, but I didn't want to kill anybody. I'd read a book called *Medal of Honor.* A Medal of Honor winner got a special pension from the government; his son could go to West Point, and other soldiers saluted him. The book was full of stories about men who had won the Medal of Honor.

Randy came over, and I introduced him.

Helen raised her left hand to smooth back her hair. She wore a large diamond engagement ring. She had one gold bracelet on her right wrist. She told us that her father was in the hospital, so he would have to see us at the ranch when he was well enough to ride in a car.

"He's sorry he can't be here to meet you. We would have liked to have you stay at our house overnight. You could go for a swim. But maybe you can do that in September when you go home. Well, would you like to go out to the Tropicana for lunch? We've got plenty of time."

"Great," Randy said. "That's out on the strip."

Helen smiled. "Haven't you ever seen the strip, Randy?"

"No."

"We'll have time to see some of it."

"Great."

"Have you seen it, Owen?"

"No, I haven't seen it."

We walked out from under the station canopy into the white sunlight and the heat. Helen stopped and unlocked the trunk of a new blue four-door Buick. We put our bags in and closed the lid.

"We can all ride in front." Helen unlocked the door for us. I walked around and opened her door after she unlocked it. The Buick had air-conditioning.

"Thank you, Owen."

Driving out, Helen asked us about our families and Provo. She said that a lot of Mormons lived in Las Vegas. They had a reputation for having strong families. She said that she had Mormon friends who had told her about the Church.

"The missionaries tracted our street two years ago, and I saw two of them on bicycles again last week. They look so clean."

"I plan to go on a mission."

"That's nice, Owen. Do you plan to go too, Randy?"

"Sure."

I didn't ask Helen if she wanted to know more about the Church. It didn't seem necessary. I sat so the cool air hit my face.

After we ate lunch Helen took us to see the other big casinos. The red-carpeted rooms were full of people gambling. Some people played two and three one-armed bandits at one time. They had stacks of coins on the trays, and they had a cigarette in one hand and a glass in the other while they played. A lot of older women played, their hair tinted blue or orange. It was like they didn't have anything else to do. All the casinos were air-conditioned, but they were still full of smoke. We drove from the Sands Hotel back into town to meet our bus.

The bus was an old school bus painted green and had all the windows down. The five other passengers stood in the shade. The driver was in the drugstore.

Helen shook hands with us, and I walked her back to her car and opened the door. She started the engine and then looked up at me.

"You do look like Brent. You remind me of him a little in other ways too." She smiled. "Goodbye, Owen. You and Randy have a good summer."

"We will."

"Say hello to everybody."

She waved as she drove away and I waved back. I turned and walked over to where Randy stood in the shade.

"How'd you like to have a woman and a car like that?

I looked at Randy. "She's a nice person."

"Did you get a good look at that ring? I'll bet it cost about five thousand."

I walked over and picked up my bag and got on the bus. We sat in the seats behind the driver.

We drove north out of Las Vegas across the flat bare desert toward Silverton, which was ninety miles away. I looked at my watch. The sun was turning orange, but it was still hot. All the low mountains were barren except at the top. I asked the driver why the desert along the road was all torn up, and he said that the Army had had tank maneuvers the previous week. Two ravens flew low following the edge of the road.

The driver turned and asked us where we were going. I told him. I had to speak loud because of the air coming in the open windows. I could see the speedometer. We were going seventy.

"Hope you boys like work."

"Do you know Staver?

"Sure. He's a good old boy. He got all shot up in Korea. You won't believe that scar he's got on him till you see it. That's when the Johnson kid got killed winning the Medal of Honor. That's a pretty ranch up there on that river." The driver lit a cigarette and reached the pack and the matches back over his shoulder. "You boys want a smoke?"

"We don't smoke. We're Mormons."

Randy started coughing. He stomped his feet and shook his head.

"Good for you. I got a brother who's one. He and his wife give up smoking, drinking, and everything else when they joined. They like it a lot. It's good for their kids." The driver flicked the ash from his cigarette. "Wish I'd never started. It'll kill you. Too late now though, so I might as well enjoy it." He blew smoke against the windshield.

"Has your brother told you very much about the Church?"

"Hey, look at those two eagles on that ledge." Randy pointed out through the windshield.

"They're vultures," I said. I had my bird-watching merit badge.

"Vultures all right." The driver blew out the smoke. "Lots of them around here. You have to be careful not to have a wreck out on any of these back desert roads. We had one last summer. Killed five college boys from Stanford. Station wagon went off a ledge; threw 'em all out. Sheriff didn't find it till the next day, and when he did there was nothing left but bones and hair. That flock of vultures even ate the clothes, including the wallets. The sheriff had to fly in all the dental records to identify those skeletons. Of course the hair helped some. Vultures don't eat hair. Happens to California people all the time. It was in all the papers. You have to keep moving in this country."

"Brother," Randy said. He leaned across me to look back at the ledge.

"That's terrible."

The driver looked straight ahead out through the windshield. He hunched forward, both hands high on the steering wheel. He turned on his lights.

I'd read about vultures. They specialized. Some had big heavy beaks for breaking bones; others had small pointed beaks for cleaning the meat out of joints. Some vultures didn't have feathers on their necks so they could reach into the stomach without getting dirty. I'd never read anything about vultures eating clothes or not eating hair.

We drove up over low hills and out into barren valleys ten miles wide where no cattle grazed. A fire had burned a big area of sagebrush along the road. Far ahead were dark high mountains. The whole land had become full of shadows. Jackrabbits ran across the road. The west sky turned red above the disappearing sun, like half the earth was on fire. Far out ahead a cluster of lights glowed at the bottom of the mountains.

"That's Silverton, boys, straight ahead."

Randy sat up. I watched the light grow closer. I looked at my watch. A dead skunk lay in the middle of the road.

"Brother those things do stink. You boys better get used to it. Lots of skunks around."

Twenty minutes later we passed the first houses, which didn't have lawns or flowers. We drove down Silver Street. The neon signs above the bars and casinos reflected red light in the windows and on the parked cars and pickups. All the pickups had gun racks in the back windows with guns in them. Two men wearing cowboy hats walked into a place called the Volcano Club. The neon sign over the door was a red erupting volcano. They were the only two people on the street.

The bus stopped in front of the World Hotel. We were the only ones who got off. I looked up. The blinds were pulled down on all the hotel's upstairs windows.

"You boys have a good time this summer." The driver didn't stand up. "Don't let old Staver kill you off."

"We won't. Thank you."

"Lots of luck."

Someone in the bus laughed. Holding my bag, I watched the bus turn the corner. A banner hung across the street advertising the Fourth of July celebration—a carnival, rodeo, horse race, and picnic.

Carrying our bags, we crossed the hot street to the Silverton Cafe, where we were supposed to meet Stan from the ranch. All the wooden buildings made it look like a street in a western. Cool air came out through the cafe screen door. A short thin bald man dressed like a cowboy sat alone at the counter smoking and drinking coffee and talking to the waitress. His hat was pushed back. He turned to look at us.

"Well, Alice, it looks like the new summer hands have just arrived."

"Looks like it, Stan. Hello, boys. Come on in."

We walked in. "Hello, ma'am."

"Hi."

The cafe was clean and cool and had a nice smell.

"So you're the ones for this year," Stan said. "Never had any from Utah before." He put his cigarette in the ash tray.

We introduced ourselves and shook hands.

"Well, I guess you'll have to do. Hope you know how to work."

"We do," I said.

"Now, Stan, they look like fine boys. Randy already looks like a cowboy. You boys want a piece of pie on the house?"

Stan got down off the stool. "Thanks, Alice, but Mrs. Cummings is waiting supper on 'em, and Staver wants 'em after that. We still got to go over to Thurman's and get their stuff. See you, Alice."

"Be good, Stan. Why don't you come Saturday night with Frank and Staver?"

"Getting too old, Alice. Can't party all weekend and go to work Monday morning anymore. Not a young buck."

She laughed and started wiping the counter again. "You never know till you try, Stan."

"I've tried. See you, Alice."

"See you, Stan. You boys have a good summer. We'll see you out to the ranch maybe. Say hello to Staver for me, Stan. Hey and don't forget to tell him Cliff got out today. He's on parole. They gave him time off for good behavior."

"I'll tell him."

"Goodbye, ma'am."

"You boys be sure and come to the Fourth of July. That's our big celebration."

"Thank you."

We walked outside.

"That's Staver's girl friend; she's a mighty nice lady." Stan stopped. He broke the paper on his cigarette, dropped the tobacco on the sidewalk and stepped on it, and then he rolled the paper into a ball and flipped it away.

"That's called field-stripping. It's something Staver learned in the army and what you're supposed to do because of all the brush fires we get up on the river."

"We don't smoke."

"Well, you won't have to worry about startin' any fires then." Stan nodded toward a blue pickup. "You boys can throw your bags in the back."

I set my bag in. Back against the cab were two empty wooden Hercules dynamite boxes. We walked down the sidewalk with Stan.

"Used to be an old mining town. Lots of fights, lots of shootin' in the old days. You could fill a five gallon bucket with the lead slugs in these walls. Maybe a ten gallon bucket."

I looked at the wooden building fronts for bullet holes.

"They'd shoot four or five men on an average Saturday night." Stan blew out smoke. "In here."

The painted sign on the big window said, "Thurman's—Groceries, Hardware, Liquor, Guns." I caught the wooden screen door behind me and walked in. It was cool. I stopped. The whole left side of the store was shelves of dark bottles all the way to the ceiling. A ladder on wheels stood by the shelves. I'd never been in a liquor store before. Provo had one state liquor store.

Drinking alcoholic beverages caused divorce, disease, bankruptcy, automobile accidents, child abuse, and murder. I'd read a book called *Drinking and the Young American.* I didn't know how anybody could drink. It wasn't very intelligent.

Stan introduced us to Mr. Thurman, who had white hair.

"Glad to know you boys."

We each had to buy a folding sheath knife, three pairs of leather work gloves, six big red bandana handkerchiefs, and a wide-brimmed straw cowboy hat. Behind Mr. Thurman was a long rack of rifles and shotguns, and shelves of ammunition; the pistols were under the glass counter.

"You can save that Stetson for Saturday nights, Randy. Wear these straw hats outside or that sun will cook your brains in about an hour. We had to haul a kid named Smith into Las Vegas to the hospital two summers ago. His momma had to come and get him all the way from Los Angeles."

We paid for our things. Randy bought a candy bar and he walked over to look at the magazines.

"That's an Eagle Scout ring you're wearing, isn't it, son?"

I looked up at Mr. Thurman. "Yes, sir."

"That's a fine thing to be. My boy Steve is an Eagle."

"Do they have Scouts here?"

"Why sure, son. The Community Church runs a Scout troop and an Explorer post, too. Have for years. They do a fine job."

"Let's go. Staver's waitin'."

"Hope you boys have a good summer. Say hello to everybody out at the ranch."

"Thank you."

Randy flipped through the last pages of the *Playboy* and laid it down.

"Say, Stan, did you hear Cliff was out?"

"Ya. Alice was telling us."

"Everybody's glad about it. Cliff just had too much to drink that night or he'd never shot that deputy. He grew up a nice kid. Nearly killed his folks when they heard about it."

"Well, he's back now."

I went out. I wanted to ask Stan about who Cliff was and what had happened, but I didn't think that I should. I didn't see how a person could shoot another person he knew.

Randy stood in front of the casino next door looking in through the open doors and eating his candy bar, a giant Butterfinger. Loud music came out through the doors.

"Let's go."

Randy turned and walked over to the pickup. I let him get in first because I wanted the window if Stan smoked. Behind me in the casino somebody started to laugh loud. I got in.

Stan started the engine and backed out and drove down Silver Street. Both windows were down. The pickup wasn't air-conditioned. I turned to look at Stan.

"Does it always stay this hot—even at night?"

"Cools off some at night up in the valley, but it's hot during the day, and it's going to get a lot hotter before you go home. A lot hotter." Randy groaned and slid down in his seat.

2

The moon was full. Trailing a plume of dust we climbed high up through sagebrush hills and then cut across through black lava ledges into the mouth of a mile-wide river valley. I found the North Star. I watched the silhouetted mountains for extinct volcanoes, but I saw none. I had my geology merit badge. I wanted to know the names of all the rocks and minerals there were. Heavy brush grew on the sides of the mountains; the river was lined with dark trees. We crossed a wooden bridge over the silver river. I watched the speedometer. Stan drove fast.

"That's Battle River." Stan blew smoke against the windshield and nodded down toward the river. "The Indians had a big fight around here. Got a monument back a ways."

I turned but I couldn't see the monument. I watched the dark trees. The Indians were the descendants of the Lamanites in the Book of Mormon. In terrible wars the Lamanites killed all of the Nephites, who had become so evil that they had lost all love for each other, and the Lord didn't help them any more.

We crossed the river again on another wooden bridge.

Jones, Blake, Taylor, Fillmore, Miller—Stan named each ranch as we passed. The lighted houses stood in groves of high trees. At the side of each front gate was a small shed painted red with "Fire Tools" written on it in white.

"Pretty ranches along this river, but the Johnsons got the prettiest. Staver's trying to buy it. Get three crops of hay a year, and we'd get more except we're too high. Got plenty of pasture, plenty of water. Only thing wrong is the summer grazing permits on the Forest Service land are too far away. Takes a week to move cattle up there, unless you truck 'em."

We drove along fields, the white-faced cattle turning to look into the lights, the high rectangular hay stacks behind them. In some fields big sprinkling systems sent out high white plumes of water. We drove down into the river trees. Stan told us that the river was good for swimming and that Alice came out to the ranch to swim. A Forest Service sign said Battle Campground. Back through the trees bonfires reflected light against the tents, campers, and trailers. Ahead the trees made the road a tunnel. A scoutmaster named Dean Jones had taught me the names of fifty different trees. I liked to know the names of things. In seminary Brother Anderson had told us that we had to love knowledge and learn everything we could if we wanted to be exalted. Knowledge was power.

We passed another pickup and had to roll up the windows against the dust, which made the cab warmer.

"Dry already," Stan said. "Going to be a hot summer. Already had two little brush fires." Stan turned the radio on and then off. "Can't get any good reception down here."

Stan swore when he talked and took the Lord's name in vain, but I didn't have to repeat the words in my mind. People didn't have to swear.

We crossed another bridge.

"The river's full of trout at the ranch." Stan put his cigarette in the ash tray. "Staver don't let anybody except us fish. He dynamites a hole about once a month for a fish fry in Silverton. He says fish is good for the girls." Stan shook his head. "Staver used to use hand grenades in the rivers in Korea. He got his share of gooks too. He'll show you how."

"That's against the law in Utah," I said.

"Is here, too, but Staver runs things his way. He got in a fight last summer with some college kid who wouldn't quit fishing. He spotted him with those binoculars of his. He likes to knock the snot out of the smart kids that come around. He always gives the summer hands pointers. He's about perfect with those hands. Really pretty. He got wounded in Korea. He's got a scar down the front of him that looks like they opened him up with an axe." Stan swore. "Wait till you see it."

A big skunk walked along the edge of the road in the lights and vanished into the grass.

"Got lots of them skunks around. You got to watch out when you're out waterin' at night. They sure like pheasant eggs."

Stan spit out the window. He asked us if we could operate a tractor, a mower, or a baler. When we told him no he said Staver would teach us.

"All the equipment is old because old man Johnson don't want to change anything. That's why we don't have these big sprinkling systems. He wants it all like it was when his boy got killed. Staver can fix anything on four wheels, so he keeps it all running about perfect."

Stan lit another cigarette, his face flaring orange from the match. The smoke made the air even warmer.

"That's the Millers' place. See that shed there by the gate, the one painted red? That's got fire tools in it. You'll get your chance fighting brush fires this summer. Kids from the campgrounds start some of 'em and lightning starts the rest. We get more fires along this river than any place in the state."

Randy turned to look. "Sounds like fun."

"Nothing but hard work. But all we get around here is brush fires. The Forest Service has got fire roads cut and they use tanker trucks with hoses. They got airplanes that drop that fire retardant stuff. You got to have timber and a wind for a real fire."

Stan pulled the front of his hat down.

"Twenty years ago I was on a big fire at Hells Canyon that killed a whole herd of elk. We ate about six of 'em. Cooked just right. We had rabbit and grouse and quail to go with 'em, all you wanted. You could just reach down and pick up one when you got hungry. The fire was so bad, they couldn't get any food up to us."

Stan kept looking straight out through the windshield.

"We had boiled trout out of Coyote Creek, that fire was so hot. Some of the boys even had duck. A flock got lost in the smoke, crashed into the cliffs and broke their necks. They just laid there on those ledges and baked."

"You're kidding," Randy said.

"Nope. It's a fact. They wrote about it in all the papers. Funny things happen in big fires. That's how those cave men first started to eat cooked food. After that they started a forest fire every time they wanted a cooked meal. Didn't they ever tell you about that in school?"

"Yes, I read about it," I said.

We passed two more campgrounds.

"That's the Benson place." Stan nodded. "Staver'll have you two down here helping out. Old man Benson got rolled on by a horse and broke both his legs. Staver's had me and Frank down twice. Staver can work all day and half the night and still go cattin'. I can't. He's got lots of friends."

Stan looked down at me. He nodded toward Randy.

"He looks pretty stout, but ain't you a little thin for ranch work, kid?"

"I can work."

"Well, stacking hay out under that hot sun is some of the hardest work you'll ever do. But we won't be cutting again for another month, so you'll have a little time to put some meat on those bones. The food's sure good, I can tell you that."

We passed Volcano Campground. I took off my glasses and polished them with my handkerchief. I put them back on and looked at my watch.

"Do we get our own horses to ride after work if we want?"

"Sure, if you got the strength. Staver teaches all you kids how to ride. He can sure ride. Got a big black stallion."

"Do we get to herd a lot of cattle?"

"Naw, just move 'em from pasture to pasture with the Jeep. Most of the cattle are up on the summer range. You won't be going up there. You're goin' to be workin' hay all summer."

"Oh."

"Nuts," Randy said.

Jackrabbits kept running across the road through the headlights.

"Four or five of those jacks will eat as much hay as a sheep. We shoot 'em by the pickup load at night. You boys shoot?"

"Sure, all the time," Randy said.

"I got my marksmanship merit badge."

"Your what?" Stan looked at me.

"He's a Boy Scout."

"I'm an Explorer. But I don't want to kill anything."

"You an Explorer too, Randy?"

"Not me."

Stan suddenly swerved the pickup toward the left.

"Did you see that big rattler?"

"Where?" Randy looked back through the rear window.

"On the side of the road there. They try to make it across, and I get 'em."

"Do you have a lot of rattlesnakes?"

"We got our share, kid, that's for sure. You got to watch yourself a little." Stan took the last puff on his cigarette and ground it out in the ashtray. "Two years ago last spring Staver knocked the top off a den with a cat while he was grading a field. He tied a stick of dynamite to a five-gallon can of gas, and that fixed all of 'em. It was like dropping a bomb. This is the start of the Johnson place."

The headlights hit a big white no-trespassing sign on a corner fence post. The dried-up body of a coyote, wired by its hind legs, hung below the sign. We passed a bobcat and another coyote. Some of the bones showed.

"Staver shoots or poisons all the varmints. He gets 'em all."

Every fifty yards a no-trespassing sign flashed white in the headlights. I watched for dead animals. I'd read *Animals that Love* and *Animal Families.* If an elephant got sick, two other elephants would help it walk, one on each side to support it. Elephants laid their trunks on a dying elephant and stroked it, and the whole herd gathered in a circle before they left. Some animals and birds mated for life and stayed in families. Whales, porpoises, and dolphins talked to each other under water. Birds and animals had spirits, just like human beings, and they would be resurrected, too. It was wrong to kill animals if you didn't have to. I didn't ever want to kill anything.

"Well, looks like we made it, boys. We're the last outfit on the river." Stan took off his hat with his left hand and wiped his forehead with his arm. "It's hot around here all summer."

A sign said "Johnson Ranch" and, under that, "Black Prince at Stud." We dipped down through the river trees, crossed a new wooden bridge, and then drove up out of the trees. Horses along the white board fence raised their heads into the lights. To the left a big tree stood silhouetted above the other river trees.

"Do you breed a lot of horses?" Randy took off his hat and smoothed his hair.

"Sure do. Ranchers bringin' in mares all summer."

Barking, a big brown collie ran ahead of us up the lane to the white frame house standing in a grove of high dark trees. Windows were lit on the bottom floor and in a low building farther back. A tall heavy woman stood silhouetted in the kitchen doorway. She waved as we passed, and I waved back. We drove under trees.

"That's Mrs. Cummings. Best cook on the river, sick or well."

"Those chickens up there?" Randy looked up into the low branches of the trees.

"Sure are. Skunks can't get 'em up there. Here's the cook's cabin where you two will be staying."

We got out and took our bags.

"Thanks."

"That's the bunkhouse. When you're through eatin', Staver wants to see you."

Two pickups, a red one and a green one, and an old World War Two army jeep stood parked in front of the bunkhouse. The collie came up and licked my hand. I knelt down and petted him.

"That's old Tobe."

Stan shifted gears and drove across to the bunkhouse.

"Good boy, Tobe." I stood up.

Randy and I walked up onto the porch and opened the screen door to the cook's cabin. We each dropped our bags on one of the two army bunks. There was a green sofa, a table with chairs, a dresser, a full-length mirror, and a closet and a bathroom. The two rotating table fans were on, and a fresh strip of flypaper hung down over the table. In the corner was a double stack of magazines.

"This place really is clean."

"Great. Let's go eat."

We washed our hands and walked back outside. Loud, long laughter came through the open windows and doors of the bunkhouse above the sound of the T.V. Stan, Frank, and Staver sat at a table.

Mrs. Cummings pushed open the screen door when we got up on the kitchen porch. A grey cat and a white one sat on the railing.

"Come on, boys. You're welcome. I'm the housekeeper, Mrs. Cummings." She shook our hands, her hand big and soft. "Your supper's ready."

We introduced ourselves. On the wall above the table were six framed pictures of Jesus showing the important events in his life.

"I'm sure you're fine boys."

Mrs. Cummings' face was big and round, her white hair tied in a bun on the back of her head. Her big white apron covered the whole front of her blue dress. She wore wide white shoes that looked like a man's. She moved slowly, and her breathing was heavy.

"That's where the summer hands sit at my table, those two places. Sit down, boys."

The white kitchen was very clean. Two rotating fans blew warm air on us and turned the flypaper hanging down from the ceiling. A big rocking chair stood between the table and the sink. Inside a door two baskets of dry laundry stood in front of an old-fashioned washer.

Mrs. Cummings brought bowls and platters of food and set them on the table and asked me to say the blessing.

"That's a nice blessing, son. Your grandmother called earlier to see if you got here safe and sound. She's going to call back."

Mrs. Cummings put a steak on each of our plates.

"I don't usually eat very much."

"I can see that by just looking at you. If you're going to work, son, you got to eat."

Mrs. Cummings sat down in the rocking chair. She took a man's white handkerchief out of her apron pocket and wiped her neck. She breathed heavy, like she was trying to catch her breath.

"You boys are both from Provo?"

"Yes, ma'am." I cut a small piece from my steak.

"Well, you're the first summer boys Staver's ever had from Utah. Provo's a nice place. I was there when I was a girl. My people were all from Manti and Sanpete County."

Mrs. Cummings smoothed her apron; she didn't rock in her chair.

"My Great-grandfather Stevenson helped build the Manti temple, and he knew President Brigham Young. At night, all lit up there on the hill, the temple looked like it was rising into heaven. We used to hear such grand sermons in our ward meeting."

My grandmother had told me that Mrs. Cummings had gone to the Community Church for forty years. She had been the only Mormon in Silverton for thirty years. She told my grandmother that she was too old and too sick to change back now.

"But that's all a long time ago, before I married Mr. Cummings and came to Silverton to live. Most of my cousins and all of my brothers and sisters are on the other side now. I'm the youngest in my mother's family."

I looked up at the pictures of Jesus. They said, "Jesus is Born," "The Boy Jesus in the Temple," "Jesus Preaching the Gospel," "Jesus in Gethsemane," "Jesus Crucified," and "Jesus is Risen."

"I've had those pictures a long time, son. We all need the Lord's help. I've waited all my life for him to come back."

I turned. Mrs. Cummings was looking up at the pictures, and then she pushed herself up from her chair.

"Here, have some more potatoes and gravy." She put more on my plate.

She sat back down and wiped her neck with her handkerchief, her breathing still heavy.

"We all need the Lord Jesus Christ, son. At least I've never met anybody who didn't. We need to let him love us and wash us clean with his blood; we all need that. It takes a lot of suffering sometimes before most people are willing to let the Lord teach them anything, and some never are. It takes a lot of faith. Isn't that right, son?"

"Yes, ma'am."

"Isn't that right, son?"

"Sure." Randy put more jam on his biscuit.

"I just got through visiting my boy Dale, who's in the state prison in Carson City for robbing a service station in Las Vegas. Dale, he needs the Lord. So do all those other poor men, hundreds of them. They got to accept love, the Lord's and everybody else's, or they're just going to get mean and stay mean. But my boy Dale didn't shoot anybody. I'm grateful to the Lord for that. All you see on these television programs is shooting and killing. And on the news they're always talking about some new war. The Lord wants us to be perfect, but he's the only one that ever was. It takes a lot of faith to believe in people being perfect some day."

Mrs. Cummings wiped her face and neck with her handkerchief.

"How are the Johnsons, son?"

I told Mrs. Cummings that Helen had said to say hello and that they would be out when her father felt better.

"That poor man. Randy, hand Owen the peas and the biscuits. He's had his share these last ten or twelve years. It all started with Brent being drafted and killed in that war. That boy loved everybody. The whole town came out here. Mr. Johnson just went up in Brent's room and sat there all day. Of course he was awfully proud of the way Brent won that big medal they gave him. A few months later Mrs. Johnson died. And now he's got this emphysema that'll take him to his grave. But that Helen is a lovely woman. She's going to marry a fine man and have a family of her own. You got to keep going in this life no matter what happens."

Helen had told us that after Mrs. Cummings' husband died she had a boarding house in Silverton. Helen told us about Dale and that Mrs. Cummings had a daughter who lived in Los Angeles. Her youngest daughter had been killed in a car crash. Mrs. Cummings had diabetes, high blood pressure, and kidney trouble. And she might have to have a kidney taken out.

My grandmother phoned, and I talked to her. I told her I was fine and not to worry, and I'd call her if I got sick. My mother was already in bed. I sat back down.

"You're blessed to have a grandmother like that, son."

Mrs. Cummings took our plates and gave us each a big piece of apple pie with ice cream and filled our glasses with milk.

"Work like a man, eat like a man. Staver will work you hard; you can count on that."

Mrs. Cummings sat back down in the rocking chair. Wiping her neck with the handkerchief, she looked out through the screen door.

"What will that boy do if he doesn't get that government loan to buy this ranch? What *will* become of him?" Mrs. Cummings shook her head and turned to look at us. "He and my Dale were friends together. Staver would have money now if he hadn't squandered every dime his father left him. Well, those who won't hear have to feel."

Mrs. Cummings got up and filled the gravy frying pan with water and put it back on the stove. She stood leaning against the counter breathing hard. She told us to bring our laundry on Saturdays and to keep the cabin clean. She asked us if we had our clothes marked.

"Some boys don't know what the word clean means. You both had enough to eat?"

"It was great." Randy had another biscuit with jam.

"Thank you." I felt a little sick; I'd eaten too much.

"Well, you don't ever have to go away from this table hungry. Too many people in this poor old world go to bed hungry every night. You see that on the news."

Mrs. Cummings followed us out onto the kitchen porch. She petted the white cat that still sat on the porch railing across from the grey cat.

"Feel that breeze." She closed her eyes. "We get a wonderful river breeze nearly every night about this time." Her eyes opened. "You get so you wait for it."

At the bottom of the steps I knelt to pet Tobe.

"He likes you. He's a good old dog. He's lasted longer than the other three or four we've had." Mrs. Cummings stopped to catch her breath. "They pick up that coyote poison Staver puts out."

I stood up and took off my glasses and polished them.

"You nearsighted or farsighted, son?"

"Nearsighted."

She turned and petted the grey cat.

"Most people are. Well Staver's waiting for you boys."

"Yes, ma'am. Thank you for supper."

"Thanks."

"You're welcome, boys."

Tobe licked my hand as Randy and I walked under the poplars to the bunkhouse. I wanted to go brush my teeth first. We walked between the red pickup and the army jeep, which still had the white army numbers on it. Two pitchforks stood in the pickup rack. A rifle with a scope and a sling hung in the rear window; on the dashboard was a pair of binoculars. We climbed the steps to the porch. Stan sat with two other men playing cards at a round blanket-covered table. They all wore white T-shirts. The TV was on.

I raised my hand to knock on the screen.

The whole wall above their heads was covered with pictures of naked and nearly naked women, all smiling. In the big yard-high center picture, a calendar for a Las Vegas tire store, a tall, naked woman holding a candle climbed a flight of stairs. She looked back over her shoulder smiling, her long black hair lying on her white skin. The big caption said, "Remember Us When You Re-tire." Next to the three army bunks was a gun rack filled with guns.

"Come on in, men."

Tobe whined.

They turned in their chairs, each of them smoking, holding cards, beer cans in front of them on the table. Flypaper hung down by the suspended globe. Two rotating fans blew the grey-blue smoky air. The TV was loud.

The pointed tip of the scar showed in the center of the younger man's throat just above the neck of his T-shirt, and I knew that it was Staver. He was tall and had hard muscles, and he looked quick and strong. His auburn hair, which was combed flat and close to his head, glinted under the light. His eyelashes were almost blond. Frank was thin and had watery eyes and looked old.

We introduced ourselves to Frank and Staver and shook hands. They didn't stand up. On the wall by the door were three sets of big deer antlers with the skulls attached.

Staver tapped his cigarette on the edge of the red coffee can in front of him on the table and looked at his cards. "Provo. That's where the mental hospital is. I had a friend there once." Staver sucked on his cigarette and blew out smoke.

"Have a seat. Stan, turn down the TV a little."

"Thank you."

I sat down next to Stan, and Randy sat between Frank and Staver.

"You men want a beer? Stan, get these two a cold beer out of the refrigerator. We want you men to always feel welcome."

"No thanks," I said. "We don't drink alcohol."

Nobody had ever offered me a beer before. I'd never been in a room where men gambled, drank beer, and smoked. I felt funny. My whole body felt heavy.

Randy looked up at the ceiling.

"That's right. I forgot. You boys are Mormons from Utah. You don't smoke either. Make that *root* beers, Stan. You look like a real cowboy, Randy."

"Thanks."

The tip of the scar was heavy and thick. On each side were double rows of puffy white stitch marks. Staver's arms were white from his wrists up to his T-shirt.

Stan handed Randy and me each a root beer.

"Thank you."

"Mormon, huh. Don't Mormons wear funny underwear?"

I looked at Frank. "They're temple garments. You wear them after you go to the temple."

"That's right. I saw the temple once in Salt Lake City. It's a nice building with a gold angel on top with a funny name."

"The angel's name is Moroni."

"That's right, Moroni."

"I was just telling Stan and Frank that we had a lieutenant from Provo in my company in Korea. Named Noral Peterson. Did you ever hear about him, Owen?"

"No, I didn't."

Staver tapped his cigarette on the coffee can. A dry three-foot-long willow lay between his beer cans and his pile of blue, white, and red poker chips. He had the most chips.

"Noral was a nice guy. He used to read his Book of Mormon a lot. He liked to talk to you about religion, but he wasn't pushy. He got killed, though; a sniper got him. Of course, he believed in God, so he was all right." Staver smiled.

"Men cause wars, God doesn't."

"You're right, Owen. Who told you that?" Staver blew out smoke.

"Brother Anderson, our seminary teacher."

"What's seminary, Owen?"

"It's a religion class Mormon students go to when they're in high school."

"Did you have any Utah boys in your outfit in Germany, Frank? Frank was in World War Two."

"Sure. They were nice boys. They held meetings on Sunday. Some of them wore that funny underwear. I asked them to tell me stories about Brigham Young."

Frank laughed and started coughing. It sounded like his lungs were full of water. Bending down laughing and coughing, he put his hand on Randy's shoulder. Staver picked up the willow switch on the table by his hand and killed a big blue fly that had lit on the blanket. He flicked it away.

Frank stopped coughing, spit in a gallon can by his chair, and straightened up. He put his cigarette back in his mouth.

"Frank, you better tell these two men here the ladies' names." Staver pointed with the willow at the wall of pictures. "The summer hands always want to get acquainted."

"Sure." Frank pushed back his chair and stood up.

Stan drank from his can of beer.

Standing between two of the bunks, Frank read the names at the bottoms of the pictures and then sat down. The woman climbing the stairs in the calendar was named Laura.

"Frank, Randy here is a wrestler. Did you wrestle back when you were to school?"

"Sure, but not on any team." Frank started to laugh again.

"Do you wrestle, Owen?"

"No, I don't."

Frank kept looking at the pictures on the wall.

"Those are all real nice girls." He spit in the can.

They all laughed, including Randy. I didn't say anything. I wanted to tell them that the body was the temple of the spirit and had to be kept clean if you wanted the influence of the Holy Ghost, but I knew they would only laugh. I watched Randy. He was enjoying himself. I knew that he wanted to play poker.

"You men like us to deal you in?" Staver took another cigarette out of the package on the table. Frank struck a match for him. "The chips are all free."

"We're not supposed to gamble."

"I know, Owen. Those Mormon boys we had in the company didn't gamble either. But you can't win any money in this game, so it really isn't gambling. It's just a game. We'll play Monopoly some night, Owen. You can come over and play Monopoly. It's nice to have high standards isn't it, Frank?"

"It sure is. Wish I had some." They all laughed. Randy, too.

Stan dealt the cards.

Staver told a story about a poker game where a soldier won and then lost ten thousand dollars. He ran up three flights of stairs in the barracks and jumped out a window.

"Happens all the time," Stan said. "I knew a rancher once named Morrison who just sold his spring lambs and had a check for twenty thousand dollars in his pocket. He got in a poker game in town and lost the twenty thousand, his sheep herd, all his equipment, and his ranch. He put up his two-hundred-dollar boots and a five-hundred-dollar turquoise-silver belt buckle, and he lost those, too. And he lost his new pickup, so somebody had to give him a ride out to his place, only it wasn't his anymore. He walked up on the porch in his socks and holding up his pants, and his wife shot him. She knew what he'd done without even asking him. She just reached for the rifle they kept behind the door for coyotes. That's a fact. Hit him in the leg. It was in the papers."

They laughed. A man was singing on TV, but you couldn't hear him above the laughter.

"Frank, did you know that the Mormon church is the richest church in America? They own more big companies than the Catholic church."

"The Church pays taxes on its businesses.

"Did your seminary teacher tell you that too, Owen?"

"Yes, he did."

Staver showed Randy his cards.

Frank struck a match with his long yellow thumbnail. He bent his head to light his cigarette.

"You play solitaire much, Randy?"

"Sometimes."

"Boys sure like to play solitaire." Frank smiled. "What about you, kid?"

"No, I don't."

"You sure, kid?"

"Yes, I am."

"Come on, kid. Ninety-nine percent of all you boys play solitaire, and the other one percent are liars."

They all laughed. I looked at Frank. My heart pounded; I breathed in deep. He meant masturbation. Brother Anderson had told us there was a joke that said ninety-nine percent of all adolescent boys masturbated and the other one percent were liars. There were jokes about boys who masterbated getting boils, having hair grow on the palms of their hands, and going insane sometimes. I'd read all about masturbation. If a boy did masturbate he could repent and not do it any more. It was just a phase boys went through.

"I don't play solitaire."

"Well maybe not now." Frank turned and spit in the can. "We'll have to keep an eye on you this summer. Never know what a boy's likely to start doing all of a sudden."

My heart kept beating hard, and I breathed fast, but I didn't say anything. I wasn't going to let Frank know that I knew what he was talking about. Nobody had ever said anything like that to me before. I watched Frank. Staver won the hand, and Randy stacked his chips.

"Too bad you two men didn't get a chance to spend a night in Vegas, Randy."

"It sure is."

"Well, maybe you'll get a chance later."

Staver told us what kind of work we would do. He asked if we could ride a horse. I told him no, but Randy could. Lana's father owned horses. Randy took out his wallet and showed her pictures.

"You got a girl, Owen?"

"No."

"He's got a girl named Becky."

"You got a picture, Owen?"

"No, I don't. She's not really my girl."

Staver told us that we could use the bunkhouse phone any time we wanted to call our girls. He drank from his beer can. He said that maybe we could find some girls in Silverton.

"Do you think these two will stay and earn their bonuses, Frank?"

"Sure. All the summer hands like their bonus." He laughed. "Except we had that Larson kid two years ago. Wet his pants when he saw that rattler in the ditch where he was cutting weeds. He didn't stay around for any bonus. You'd have had to whip him to make him stay. His momma had to come and take him home." Frank spit in the can.

I stood up. "We'd better go."

"You boys will need lots of sleep." Staver discarded two cards and Stan dealt him two more. "You look a little thin, Owen. We don't want you getting sick." Staver smiled.

"I won't get sick."

Staver put down his cards and stood up. "You men shoot?"

"Sure."

"What about you, Owen?"

"Yes, I have my marksmanship merit badge."

"He's a Boy Scout."

I looked at Randy. "I'm an Explorer."

"Well, it's nice to have an Explorer for the summer. You can help keep the rabbits and the gophers down."

"I don't want to have to kill any animals."

"Just think of it as part of the job, Owen, and it won't bother you. We furnish the guns and all the ammunition you can shoot. On anything bigger than a jackrabbit we use a special lightweight slug that explodes on contact so it won't suffer." Staver smiled.

There was a loading bench by the gun rack. The row of guns gleamed.

Staver turned and picked up something from the stack of magazines.

"Here, Randy. You better take this with you. I don't think you've got a calendar in the cabin." He handed Randy a *Playboy* calendar.

"Thanks."

"We want you men to feel welcome to come to the bunkhouse any time. There's always plenty of root beer. You can watch television, and we'll play Monopoly sometimes." Staver followed us to the screen door. "You're welcome to use the phone to call Provo."

We stepped out onto the porch.

"If you walk up to the corral, don't try to pet that stallion. He'll take your hand off, maybe your arm. A stallion can bite worse than a bear."

"Thanks."

"Nice dreams, Boy Scout." It was Frank.

"My name is Owen."

"That's right. Sorry, Owen."

We walked down the steps and under the trees. I looked back; Staver stood silhouetted in the doorway. I was glad to leave the bunkhouse. Suddenly behind us they all laughed, the laughter followed us across the yard. On the cabin porch I knelt down and petted Tobe. When I went inside, Randy was hanging the calendar on a nail that stuck out of the wall across from the bunks. He looked at all the pages and then turned the calendar to May.

"That's a year old." I sat down on my bunk facing Randy.

"Who's worried about what year it is?"

Randy set one of the fans so it blew on his bunk, and then he undressed and lay down in his shorts and T-shirt. He put his hands under his head.

"It won't be too bad around here."

"Are you going to play poker? You know that your father doesn't like you playing poker."

"Oh, come on, cousin. Who cares out here? What can it hurt? It's just for fun. They don't play for money. It's just like playing Monopoly. My dad doesn't care as long as I don't play for money. He wants me to have fun, not get bored to death." Randy kept looking at the ceiling. "Sure I'm going to play a little poker."

"We're supposed to be examples."

"Oh brother." Randy turned on his face and covered his head with his pillow. He raised the end of the pillow. "Why don't you wait until you're on your mission."

"The prophet says that every member is a missionary. You're a Priest."

Randy groaned. "Well, you better keep preaching to Staver then. You can preach to Stan and Frank, too, if you have any time left over. You sure made a lot of progress in there tonight."

"If we work hard this summer and are good examples for the Church, we could make a lot of difference. The gospel changes people's whole lives."

Randy pulled his pillow down tight over his head.

Outside in the yard, one of the pickups started. I looked up. The dark red pickup went past.

Randy sat up. "I wonder where those guys are going."

Randy lay back down, and I walked out on the porch. Tobe nuzzled my hand. Lightning flashed back behind the west mountains, but I heard no thunder. I felt the breeze. I decided to walk down to the river bridge. I followed Tobe. The big cottonwood I'd seen when we drove in was twice as high as the other river trees.

I stood on the new bridge listening, feeling the coolness over the water. I listened. Upstream something big splashed, a big fish. I leaned out over the rail. He jumped again, but I couldn't see him. I walked up through the trees to the old bridge. The center was gone, the heavy planks hanging out over the dark water. He jumped and I saw him, silver-gold against the willows, holding in the air, then vanishing. I waited, my heart beating hard, but he didn't jump again. I knew that it was a very big German brown trout. He was beautiful. But he didn't jump again. A great horned owl hooted. I listened. It was my favorite bird. The calls of the male and the female were different. I'd learned that when I earned my bird-watching merit badge.

I walked back up the road to the cabin and stopped. I wanted to go up to the barn and climb to the top of the high haystack to see everything and listen for coyotes, but it was too late.

Randy was asleep when I got back to the cabin. In the shower I washed my face with the special soap the dermatologist had told me to use. I felt my face with my fingers. When I was drying myself with my towel, I looked at my appendectomy scar. It was the only scar I had. I put on clean shorts and a T-shirt. I liked boxer shorts because they felt more like clothes. I put on the new blue summer pajamas my grandmother had bought me.

I knelt down by my bunk. I prayed for Randy, that I could help him. I prayed that he would keep the commandments, have a good summer, and be an example. I prayed for Stan, Frank, Staver, Mrs. Cummings, and my mother and grandmother.

I opened my eyes and raised my head. Randy lay looking at me.

"You praying?"

"Yes."

"Oh." Randy turned to the wall.

I stood up and got in bed. I pulled the sheet up. I lay on my side looking out through the screen door at the dark house. I wondered which of the upstairs bedrooms had been Brent's and if his Medal of Honor was in his room. Tobe lay against the screen door. Across the yard the kitchen screen door opened, and Mrs. Cummings stood in the doorway under the porch light in a long white nightgown. Her long white hair fell down over her shoulders. She stood there looking toward the cabin. She didn't move. Tobe raised his head. Mrs. Cummings stood there, and then she stepped back, the screen door closed, and she vanished into the dark kitchen.

I turned on my back and put my hands under my head. I smelled my new pajamas. I wasn't homesick; I didn't feel that hollow pain in my chest now like I had when we left Provo. It was going to be a good summer. I took off my glasses and reached out in the dark to put them on the night stand between the two bunks. I listened to Randy breathing. I was glad that we had the cook's cabin to sleep in and had our own bathroom. The spiral of flypaper hanging down by the light gleamed. I closed my eyes and lay listening to the thunder.

3

I set the alarm for five-thirty because we were going to eat breakfast at six, but Staver and Frank woke us up at five-fifteen. Randy pulled the sheet over his head and didn't get up, so Frank tipped him out. Staver said that's what they used to do in the army when a dogface wouldn't get up. Frank said he liked my pretty blue pajamas. Staver said we wouldn't have time to shave if we didn't hurry. Walking down the steps they laughed. Staver wore a straw cowboy hat, a blue cowboy shirt, Levis, and cowboy boots.

When we left the cabin, the sun was just coming up over the east mountains, but it was already warm, and I saw no clouds. Out in the fields rooster pheasants crowed. Tobe walked ahead of us. Mrs. Cummings made me eat a big breakfast. When Randy and I finished and got outside, Stan, Frank, and Staver stood at the bottom of the steps lighting cigarettes. Staver told me that he wanted me to mow the lawn, wash off the walks, and sprinkle down the yard. He said that I would be taking care of the yard and Mrs. Cummings' vegetable garden all summer.

"Can I go brush my teeth first?"

"Sure. How about you, Randy, do you want to go brush your teeth?"

Frank laughed and had to take the cigarette out of his mouth, his watery eyes glistening. I didn't like to be laughed at. Nobody laughed at me in Provo.

When I got back they were up at the barn. I got the lawnmower and catcher from behind the house. The lawn was all shaded. I put on the catcher and then stood looking at the river trees, the foothills, and the mountains. Already the sun hit the whole valley. The wooden corral fences, all the outbuildings, and the barn were painted white. It was a beautiful ranch. The big cottonwood was the biggest one I'd ever seen. I liked high places. I looked for Staver, but I couldn't see him anywhere. A dead animal hung from the fence across the field from the house. The pheasants had stopped crowing.

I started to cut the lawn. I liked to cut and trim lawns and wash off sidewalks and driveways. I liked things to look nice. I dumped the grass over the fence for the horses. Tobe lay on the lawn watching me. The heat waves rose above the fields, and it was hot already. After I finished the lawn, I wet down the yard and washed off the porches and walks. Through the screen door I saw Mrs. Cummings in the kitchen. The grey and white cats sat on the back porch railing watching me.

"Be sure you coil that hose."

I turned around. Staver sat in the red pickup. I hadn't heard him drive up. I didn't know how long he'd been watching me.

"When you get through, go up to the barn. You and Randy are going to finish painting the tractor shed. Frank will show you what to do."

Smiling, Staver shifted and drove down the lane. I watched the red pickup vanish into the trees. When I cut my grandmother's friends' lawns, they always told me what a good job I did. They brought me out tall glasses of cold lemonade and told me to sit down and rest. They had all known my father when he was a boy, and they told me what a wonderful son he was all his life. The money I earned cutting lawns I put in my missionary savings account.

I got another drink out of the hose and walked out of the shade into the hot sun, Tobe ahead of me. I couldn't see one cloud in the pale blue sky. Black Prince stood in the barn corral watching me. He moved his head up and down and pawed the dirt. He gleamed when he moved. He was a big horse. A ladder had been built up the front of the barn, and on the top was a small railed platform.

Frank and Randy came out of the barn. Randy carried a full canvas water bag.

"This way," Frank said. He took out a cigarette and lit it as we walked. "You boys get to do a little painting."

We went to the equipment shed to get brushes and paint. Three boxes of dynamite stood stacked by the five-gallon cans of white paint. Frank led us toward the tractor shed. The bay doors were open. In the last bay at the end of the line of tractors and balers was a pickup. The paint was new, but it was an old model. Randy stopped.

"Whose is that pickup? It sure is in good shape."

Frank stopped and turned.

"It belonged to that Johnson kid. His dad put it there after he got killed in Korea."

"Can I go look at it?"

"Sure, go ahead."

Randy and I walked over. Randy opened the driver's door. The keys were in the ignition. Randy looked at the registration tag on the steering column.

"It's a nineteen-fifty. I know a lot of guys who sure would like to have something like this. It's almost new."

The pickup was dusty, but the paint still shone. A graduation tassel hung down from the mirror. I wanted to see a picture of Brent so I could know how much we looked alike. I wanted to know what he'd done to win his Medal of Honor.

"Come on, you two. You got to get some painting done."

Randy closed the door, and we followed Frank around to the back of the tractor shed, which was about two-thirds painted. Two aluminum stepladders stood by the wall. Frank showed us how to clean off the old paint with our wire brushes and how to paint the weathered boards.

"This ought to keep you two boys busy till noon. Don't fall off a ladder." Frank laughed. "My old man whipped me once for falling off a ladder and breaking my arm. He claimed I did it just to get out of loading hay. But he didn't touch me till after I had the cast on. Your old man ever use a belt on you, Randy?"

"Nope."

"How about you, kid?" Frank turned to spit.

"No." My grandmother had told me that neither I nor my father had ever had a spanking.

After Frank left, I asked Randy what he'd been doing.

"Working." Randy cleaned off a board with his wire brush and then stood back and looked at it. "Working on this ranch all summer ought to be worth at least a Triumph."

Tobe lay in the shade watching, his head on his paws. I kept turning to see if Staver was watching through his binoculars. I felt like he was always right behind me.

Standing by the board wall was like being near a fire. My brush stuck on the hot boards, and the paint ran down the handle onto my hand. Randy swore. My glasses kept slipping down. I got paint on them trying to push them up. I felt a little dizzy; my stomach felt funny. I looked up. Two vultures circled in the sky, disappearing against the mountains, then coming out into the sky again. When I painted I kept seeing my watch and what time it was. I stopped and got a drink from the canvas bag. I tried not to touch the metal with my lips because of germs; there weren't any cups. I went back and started to paint again.

Randy stood looking at the shed, his paintbrush held down by his side.

"It'd be fun to have a gun in your pickup and stop and shoot when you saw something."

I felt like I might vomit, but I kept painting. I didn't want to get sick. The sun flashing off the windows and chrome, the red pickup came around the equipment shed and stopped. Staver and Frank got out. Tobe stood up. Staver stopped by me.

"You got to fill up the cracks, Owen, or it doesn't do any good. Give me that rag." Staver wiped off the paintbrush handle. "It's a paintbrush, not a broom." He dipped the brush into the paint. The paint went on heavy and filled the cracks where I'd already painted. None dripped off the brush down onto his fingers. He held the willow switch in his left hand. "Here, try it. Keep the brush moving. Keep it pointed down on an angle. Use your ladder; that's what it's for. The paint is supposed to go on the boards. You, too, Randy."

"Sure." Randy kept painting.

I painted. I didn't say anything. I knew that Staver was right. I should have seen what I was doing wrong. I liked to figure things out and do them right. But Staver could have been more polite.

Staver and Frank squatted in the shade at the end of the tractor shed smoking. We had painted almost to the end. Tobe had lain down again.

Staver drew lines in the dirt with the willow switch. He asked Frank about the German women. Frank said that after

World War Two all an American soldier had to pay a German woman was a candy bar, a cake of soap, a pair of nylon stockings, or a package of cigarettes. Frank repeated the first names of the German women. He said the women walked around the high barbed-wire fence outside the barracks calling to the soldiers standing at the barracks windows to come out.

"That's what they wanted right there." Frank took the package of cigarettes out of his shirt pocket. "Good old American cigarettes. Better than money. They could trade them for whatever they wanted."

I tried not to listen to Frank's stories, to the obscene words he used when he talked. I always walked away if a boy in the hall or in gym started to tell a dirty story. The Prophet Joseph Smith when he was in prison commanded the guards to stop telling their obscene stories. And they did, and they apologized to him. But I knew I couldn't walk away now. I didn't know where to walk to, and Staver would ask me where I was going and if I wanted to keep my job. My whole body was tight. I could feel my heart beating, and I was breathing hard. I wanted to be taller and stronger. Frank kept talking about what the German women did for a pack of cigarettes.

I turned and looked at him. "Marriage is sacred. A man and woman get married for eternity."

Squatting there in the shade, Frank blew out smoke and then spit. "Sure they do, kid. It seems that long. I tried it twice."

Staver and Randy laughed.

"You'd try on a pair of shoes before you bought them wouldn't you, kid?"

"Yes, I would, but a girl isn't a pair of shoes."

"Who told you that, Owen, your seminary teacher?" Staver smiled.

"No, he didn't. It's just true."

"Maybe Owen here is right, Frank." Staver drew a line in the dirt with his willow. "Maybe you've been wrong for a long time. A woman isn't like a pair of shoes."

"Maybe not. Guess you're right, Boy Scout."

"My name is Owen."

"That's right. I forgot again. I'll remember next time for sure."

I turned and started to paint again. I watched the white paint fill the cracks in the old wood, felt my heart beating hard. I breathed deep.

Brother Anderson had Doctor Rogers come and talk to our seminary class. He showed a film on human reproduction, and he explained all about human sexuality. At the end of the class, Brother Anderson read the list of words Doctor Rogers had written down. And then he told us that the words meant exactly what they said and that part of being virtuous was using the right words. I liked the words. "Loins" and "beget" were good words.

Frank and Staver got back in the pickup. Frank stuck his head out of the window.

"You boys watch for skunks. They like to get under sheds. Don't want you stepping on a skunk." Frank laughed. "That'd be terrible."

I kept painting. I didn't turn to watch them drive off. You hated the wrong things a person did. You didn't have to hate the person. That's what you concentrated on. I just had to hate the obscene things Staver and Frank talked about, not them. I felt dizzy and sick.

"Look, will ya lay off the Church stuff around Staver and Frank."

I lowered my paint brush and looked at Randy standing on his ladder.

"They're just kidding you. They're good guys."

"Good guys don't tell obscene stories."

"Just take it easy. You don't have to change the whole world."

"That's what missionaries are supposed to do."

"Oh brother." Randy turned and started painting again.

I kept watching Randy. I wanted to help him. I didn't want him to get into any trouble during the summer.

At noon we went in for lunch. We cleaned our hands with paint thinner, but I couldn't get my hands clean. I washed them with soap and hot water in the cabin, but they still smelled of paint thinner.

Mrs. Cummings told me I looked pale, but I told her I wasn't sick.

"Well, hard work never killed anybody, not as far as I know anyway."

Every time I brought my fork up to my mouth I smelled the paint thinner on my hands. I didn't talk. For dessert Mrs. Cummings opened the refrigerator and brought out three chocolate pies with whipped cream. She gave me a big piece.

"There, that's good for what ails you, son."

Stan ate three pieces.

After lunch it was hotter painting. Randy kept talking about going swimming in the river. I kept my mouth closed. I couldn't look up. I breathed deep. But I vomited. I couldn't help it. I vomited up everything.

"Hey, you're sick."

I stayed leaned over. "I'm not sick. It's just the chocolate pie." I vomited again.

"You better go lay down in the cabin. I'll go tell Staver."

"I'm not sick." I straightened up. I wiped my eyes and nose with my blue bandana handkerchief. I felt my forehead and took my pulse. It wasn't sunstroke or heat exhaustion. I was a certified first-aider, but I'd never had to help anybody before.

"Get me the water bag and pour it over my head."

The cool water made me feel better. With my foot I scraped dirt over the vomit. I looked to see if Staver was watching me with his binoculars, but I couldn't see him.

"What you doing that for?"

"Because I don't want Staver to know. And I don't want you to tell him either."

"Don't get excited."

I felt a lot better.

We finished painting the storage shed at three, and Staver took us out to clean ditches. Randy rode in the cab with Staver and Frank, and I rode in the back. Holding onto the rack, I stood next to a dynamite box with the lid on. We passed four haystacks. The cattle along the fences lifted their heads to watch the red pickup go by. Staver drove fast. When we stopped at the south end of the ranch by a ditch, the pickup dust settled slowly. It didn't drift. No breeze had blown all day. The mountains on both sides were bleached and hazy with heat. I kept looking for clouds.

Staver showed us how to sharpen our shovels with a file and how to clean out a ditch.

"You two keep your eyes open. Rattlesnakes like these shady ditches during the day. With a shovel you're all right."

Frank smiled and shook his head.

"That Larson kid came out of that ditch a jumpin' and a yellin'. He ran all the way back to the yard before he stopped. Sixteen years old and he wet his pants. Of course he was bothered with boils too. That's not a boil coming on the back of your neck is it, kid?" Frank reached up and touched my neck with his finger.

I pulled away. "No, it isn't."

"Well, you want to be careful of boils. 'Course, you know what causes 'em."

I didn't say anything. A boy didn't have to masturbate.

Frank talked with his cigarette in the corner of his mouth. He swore almost every time he talked. They got back into the red pickup and Frank shut the door.

"You be careful now, kid. We don't want any more accidents."

Staver and Randy laughed. I kept working. Staver shifted gears, turned, and drove back down the road, the yellow dust rising behind the pickup.

"Hey, why didn't you laugh? Frank told a joke." Randy was ahead of me in the ditch.

"I didn't feel like it." I kept cutting weeds.

"He was just kidding you a little."

"Maybe."

"They were just trying to scare us. They probably do it every summer."

"I know that."

I kept working. A zoology professor from B.Y.U. had given our Explorer post a demonstration on snake safety. He brought a rattlesnake in a wire cage so we could learn what one looked and sounded like. The amount of venom depended on the snake's size and whether it had just eaten or not. A rattlesnake could only strike about the length of its body. We learned snake-bite first aid and how to use a snake-bite kit. Snakes were very beneficial to farmers and ranchers because they ate rodents.

When I hit rocks with my shovel the feeling came up through the bones in my arms into my whole body. I sweated. My glasses kept slipping. My Levis were hot. I'd never worked hard all day before. My hands and arms, shoulders, and back ached. I kept taking off my gloves to look at my dirty hands; I liked to watch my hands when I played the piano. I didn't raise my head to see if Staver were parked somewhere watching through his binoculars. I kept working except when I stopped to drink from the water bag.

I heard the rattlesnake before I saw it, the hard buzz close in front of me. I jumped back, saw it coiled near a smooth white rock, brought my shovel up without thinking. I hit it again and again, smashing it, raising the shovel high above my head like a club, smashing it against the white rock. My whole body was tight and trembling.

"Hey, he's dead. You got him."

Randy stood on the bank. I lowered the shovel.

"You really mangled it." Randy lifted the rattlesnake with his shovel and tossed it on the bank. "It's a little one."

The rattlesnake lay on its back, its yellow-white belly up. Its head and body were smashed.

"Do you want the rattles? It's only got three."

"No." I kept swallowing and stiffening my body against the trembling.

"Hey, what's that?" Randy turned. "Was that thunder?" Randy looked up at the sky. "It must be old Staver dynamiting something." Randy listened but there were no more explosions. "That would be fun."

Randy picked the snake up again with his shovel. "Better give him the old heave-ho. You really flattened him." Randy threw the snake over into some high weeds and walked back up the ditch. "I'd like to see one about six feet long. I'd send the rattles to Lana."

I cut the weeds. I'd stopped trembling. I shouldn't have gotten scared; it wasn't necessary. I didn't like to let things scare me. The sun had started to slant down toward the west mountains, but it was still hot. I watched the high willows along the ditch bank. I'd read of snakes in Africa dropping out of trees onto the people in the safari. I looked over the high weeds where Randy had thrown the snake. It was the first thing I'd ever killed.

Stan, Frank, and Staver came to get us just before six. The fields, river trees, mountains, sky, and sun had all grown darker. But there was no breeze yet. Randy told Staver I'd killed a little rattlesnake.

"Well, let's look at you." Frank put his hand on my shoulder and turned me to face Staver in the pickup. "Doesn't look like you had any accidents."

I sucked in my stomach, tightened my groin. But I didn't say anything. I knew they were trying again to make me angry.

"Owen needs a good night's sleep, Frank."

"He can wear those nice blue pajamas and say his prayers."

"What did you wear to bed when you were sixteen, Frank?"

"Sheets."

They all laughed.

"Do you say your prayers every night, kid?" Frank's cigarette hung from the corner of his mouth.

"Yes." I looked at Randy. I knew he had told them that I said my prayers. "And every morning."

"That's wonderful, kid."

"It certainly is, Owen." Staver smiled.

I didn't say anything. I climbed in the back of the pickup. Driving back I asked Randy why he'd told them I said my prayers. "That's private."

"Ah, come on. Frank asks questions about you. He wants to get to know you. These are good guys."

"Some things are still private."

"Okay, I'm sorry."

The pickup slowed down and stopped by a clump of trees. Staver got out of the cab and reached back in and brought out his rifle.

"Come on down here, Owen."

Randy and I climbed out of the back of the pickup, and Staver handed me the rifle.

"Let's see you drop that magpie out of the top of that dead cottonwood over there. It's about fifty yards."

I held the rifle. "I don't kill birds."

"Just put the scope on him. You can use a scope can't you?"

"Yes."

I raised the rifle and put the cross hairs on the magpie. The rifle felt heavy and smooth. I'd always wanted to do courageous things and defend people. Every month in *Boy's Life* there was an illustrated story of how a Cub, a Scout, or an Explorer saved somebody's life. The magpie dipped its tail. I lowered the rifle and handed it back to Staver.

"No, thanks."

"Magpies are pests. They eat other birds' eggs."

"I know that."

"You ever eat meat, Owen?"

"Yes, I have."

"Was it dead?"

Randy and Frank laughed. Frank had gotten out of the cab. He spit on the ground.

"Yes, but that's different. It's food."

"You killed that rattlesnake didn't you?"

"Yes, I did."

"So killing's all right if you do it for the right reason."

A thread of shining spittle hung between Staver's lips. The tip of the scar on his throat moved when he talked.

"If you kill this one magpie you'll save the lives of other birds. Isn't that a good thing?"

"Yes."

"Well, here then. Save lives." Staver held the rifle out to me.

"I don't kill birds."

Staver smiled.

"Here, Randy, you try. Killer doesn't want to."

Randy rested the rifle on top of a fence post to shoot. The magpie exploded in a puff of feathers.

"Good shot. Let's go."

Standing in the back of the pickup hanging onto the rack, I turned and watched the top of the cottonwood. Brother Anderson had told us that war was the greatest form of human violence. On the board he wrote the names of the Nazi concentration camps—Treblinka, Belsen, Buchenwald, Dachau, Auschwitz, and a lot of the others. He pronounced the names and made us pronounce them and assigned us to memorize them. He said that every human being should memorize these names because that kind of violence was all over the world, and we were all capable of it, every nation, every people. He said that was why the atonement was necessary, and being baptized, and taking the sacrament every week to renew our covenants. He told us to lay our hands on top of our desks, palms up. He said to look at our hands and think about what they would do. I knew I couldn't torture and kill people.

I turned and looked at my hand holding onto the rack. The rattlesnake had really been the first thing I'd ever killed. I wished I hadn't had to kill it.

Randy and I had a half an hour before supper to go swimming. I got my athletic supporter and my swimming suit out of my drawer.

"What are you taking that for?" Randy stood at the screen door looking at me. "You afraid some girl's going to see you out here?"

"I like to wear a suit."

"Do you shower in your jock strap at school?"

"No, I don't. I wrap my towel around me when I go to the showers."

Randy shook his head. "Try that in the varsity showers and you wouldn't get out alive."

"Maybe."

I followed Randy off the porch. Tobe was between us. The path behind the cabin led toward the river tree and the big cottonwood. We walked out onto a wide flat ledge down the whole side of a long deep wide hole the river had hollowed out of the lava. The deep clear water was almost still.

"Great." Randy pulled off his clothes. "I've been waiting for this all day."

I turned and looked up. The big cottonwood, its main trunk twice as big as a car, divided into three trunks, the right trunk bending out over the river fifty or sixty feet high. A ten-foot piece of heavy swing rope hung down. Cleats led up the trunk and vanished into the leaves. Sets of initials filled a two-foot square where the bark had been cut away, but you couldn't read them now. I looked back up at the high limb. I knew that boys dived from there. My hands tingled when I thought of doing that.

Randy yelled and hit the water.

I sat down on a log by a circle of black fire rocks to unlace my boots. The fire circle was full of crumpled burned beer cans. I looked down. Some of the scattered cigarette butts had lipstick on them. A red coffee can held two used bars of white soap. I didn't think that Alice could be immoral. She wasn't that type of person. She would come swimming and enjoy herself, but she wouldn't be immoral. I wanted to ask her what she liked about Staver.

I put on my athletic supporter. I wanted to wear one all the time, but it embarrassed me when I thought of my grandmother washing them separate from my gym trunks and putting them in my drawer, so I didn't. I needed my father to ask him questions about things like that. Pulling on my swimming suit, I ran across the ledge and dived as far out into the river as I could.

I went down, down, went deep to find the best coolness, didn't want to come up. I wanted to be like the water, not feel the difference where my body touched it. I'd never swum in a river before, only swimming pools. I'd had swimming lessons for two years. I rose slowly to the surface, took air, and sank again into the coolness, closed my eyes again to feel only the cool water.

I rose slowly up toward the light. I floated, looked up into the roof of trees that held out the sunlight. We had to get back to supper. I told Randy. He groaned. I went under again, held my breath as long as I could. River water felt softer than chlorinated water. I came up and went under again, and then I swam to the ledge and took off my suit and athletic supporter and got my soap.

I soaped my whole body and then sank back down into the water. Before, I had never thought I would feel my body so much. In my grandmother's albums I found all the pictures of my father in a swimming suit, tennis trunks, and gym trunks. I wanted to know how his body felt when he turned sixteen. My whole body seemed to swell sometimes, grow tight, be full of pain. I didn't know what to do with my body. The Holy Ghost could fill your whole body with light and knowledge. You could have complete control over your thoughts and actions. You didn't have to break any commandments. At night sometimes I curled into a ball, put my arms around my knees and pulled tight so I didn't feel the parts of my body. I wanted to ask other boys what it was like to feel the Holy Ghost and how many times they'd felt him.

I soaped myself again, rinsed off, and then got out. I'd brought clean socks, T-shirt, and shorts. Mrs. Cummings had told us that we couldn't change our shirts and Levis every day because she wasn't going to do all that washing. I changed all my clothes every day at home. In the summer I took two showers and changed twice.

At supper Mrs. Cummings said that I looked a little pale, and she asked me how I felt. Stan said the blessing. We had pork chops and hamburger steaks. Both fans blew across the table, and all the hot food was covered so it wouldn't cool.

"You'll get used to hard work, son. Work's like everything else. Eat a good supper and get to bed early. You'll be all right."

Mrs. Cummings didn't sit down with us to eat. She sat in her chair and wiped her neck with her handkerchief. She didn't rock.

"Is that from ol' Lana?"

Randy had a pink envelope by his plate when we came in. He'd picked it up before the blessing and put it in his shirt pocket.

"It sure is. She wrote it two days before I left. She's going to write me every day."

"Let's see, lover boy." Frank reached over, and Randy handed him the letter. Frank smelled it. "Ol' Lana's got class." Frank smelled the letter again and handed it back to Randy.

I was surprised that I was hungry. For dessert there was chocolate pie with whipped cream again and peach cobbler. I had the cobbler.

I helped Mrs. Cummings clear the table. I told her that I'd like to stay and help her with the dishes, but Staver wanted to show Randy and me our horses. She thanked me. She said that she'd do them and then sit down and rest and watch television.

The sunset was turning the tops of all the north mountains orange-red. The air was still. The white chickens already roosted in the trees. Black Prince watched me as I passed. Randy, Stan, Frank, and Staver stood by the corral at the back of the barn. Staver showed us our horses. Mine was a sorrel gelding named Blade and Randy's was a black named Miser. Staver took us to the tack room in the barn to show us our saddles. I liked the smell of leather and horses. All the saddles hung from the rafters on ropes tied around the saddle horns. I rubbed mine with my flat hand. Next to mine was a beautiful new saddle with the initials "BHJ" inlaid in silver. Mr. Johnson's first name was Harold.

"Is that Brent's?"

Staver turned and looked at me.

"Who told you about him?"

"My Uncle Mark first, and Helen Johnson."

"Yes, it was his. Come on, let's get out of here."

I looked at the saddle. I walked to the door and turned and looked at it again. The silver was polished. I turned. Staver stood lighting a cigarette. I wanted to ask him why Brent liked him and why they were such good friends, and if he thought that Brent would still like him. I wanted to ask him if he'd won any medals besides the Purple Heart. I knew that every soldier who was wounded received the Purple Heart.

Walking back to the yard, Frank asked Randy if Lana was on the girl's wrestling team.

"Girls don't have wrestling teams."

"Too bad." Frank closed his right eye against the smoke from his cigarette. "Some of those girls would probably be pretty good."

"We'll see you in the bunkhouse, Randy."

"Sure."

Staver turned to me. "You're welcome to come, Owen. You can have a root beer and watch TV."

"No thanks. I need to go to bed early."

"Well, the invitation is always open." Staver smiled.

"Thank you."

I followed Randy into the cabin. I sat down on my bunk. When he came out of the bathroom, he stopped in front of the mirror to comb his hair.

"Why do you have to go to the bunkhouse and play poker?"

Randy ran his hand down over his hair to smooth it behind the comb.

"Because it's a lot better than being bored to death. They're interesting guys. You think they're going to get me to smoke or get me drunk or something?"

"No."

"Then what's the problem? They don't play for money, so I can't lose anything. Come on over. You're invited. You could take care of me so I didn't do anything wrong."

"You'll watch them drinking beer and smoking. You'll listen to their bad language and their obscene stories. Even if you don't play for money it's still gambling. Your dad doesn't want you around things like that."

Randy patted his hair to make it stay down.

"You ought to have been in the locker room the night we lost the state wrestling championship to East High last year.

My dad was there, and he didn't say anything about the language. He knows guys talk like that. Some guys were crying they were so mad. He wants me to wrestle. I might be captain this year." Randy put his comb in his pocket. "You're going to let Staver teach you how to ride."

"That's different. Learning to ride a horse is a good thing to do. We could go swimming again or play football maybe. You brought a ball."

Randy stood at the screen door.

"You need your rest. Look, don't worry about me. I'm okay. I've been around a little. I'm not just a kid. You ought to try to have a little fun too."

"I have fun."

"Well, try having more. See ya, cousin. You better get lots of sleep so you can work tomorrow and not get sick."

The screen door shut behind Randy. I stood up and walked out on the porch. Tobe stood up and touched my hand with his nose. Randy walked into the bunkhouse without knocking. Through the window I saw him sit down at the table with Stan, Frank, and Staver. Smoke rose above all their heads. I knew that I had to find other things for Randy to do that he would enjoy more than poker. We could really be good friends. That's what Uncle Mark wanted.

"Son! Son!" I looked up. Mrs. Cummings stood on the kitchen porch. She waved me to come over. When I got in the kitchen she told me that my grandmother had called to ask her if I was all right. Mrs. Cummings put a plate of cookies and a glass of milk on the table and told me to sit down. She sat in her rocker.

"She told me how sick you've been. She's worried about you."

"I was born six weeks premature and had to stay in an incubator. I had ear infections till I was three. I had to have my tonsils and appendix out. I've had mumps, measles, chicken pox, scarlet fever, rheumatic fever, and double pneumonia."

"Well, dying's a lot easier than living. We all know that. Eat those cookies; that's what they're for."

I bit into the cookie.

I'd almost died when I had double pneumonia. I was so weak I couldn't lift my hand to touch myself. I got smaller and smaller inside my body so I could leave it, but I didn't. I waited for a light to grow bright in the corner of my hospital room and my father all dressed in white to step out to come and get me. But he didn't. Bishop Matthews gave me a blessing and I got better. Afterwards, sitting in school, I'd look around the classroom and think about how sad everybody would have been if I'd died, and my eyes would fill with tears.

"That Randy's over at the bunkhouse playing poker I suppose?" Mrs. Cummings sat in her rocker breathing hard. She wiped her neck with her handkerchief. "A person can't tell a boy that age anything; he's got to learn it all for himself. We taught Dale all his life, but it didn't help. He drank and gambled. He got married and divorced twice, so he's got no family now except me and his sister. Now he's in prison and will be for another two years." Mrs. Cummings shook her head. "At least he didn't shoot that gas station attendant. He had enough good in him not to do that."

Mrs. Cummings looked up at the pictures of Jesus on the wall.

"The Lord had to pray. He needed help. You pray don't you, son?"

"Yes." I drank some milk.

"Boys stop praying just when they need the help the most. The Lord's blood washes away sin. All that sin in the world's got to be paid for with suffering, either his or ours. They're talking about another war now in some place there next to China. It was on the news tonight. There's so many terrible things happening you wonder how the Lord puts up with it all."

I looked at my hand holding the glass of milk. I didn't need to pray for myself before except when I was sick. I hadn't done anything wrong. I prayed for my mother and grandmother and for people I knew who were sick or in accidents. Even though I thought about myself a lot now and my body was different, I didn't know what to ask for. I hadn't done anything wrong. I prayed that I would always be able to keep the commandments. I didn't ever have to smoke or drink or swear or lie or steal, or be immoral. I would be a Priest, receive my Duty to God Award, be an Elder, go on a mission, be married in the temple. Everybody could become a god and create worlds of their own if they kept the commandments and became perfect.

"I married Mr. Cummings when I was seventeen. He herded sheep for my father. And we came here to Silverton, where he was from. Maybe if we'd stayed there in Utah and he'd joined the Church things might have been different for Dale. He would have had the Priesthood and gone on his mission. He would have had all of his cousins and aunts and uncles around him. His great-grandfather knew the Prophet Joseph Smith and Brigham Young both."

Mrs. Cummings began to rock slowly in her chair.

"But we had good neighbors here and we went to the Church of Christ, and they're good people just like in Utah. You just don't know I guess. Whatever church you're in you got to have faith and you got to love people."

"You could go to meetings with me and Randy every Sunday."

"No thanks, son. The Church of Christ will have to do me for what time I've got left. They're fine people, and I'm too tired. You had enough, son?"

"Yes, ma'am. Thank you."

"You better go get to bed then. I've seen boys quit the second morning they were so tired."

"What did they do?"

"They just couldn't get out of bed. They didn't know how to work and they didn't want to learn. They couldn't stand the awful heat. It stays hot here until September."

"Good night, Mrs. Cummings. Thank you for the cookies and milk."

"Good night, son. You get a good night's sleep now. I'm going out on the front porch and sit. That breeze is so nice at night. I look forward to it."

I walked up toward the barn. Black Prince stood in the middle of the corral watching me. I walked to the ladder that went up the front of the barn. Tobe whined.

"It's okay, boy."

I climbed to the top and stood on the platform, held onto the railing. I liked to be up high. I looked out over the whole ranch, all the shapes grey-blue and black, the darkness heavier along the ground. Above the big cottonwood and the river trees were the foothills and the mountain peaks—Lava, Battle, Volcano, Spanish, Black, and Fire. Stan had told me their names. Above them I saw the North Star. I'd read a book called *The North Star.* It was my favorite star. The Chinese, Greek, Phonecian, Viking, Roman, Elizabethan, and Spanish sailors had all used it to guide them. Columbus used it to find America. The valley breeze blew against me. I liked the ranch. I wasn't homesick. I listened for coyotes, but I didn't hear any. I turned and climbed down, and walked back to the cabin.

After I put on my pajamas and brushed my teeth, I said my prayers. I prayed for my mother and grandmother, and Helen and Mrs. Johnson and Mrs. Cummings, and for Dale. I prayed for Randy, Stan, Frank, and Staver. I prayed that Randy and I could be good examples.

I got in bed and lay looking out through the screen door. Mrs. Cummings' bedroom light went out. Her window was on the opposite corner from Brent's. She'd told me which was Brent's bedroom. Brent's saddle had probably been a birthday or a Christmas present. Tobe lay against the screen door. A horse running past the cabin and out of the yard woke me up. I raised my head. I listened. I knew that it was Staver riding Black Prince. Stan told me that at night Staver rode the big black stallion down the empty river road past the campgrounds and ranch houses. I lay back on my pillow.

Randy lay on his bunk in his T-shirt and Levis. He had his boots off; he wore white boot socks. A long centerfold picture hung on the wall by the *Playboy* calendar, but I couldn't see what it was.

4

We cleaned ditches Wednesday and Thursday, and both nights Randy played poker. Both evenings ranchers brought mares to be bred, and Randy went up to the barn with Staver and Frank. I slept ten hours. I didn't even go swimming I was so tired. I lay, eyes closed, just feeling my body being still and not in the sun, the fan blowing on me. All the muscles in my whole body were sore and tight against my bones. I felt my muscles. Both nights I fell asleep feeling them, even the little ones in my fingers and toes. I'd never really felt my muscles before. And looking up at the gleaming spiral of fly paper I thought about being sixteen Saturday. Nobody had said anything about my birthday. I hadn't received any cards from home yet. Flies were stuck to the new flypaper now.

Friday morning after breakfast we stood by the red pickup. Frank put his hand on Randy's shoulder.

"Old lover boy here's going to make a good poker player, don't you think." The cigarette in the corner of Frank's mouth hardly moved.

"I think he will." Staver let smoke out of his mouth. It went up past his pale blue eyes and spread out under the brim of his hat. "He just needs practice."

"All boys need practice, but it's a lot better than playing solitaire." Frank laughed and started to choke. He turned to spit on the ground, but he kept his hand on Randy's shoulder. He turned to me. "Randy here told us about all those pretty girls you boys have in Provo. He gets nice letters from Lana."

"Provo girls are nice girls."

"Sure they are."

I had received my first letters from my mother and my grandmother. My mother said that she had met Becky in Allen's Market and Becky had asked how I was.

"You feel strong enough to work this morning, Owen?"

"Yes, I do." Staver had asked me that the last two mornings. Randy had told him I was sick on Tuesday and vomited. I told Randy that he didn't have to tell everything he knew about me.

Staver field-stripped his cigarette and then looked up.

"Okay. If Owen can work, let's move out."

Randy and I climbed into the back of the red pickup. I looked down at Mrs. Cummings' vegetable garden behind the house. Staver had me weed it Thursday morning, and he told me to get one of the Browning .22's out of the bunkhouse and kill the family of gophers that had moved in. When I told him that Randy would like to do it, he told me that Randy was busy, and it was part of the job. I shot five gophers. I put the cross hairs on their front shoulders so that when the bullet hit them they didn't suffer. They flipped in the air and lay on the ground. Blood came out of their mouths. They were the first animals I'd ever killed. I dug a hole and buried them and put a big rock on it so the skunks wouldn't dig them up.

Staver drove out of the yard slowly so he didn't make a dust, then picked up speed. Standing holding onto the rack, Randy had his face turned looking at the horses in the pasture. He shaved every morning. Last night he'd stood in the cabin doorway, his hand on the screen door, just leaving for the bunkhouse. I'd been trying to get him not to go.

"Look, these guys are interesting. Staver was in the army in a war and so was Frank. Stan's been a cowboy all his life since he was fourteen. You should hear some of the stories those guys tell. Staver was an all-state tackle, and he took the Golden Gloves final in his weight class in the western region. Frank worked in a gold mine for five years; he worked on the railroad and did a lot of other stuff. What are you going to do all summer, sit in the kitchen and talk to Mrs. Cummings? Maybe you could earn your cooking merit badge."

"I've already got it." I looked at Randy. "You don't have to play poker. We can do other things together."

"Okay, I'm sorry. Don't get mad."

"I'm not mad. I just don't know why you have to play poker."

"Look, Staver is going to take me into Silverton at the end of the summer for a real poker game if I get good enough by then. All I want is just to play in one real poker game just once in my life. I'm going to quit playing after that. What's so terrible about playing just this summer? I'm going on a mission. Are you scared of having fun or something? There's no girls around here, so what else is there to do?"

"I know that your dad doesn't want you to play poker."

"Look, I haven't smoked one cigarette or drunk even one beer, and they don't offer me any. I don't have to do that. My dad got mad before because I sold a camera he gave me to get money for poker. I'm not even playing for money now. I want that VW so I'm not going to louse things up for myself. That'd be dumb. Nothing's going to happen. You worry too much, cousin."

"We both bear the Aaronic Priesthood."

"What?" Randy had a funny look on his face. He almost closed his eyes.

"We both bear the Aaronic Priesthood. We're supposed to honor our priesthood."

"I *know* that, but we're on a ranch in the middle of Nevada. I told you that our first night." Randy shook his head. "Wait till you get on your mission. Don't louse things up for us this summer with these guys. They don't care about religion. If we get 'em on our backs they'll be riding us all summer. You got to get along with 'em."

"I will."

"Good."

Randy pushed open the screen door and went out, vanishing into the darkness beyond the porch light. Staver had showed him how to put a fuse in a stick of dynamite. Staver had crimped the dynamite cap around the fuse with his teeth and then let Randy light the fuse to blow up a tree stump. I'd heard the explosion.

We cleaned ditches Friday morning, but after lunch I drove the blue pickup up to the kitchen porch to take Mrs. Cummings into Silverton to buy groceries, and I was supposed to get my driver's license. It was legal to drive on the ranch without a license, but not off. I wasn't supposed to get my license until Saturday, when I was sixteen, but Staver had called the sheriff so he would give me my test and postdate the license. I told Staver it was illegal for me to drive into Silverton without a license.

"Well, Owen, I need everybody else here, so you're the only one I've got. If we don't get groceries we don't eat. You want to eat don't you? You don't want to cause Mrs. Cummings any worry do you?"

"No, I don't."

"Well, you got to go in anyway to get your license, so you're saving time. Nobody's going to take your Eagle Scout badge away because you drive into town to take a driver's test a half a day early."

Mrs. Cummings wore a straw hat, and she had a package to mail to Dale. Driving out of the yard, I asked her if she was going to see her doctor about her operation and she said no. I told her that I was going to be a doctor.

"That's nice, son."

"I want to be a surgeon. My father was going to be a surgeon."

"That's nice, son. Doctors can do a lot of good if they don't get all crazy for money."

I watched the fence to see if Staver had killed a great horned owl and hung it up, but he hadn't. We passed the last no-trespassing sign. We passed Porcupine Campground. Mrs. Cummings wiped her neck and breathed heavy. Her open purse was full of men's ironed white handkerchiefs. She shook her head. Two ravens and a magpie flew up from a dead jackrabbit.

"I never cross this bridge but what I think of poor Vera Swenson. She lost a son here in a brush fire twenty years ago. It broke Vera's heart; she died herself a year later. Terry was her only child and a fine boy. It was a terrible fire."

I watched the side of the valley to see where fires had been. I wondered what it was like to fight a fire, how dangerous it was. A fire shed stood by every main arch gate.

Riding my bike at night down the Provo streets, I watched every house for flames and smoke coming out of the windows. I would ride up on the lawn, break open the front door, and rescue the sleeping family so that nobody got burned but me. The police would check my wallet, and as the attendants lifted me onto the stretcher, the people standing on the lawn would all whisper my name. Even the policeman who helped close the ambulance doors would have tears in his eyes. And *Boy's Life* would print a story about me, and I would receive the Boy Scout medal for saving a life.

The cattle along the fences turned their heads to watch us pass. The sprinkling systems sent great fans of water across the green hay fields. Dust covered the weeds along the fences, and a dust haze hung over the road. I kept glancing in the rear-view mirror. I'd never broken the law before; I didn't ever want to break the law. I drove the Utah speed limit. It made me feel funny that there weren't any speed limit signs. Riding my bike, I always stopped for stop signs and red lights.

Mrs. Cummings talked about her friends who had lived on some of the ranches we passed. She described one flash flood that had killed a whole herd of cattle, and the rancher went bankrupt. A rancher named Taylor had shot his wife, who had suffered great pain from cancer for two years and couldn't die. Another whole family had been killed in a wreck caused by a truck driver who was drunk. A girl fifteen committed suicide because her father had gotten her pregnant.

"Terrible, terrible." Mrs. Cummings wiped her face. "It all keeps you humble, your sorrows and everybody else's. It's when you're hurt that you turn to the Lord and he teaches you. He's your friend. He's the one who died for you. A lot of people love you, but not like he does, son."

I looked up at the mirror and down again. A dead rattlesnake lay in the middle of the road.

"That was a big snake."

"Folks get used to snakes around here."

Mrs. Cummings took a clean handkerchief out of her purse and lifted up her hat to wipe her forehead.

"We know what's right, son, but we just don't do it. Now Dale knew right from wrong. Cliff Hinckley knew what was right too when he shot that deputy through the heart and left a widow with five children, even if he was drunk. It cost him ten years of his life, and he'll die with it on his conscience. I thank the Lord every night on my knees that Dale didn't shoot the boy at that service station. He had a gun."

Mrs. Cummings breathed deep and put her hand on her chest.

"But look at the Bible. Cain killing his own brother, all those wicked people at Noah's time. Sodom and Gomorrah, the Children of Israel and their gold calf. And just think when the Lord himself came, how they treated him. They all knew what was right, but they didn't do it. Why, remember how the Lord had to strike Saul blind and send an angel to him before he changed his ways. And the Book of Mormon is full of it, too, as I remember. It's life makes us need the Lord, son. Who but him can save us from it?"

I turned to look at Mrs. Cummings. She put both her hands on the package on her lap. I looked up at the mirror and then straight out through the windshield. I saw my hands on the steering wheel.

When I was twelve and had my interview to receive the Aaronic Priesthood and be a deacon, I told Bishop Matthews that I was going to keep all the commandments. I had written down a list of the Ten Commandments, the Articles of Faith, and the Boy Scout oath and law with little boxes to check off to see if I was doing all those things. And not even my grandmother knew about it because it was secret. Every night I checked the boxes. I had a new page for every month and I kept the old pages so I could look at all the filled boxes. I knew that if I kept all of the commandments, I would be perfect. But when I was fourteen I stopped checking the boxes because I began feeling things I didn't have any boxes for.

I looked up at the rearview mirror. We came out of the mouth of the valley and passed the Indian battle monument. Stan had told me that the first ranchers used to find skulls and bones when they plowed their fields. We climbed up through the black lava ledges and dropped down into Silverton. I slowed down to five miles under the speed limit. I watched to see if missionaries were knocking on doors, but they weren't. I turned and drove down Silver Street under the banner about the Fourth of July.

"Stop at the post office first, son, and let's get this package mailed." Mrs. Cummings wiped her face and neck. "It's too hot even for vultures. You take it in, and save me those steps. Here's the money."

I mailed the package and got back in the pickup.

"Thank you, son. I send Dale packages, I write him, and try to visit him every two or three months, and I pray for him. That's all I can do now."

I backed out very carefully. I checked the rearview mirror to see if the sheriff was following me. The neon signs burned above the saloons and casinos, the parked cars and pickups glaring in the sun. A cowboy with his arm around a girl's waist walked into the Volcano Casino. All the blinds on the upstairs windows of the World Hotel were still pulled. The movie at the Silverton was *Fort Apache.* We passed the Silverton Cafe.

Randy and I weren't coming in to the movie Saturday night because we had to irrigate. We had to irrigate until ten Sunday morning, so we couldn't come in to church either. I'd never worked on Sunday before. It made me feel bad, but I knew that we had to take the water when it was our turn.

Driving down Silver Street, I wondered which buildings men had been killed in front of in the gun fights. We went to a grocery store called Bob's. I had to help Mrs. Cummings out of the pickup. She was very heavy. The air-conditioner hung down from the ceiling and blew cold air down the aisles. Mrs. Cummings introduced me to Bob.

"It's nice to meet you, son. Hope you're having a good summer. Mrs. Cummings here is my oldest customer. I opened my store the year she moved to Silverton."

"You always sell good meat."

Mrs. Cummings pushed the cart so she would have something to hold onto. She pointed to the things she wanted and I put them in the cart. When we filled a cart I pushed it to the front and got an empty.

Mrs. Cummings sat down on the bench by the meat counter breathing hard, and Bob came back to wrap the meat she wanted.

"Anna Rhodes just came in. She'll be down here in a minute."

"I haven't talked to her on the phone for over a week. Nora Williams told me that Anna was feeling a lot better." Mrs. Cummings turned to me. "Son, you better go over and get that driver's license. He's sixteen tomorrow and has to have his driver's license."

"Happy birthday, young man."

"Thank you."

I drove over to the sheriff's office. I showed the deputy my Provo High School driver's education certificate, and he issued me a Nevada driver's license without testing me. He didn't postdate it.

"So you're working out at the Johnson place. Sign here."

"Yes, I am. Thank you." I signed the license and picked it up. I'd already paid the three dollars.

"Don't let old Staver teach you too many bad habits." He laughed.

I opened the door. "I won't."

In the pickup I took out my wallet and looked at my Nevada license. I read all the information. I'd never thought that I would have a Nevada license. Now I could go on dates in my grandmother's car.

When I got back to Bob's I put twenty-five pounds of ice in the insulated box we brought for the things that had to be kept cool. I bought Randy a box of Butterfingers and five sports car magazines. He said to buy all the new ones they had.

Bob helped me carry the groceries out to the pickup. He asked Mrs. Cummings if it looked like Staver was going to get the ranch, and she said that she hoped so but they were still waiting on the government loan because he was a veteran. He said goodbye, and I helped Mrs. Cummings get into the pickup and then got in.

"Hello, Grace."

I turned. I had my fingers on the key. A woman in a tight red silk dress stopped on the sidewalk. Her long black hair fell down over her bare shoulders. She wore a lot of makeup.

"Hello, Mrs. Cummings." She didn't walk closer.

"How are you, Grace?"

"Okay, I guess."

"You're a lovely girl, Grace."

She didn't smile. "You were always kind, Mrs. Cummings."

"It's nice to see you, Grace."

In the side mirror I watched her walk down the sidewalk and go into a casino. Her shoes and small purse were gold.

"That poor miserable soul. It's a blessing her mother's gone." Mrs. Cummings shook her head.

"Is she sick?" I turned the key, shifted and pulled out.

"Never you mind, son. Never you mind."

Turning the key, I looked in the side mirror at the closed casino door. I drove out to the Silverton cemetery. Mr. Cummings's birthday had been Wednesday. The cemetery was on a hill and had a barbed-wire fence around it, but it was all dirt and weeds, with no lawns or trees. I parked as close as I could. Mrs. Cummings carried a wreath of paper flowers she'd bought at Bob's. She bent down and put it on the grave. The headstone was long and flat and had Mr. Cummings' name and birth and death dates on one side and Mrs. Cumming's name and birth date on the other side, with a space for her death date. I'd never seen a stone like that before.

"Pull those few weeds will you, son. It's too much for me to get down anymore." Mrs. Cummings wiped her face. "Fred had his faults, like all of us, but he was the Lord's blessing to me, I know that. My little girl is right there. She's been gone nearly forty years now."

I stood up and brushed off my knees, and then I knelt down again and pulled the weeds on her daughter's grave.

"You've got a good heart, son."

Mrs. Cummings wiped her neck.

"Staver's people are just over there."

I stood up. "Where?"

"There, just over there." Mrs. Cummings pointed to two white markers by the fence. She took my arm and we walked over to them. She read the names aloud.

"Good people. No woman ever did more for others than Etta did. She's one of the first people I want to see. You wear out, son. You just wear out and there's nothing you can do about it. We just live till we die."

"Does Staver ever come here?"

"Why of course he does. He's like the rest of us."

I didn't say anything. I wondered what Staver thought when he looked down at his parents' graves and if he was sorry for all the things he'd done.

Mrs. Cummings took my arm again to walk back. "Thank you, son." She walked slowly. "This sun and heat are too much for me anymore, but I know that Glenna Marshall comes out here every day of her life. Herb's been dead ten years, but Glenna still keeps his hat hanging on the nail in the hall. She still sets a place for him at the table. You got to let go of the past and go on living when you're young. When you get old it's different because you'd just as soon be there as here, but Glenna can't be sixty yet, and that's no age."

The hot gravel cracked under our shoes.

"That's Doris Johnson and Brent right there."

"Brent Johnson?" I looked where Mrs. Cummings nodded.

"Yes. They had him brought home from Korea. Everybody loved that boy. What a dirty shame. What that boy must have suffered fighting that war. He was a gentle boy."

A bouquet of dry red roses lay on each grave. I read Brent's name and the dates. Brent was twenty when he was killed. Below his name was written his military unit, then it said, "Recipient of the Medal of Honor. Posthumously Awarded May 1, 1951."

"The governor of Nevada came to Silverton when they gave the Johnsons Brent's medal. It was a big military ceremony with a lot of people, but of course that poor boy was dead."

I turned to look at Mrs. Cummings.

"What did Brent do to win the Medal of Honor, Mrs. Cummings?"

"Oh, son, it's been over ten yers, but I think it was for saving a lot of other men's lives. But of course he was a soldier and that was what he was supposed to do."

"Did he save Staver's life?"

"No, Staver wasn't wounded until after Brent was killed. Those two boys were drafted and went in the army together."

Mrs. Cummings wiped her neck with her handkerchief and nodded down at the headstone.

"I wash all his clothes and all his bedding and the curtains every summer so his room looks nice. Mr. Johnson might open up a closet or pull open a drawer when he goes up there to sit. I want it to look nice for him. Poor man. He's so sick with that emphysema."

I drove slowly so I didn't make a dust leaving the cemetery. Mrs. Cummings sat with her head resting against the corner looking down at the headstones. She fanned herself with her hat. Her open purse was full of wrinkled white handkerchiefs.

"You know, son, my mother used to do a lot of genealogy work. And then as children we would go to the temple to be baptized for all those dead family members, and the older people would be sealed for them. So the family is there, all joined clear back to Father Adam. Of course Fred and me weren't married in the temple, but the Lord will find a way for us. There couldn't be no heaven without the people you love being there too, could there, son?"

"No, I guess not." I told Mrs. Cummings that my grandmother did genealogical research on our family all the time and went to the Salt Lake Temple to do work for the dead.

I turned left onto the main road, and we started up through the black glaring ledges. In the rearview mirror the dust hung over the road as far back as I could see, the land all pale under the white sun.

"How long have you known Staver, Mrs. Cummings?"

"Goodness, son, I knew his mother when she was carrying him. I've got pictures of him in my album when he was just a baby." She shook her head. "Etta died just before he and Brent left to go to Korea, and she had a terrible death from cancer, and Bill died just two weeks after he got back. Brent was dead, and Staver had that terrible wound in his heart." Mrs. Cummings wiped her neck. "I tell that boy he's got to let the Lord teach him and love him, but he won't listen. He better let somebody love him or he's just going to have the devil's meanness in him finally and nothing else."

We crossed the first river bridge. Kids from Battle Campground were diving off the railing into the shining water.

"Staver and his sister Carol sold the ranch. It wasn't a big place, but he spent and gambled and gave away twenty thousand dollars in six weeks. He threw big parties in Las Vegas for all his friends. He got in poker games that lasted three days, and got in fights. They say he wrecked two new pickup trucks. Now he wishes he had that money."

Mrs. Cummings pushed her hair back up under her hat.

"Married, that's what he needs to be. He's going to end up just like Frank, with nothing, that poor lonely soul. Whether Staver gets that ranch or not he ought to marry Alice. She's a good woman in her heart, and she'll work hard. Helping everybody and having party friends ain't enough. A man's got to have the love of a wife and children to make any sense. Staver's got a lot of good in him. He earned medals in the war. It was in the Las Vegas paper."

I turned and looked at Mrs. Cummings.

"Did he win the Medal of Honor?"

"No, son, he didn't win that because it wasn't the same as Brent's. You'd have to ask him."

Ahead a freshly killed jackrabbit lay in the road, its head bloody. I turned so I didn't hit it with the tire. The ravens and magpies hadn't found it yet.

If you'd been wounded, in the hospital you could take your medals out and look at them and show them to people. You could see your scars and touch them. At night you could feel under your pajamas and T-shirt and touch them. You could think about everything that happened when you got wounded and how brave you were.

"A wife and children, that stops a man from thinking about himself too much. A man's got to love somebody and somebody's got to love him. That's why he gets married and has children. It's only common sense."

On both sides of the roads the long rows of sprinklers swept the hay fields with high plumes of white water.

Mrs. Cummings looked out the window.

I'd read *How Youth Prepare for Temple Marriage.* You were married in the temple for time and eternity, had a reception, and went on a honeymoon. Sexual love was sacred. It was the way you cooperated with God to create bodies for the spirits still in heaven. God commanded Adam and Eve to have children. In the *Deseret News* and *The Provo Herald* I always looked at the pictures of the brides, who were always smiling and pretty, to see if they'd been married in the temple.

I unloaded all the groceries and put them on the shelves when we got back to the ranch, and Mrs. Cummings gave me a glass of lemonade and some cookies, and thanked me. Later, outside, I looked at my watch. We were going to irrigate all night. Staver told me that when I got back from Silverton I should go down to the Bensons' and clean out some ditches so that we could irrigate down there, too. I took out my wallet and read my license again and put it back.

I walked over to get back in the pickup. The left rear tire looked low. I bent down and looked at it and then drove up to the equipment shed and put some air in. The other tires looked a little low too, so I also put air in them. The compressor started. Tobe stood looking at me. I got back in and turned the key.

I heard a loud bang. I listened. I turned off the engine to listen. I couldn't hear anything. Dust drifted by my window. I got out. Dust settled by the back of the pickup, which was tilted to the right. The tire was flat. I squatted down to look at it.

"Bang!"

I jumped up. Dust spurted up from the right side of the pickup. I ran around. The whole back of the pickup tilted down. The other back tire was flat. My heart pounded hard; my hands tingled. I'd put in too much air. I ran to the front of the pickup. I felt in my pockets. I didn't have anything to let air out with. I looked on the ground. I yanked open the pickup door. A match stick lay on the floor. I grabbed it. I let air out of both front tires. My hands trembled. I wanted to close my eyes.

A pickup drove up behind me, but I didn't turn around. They all got out.

"What happened, Owen?" Staver stood next to me. Frank squatted down by the right tire and put his hand on it. He took his cigarette out of his mouth to look closer, and then he spit on the ground. Randy and Stan stood by Staver.

"I put in too much air. I'm sorry."

"How much did you put in?"

"I don't know. I tried to be careful."

"Did you use the gauge?"

"No. I didn't know there was one. I'm sorry."

"Did you put air in all of them?"

"Yes."

"How much does a tire hold in this heat?"

"I don't know."

"You don't know?"

"No, I don't. I'll pay for the tires."

Frank stood up. He shook his head. "Got a rip on the inside."

"That's kind of a dumb kid trick to pull isn't it?'

"I didn't know . . ."

"Well, you know now. It's a dumb kid trick isn't it?"

My whole body felt like hot metal inside. I held my breath, spread my fingers, curled my toes inside my hot boots. I watched Staver's mouth. I wanted him to stop talking to me about the tires. I'd said I was sorry and that I would pay for the tires. I got A's in school, my piano teachers had always told me I was their best student, and in the ward I was an example for other boys. Staver kept talking. I wanted to hit him in the mouth, double up my fist and hit him just once quick and hard. He didn't have to keep talking about it.

"Isn't it a dumb kid trick, Owen?"

"Yes, it is. I should have been more careful. I'll pay for the tires out of my first check. I didn't bring that much money with me."

"Oh, we expect you summer hands to pull a few dumb tricks. Just don't break old man Johnson while you're doing it." Staver smiled.

"I still want to pay."

"Good, we'll put it on your bill. For right now you can change these tires."

I looked at Staver. I breathed in deep.

"I don't know how to change a tire. My grandmother always had our tires changed at the service station."

Staver pushed his hat up with his index finger.

"You're a winner, Boy Scout, a real winner. It's a wonder they let you loose. Don't they have a merit badge for tire changing?"

"No, they don't."

"I'll show him how." Stan bent his head down to light a cigarette. He took it out of his mouth and looked at it. "I've got a cousin who works for Nevada Cement. It's the biggest batch plant in Las Vegas. They had a summer kid three years ago on the night shift check the tires on their ready-mix trucks. The next day by two o'clock it was a hundred and twenty degrees. Blew out every tire on all twenty trucks. They had to dump their cement right there where they were or it'd go hard in the barrels. Those trucks were stuck in three feet of hard cement. Had 'em all over Las Vegas. The cops were going nuts putting up roadblocks and directing traffic. Took three days to cut those trucks out with jackhammers. The batch plant boss went out hunting that kid with a gun. But he joined the navy."

"I read about that." Frank turned to spit on the ground. "It was the hottest summer they'd had in fifty years."

Frank and Staver got back in the pickup. Frank laughed. "His grandmother . . ." He laughed harder. "My old man would have beat me till . . ." He laughed. "His grandmother." Staver started the engine. Frank took off his hat and stuck his head out the window. "See ya, Careful." He whooped and laughed and waved his hat as they drove away. Tobe stood watching me.

Randy stayed to help change the tires. And he talked all the time about dynamiting a hole on the river that afternoon for trout, and how great it had been. He, Frank, and Staver had taken off their clothes and waded in the river chest deep with pitchforks to throw out the fish, some four and five pounds and twenty inches long. They got two gunnysacks a third full, which Staver had given to some friend who came out from Silverton to get them. Randy described Staver's scar. He said you couldn't believe it. It was two feet long, and two inches wide in the middle.

Before supper we went swimming. I went deep, coming up just for air. I wanted to stay under and not think about anything. Every time I thought about the tires I rolled into a ball under the water and squeezed tight. I wanted to stay down forever. I'd never made a mistake like that before. I'd never wanted to hit anybody in the mouth before or been that angry. I couldn't believe what I had felt. I wanted the water to wash all that feeling away.

I floated slowly to the top again.

"Hey, Randy, how's the water?"

I turned.

Staver and Frank stood on the ledge, each holding a can of beer; Frank had a cigarette. Frank knelt down on the ledge, put his cigarette in his mouth and reached down to touch the water.

"How is it, Randy?"

"It's great."

"Is Careful wearing a jock strap with that swimming suit?"

"Sure."

"What for?" Frank laughed. I looked at Randy. He'd told Frank and Staver even about that.

"Is his swimming suit a pretty blue?" Frank laughed again, took his cigarette out of his mouth and spit on the ledge.

"Ya."

"I thought it would be."

I turned back to watch them. They sat down on the white log, but they didn't start to pull off their boots. I didn't want them to come in swimming. I didn't want to see them undressed and hear their jokes about their bodies and what they'd done with women. I didn't want to be in the water with them.

Staver stood up from the white log and walked to the ledge.

"What about Adam, Owen? Did he wear a swimming suit when he was swimming around with Eve? I'll bet they went swimming all the time." He drank from his can of beer.

"They didn't need suits. They couldn't do anything wrong." I kept treading water.

"Well, you're a nice clean Mormon boy aren't you? Can't you swim like they did?"

"Hey, maybe old Owen isn't a virgin after all. Maybe just old Randy here." Frank squeezed his beer can and dropped it by the white log. "It's the quiet ones you got to watch. Still water runs deep. Anyway that's what my daddy used to tell my sisters." They all three laughed. "How about it, kid, you still a virgin too, or is old lover boy here wrong?"

"I think that's personal."

"It's what?"

"Personal."

"Owen's right, Frank. It's personal. You shouldn't ask a personal question like that. It's embarrassing."

"I'm sorry, kid. I'm just trying to find out the facts. You got to know the facts of life."

They laughed. Randy climbed out on the ledge to dive and Frank whistled. Randy ran across the ledge and dived in and came up.

"Hey, Randy." Frank flipped his cigarette butt into the river. "You sure old Owen here is all boy? He looks a little thin."

"Yeh, I'm sure."

"Just checking. You can't always tell these days."

I went under the water. I didn't ever want to come up. I wanted to turn into a fish. I held my breath as long as I could. I rose slowly.

"There he is. How about you, Owen?" Staver pointed at me with his beer can.

"What?"

I was just asking Randy here if he didn't want to climb up those cleats and dive off. You get to carve your name on the trunk. It's about sixty feet. You want to be sure and hit the water."

I looked up. A sharp clean feeling of fear came from down in my groin up through my body.

"Hey, Staver, did you climb out there to put that swing up?"

Treading water, Randy looked up at the limb.

Staver didn't look up. The swing was farther out than where they dived from, which was an opening in the branches.

"Did you do it?"

"No."

"Who did?"

"Somebody else."

"He must have had guts."

Staver threw his beer can back into the trees. "Maybe too many." He turned and walked back through the trees.

Frank stood up from the log. "See you boys later."

"Yeh. See ya, Frank."

I watched Frank and Staver until they vanished into the trees.

Randy floated on his back, and when I asked him why he still told Frank and Staver things about me, he just laughed and told me I worried too much. He took a bath and got dressed. He told me not to drown and then left. We were going to eat supper late because we would be irrigating all night, and we were supposed to sleep for a couple of hours before supper. I took a bath, wrapped my towel around me and sat down on the ledge. Tobe came over and lay down beside me.

I pulled my legs up, put my arms around them and rested, my forehead on my knees. I pulled tight. I wanted to feel like a ball, have all my body connected, not have any ends or edges. I wanted words for what I felt so I could say them and know what it was and understand. I couldn't find the words in any of the books I read or in the dictionary. When Brother Anderson bore his testimony he said, "The Holy Ghost will fill you with light and understanding if you live humble worthy lives. I know this is true."

I opened my eyes and raised my head from my knees. I was looking at the initials carved on the trunk of the big cottonwood, which was where the cleats started and the three trunks divided. I looked up where they dived from. The tingling electric feeling came up from my groin into my stomach and chest. I knew that I was going to dive because Staver had and because of what he'd done to me. I knew I would. Tobe stood up and whined. I stood up slowly. I kept looking at where they dived from. I spread my fingers and shook my hands like a swimmer before a race. I was scared. Behind me in the fields beyond the trees a pheasant crowed.

I took off my towel and put on my swimming suit again. Tobe whined. I walked to the tree and started to climb the cleats. I climbed into the leaves, which touched me. The cleats ended where I could stand up leaning forward on the sloping trunk if I held onto the limbs. I walked slowly, my heart beating hard. Ahead I saw where they had cut the limbs away to make the hole to dive through. Far below the river shimmered like a pond. Holding onto a branch with one hand, I stopped and turned. I looked at the mountains and the sky, but my chest was caving in. I had to do it fast.

I reached under my suit with one hand and pulled my supporter up tight. I let go with the other hand and stood without holding on. I tipped forward and pushed with my feet, lifted my arms, fell, kept my eyes open, fell, fell against the air. I closed my eyes, hit, went down, down, opened my eyes in the dark water, flattened out and came up slowly, broke surface. I reached up and touched the top of my head, which hurt. I looked up at the diving place. I didn't say anything to myself.

I swam over to the ledge and climbed out. Tobe nuzzled me and I knelt down and petted him.

"It's okay, boy."

I stood up. I looked up at the high limb. I took off my suit. I looked up at the limb. I looked down at myself. I held out my arms and looked at them. I looked down at my feet and legs. I ran my hands down over my arms, chest, stomach, groin, and legs. I held my head in my hands. I wanted to see myself in a room of mirrors. I looked up at the diving place again and down at the river. I'd never done anything like that before.

I got dressed. I didn't carve my initials in the tree because I didn't want Staver to know what I'd done. I didn't want anybody but me to know. I liked to know things about myself that nobody else knew. I wanted to see the big trout. I walked up to the old bridge and crawled out on the planks. I lay down, edged forward, and looked down into the water.

I saw the big German brown trout. He moved his tail slowly, hung in the water beneath me, turned a little, his whole broad side gold. I tried not to breathe. He was two feet long and thick, a big German brown trout. Slowly, slowly he sank, disappeared down into the dark water without moving any part of his body. I waited but I didn't see him again. He was a very beautiful fish. In the trees above me a male great horned owl hooted.

I stood up and walked back off the plank. Staver would dynamite the hole if he knew the big trout was there. I'd decided to make a screen trap and catch minnows and put them back in the holes Staver dynamited. I turned once to look back. The big cottonwood tree, becoming dark now, was the biggest tree I'd ever seen. I liked trees. In Provo in the evening riding my bicycle, I stopped to touch the trees. Sometimes I put my arms around them and pulled tight. At night I rode my bicycle fast under the dark trees, which was like flying.

Walking toward the lit house, I thought about how I'd wanted to hit Staver in the mouth. I was sorry about feeling that way. I wanted to be friends with him.

5

I slept for two hours, and after supper I helped Mrs. Cummings clear the table. Stan, Frank, and Staver went outside to smoke, and Randy went with them. A rancher was bringing a mare to be bred.

"You're getting your color back, son. You keep eating and getting your sleep, and you'll be all right."

Mrs. Cummings carried the plate of meat scraps out to the back porch for her two cats and Tobe. The rancher drove into the yard pulling a black horse trailer. Staver got in the pickup, and Randy and Frank walked up toward the corral behind the trailer, Frank with his hand on Randy's shoulder. Stan sat on a bench under the first tree smoking. Mrs. Cummings came back in carrying the empty scrap plate. The whole west sky was red with the setting sun.

Mrs. Cummings put the plate in the soapy water.

"Staver and that horse. He needs something to grab onto, and he'd better be finding it. A man gets so he only answers to the devil after a while." She rinsed the soap off the scrap plate and put it in the drainer. "Of course, he's always been good to me. He couldn't have been better to his own mother. He's always been good to help people and do for them, but that isn't like doing for a family of his own."

I wiped the dish and put it in the cupboard. I knew where everything went now.

Mrs. Cummings lifted her soapy hand out of the water to push back her white hair with her forearm.

"It's hot this evening, and going to get a lot hotter. You'd think after forty years living on this desert you'd get used to it, but you don't. I don't know what I'd do without that evening breeze." She turned to look out the screen, then turned back. "We used to get such lovely summer rainstorms at home in Manti when I was a little girl. Everything was so pretty and fresh afterward, the air so clean. We didn't have the dry thunderstorms and the brush fires, not all this dust either. It was such a nice place. But that was a long time ago."

Both the fans were on. Mrs. Cummings dried her hands and arms on her apron and walked over and sat in her rocking chair.

"I just need to sit down and rest for a minute before we finish those pots and pans." She sat back in the chair. "It's a hard life, son; you don't know what will happen to you till it's over, or how you're going to deal with it all. Just look at my sister-in-law Beth. Her husband Ron killed himself with drink, and he was a good man when she married, just as good as my Fred. The suffering that man caused. He drove all his children away and broke poor Beth's heart. There's so much meanness in the world, son." Mrs. Cummings looked up at the pictures of Jesus above the table. "He knows all about it."

"I'll do the pots and pans, Mrs. Cummings."

"Thank you, son. I'm tired." She leaned back in the rocking chair and closed her eyes. Her breathing was heavy.

I put the frying pan in the soapy water. Through the laundry room door I saw our dirty clothes and bedding for the week. We'd all brought our laundry when we came for supper because we'd be irrigating tomorrow morning and couldn't bring it then. Mrs. Cummings liked to have everything ready for Monday morning, when she washed. We changed our bunks on Saturday. Frank had asked me if I had another pair of new pajamas.

I'd put on a clean work shirt before supper. Dirty collars could give you boils on your neck, and I'd never had a boil. My grandmother sent me to Dr. Parker when I first started to have pimples. He said that all boys had pimples. I washed my face four times a day with a special antiseptic soap. I didn't like anything to be wrong with my body.

I finished the pots and pans and put them away and cleaned the sink. I kept expecting Mrs. Cummings to say something about it being my birthday Saturday, but she didn't. The rancher drove back past the kitchen door pulling the horse trailer. I hung up the wet dishtowel.

"I guess I have to go, Mrs. Cummings."

"Well, bless you, son, for your help. There's five sack lunches in the refrigerator if you'll take them with you."

She didn't get up. I got the lunches. "You be careful now out there irrigating all night."

"Yes, ma'am."

Staver, Frank, and Randy sat in the first pickup; Stan was in the second. The halo of light above the west mountains faded into the darker blue. I passed out the lunches. Stan handed me a pair of heavy knee-length rubber boots out the window.

"You'll need these, kid."

"Thank you."

I sat on the porch steps and put on the boots. Tobe sat by me.

"Hey, Owen, Frank here wants to know if you've got a merit badge in irrigating."

"There isn't one."

"You'd better watch our Eagle Scout then, Stan. We don't want him to fall in the canal and drown."

"Don't let him get too close to that air hose, Stan." Frank laughed.

"I'll watch him."

I pulled on the second boot. I didn't say anything. I didn't even look up. I'd decided not to let Staver or Frank get me angry again. I was just going to work hard and be an example. That was all I could do. They wouldn't listen to anything I said about the Church. I didn't want to hit Staver or anybody else. It wasn't necessary to get that angry. I could control my emotions. I just wanted to be their friends.

"Good." Staver shifted and drove off.

I put my work boots in the back of the pickup and got in. Stan drove down across the bridge and turned north at the gate. Two jackrabbits sat together at the edge of the road staring into the headlights. Stan leaned forward over the steering wheel to light a cigarette. In the dark windshield the match flared against his face. He blew out smoke and sat back.

"You got to learn how to take Staver, kid." He put the match in the ashtray. "Just don't get your back up, and you'll be okay. He's a good foreman; never seen a better one. You can learn a lot from him if you keep your eyes and ears open.

The Johnsons know that Staver will take care of this place the way they would; that's why they want to sell it to him. A big California outfit buys a nice place like this and it's just an investment. I guess Staver having it is the next best thing to old man Johnson's boy being alive. Those two was like brothers from all I hear."

I looked straight out the windshield. A jackrabbit ran across the road and back into the darkness.

"Staver doesn't bother me."

"Good."

We drove along the canal. I watched the black, smooth water, the dark haystacks in the fields. I didn't want Staver to own the ranch; I wanted Helen to inherit it.

"Was Staver with Brent when he got killed in Korea?"

"Some say he was and some say he wasn't, but he don't talk about it. He talks about the war and killin' gooks, but he don't say nothin' about what happened to the Johnson kid or gettin' wounded himself. I talked to a fellow once who said he was in the same outfit with Staver, and he said that Staver sort of went crazy after the Johnson kid got himself killed. Staver got wounded the next day and won a medal. That's sure some scar he brought home with him. Never seen one like that on a man before."

I watched the dark canal.

"What did Brent do to win the Medal of Honor?"

"I don't know that either. I wasn't working around here when they had the big ceremony in Silverton. People say he saved a lot of lives. Both him and Staver got drafted and went in together and stayed in the same outfit."

Stan stopped at a headgate on the canal, and we got out. I got the shovels out of the back. He handed me a flashlight and shined his on the headgate.

"Plenty of light to see what you're doing, so about all you need a flashlight for is to check the headgates for rattlers. You can expect to see one or two in a summer. They like the warm cement. All you have to do is hit 'em good and hard once with the flat of your shovel. Don't try to cut their heads off; you might miss. Just pound 'em. Don't worry about stepping on one. They can't get through these heavy boots. And you have to watch out for skunks too; they come out at night. You don't want to tangle with any skunks."

Stan bent down and unlocked the chain around the headgate.

"I knew a rancher named Simmons once that stepped on a skunk out irrigating one night. Stepped right on it. They had to bury him up to his neck in a manure pile for a week. Manure's good for drawing out stink. Gets it off a lot better than washing with tomato juice, which is what most people use. A lot of car wrecks are caused by skunks. You hit a skunk and that smell gets inside and people just go crazy. Simmons' wife would carry his meals out to him. They had to put a fence around that manure pile to keep the pigs and chickens off."

"How could he stand it that long?"

"Didn't have any choice."

Stan stayed with me for two hours. He showed me how to work a headgate, build sets with canvas and sod, and how to get the water to spread out over the pasture. You had to use the grade and keep the ditch full so that the water flooded over all along the top of the field.

"Okay, kid," he said. "You learn fast, so I'm going to leave you. But be careful. You let one of those big ditches get away from you and you can tear up a lot of country. One summer we had a kid from Las Vegas that ruined a couple acres of young hay. Staver ripped the hide off that kid, and he just broke down and bawled. But he stayed all summer, stacked hay, and got his bonus. Staver's okay as long as you don't make the same mistake too often."

Stan looked at me. "You better put on some weight before we start stacking hay. That's about the hardest work you'll ever do. Do that twelve hours a day and you can do most anything."

He walked over and got in the pickup. "Watch out for those skunks. They like to hunt for pheasant nests along the ditch banks at night. One cuts loose and it'll blow your hat off fifty yards downwind. You can smell one for ten miles if the wind's right."

I watched the pickup lights disappear down through the fields. I wanted to ask Stan about what the farmer did in the manure pile for a whole week.

I worked hard. The breeze had started. I listened for coyotes. The North Star hung like a lamp over me. I named the constellations to myself, spoke the names out loud, knew there were other worlds there, and kept looking up to see the moon. And I liked to control the water, hear it spreading out over the dry fields, smell it, whole patches of the fields silver where the pasture grass was low. Through my boots I felt the water cool and pushing. I liked to make it go where it was supposed to, to the waiting grass, my feet cool in the boots in the water. I looked at my watch. It was past midnight. Twice I shouted up at the sky, "I'm sixteen! It's my birthday!" And I wanted to climb up on a haystack and shout that, but I was afraid Staver might be watching and hear me.

Stan came back at one o'clock and we drove down to the canal to the next headgate. We sat in the pickup with both doors open and opened our lunch sacks. I wanted to say, "It's my birthday, Stan." But I didn't.

"See any rattlers?"

"No."

"I got a little one."

Stan ate his chocolate cake first. With his finger he scraped the frosting off the sides of the plastic container Mrs. Cummings had sent it in.

Stan told me how rattlesnakes crawled down into Silverton out of the lava ledges to strike children playing in backyards, and their mothers found them dead in their sandpiles. Snakes crawled into two boys' clothes while they were swimming in the river, and a fisherman found their bodies. Ranchers baled snakes in the hay in the summer, and when they broke the bales in the winter to feed the cattle they got struck. Their wives found their bodies in the barn or the feed lot.

I lowered my sandwich. "A snake would die; it'd suffocate." Stan was eating an apple.

"Well, I only knew of that happening once myself. A rancher named Roberts baled his last crop of hay in October when one of those big arctic cold fronts blew in and it dropped to ten below overnight. It was a cold year. That snake was froze stiff. It just stayed in that bale and thawed out. When Roberts broke that bale open in the spring it got him right in the neck. He must have been leaning over to break the bale apart with his hands. He had two boys in high school, so his wife had enough help to run the ranch. The oldest boy's got it now."

Stan turned to look out his door. He tossed the apple core out into the weeds. I'd read about experiments where they quick-froze tissue and then thawed it out and it lived.

After we ate we moved further down the canal irrigating pasture where the cattle had been moved out. I watched the dawn come slowly, the faint light about the mountains first, and then the shapes of the rectangular haystacks, the trees, willow hedges, and then the colors coming back until the sun hit the valley floor and moved across to us bringing the heat. Magpies and ravens flew out of the trees down to the irrigated fields in small flocks to feed, jackrabbits and pheasants standing at the edges of the field.

Stan and I checked to see that our headgates were chained and locked. He said that fishermen and kids from the campgrounds opened them sometimes just to see the water go down the ditch.

"That's why Staver keeps 'em chased out of here."

"What are the magpies eating?"

"Fish." Stan stopped to light a cigarette.

"What fish?"

"Trout. They come down the canal from the river and then get caught when we cut the water out of the ditches. Skunks get a lot of them. I've seen vultures after 'em once or twice, if they're big enough."

"Can't we put up a screen at the river?"

"Guess you could, except nobody ever has. You'd have to keep it cleaned off."

I watched the magpies.

"There's a big one right there." Stan pointed down behind a headgate.

"Where?"

"In the hole."

Each headgate was cement, and at the downstream lip there was always a hole worn where the water hit the dirt.

"He's about three pounds. That's a nice fish. Staver likes that kind to take into Silverton to his parties."

The dorsal fin stuck out of the water, the trout not moving. I saw under the water the eyes. His sides were gold with orange and red spots circled by white. I climbed down into the ditch behind him. He moved his tail slowly. A trickle of water came under the iron gate and into the pool. His gills opened and closed, but he didn't move except for his tail. He was beautiful, a German brown. I'd studied all the game fish of the Rocky Mountain states for a special project in biology.

"Come on, kid. I want a cup of good coffee. Some skunk will get him."

"I'm going to put him back in the canal."

"How you going to do that?"

"With my hat."

I caught the trout on the third try. I hugged the hat against my chest, and I could feel him. I climbed out of the irrigation ditch and hurried to the canal. I pushed the hat deep into the water and opened it. The big trout vanished into the deep water. I knelt there watching the place he'd gone.

"He'll just get caught in some other ditch."

"Maybe."

"Staver fills half a gunnysack with trout every time he dynamites a hole. Sometimes two."

"That's against the law."

"Well, they're awful nice parties. The girls always invite the summer hands out a time or two. You'll enjoy 'em."

Stan told me to drive the pickup back. A faint breeze, just barely moving the willow leaves, blew down the valley. I looked at my watch. The road went through some willows along the canal. I felt good. I liked to irrigate. It was my birthday, and I was sixteen.

"Hey, watch out for that big skunk!"

I put my foot on the brake.

"Where?"

"Keep going, kid! Keep going!"

"Where is he?" I shifted to neutral and pulled on the brake.

Stan looked out the rear window, opened the door, and jumped out. "Run, kid!"

I got out. I looked back along the road. The skunk was about twenty feet behind the pickup lying on his back, his hind feet still moving.

I turned to look at Stan. He was standing about a hundred feet down the road.

"What's the matter, Stan?"

Suddenly I went blind. I gave one shout. I fell to my knees. I grabbed my throat, choking and gagging. I tipped over and fell on the ground. I was blind. I touched the willows. Feeling with my hands I crawled through them and down the bank and rolled into the canal. I stayed under. I didn't ever want to come up, but I had to. I could open my eyes. Stan stood on the bank laughing and slapping both thighs with his hands. I could breathe.

"Kid, you got yourself about half-skunked." He shook his head. "I thought you were going to drowned yourself. You sure did a dance."

"It's awful. It's terrible." I breathed deep; I could still smell the skunk.

"I hollered at you, but he didn't get you. That was just the vapor cloud. He didn't get the pickup either. You must have run over his head, so you won't stink very much. But you better ride in the back going in. I sure wish I had a movie camera."

Holding onto the rack I stood up going back. I kept breathing deep. That's all I wanted to do. I kept taking big deep breaths of fresh air. I hadn't turned to look at the dead skunk. I just wanted to breathe fresh air. I couldn't believe it had happened to me.

Frank and Staver stood by the kitchen porch smoking when we drove into the yard. Randy was with them. Stan pulled up and stopped. He got out.

"What happened? Did he fall in?" Staver took his cigarette out of his mouth. He was already smiling.

I didn't get out. Randy looked up at me, and Mrs. Cummings came to the door.

"The kid here got himself about half-skunked."

"What?"

Stan told them what happened. They all started to laugh, Stan again, too. Frank laughed so hard his cigarette fell out of his mouth. He reached down and picked it up. Mrs. Cummings had gone back into the kitchen.

"Don't get too close. Kid, you stink."

They all laughed.

"Very funny."

I knew that they were just kidding me, trying to make me mad. My hands tingled. I let my hands hang down, my fingers spread apart.

"Here, Randy, give these to Owen." I looked up. Mrs. Cummings stood on the porch. She handed Randy two quart cans of tomato juice. "Son, you go down to the river and take a bath. Pour this all over you and rub it in. You leave your clothes down there in the river with a rock on them for a day or two. Randy, you go get Owen some clean clothes and a towel. Breakfast will be ready in ten minutes. You hurry up, son. Don't you go in that cabin till you take a bath."

"Yes, ma'am."

When I got down from the truck they all backed away.

"Hey, Randy. Stack that stuff on the porch. Don't get too close."

"Be sure to stay up wind from old Skunky here." Frank turned and spit on the ground.

"I'll watch it."

They laughed.

Carrying the two cans of tomato juice, I walked under the trees to the cabin to get my clothes. Tobe walked ahead of me. I wanted to close my eyes. I still couldn't believe it had happened to me. I tried not to breathe deep enough to smell. I shouldn't have stopped the pickup and gotten out. I couldn't believe it.

At the swimming hole Tobe lay on the ledge and watched me. I put all my clothes except my boots in the shallow water under a rock. Mrs. Cummings had punched the tomato juice cans. I poured the juice over my head with one hand and rubbed it in with the other. I put the can down and rubbed with both hands, and then I poured more juice on my head. My whole body was red. The red juice ran down off my legs and onto the ledge. I smelled my arms; I bent down to smell my legs. I poured the last bit of juice on my boots and rubbed it in. I had only one pair of work boots. I rinsed off in the river and washed myself with soap three times. I kept smelling myself. I smelled my towel after I got dry. Going back up the trail I stopped twice to smell myself. I heard a roar and looked up. Six jet fighters flew low up the valley and disappeared over the mountains. I walked across the yard.

Mrs. Cummings pushed open the screen door for me. She turned to the table. "Now you four can stop all the laughing and jokes. Owen's just fine. He doesn't stink."

I sat down. Randy moved his chair away from mine a little.

"Randy."

"Yes, ma'am."

They all looked down at their plates. Nobody wished me a happy birthday, not even Mrs. Cummings. I didn't really care. I hadn't received any birthday cards yet either. I knew that my mother and grandmother were keeping all my presents until I got back on Labor Day.

After breakfast I went back to the cabin. We could sleep until noon and then Randy was going to irrigate with Staver while Stan and Frank rested. I had to clean a section of ditch that Staver wanted done. We had the water for two days.

I was so tired I just pulled off my boots and fell on my bunk. Randy lay in his shorts and T-shirt reading a *True West* magazine. When he wasn't playing poker, he read magazines from the stack against the wall. He had four on his bunk. He'd put another *Playboy* picture on the wall by the *Playboy* calendar. He had three now; they were all centerfolds. I'd told Randy I didn't like the pictures on the wall. When I told him they made you think about girls too much, he said that's why he put them up. At night lying in my army bunk, my glasses off, the pale bodies were blurred.

Randy looked up. He'd gotten back to the cabin first.

"I can't smell any stink. You don't stink anymore."

"Thanks."

Randy reached up and moved his fan so that it went up and down his whole body.

"Hey, you ought to hear some of the war stories Frank and Staver tell." He lay back down and turned the page of his magazine. "They were both in a lot of big battles. Staver's a real boxer, too. Frank told me that nobody in Silverton ever beat him in a fight. He won his weight in the Golden Gloves championships for all the Western States when he was seventeen. He boxed in the army, too. Nobody ever hits him in the face. He's going to give us lessons. He wants to play football with us, too, on the lawn. He was all-state."

"Does he say anything about being wounded or Brent Johnson being killed?"

"No, but he talks about everything else. He really killed a lot of gooks. Why?"

"Nothing. I was just asking." I looked at all the dead flies stuck on the flypaper. "Do you have to play poker over there every night?"

I heard Randy turning the pages of the magazine.

"No, I don't have to. I don't *have* to do anything. I just want to. There's nothing wrong with it. What're you so worried about. What do you think they're going to do to me? They keep inviting you to come and watch TV and have a root beer."

I turned on my side away from Randy.

"I want to go to sleep. We've still got to work all afternoon and half the night."

"Did you hear the shooting this morning? Staver shot three jackrabbits. One shot each at a hundred yards. Pieces flew all over. That .22-250 of his really blows things apart with those special shells he loads."

"I need some sleep."

"I wish we were going into Silverton tonight. I haven't seen a girl for a week. I'd like to go to Las Vegas."

I pulled the ends of my pillow up over my ears, but I couldn't sleep. I breathed deep; I couldn't smell anything. I thought about Brent and what it felt like to rescue all those other soldiers, and if he got wounded and knew he was dying. I wanted to know what that felt like and if Staver talked to him before he died and what they said. I'd always wanted a friend like Brent. I'd never had a really good friend yet. I wondered if Brent had to kill any Korean soldiers. In the Book of Mormon the Nephites and the Lamanites hated each other so much that they killed their prisoners and ate their flesh and drank their blood. Brother Anderson said that both sides kept prisoners in concentration camps.

The alarm clock went off at noon. Randy didn't want to get up. The heat was like waking up under a wool blanket. I took a shower. After lunch Stan drove me out to clean the ditch. Nobody had wished me happy birthday yet. At the table I almost said, "It's my birthday today. I'm sixteen." They knew it was my birthday because I had to get my driver's license.

Stan held the steering wheel with his wrists while he lit a cigarette. He shook the match and put it in the ashtray.

"You two kids know that Staver's watching you when you're out here alone don't you? He's always looking for trespassers, broken fences, looking at the cattle, and for varmints to shoot, but he's looking at you, too, with those binoculars of his. You don't have to kill yourself, but stay busy. Staver expects a day's work out of you summer hands, and he gets it, too. He knows everything that happens on this whole place."

"I work hard."

"Good. Just remember that you don't even know when he's watching you. He could be two or three miles off. Those are big army binoculars he's got."

Stan stopped by the ditch I had to clean, and I got out. I got the water bag and my shovel out of the back.

"See you about six, kid. Watch out for rattlers around here. This is the kind of place they like down below those ledges."

"I will."

I watched Stan's plume of dust getting longer and longer. I looked up. Not one cloud. A vulture circled. I hung the water bag on the fence and started cutting weeds. Vultures didn't come down unless they were sure there was something to feed on. They couldn't waste energy. Each vulture had a certain territory to patrol, and he watched to see what the other vultures did. If one vulture went down, the others followed him. I'd read a book called *Desert Birds.*

I chopped the weeds. The heat was like standing in front of a bonfire. My clothes were hot, even my boots. But I liked my work clothes; I liked the way my body felt inside them. It felt stronger and bigger, the new Levis heavy and stiff on my legs. I liked my leather gloves, which fit my hands now.

I worked hard. I didn't look at my watch. I didn't care if Staver was watching me or not. It was my birthday. I took out my driver's license and looked at it and the word "Nevada" and put it back. I pulled off my shirt and T-shirt for twenty minutes to tan. I did that twenty minutes each day so I wouldn't burn. The sun was good for my face, too. I watched the muscles in my arms. I'd never needed to be strong for anything before in my life. I wanted to be able to work as hard as Staver. I liked the feel of not wearing a T-shirt or a shirt.

I didn't see Staver's pickup coming until it was close enough to hear. I hadn't looked at my watch. Randy, Stan, Frank, and Staver were all in the cab. Staver pulled past me to a wide place in the road. They all got out, the dust settling around them. Staver carried a willow switch. Frank said something to Randy, and he nodded his head and then turned to face me.

"Come on, kid, let's go. Time to go, kid." I climbed out of the ditch and took the water bag from the fence. "I guess you're tired after irrigating all night. Stan was telling Staver you did a good job."

They all stood near the back of the black pickup.

"A little."

"Well, let's go," Staver said. "You and Randy climb in the back, Owen. Let Frank take your shovel."

"Thanks."

Randy stood behind me. I stepped up on the rear bumper and put my leg over the tailgate. My foot came down by a large coiled rattlesnake. I yelled, screamed, and threw myself back, letting go of the water bag. I rolled in the heavy dust and lay there dazed. I didn't move. I heard the loud laughter. I raised my head.

They stood together laughing. Bent forward, Frank kept slapping his leg with his hat. He started to cough, but he still laughed. He turned to spit, and when he straightened up he picked up my hat.

"Here, kid, you dropped this." He pushed my straw cowboy hat down on my head. "Let me give you a hand." He helped me up. "You got all dusty, kid." He brushed off the back of my shirt with his hand. I reached up and felt my glasses.

"Better take a look and see what scared Owen, Frank."

"I was just going to." Frank walked up to the tailgate; he leaned over and lifted the rattlesnake out by the tail. "Was it him? Why he's dead, kid. Somebody shot off his head." Frank walked over and held the snake out to me. I stepped back. It was four feet long and thick as my wrist in the middle. "Nothing to be scared of, kid. It's the live ones you want to watch out for." Frank turned toward Staver and held the snake up higher. "It's dead."

Holding the switch in his hand, Staver lit a cigarette and rubbed the head of the match between his thumb and finger. "Snakes are dangerous, Frank. We had a corporal in the outfit in Korea that was in a foxhole one night when a little green snake crawled in and bit him on the lip. He killed it with his bayonet, but that didn't do him any good. A good man, too, an Eagle Scout." Staver inhaled deeply, took the cigarette out of his mouth and blew out the smoke. "How does Owen look, Frank? Is he okay?" Staver smiled.

Frank looked down at the front of my Levis. "Fine, just fine. No problems."

They laughed.

My whole body swelled, getting hard, bigger, my eyes closing tight. I wanted to hit Staver, knock him down, and when he fell I wanted to pick him up and hit him again, keep picking him up and hitting him until he crawled away begging me not to hit him anymore. I would reach down and grab him by the collar, lift him up and push him against the cab of the pickup. I'd tell him never to laugh at me again and push him toward Frank, who would catch him.

"You okay, Careful?"

I opened my eyes. "Yes."

"Thought something might be wrong. Here, you dropped this." Frank handed me the water bag.

"Let's move it." Staver turned and got in the pickup.

Riding back, Randy and I stood up behind the cab. Randy would look at me, shake his head and start to laugh. "Brother, they really sucked you in on that one." He held on to one of the pitchforks in the rack to keep his balance when he laughed.

"Very funny."

"It sure was." Randy put his foot up on the box of dynamite.

I felt dumb. I knew that Staver scared the summer hands every year with a dead snake in back of the pickup. They'd made me feel really dumb again, and I didn't want to do anything dumb again all summer. It scared me how angry Staver made me. I didn't want to feel that way toward any person. I knew I had to really think about how I felt and control it. I had to hate the bad things Staver did, but not him. You had to love everybody. I kept thinking about how I'd felt. I'd never felt like that toward anybody before in my whole life. I wanted to love everybody.

I watched the high dark green river trees across the dark green fields. I wanted Brent Johnson to be alive and be married and have the ranch and be his own foreman. And have Mrs. Cummings as the cook and Stan as the permanent hand. Randy and I would sleep in the bunkhouse. The ranch would really be wonderful without Frank and Staver. We wouldn't even know their names or where they lived. I turned my Eagle Scout ring on my finger.

The cattle lifted their heads to watch us go by. Dust covered the mowed weed stubble along the fences.

I wanted to live in Provo all my life in our house and in our ward. My grandmother had left the house to me in her will. One night when I was fourteen I got up to touch all the furniture in my bedroom with my hands in the darkness; I touched the walls, windows, doors, and the full-length mirror. Some of my school teachers knew my father. Old clerks in the stores my grandmother took me to knew my father. Ward members and neighbors knew him. Until I was fourteen, at night, I expected a light to start growing in the corner of my room and get brighter and brighter, and it would be my father. But he didn't come, and I woke up in the mornings still wearing my glasses. Some nights I climbed out through my windows to sit in the sycamore tree and listen to the owls. One night Uncle Mark told my mother that my room needed more than new paint, wallpaper, and carpet.

Barking, Tobe ran down the lane toward us.

At the end of supper Mrs. Cummings came out of the pantry carrying a chocolate birthday cake with sixteen lit candles on it. Everybody sang happy birthday and shook my hand. Stan, Frank, and Staver gave me a silver inlaid cowboy belt buckle and Randy gave me the belt. Mrs. Cummings gave me a shaving mug and brush, and a dozen disposable razors. I got a lot of birthday cards, including one from Becky and one from Helen Johnson. Mrs. Cummings had been keeping them. My grandmother and mother called. Mrs. Cummings served ice cream with the birthday cake, and Frank asked me four times what it felt like to be sixteen. I thanked everybody for being so kind. I really felt good about everything, and I knew that Randy and I were going to have a good summer. I really appreciated the belt buckle. I shook everybody's hand.

Randy and I slept until two o'clock Sunday morning and then got up to irrigate. It was the first time in my life that I'd ever worked on Sunday, and I felt all day like I was doing something wrong, but I knew that we had to irrigate because we had the water. Staver told Mrs. Cummings that I could drive her into Silverton to her church, but she wasn't feeling very well and didn't want to go.

6

Monday morning Mrs. Cummings was already hanging the sheets on the line when Staver took me and Randy up to the equipment shed to show us how to operate the two small tractors and the power takeoffs and the knives for cutting hay. We were going to cut weeds along the road fences for practice. First Staver showed us how to sharpen the long silver knife. We were responsible for sharpening our own knives. We would take an extra knife with us when we cut hay so we would always work with a sharp knife. Staver showed us how to fit the knife, oil it, how to raise and lower it, and how to fold it up on the hinge and bolt it with the bar for traveling. I liked to see the weeds fall in front of the knife, the pheasants flying out ahead, see behind me everything cut clean. The diesel exhaust didn't bother me.

I wore my wet red bandana handkerchief down over my nose and mouth because of the dust, and I took long drinks from the water bag. I felt my whole body inside my clothes. The vibration of the tractor came up through the iron seat into my bones. In the late afternoon I took off my shirt and T-shirt to tan more. I looked down at my naked arms, chest, and stomach. The weed dust made black sweaty lines where my stomach creased in the light hair above my belt. When the tractor got close, the magpies and ravens flew away from feeding on the dead badgers, coyotes, wildcats, and hawks hanging on the fence.

After supper Staver gave Randy and me our first boxing lesson. Randy put on the gloves first to box with Staver in front of the bunkhouse and then I did. I was tired. All I wanted to do was take a shower and go to bed.

"Jab. Keep that left moving. Jab, jab, Owen. Keep the other guy off balance. Keep dancing, Owen. You're always dancing so you're hard to hit." I wanted to stop and take off my glasses, but Staver said I didn't need to. He hit me on the forehead and the jaw, just tapped me, his gloves so fast I couldn't see them coming. He hit me harder on the chest and stomach, but it didn't hurt. "Keep your elbows in. Protect yourself, Owen. Keep those gloves up. Dance. Come after me, Owen." He kept talking all the time telling me what I was doing wrong. He was quick and tall and very strong, and I couldn't hit him even once. Staver said that by the end of the summer I ought to be able to take care of myself.

"Sure the kid will." Frank turned to spit. Stan sat in a chair on the porch watching.

Afterward Randy showered and went to play poker. I went to bed.

We mowed weeds again Tuesday, and in the afternoon I hit a rock and jammed the knife. I couldn't believe it. The shear pin broke so that the whole knife came back, but it was still jammed. I'd been careful. Staver had told us to watch for logs, stumps, and rocks. I got my tool box off the back of the tractor and tried to fix it, but I couldn't. I stood up. I held the wrench tight. I wanted to throw it clear across the field.

Staver's red pickup stood parked by the tractor shed when I drove into the yard. I turned off the engine and got down. Staver came out of the tool room. Frank stood behind him in the half shadow of the doorway. Tobe reached up and licked my hand. Staver wore a blue cowboy shirt with pearl buttons. Every day he wore a cowboy shirt with pearl buttons.

"What's wrong now, Owen?"

"I hit a rock and jammed the knife. I couldn't fix it." Staver knelt down on one knee to look at the knife. "I didn't see it. It was behind a big weed."

"Do you want me to have Frank paint all the rocks white? Get your tool box."

"I'd paint rocks for Skunky." Frank walked over to us and squatted down. "He's kind of hard on old man Johnson's equipment though."

"You didn't see Owen put any air in the tires when he drove up did you, Frank?"

"I don't think so."

"I'll pay for any damage I've done." I wasn't angry; I wouldn't let them do that to me again.

"Frank, put this on Owen's bill, will you?"

"Sure." Frank laughed. He turned his head to spit and then took out his pack of cigarettes. "Old Careful's going to have quite a bill."

"Well Owen's sixteen now, got a driver's license, and he's an Eagle Scout, so maybe there's some hope." Staver looked up at me. "You going to stand there all day or are you going to help?" I knelt down by Staver. "Maybe you'll be able to fix it yourself next time."

I wanted to say that there wouldn't be any next time, but I didn't. I wanted to take out my wallet and pay Staver, but I didn't have enough money. I'd just hand him the bills and say, "Here, this is for the parts and labor, and here's the money for the pickup tires too."

Frank blew out a lot of smoke. "I got a flashlight back here in the tool room, kid. You want it to see behind those weeds?"

"It probably wouldn't help, Frank. Maybe Owen will have to get his glasses fixed. There's some pretty small trees out along that fence."

Frank laughed. I got on the tractor, started it, and turned around in front of the tractor shed.

"Hey, Careful, don't go so fast. That yard's full of trees."

"Sorry." I slowed down. I wasn't angry.

After supper that night I helped Mrs. Cummings with the dishes again because she was tired, and when I came out of the house Randy and Staver were passing Randy's football in front of the bunkhouse. It was still light. Frank sat in a chair on the porch smoking. Staver had given Randy a new deck of cards so that he could practice dealing and shuffling, and Randy carried it in his shirt pocket. Randy and I were going to go into Silverton on Saturday to go to a movie and buy a malt and a hamburger. Randy wanted to see some girls. He kept saying that it would be two weeks since he'd seen a girl. Every day he talked to the *Playboy* girls on the wall. Frank and Staver were going to a birthday party in Silverton on Saturday. Randy wanted to go, but we weren't invited.

I walked under the trees to the cabin and brushed my teeth, and then I went down to the river. I was too tired to go swimming. I just wanted to go down along the river under the trees. Tobe was ahead of me. I stood back in the trees to watch the fish rise to feed on insects in the holes. I listened to the evening birds above the sound of the river.

I walked to the head of a long deep hole. I stood in the trees watching, but no trout rose feeding. I waited. None rose. I walked out onto the grassy bank. Insects touched the water. I walked slowly down the bank. At the end of the hole on the bottom in the shallow water lay small trout bleached white and strings of fish entrails. I turned and looked at the grass. By my feet it was black with dried blood where they'd cleaned the fish. I knew it was the hole Randy had helped Staver dynamite. I stepped back from the patch of dark grass. I sat down on a rock and watched the hole for twenty minutes. The dynamite explosion had killed everything in the water. A dead muskrat was caught in the rocks at the bottom of the hole. I wanted to ask Staver why he had to kill everything, and how it made him feel. I watched the dark smooth water. It scared me that Staver liked to kill things so much and that people could be like that.

I stood up and walked out from under the trees to the pasture. In the middle was one of the high rectangular haystacks. The sun was just setting, the whole western sky pink-red above the mountains. I went through the barbed-wire fence. The cattle turned to watch me as I walked across the pasture. I climbed the haystack and stood looking down the river valley. I turned. The white barn, outbuildings, corral fences, and house were turning grey. I breathed deep. I liked the smell. I looked up at the billion stars. I'd buy the screen wire for the minnow trap on Saturday when Randy and I went to Silverton. I'd learned how to make a minnow trap in the Explorers when we had survival training. You could bake minnows on hot rocks in front of a fire. They were high in protein.

Wednesday, Thursday, and Friday we irrigated, and Randy kept talking about girls. He said that he didn't have to talk to any girls in Silverton; he just had to see some. Saturday morning I mowed the lawns, washed off the sidewalks and porches, sprinkled down the yard, and weeded the vegetable garden, and then I went to work with Stan building a new canal bridge. I liked to drive the big sun-hot sixteen-penny nails into the new two-by-eight planks without missing. The sound was hard and clean, and the feeling came up through the hammer into my arm bones and my body. I liked fitting the parts of the bridge together and seeing what I'd done. Stan told me that I was going to make a pretty good hand.

"At least you ain't afraid of work. Most of 'em are. But you're going to need a little more weight stacking hay all day. That's real work."

I weighed myself every day on the feed scales in the barn. I'd gained three pounds in two weeks. Mrs. Cummings said that I was looking much better.

I asked Stan why he wasn't going into Silverton to the birthday party.

"Well, kid, I don't go no more because I had about all the partying I want. I'll just stay here and play my banjo a little bit and watch TV. It's restful not having everybody around. I'll go over to the kitchen later and eat about half of one of them custard pies that's left from supper and drink two or three cups of good coffee. That makes a lot more sense than most things when you get my age. They always invite me, but I don't go much."

We quit at six. Randy wore his Stetson and his shorts while he shaved. He hadn't shaved for three days. He was always reaching up to feel his beard. Now he held his face close to the mirror and felt his chin. He rubbed on his skin bracer, Big Sir. He put on his T-shirt and his cowboy outfit and combed his hair again.

"You ready, cousin?"

"Yes." I felt my wallet in my back pocket again. Staver had paid us, and my check was in my wallet. It was the first paycheck I'd ever recived and the most money I'd ever earned at one time in my life. I'd taken the check out twice to unfold it and look at it. I liked the heavy paper. I liked knowing I'd worked and earned that much money. It made me feel older and better. I'd asked Staver about paying for the tires and the bent mower blade, but he said to wait until the end of the summer and he'd total everything up.

"I'd rather have you take it out of my check now."

"Let's just wait, Owen. It's easier to keep track of it that way."

Randy stopped and asked the girl in the *Playboy* calendar if she would like to go for a ride in a Triumph. He had a picture of a blue Triumph tacked up between the calendar and the four centerfolds. The girl's name on the calendar was June. The girls' names were the names of the months. I hadn't known that before.

"Let's go."

Stan and Frank sat on the bunkhouse porch. Frank whistled.

"You look nice, Randy. You look like a summer hand who's going to get his bonus in September."

Randy laughed. "Hope so. I could use it."

"Sure you could. You boys have a good time now." Frank held a red coffee-can ashtray in his hand. "Don't spend all that hard-earned money in one place. You better watch old Owen there. You never can tell what he might want to do now he's sixteen." Frank spit out on the ground and tapped his cigarette on the edge of the can. "Some boys stop getting boils after they're sixteen."

Frank laughed. I didn't say anything.

Staver came to the doorway and stood there silhouetted.

"You going to check the air in those jeep tires, Owen, before you go?"

"No. I don't think they need it."

Frank laughed.

We got into the jeep. The keys were in the ignition. Randy was going to drive in, and I would drive back.

"Keep an eye on that Boy Scout, Randy. That Silverton's a wild town on Saturday night."

"I will," Randy waved.

I knew that they were just trying to kid me. They liked to do that.

Mrs. Cummings stood on the kitchen porch. Randy stopped.

"Now you boys be careful driving."

"We will," I said across Randy.

Randy shifted and let out the clutch. Tobe ran ahead of the jeep down the lane. I looked back, but Mrs. Cummings had gone in. She was sick. She had told me that she wouldn't be going into Silverton in the morning with us to go to her church. The headlights hit the hanging dead animals and birds and the backs of the white no-trespassing signs. Every two or three hundred yards a dead rabbit lay in the road. The valley breeze hadn't started yet, and the air was still hot. I told Randy he was driving too fast, but he told me I worried too much. The fire sheds by the gates didn't have padlocks on them.

We cashed our checks at Thurman's. Mr. Thurman asked us how we were getting along. He said I looked like I'd put on a little weight. I bought the screen and the wire I needed for my minnow trap and an elastic head strap to attach to my glasses to keep them from slipping while I was working.

"I guess you're nearsighted, aren't you, son?"

"Yes."

"A lot of people have that problem."

I arranged all the bills neatly in my wallet.

"That's hard-earned money."

"Yes, it is."

Mr. Thurman tied a string around the screen. "What are you going to use this for?"

I told Mr. Thurman about the minnows.

"That's a fine thing to do. Staver ought to quit dynamiting that river. It don't belong to him. He's got used to blowing up things in Korea I guess."

Randy set the *Playboy* he was looking at back on the stack, and we left. I put the screen and wire in the jeep.

"What are you going to do with that stuff?"

"Make a minnow trap and catch trout minnows to put back in the holes Staver dynamites."

"They'll just come back in anyway on their own."

"If I help it will be faster."

"Who cares?"

"I do."

We went to the Silverton Cafe to eat. Alice served us.

"You boys in town to go to a movie?"

"Yes."

"That's nice. You're both looking fine. Is Staver on his way in?"

"He was going to eat supper first."

Alice looked up at the clock on the wall. "He ought to be getting here."

"You're going to a birthday party aren't ya?"

"Yes, Randy."

"That ought to be a lot of fun."

"We'll be having one for Frank in about a month, and you can come to that."

When we went to pay for the malts and hamburgers, Alice said it was on the house.

"You boys have a good time now."

We both thanked her. She smiled. She was clean and pretty. I knew that if I asked her whether or not she was immoral, she would say no. I couldn't believe that she would be immoral. She was too nice.

The movie was *Treasure of Sierra Madre* with Humphrey Bogart. All the girls we saw at the candy counter and sitting down were with boys. Before the movie started, Randy kept raising up on his seat to look around. After the movie I stood with Randy in front of the open doors of the casinos and saloons to watch the miners and ranchers with their wives and girl friends play the rows of silver one-armed bandits. The cool air smelled damp and smoky. We went back to the Volcano Casino twice. People stood at the tables to gamble, the smoke rising toward the lights like the gamblers were standing around a campfire.

"Nuts. Why can't we go in? All we want to do is watch." Randy turned and looked up Silver Street. "Casinos have big rooms in the back for private parties." Randy had looked for Staver's pickup. Randy said that the Volcano was Staver's favorite casino.

Some of the saloons were old and had long mirrors behind the polished wooden bars. Men had been shot in the old saloons and on the streets in front of them. People would crowd around to look at a man who lay in the dusty street dead. The man who shot him would look down at the dead man's face. He would pick up the dead man's gun and put it in his belt. The other men would congratulate him and take him back into the saloon to buy him a drink, and they would laugh. I watched for painted-over bullet holes in the fronts of the old wooden buildings as we walked down Silver Street, but I didn't see any.

Randy kept looking for high-school girls, his face changing colors under the neon signs. I tried to recognize the Las Vegas prostitutes that Frank said came on weekends to Silverton. I'd read a book called *Women Without Hope.* Prostitutes became alcoholics, dope addicts, suicides, and they had a high incidence of venereal and other diseases, and they got assaulted a lot and murdered. Nevada was one of the states that registered prostitutes.

In Utah prostitution was against the law and the police arrested prostitutes. I'd told Frank and Staver that no prostitutes lived in Provo.

Staver smiled. "What makes you think that, Owen?" He rubbed his tongue across the bottom of his top front teeth.

"I've never seen any."

"What does one look like?"

"They look different."

"Is he right, Randy?"

Randy laughed. "Don't ask me."

"What about it, Frank?" Staver took a cigarette from the pack that Frank held out to him.

"Maybe so. Maybe Careful here is right. They got all those nice high-school girls in Provo."

I looked at Frank.

I knew about girls at Provo High who were immoral; everybody did. But the immoral girls didn't seem different. They smiled, laughed; they weren't embarrassed. They wore clean clothes and asked questions in class. I wanted to ask them what they thought about and what they said to the boy the next day in class after they'd been immoral the night before. I wanted to ask the immoral boys what they felt when they looked at their fathers' hands and then looked at their own hands and what they felt in seminary when Brother Anderson talked about repentance and their bodies being temples. They had to go to their bishop and repent if they wanted to be clean again and experience the Holy Ghost.

I turned once in seminary and looked at a boy who everybody knew was immoral. He had his arms folded tight, and he looked down at his desk.

Randy and I left Silverton at midnight to start back to the ranch. I drove. Randy sat turned in his seat looking out the rear of the jeep back down toward Silverton as we climbed up through black ledges.

"I'll bet Frank and Staver are having a good time at the party. I wish I was twenty-one. You can have more fun."

I looked down. Silverton was a glow of red-blue neon light in the darkness spreading out to the east mountains. We came to the top of the ridge and started down toward the mouth of the Battle River, and the monument marking the old Indian battlefield.

Randy and I drove back into Silverton the next morning for church. The branch was small, but the people were very nice. They only had one meeting, and it was short. Frank and Staver didn't get back from Silverton until supper time. Frank asked Randy if he'd had a good time, and Randy said it was okay.

"Meet any nice girls?"

"No."

"Maybe you'll have better luck next Saturday. We got lots of nice girls in Silverton, just like Provo."

"I sure hope so."

After supper I helped Mrs. Cummings with the dishes. Sitting in her rocking chair, she read me a letter from Dale. When she finished she still held it open looking at it, the fans moving the pages. I sat at the table drinking a glass of punch.

"I tell him in my letters to love and not to hate. I don't want him to be worse when he comes out of prison than when he went in. I don't want my boy to be mean. I pray every night and morning on my knees for the Lord not to let him get mean." Mrs. Cummings looked up at the line of six pictures on the wall. She still held the letter.

"Cliff Hinckley called me last night to tell me Dale was fine. Cliff talked to him just before he got out. Cliff's going to come and see me. I sure hope that boy does the right thing now he's home. I told him that he can't start drinking again. He knows that."

Mrs. Cummings reached in her apron pocket and got a handkerchief to wipe her neck.

"All those poor men locked up. What a terrible thing."

I drank my punch and listened to Mrs. Cummings talk about the men in prison with Dale.

At night in our car riding back from Salt Lake I would look out when we passed the Utah State Prison, watch the fences, towers, and yards under the lights. Men had forged checks, embezzled money, stolen cars, robbed stores, committed rape, and murdered people. I'd read a book called *Those Who Got Caught.* Prisoners became homosexuals, went insane, murdered other prisoners, and committed suicide. I rode my bike to see the houses of men in Provo who were sent to prison. Their names and addresses were in the *Herald.* There were two who lived in nice houses with flowers and big green lawns and had the Melchizedek Priesthood and went to church.

"Maybe Fred and me should have stayed in Utah. But Dale went to Sunday School every Sunday of his life and was in the Boy Scouts in Silverton. So was Cliff Hinckley. And Staver, too, when his family moved back to town from the ranch for the winters so him and his sister could go to school. A boy starts to get the devil in him and you don't ever know what he'll do next."

"Was Staver a Boy Scout?" I sat up straighter in my chair.

Mrs. Cummings folded Dale's letter and put it in the envelope.

"Of course he was." She shook her head. "His mother's death was hard on him. But I didn't hear Etta complain very much, and she was doing the dying. I was with her every day helping where I could. The way that poor woman suffered. That cancer is awful. It was hard on a boy that young, but other boys have had worse and put up with it somehow."

Mrs. Cummings smoothed the envelope with her hand.

"Dale and Cliff were Boy Scouts, too. I've got pictures of all those boys if you'd like to see them."

"Yes, I would."

"The book's upstairs in my room on the table by the bed. You go get it, son, and save me climbing those stairs. It's the first door on the left. It's Helen's old room."

The door was open, and I walked in. I stopped and looked all around the room at the furniture, curtains, and wallpaper. I wondered if it was the same when it was Helen's room. I'd never been in a girl's bedroom before. Mrs. Cummings' clothes hung in the closet. The door was open. A large Bible lay beside the photo album on the small table in front of the window. I walked over and picked up the photo album.

When I came out, I stopped and turned. The door that I knew had to be Brent's because his window was next to Mrs. Cummings' was closed. I wanted to walk over and open the door and walk in. I turned and walked down the hall and down the stairs with the album. Mrs. Cummings got out of her rocking chair and sat down at the table.

"I look at my pictures a lot now, son. That's me just a year before I married Fred, and that's my family in Manti. That's my mother. You'd never believe it now would you? How we change, how we change. And I'm the only one left."

"You were very beautiful."

"That's my Fred when he was young and herding sheep for my father. Oh, how I miss him. What would I have done in this life without my Fred? I see him in my dreams just as plain as day. He just smiles. He knows I know he's waiting." Mrs. Cummings turned the pages showing me baby pictures. "That's my Ann, who was killed. What a beautiful child. Oh, I'm waiting to see her. And that's Dale and Staver together. They were in grade school then."

"That's Staver?" I bent closer. He wore Levis and a long-sleeved shirt.

"Yes. He was always a fine looking boy and a good boy. There wasn't a better boy to help his mother than Staver, even before she got so sick."

"Did Staver earn his Eagle Scout badge?"

"I don't know about badges, son. You'll have to ask him about that. All the boys had a wonderful time. Sam Clayton was the scoutmaster then. He worked hard with those boys."

"Did he have a uniform?"

"I suppose he did. I don't know."

Mrs. Cummings turned the pages slowly. She showed me pictures of Dale, Cliff, and Staver, but none with them in their Scout uniforms. She talked about every picture.

I'd always liked to wear my Scout uniform. My grandmother washed and ironed it every week. I got Boy Scout posters for my room, read *Boy's Life* all the way through every month, and bought only official Boy Scout camping equipment. I carried my Boy Scout Handbook with me to junior high school to read, and my newest badge in my pocket to take out and put on my desk and look at. I wanted to walk up to other boys on the playground who I knew were Scouts and give them the Scout sign and handshake and ask them what rank they were, but I never did that. I always looked to see if a boy wore a Scout ring. I applied the Scout Oath and law to everything I did. And at night, after my prayers, lying in bed, I repeated them aloud to myself to hear the words. On my dresser was a picture of my father in his uniform the day he received his Eagle.

On every page that Mrs. Cummings turned I watched for a picture of Staver in his uniform. I wanted to see him in it so that I had proof. And I could tell him I'd seen it so I knew he'd been a Boy Scout once, or I could borrow it from Mrs. Cummings and show it to him and ask him why he'd changed and stopped keeping the commandments, and why didn't he change back and be like he was before. I couldn't understand why he'd changed. I wanted him to tell me. I wanted to understand. And I wanted him to see what he'd done to himself and change back. I thought that he would thank me and ask me about the Church.

"That's Brent Johnson right there at the church picnic with his family. Helen was always a pretty little thing."

Brent stood next to Helen. He looked like he was in the ninth grade or maybe the tenth. He was tall and thin and wore wire-rimmed glasses, and he was smiling.

"Brent was a fine clean religious boy. You don't see real gentleness in a boy very often, not real loving gentleness. What a dirty shame that boy had to die in a war like that. His mother never got over it. Mr. Johnson never let anybody ride his horse after that. Just kept him till he died. And he put his pickup in the shed. But you can't hang onto the past like that, son. You got to go on. Somebody could have got some use out of that saddle and that nice truck, and that horse too, and all those nice clothes."

"I saw Brent's saddle in the tack room."

"Yes, that's a beautiful saddle. Staver worked all one summer to earn the money to buy that for Brent. They were like brothers. Brent's being killed like that was a terrible thing for Staver."

"Staver? I thought that Brent's father gave the saddle to him."

"No. It was Staver."

I kept looking at Brent's picture until Mrs. Cummings turned the page. I wanted to be able to ask Brent why Staver gave him the saddle and what Staver said and how he acted, and if Brent gave him a present like that. I wanted to ask him why he and Staver were such good friends, why he liked Staver so much, and how Staver talked and acted around him. I wanted to ask if he swore, smoked, drank, told obscene stories, and was immoral, and if he always killed things, and fought other boys all the time and gambled.

"That's a lot of years." Mrs. Cummings closed the album. "There's a lot of heartache and a lot of happiness in a family. My mother used to say that a family was the only thing that made heaven worthwhile. Oh, but she was disappointed when Fred didn't join the Church and me and him get married in the temple." Mrs. Cummings leaned forward. "Is that a sliver you've got in your hand, son?"

I looked down. I was rubbing my palm.

"Yes, but it's okay."

"Well, let's get it out before it gets infected."

Mrs. Cummings told me where to get the alcohol, cotton, and the needle in the bathroom.

"Sit down here by me. Hold your hand up where I can see. Oh, the slivers I took out of my Fred's hands. He had such lovely big hands. The Lord bless him."

I felt the needle. I looked at my other hand, held it palm up. One day in class when Brother Anderson was teaching a lesson on the crucifixion, he passed out pins to all of us and had us prick one palm. I rested the back of my hand on my desk so that all during the rest of class I could look at the bead of blood in the center of my palm.

"There." Mrs. Cummings handed me back the bottle of alcohol, the needle, and the roll of cotton. She smiled and shook her head. "The alcohol Dale used to use on his face because of his pimples. That's something every boy has. Some things you just have to put up with."

When I came from putting the things back in the bathroom, Mrs. Cummings pushed herself up from her rocking chair.

"Let's go out on the front porch. The evening breeze will be starting pretty soon. There's nothing on television but talk of this new war starting. War, war, and more war. They never talk about anything else."

Mrs. Cummings held onto the doorway and then the front-room table as she crossed the room. I opened the screen door for her. She stood holding onto the door.

"Son, it's Sunday evening and I'd like to hear you play some of the old Mormon hymns. I haven't heard them for years. Could you do that for me? Your grandmother told me that you played the piano in church."

"Yes, ma'am."

I played "Come, Come, Ye Saints," "We Thank Thee, O God, for a Prophet," "Zion Stands with Hills Surrounded," "I Know that My Redeemer Lives," and "Hope of Israel." Mrs. Cummings sang; she knew all the hymns.

I watched my hands. It was the first time I'd played the piano since we'd left Provo. I liked to play the piano. I liked to practice. I practiced for two hours every day. I liked to practice a phrase over and over again until it was perfect, watch my fingers, make them do what I wanted, and then I practiced another phrase, and another, until I played the whole line perfectly, and then I started another line. I liked the big quiet house to practice in. On the piano was a picture of my father practicing. My grandmother told me he had practiced two hours every day.

When I went back out on the front porch, Mrs. Cummings was petting her two cats, the grey and the white, both of them curled up in her lap. Pheasants crowed out in the fields.

"That was lovely, son. Thank you. They're fine old hymns. I used to sit in meeting and listen to my mother sing them. She was a wonderful woman. When she got old she wrote and told me that my Grandmother Peterson used to come and stand in her kitchen some evenings. She would just look at her and smile, not saying a word, and then be gone. My mother didn't have long. They were going to operate and then decided there wasn't any use."

The two cats lifted their heads into Mrs. Cummings' hands as she petted them.

"Feel that breeze starting."

I turned and watched the mountains. Far away to the northwest lightning flashed under dark clouds.

"It'll get cooler here in September. And you'll feel like you got a right to rest a little then. But, 'course, you won't be here then."

I sat down on the top step. Tobe walked up and lay down beside me with his head on my lap. I petted his head.

"He's a good old dog. He never bothers the cats or the chickens."

The grey cat suddenly lifted its head, stood up, and jumped down from Mrs. Cummings' lap. It ran down the steps and out onto the lawn, stopped, and then disappeared into the darkness beyond the light from the porch.

"Now where is that fool cat going?"

Mrs. Cummings petted the white cat.

"Where's that Randy? Playing poker I suppose, even on Sunday." She shook her head. "Staver has all the summer boys doing that sooner or later. Not that they need much encouragement. It's something a boy has to get out of his system I guess. But that gambling's a fool's paradise. Oh, the misery it brings with it."

"I try to get Randy to do other things."

"Well, you might as well save your breath. Some things you can't tell a boy or a man either. They'll be playing poker when the Lord himself comes. I keep telling Staver that he's going to end up just like Frank if he isn't careful, a poor lonely sick man with nobody to care, but he won't listen to me. His fighting is the worst. It's nothing but meanness. I pray on my knees that boy gets this ranch and settles down with a wife and family of his own." Mrs. Cummings shook her head. "If he won't accept the Lord's love, then at least he can accept a woman's."

Mrs. Cummings put the white cat down and held onto the porch railing and stood up. She watched the white cat run across the lawn and disappear into the darkness.

"Prayer, son, that's what this sad world needs. You pray for what's inside of you and what's outside trying to get in. You start out praying on your knees, and then after you get older you're praying all the time."

Mrs. Cummings turned from the railing.

"Don't ever stop praying, son. You're going to need the Lord more all the time now. You got to ask him to help you. Praying makes you different if you keep at it. It teaches you a lot of things. Trouble is most people stop. They think they don't need their own prayers anymore, especially you boys."

Mrs. Cummings walked to the screen door.

"I'm tired. You go to bed, son. You still need plenty of rest, but you're looking a lot better."

I stood up and held open the screen door.

"Thank you."

Mrs. Cummings didn't turn on the light. She held onto the furniture she passed and then put her hand against the wall.

I walked down the steps and out into the pasture. I liked being out away from the trees under the stars. I decided to walk up to the barn and get some sugar cubes for Blade and Miser. I petted Blade. I climbed through the fence so I could stand and put my cheek against his neck. I could ride at a lope now. I liked the pounding, the feeling coming up into my whole body, the noise, the wind, the rhythm, seeing Blade, really feeling him. I wanted all the pasture fences to be down so I could lope for miles and have that feeling for a long time.

I gave Blade the last lump of sugar and patted him on the neck.

"Good boy, Blade. Good boy." He pushed against my chest with his nose. "It's all gone, boy."

I climbed back through the wooden fence.

"Come on, Tobe."

I climbed to the top of the haystack and stood looking out across the dark fields, the cattle darker than the fields. The canal shone silver, the river trees a dark border, the mountains growing bluer toward the top. I turned and looked down the valley, but I saw no lights. I listened. A bird called above the sound of crickets. I breathed in deep the hay, pasture, cattle, and barn smell. I lay down with my hands under my head and looked up at a billion galaxies, a hundred billion universes, and a hundred hundred billion stars with god-created worlds in orbits. I'd read *Beginning the Pathway to Godhood.* I looked at the beautiful sky. The Holy Ghost could give you knowledge about everything.

I liked the ranch. I was getting stronger and could work harder all the time. I hadn't been homesick. I didn't have to let Frank and Staver bother me. I could be an example without their even knowing I was, so they wouldn't know how they were being affected. It was going to be wonderful to go home after I'd worked all summer. I'd have a good tan, be bigger and stronger, have had a lot of good experiences, and have saved my money for my mission and college, except what I was going to spend for my new bicycle. And I could help Randy a lot. There were a lot of things we could do in the evenings. He didn't have to play poker all the time. I could really help him. Randy was a good person. He wasn't playing poker for money, and Staver hadn't got him to drink beer or smoke.

Lying there, my hand on Tobe's head, I tried to count the stars.

7

Thunder and flashes of lightning woke me during the night and I heard rain on the roof, but the yard was still dusty Monday morning under the film of dampness. It wasn't cooler. Mrs. Cummings already had clothes on the line.

In the yard after breakfast I took out my wallet with the money from my cashed check and asked Staver how much I owed Mr. Johnson.

"Oh, we'll just put it all on your bill, like I told you Saturday, Owen."

"I want to pay." I took all the money out. "I can pay the rest when I get my next check if this isn't enough."

"Oh, you can't pay, Owen. It just goes on your bill. Isn't that right, Frank?"

"That's right."

"We'll see how you do by Labor Day."

"I'd like to pay." I held out the money. "I don't like to have bills."

"No, no, Owen. Mr. Johnson doesn't want it that way. We'll just put it on your bill."

"I don't like to have a bill."

"Well, that's the way it is. Even Frank here's got a bill. Everybody's got one."

"That's right."

"It's very nice of you to want to pay now."

I put the money back in my wallet and put it in my back pocket. I really wanted to pay. I didn't want to owe anybody anything. I turned to go help Stan load the blue pickup with cedar posts and bales of barbed-wire. We were going to work on fences all day.

"Hey, Owen, did you get that minnow trap built yet?"

I stopped and turned around and looked at Staver.

"No, I haven't." I knew Randy had told Staver.

"Well, it's a nice thing to do. We all appreciate it, especially the girls in town. They sure like fish."

Frank laughed and spit on the ground.

"I like fish to be alive. They're beautiful."

"Yes they are beautiful, Owen, especially on a plate."

I walked over and got in the pickup. Stan always let me drive when I worked with him. I backed out.

"Bye, Careful." Frank took out a cigarette to light it and then started to laugh.

I didn't say anything. Randy stood next to Staver with his thumbs hooked in his front Levi pockets. Frank was going to take Mrs. Cummings in to Silverton to buy groceries. He had to go to the dentist because he had a toothache. I wanted to ask him if he brushed his teeth after every meal, but I didn't. I wanted to ask a lot of questions I didn't. I knew that I couldn't make any progress if I antagonized Frank and Staver.

Staver turned to say something to Randy, and Staver's big oval silver belt buckle glinted in the sunlight. He always wore the same big silver buckle on his belt.

I drove up behind the equipment shed to get the cedar posts and then around the front to get the barbed wire, staples, and tools. Stan drove one of the red tractors with an auger mounted on the power take-off for digging the post holes.

When we went through the yard, Mrs. Cummings already had the washing on the line, the sun hitting it. All the shirts, Levis, socks, undershorts, and T-shirts hung in groups. The boxer shorts were all mine, and I could see my shirts. All the other clothes looked the same hanging together. Mrs. Cummings' clothes basket sat on the back porch where she stood to hang the clothes.

I drove up to the west fields and was unloading when Stan got there on the tractor.

"Be careful with that wire, kid. Even in a bale it'll cut you worse than a knife."

We heard a shot. Stan finished lighting his cigarette and turned to face the direction of the shot. He rubbed the head of the burned match between his fingers before he dropped it.

"That one shot means Staver got what he was shooting at. He sure keeps the coyotes and wildcats out of sight around here." Stan sucked deep on his cigarette, his lips pulling in, his chest swelling. He let out the smoke. "That poison bait he sets out helps too. You wait till we get the hay cut and baled and start stacking. If we catch a rattler out under a bale in the open field, Staver won't use a gun. He'll just plain stomp it to death. Nobody else in the whole county does that but him."

Stan put his hand on the side of the pickup bed and then jerked it away.

"That's hot."

"Just with his boots?" I stopped lifting the come-a-long out of the back of the pickup.

"Just his boots, that's all. I've seen him do it, so I'm not just talking, and that's something to see."

I leaned the come-a-long against the side of the pickup. There was another shot.

Stan nodded down the valley and took the cigarette out of his mouth.

"Three years ago I saw Staver shoot a hawk right out of the air. It was hanging in the air, not flying fast, but it sure was up there in the air. It blew all to pieces. We had a kid named Christensen working here, and he had time to run out and grab some of the feathers coming down. He'd never seen shooting like that before. Me either."

"Hawks are beautiful. They have a right to live. Staver doesn't have a right to kill everything he wants to. It's against the law, too. Why does he do it all the time?"

"Guess he likes to, kid."

Stan reached out and ran his finger over a weld on the handle of the come-a-long.

"That's a perfect weld. Staver can weld anything you got. Any rancher on the river who's got a tough piece of welding they bring it up here. Staver doesn't charge nothing. He likes to help people out."

I unhooked the water bag from the side of the pickup and drank from it.

"Okay, kid, let's show you how to build a fence."

We tore out the old fence to the corner, drilled holes, and dropped the posts in. I liked to operate the auger, dig the clean deep holes, back off and take another bite, make the auger do the work. The sun got hotter every day now, the whole cloudless sky white around the sun. I took off my shirt and T-shirt so I would tan. Using the heavy metal tools made me feel strong in my shoulders and arms and hands, and I liked to see the new muscles in my stomach. I took off my gloves to wipe my sweaty hands on my Levis. I spread my fingers and kept curling them in and straightening them, my hands sweaty and slick from being in the gloves. I put my gloves back on. I'd never worn leather gloves all day to work in so that I didn't see my hands.

When I was fourteen it was like my hands changed. I kept them in my pockets, squeezed them under my arms, kept my arms folded, or sat on my hands. It was like all my feeling was in my hands and I didn't know what they would do. At night in bed I put my arms outside the covers straight along the side of my body where I could watch them, or I raised them to see my hands in the moonlight coming through the windows. From my bed I saw my hands in my full-length mirror. When I practiced the piano or did homework I saw what my hands were doing.

After I saw my hands I started seeing my whole body, like it had been invisible before, or I hadn't noticed it. I saw it in the showers, felt it inside my clothes, and for weeks at night I lay still thinking about having a body and trying to feel it without touching it. I looked at myself in the full-length mirror dressed in my shorts and T-shirt, and then in my pajamas. I looked at myself in my school clothes, my Sunday clothes, my Explorer uniform, in my swimming suit, and in my gym clothes, and in just my supporter.

I stood before the mirror undressed. I looked at my head, my arms and shoulders, my stomach, my sex organs, my legs. I turned to see my back, and I wanted mirrors all around me. I stood on a chair to see my feet. I stared at my eyes, opened my mouth to see my teeth, stuck out my tongue, got my father's stethescope to listen to my heart, felt my pulse, listened to myself breathe.

I touched myself with my hands, held myself tight, and I tried to feel through the skin and muscles to the bones. I wanted to see all my organs, my bones, my blood. I pricked my finger with a needle to see my blood. I touched it with my tongue to taste it. It was like my body was a secret, and I felt separate from other people that I watched. I wanted to ask other boys how they felt about their bodies. I stopped before the pictures of my father in the house. I wanted to ask him about his body and about my body.

"You have to go deeper than that, kid."

"What?"

I looked at Stan. I was using a bar to clean rocks out of a hole he'd started with the auger.

"Staver likes these post holes about thirty inches."

"Okay."

After I finished the hole we started tamping all of the posts in place. We heard three dynamite explosions and Stan said that Staver was blasting the lava ledges where they poke up through the fields.

"He likes smooth fields."

After lunch we strung wire. I pulled the wire tight with the come-a-long chained to the bumper of the pickup, and then we drove in the staples.

Stan told stories about how riders crashed with their horses into barbed-wire fences or were thrown into them and lay for days out on the range until they died of thirst, or hunger, or bled to death, because the pain was too great for them to fight the wire or even move. A man named Peters on a fence crew Stan worked on got his throat cut by a strand of broken whipping wire and died. They'd pulled the wire with a pickup and got it too tight.

Stan hammered the last staple in on the post.

"You just lay there and wait for somebody to come along and cut you out, or shoot you, and your horse. Worst I ever knew of though was a rancher named Perkins I worked for. He strung some new wire too tight on some old posts and then mowed the field the next day right next to the fence. About a hundred feet of that wire broke loose and whipped out and cut his head off. They figured the noise from the tractor got that tight wire vibrating and it broke and pulled those staples loose out of those old posts."

Stan walked up to the next post and pounded in another staple. He didn't look up.

"His wife found him when he didn't come in for supper. That tractor just kept going in a circle with him sitting there. They had to pry his hands loose from the steering wheel. I guess it was like in World War Two when a pilot would get his head shot off and still land his plane. They'd find him just sitting there in the cockpit."

"That's impossible." I pounded in a staple.

"Hard to say what's possible and what's impossible these days, kid. A lot of strange things happen. You read about it in the Las Vegas newspaper all the time." Stan turned to spit and wiped his mouth with the back of his glove. "I went to the funeral. Of course that mortician had Perkins' head right back on him. They do things like that. He had Perkins' collar up high so you couldn't tell anything was wrong. That mortician had some sense. He went out with a flashlight that night in the field to find Perkins' head before the skunks or some badger beat him to it. Badger find something dead and he'll dig a hole under it and stay there till he's got it all eaten up. Fight you for it, too."

Stan stood back and then hit the last staple on the post one more time.

"I knew Perkins was stringing that new wire too tight for those old posts. They get rotten and soft and won't hold a staple. And the muffler on that old tractor was about half gone, so it made plenty of noise. Too bad. Mrs. Perkins was a nice woman, a good cook. She sold out and moved. I guess she'd had about all the ranchin' she could take."

I undid the come-a-long and fastened it to the next strand of wire down and started to tighten it.

"You do a good job, kid. Give that thing about one more pull."

Stan walked back down the fence to start driving in the staples.

"Give her one more pull, kid."

I watched Stan. He didn't laugh or smile or even look up from pounding in the staples, so I didn't know if he was kidding me or not, or if I was supposed to laugh. I'd read that sympathetic vibrations could make the strings on a piano hum, break thin crystal, and damage delicate instruments. But I hadn't read that they were strong enough to break barbed-wire and pull out staples. I looked down the long strands of new wire glinting in the late afternoon sun. I raised my head. It was almost time to go in. Across the field a badger hung from the corner fence post. It hadn't been there last week.

Randy was in the cabin when I got there to clean up for supper. He told me that he'd cut the head off a big rattlesnake with a shovel. He showed me the rattles.

"I'm going to send them to Lana. She asked me for some."

"I hope she enjoys them."

"Hey, Frank told me that Staver was in a fight Saturday night in Silverton when they went to that birthday party. It was some kid who just graduated from high school. Staver broke his nose, and the kid's shirt was all covered with blood. Staver knocked him down twice, but he kept getting up. Staver took him to the doctor and paid the bill and then took him home. He didn't hit Staver once. Frank says that every year one of the local kids has to try Staver. Sometimes there's fights at the rodeo on the Fourth."

Randy stood in front of the mirror combing his hair when I came out of the bathroom.

"Wonderful. You'll have to ask Staver what it feels like to break somebody's nose so they bleed all over their shirt."

"Ah come on. It was a fair fight. The kid asked for trouble. I'd liked to have seen it." Randy turned from the mirror. "Hey, Staver wants us to come up to the corral right after supper." Randy put his comb in his pocket.

"What for?"

"I don't know. He just wants us."

After supper I told Mrs. Cummings.

"You go along, son. I'm just fine. I feel fine today. I can do these dishes all right."

Tobe walked ahead of Randy and me. Black Prince stood in the center of his corral watching us. We walked through the long dark shadow of the barn. The bottoms of the mountains had all turned dark.

Two horses I hadn't seen before stood in the corral, both of them saddled. One, a black, was tied to the fence by the hackamore. Stan stood in the corral holding the other one, a sorrel, by the head strap. Frank and Staver sat on the white fence. A lot of fresh manure was on the wet soft ground. Cows had been in the corral. Someone had irrigated the pasture and got the corral wet.

"Here they are," Frank said. "Come on, boys. We've been waiting for you. Staver wants you to finish breaking these two little mares. They're almost broke now, so they're just about right for you two summer hands. They'll teach you a lot about riding."

My heart started to pound hard in my chest. I swallowed hard. My fingers tingled. I'd been to a rodeo once with the Explorers.

"How about you, Randy, you want to go first?"

"What about all that cow crap?"

"That just makes it softer if you fall off." Frank laughed.

Staver struck a match on the fence rail he sat on and lit his cigarette. "Not afraid are you, Randy? We could have Owen ride first if you're afraid."

"No. Come on. Let's go."

Randy climbed through the fence. Stan held the mare while Randy got on her. The cows had chopped up the wet dirt with their feet so that it was soft. I stood by the fence.

"Hold the hackamore tight, Randy." Staver took the cigarette out of his mouth. "You only use one hand. Don't let her have her head. Hold on with your legs."

"You ready?" Stan stood in front of the sorrel holding her head down by both straps.

"Sure."

"Okay. She's all yours, kid." Stan stepped back from the mare and walked over to the fence.

The mare ran forward kicking out with her back feet but not high.

"Ride her, Randy, ride her! Don't let her do that to you!"

Frank pulled his hat down tighter on his head and turned to spit.

The mare hopped forward across the corral, but she didn't really buck. Randy pulled tight on the hackamore. She reared up on her hind legs and then just stood in the middle of the corral.

"Come on," Randy hollered, "buck, buck!"

The mare walked around the corral.

Frank jumped down from the fence. "Well, looks like you finished breaking this one, Randy."

Randy got off. "Some horse." He walked over and climbed up on the fence by Staver, who put his hand on his shoulder. Randy tipped his hat back with his finger and spit down between his knees.

Frank tied the sorrel to the fence and untied the black.

"Looks like it's your turn, kid. If you're scared, Randy can break this one, too. Can't you, Randy?"

"Sure." Randy spit again.

"I'll ride it." My heart beat loud in my ears. I handed Randy my glasses.

I put my foot in the stirrup, grabbed the saddlehorn, and lifted myself up into the saddle. I took the hackamore from Frank. I held on as tight with my legs as I could.

"You ready, kid? Use your legs."

"Yes."

"Be careful now, Owen. We don't want you to get hurt." Staver smiled. He had his straw cowboy hat pushed way back on his head.

"Ride 'em cowboy!" Frank stepped back.

The mare stood still. Through my legs I felt her trembling. I didn't know what to do. I held the hackamore tight, but she still lowered her head. I pulled hard. I wanted to use both hands. The first buck wasn't high. I hung on tighter with my legs. She started to hop and buck. My head kept snapping, and I tried to balance with my free arm like I'd seen in the rodeo. The jolts came up through my spine to my head. My legs were coming loose. I heard hollering and cheers. I grabbed the hackamore with both hands. My knees came up toward my head. It was like I was standing on my head being towed above the mare.

I hit sliding on my face and chest. I couldn't see. My eyes, nose, and mouth were full of mud. I didn't hurt anywhere. I sat up; I kept spitting. They were all laughing.

"Hey, cowboy, you all right? You're a real broncobuster."

They took me by both arms and stood me up. They kept laughing.

"Kid, you look a mess."

Somebody took my bandana handkerchief out of my back pocket and handed it to me. I wiped my right eye clean. I opened it. They stood around me laughing. Frank kept slapping his leg with his hat and shaking his head. My hair was heavy and wet. I looked down with my one eye. Mud and fresh yellow-green manure covered the whole front of my shirt and Levis. It slid off in lumps. I kept spitting.

"Owen, did you aim?"

I smelled the stink. Manure dripped down my face from my hair.

"You ought to join a rodeo, Owen. You could make a lot of money. You did that better than any professional rider I've ever seen."

I saw Staver. I knew he'd done it on purpose. It was one of the things he did to the summer hands, like the snake in the pickup. I wanted to run and tackle him, knock him down in the mud and manure, get on top of him and push his face down in it and keep doing that until he pleaded with me to stop, and I stood and pulled him up and shoved him against the fence, and then I climbed through the fence and walked away. I wanted Staver to feel what it was like. That's all I wanted, so he wouldn't do it to other summer hands. My body was tight and hot inside like something would melt or break, and I knew how easy it would be to hate Staver. I'd never hated anybody in my whole life before or wanted to hurt anybody. I knew that it was wrong. You had to love people.

They all started laughing again.

Manure dripped into my open eye, and I couldn't see again. I kept spitting. I felt like vomiting. I still couldn't breathe through my nose.

"Take hold of Owen's arm, Randy. We got to get him cleaned up. His own mother wouldn't recognize him. Frank, you take his other arm."

Frank started to laugh again. They took my arms and started to walk me across the corral. I pulled against them to stop and spit. I spit and spit. I bent over to spit. I couldn't talk. I bumped my head when they took me through the fence.

"Take him over to the barn."

I kept spitting.

They stopped me. Somebody turned on a hose. "Bend down, cowboy." The cold spray hit my face. I blinked both eyes open. Frank was squirting me off with the barn hose. They all stood there watching me. Randy shook his head.

"What would your grandma say if she could see you now, cousin?" He laughed. "You'd better take your shirt off."

I took the hose from Frank and took big mouthfuls of water to spit out. I kept doing that.

"What does it taste like, kid? Randy, you better go get old Owen's toothbrush."

I took off my shirt and T-shirt. My levis felt like wet iron. Stan handed me a feed sack to wipe off with.

Staver lit a cigarette. "You're kind of black all over, Owen. I thought that they didn't like black people in the Mormon Church."

I stopped rubbing the front of my Levis with the sack and straightened up.

"Black people can be members. The men just can't hold the priesthood."

"Was that one of the things that angel Moroni came down and told your Joseph Smith?"

"I don't know."

"He's the angel that gave Joseph Smith the gold plates so he could translate the Book of Mormon. Isn't that right, Owen?"

"Yes."

"Frank, you ever heard how Joseph Smith got the gold plates?"

"No, I ain't ever heard that story. I know he got 'em, but I don't know how."

"Why don't you tell Frank, Owen. You might convert him. You'd like to hear about that wouldn't you Frank?"

"I sure would."

I dropped the feed sack on the bale of straw by the tap and picked up my shirt and undershirt. Randy handed me my glasses. I put them on, and then I told Frank about the Prophet Joseph Smith. They all stood and listened. It made me feel good to tell the story.

"Well, what do you think, Frank?"

"I want to know what Joe Smith did with those gold plates after he got through with that Book of Mormon."

"What did he do with them, Owen?"

"The Angel Moroni came and took them back."

"That's too bad, I'd like to've seen 'em."

"Well, are you converted yet, Frank?"

"I'll think about it." Frank laughed.

"Get cleaned up, Owen, and come on over to the bunkhouse. We're going to have another boxing lesson."

Frank laughed.

"The kid here is going to be a real cowboy someday." He turned to spit.

I watched them walk out of the barn, Staver the tallest. Tobe came to the door and stood looking at me. I took off my boots and socks and Levis and washed off with the hose again. I washed my Levis and wrung them out and put them back on. I sat on the bale of straw to wash my socks and my boots. I put them on and went to the cabin and took a shower.

I stood in the shower and let the water pour down over my head. I trembled. I'd never been dirty like that in my whole life. I closed my eyes, pressed my head against the shower wall. I felt terrible. I didn't want to hate Staver or anybody ever. I knew that Staver did it just for fun. And if I got mad or said anything they'd just laugh at me and treat me like a little boy and talk about it all the time and kid me, and everything would be worse than ever. And they wouldn't listen to anything I said about the Church then and being an example wouldn't make any difference. I opened my eyes and pulled my head back from the shower wall and got out. I wrapped my towel around me and brushed my teeth three times. I got dressed and went outside, and I kept spitting.

At the bunkhouse Staver had Randy and me box, but we weren't supposed to hit each other. And Staver kept stopping us to show us how. He pushed me down to make me crouch more, held me there, and made me lift my gloves higher. He kept showing me how to jab and move my feet at the same time.

"Not bad, Owen. By the end of the summer you might be able to take care of yourself. We'll work on it."

Staver invited me to come in and have a root beer and watch television. I did because I wanted to be friends and show him that I wasn't mad. There was a documentary about the concentration camps because it was an anniversary since the first concentration camp had been built. Brother Anderson had made a trip to Europe to visit all the concentration camps that had been made into memorials. He said that he wanted to do that every ten years so he wouldn't forget what the gospel was for.

After the program I went back to the cabin and built my minnow trap and took it down to the river and put it in. I baited it with bread crumbs. I put on my suit and climbed the big cottonwood, stood looking down, pulled my supporter tight, and dived. I stayed underwater as long as I could, with my eyes closed. I climbed up again and just stood there on the limb staring up through the leaves at the stars and feeling cleaner high up in the air like that in the tree. I dived. It didn't scare me anymore to dive. I got out and got my soap and took a bath, but I still kept spitting. And when I thought about what had happened, I wanted to start running down the road as fast as I could so I wouldn't think.

8

We had thunderstorms nearly every afternoon, but it didn't rain. Thunder boomed down the valley but with no ground lightning, just great flares of light against the wall of black late afternoon clouds over the mountains. In the evening and at night I sat on the roof of the barn to watch the sky. Stan said that we might get a fire out of the storms because it was about time. He pointed to places where the valley brush fires, pushed by winds, had jumped the fire lines and burned up the sides of the mountains. I kept waiting for the Forest Service to call us to come and fight fire, but they didn't call. Stan said that to have a real fire you had to have a wind. I worked with Stan most of the time, and Randy worked with Frank and Staver.

One evening we all drove down to irrigate at the Bensons'. Staver didn't let us help earlier because he said that we needed more experience before he could turn us loose on somebody else's place. When we finished, Mrs. Benson pushed Mr. Benson out through the back door in his wheelchair, both his legs still in white casts from the horse rolling on him. Mrs. Benson gave us punch to drink.

"You're just saints, that's all there is to it." She hugged Staver and kissed him on the cheek. "We sure love this boy. We've known him since the day he was born."

Staver introduced me and Randy. Mrs. Benson said that we were fine young men. She filled our glasses with more punch. I looked at the red punch in my glass. I wanted to ask Mrs. Benson if Staver was a mean baby.

The next night I went to the bunkhouse to play Monopoly. I knew that I had to be friendly, and I wanted to be with Randy as much as possible so I could help him. Every day Staver invited me over to watch TV and have a root beer. He wanted to know if I played Monopoly, and I told him yes. When I walked across the yard at night and Randy was playing poker, Frank came to the door to invite me in.

I went over at seven. The top third of the bunkhouse was already full of smoke. The fans moved the smoke, but they didn't blow it out through the opened screened windows and door. Where they told me to sit I faced the pictures of girls and women on the wall. I looked down. The TV was on. They drank beer and had root beer for Randy and me. Staver had a peeled willow by his hand to kill the big blue flies that lit on the table. It was my turn to throw the dice. They all wore T-shirts, including Randy.

Frank asked me if I'd ever dated a blonde or a redhead. I'd received my first letter from Becky, and he'd asked me when I first came in if I'd brought it with me. I'd left it in the cabin on purpose because I didn't want to have to read it to them. It was the first letter I'd ever had from a girl.

"Well, what about it, kid, did you ever date a redhead or a blonde?"

"I've never dated a girl. We aren't supposed to date in our church until we're sixteen." I threw the dice again and moved my man on the board.

"Ah, come on, kid, you don't expect us to believe that do you? You mean you never dated a girl?"

"I go to parties and dances all the time where there are girls."

"What about it, Randy? Didn't you date girls till you were sixteen?"

Randy threw the dice and then looked up. "I got started a little early."

"How can you stand not being around girls, kid?"

"You can stand it."

Frank laughed and spit in a gallon can he had by the side of his chair. He asked me the names of girls at Provo High that I liked, but I didn't want to tell their names.

"Come on, kid. You like some don't you?"

"Yes, I do."

"Ever go with a girl named Lucille?" The water in Frank's eyes glistened.

"Maybe Owen can't remember, Frank." Staver threw the dice. When he moved, his combed, flat auburn hair glinted under the light.

"No, I haven't."

"How about Erica?"

"Maybe Owen can't remember all their names, Frank. Maybe there are too many."

Staver picked up a card from the center of the Monopoly board. The blunt tip of the puffy white scar showed just above the bottom of his T-shirt collar. It had a double row of stitch marks on each side.

"You can remember 'em can't ya, kid?" Frank spit in the can.

I had memorized the names, addresses, and phone numbers of six girls I wanted to date when I turned sixteen. I studied their pictures in the yearbook, and I watched them in class and in the halls. In the evening I rode my bicycle past their houses. And in my room at night I practiced saying their names and asking them for dates. I wrote each girl's name down in a notebook and listed under it the things I would say on our first date and places we would go in the car alone. But I was going to date Becky first.

"What were the names of the girls you went with, Frank?" Staver bought a piece of property Randy didn't want.

"I didn't worry much about their names." Frank started to laugh and had to put his beer can down, and then spit again.

"What about you, Stan? Do you remember their names?" Staver killed a fly with the switch and flipped it off the table.

"A few. It's been a long time." Stan threw the dice and moved his man.

Frank turned in his chair to look at the pictures on the wall. "All those girls have nice names, kid, real nice."

I threw the dice and reached down and moved my man.

Frank described the girls he'd gone with. He remembered some of their first names and what they looked like. He told stories about what he and his friends had done. He used obscene words and he made it all funny so that Randy, Stan, and Staver laughed. The girls were always dumb.

"Come on, kid. You don't chase girls and you told us you don't play solitaire. What do ya do for relaxation?" Frank reached down and picked up the dice, but he didn't throw them. He held them and picked up his can of beer with the other hand. "Maybe you and Randy got something going in that cabin every night."

"What?"

"What about it, Randy, you two pushing those bunks together after you turn off the lights?" Frank spit in the can on the floor.

"You know that's a possibility." Staver leaned back in his chair. "I never thought about that. Maybe you got something there, Frank."

I looked at Staver. I knew that Frank just said the things he wanted him to. Staver ran everything on the whole ranch. Frank was joking about homosexuality. Nobody had ever said anything like that to me before. My heart beat hard, my mouth was dry, and my hands sweated. The top of Staver's scar was right in the middle of his throat.

"Boys can be chaste."

"What?" Frank leaned across the table toward me.

"Owen said that boys don't have to sleep with girls all the time." Staver tapped his cigarette on the edge of the red coffee can. "Did Brother Anderson tell you that too, Owen?"

"Yes, he did."

"What Anderson?" Frank still leaned toward me.

"He was Owen's seminary teacher. Remember. He told us, Frank."

Randy slid down in his chair and pulled his hat down over his eye.

"Did Brother Anderson ever say how much fun it was to sleep with girls, Owen?"

"No, he didn't. It's against the commandments."

"But what if you don't believe in God, Owen? A lot of people don't even think about God—do they, Randy?"

"Immorality spreads venereal disease. Babies are born blind if their mothers have gonorrhea. Some kinds of venereal disease have no cures. People go insane years later because they had syphillis and didn't know about it."

I'd read several articles on venereal disease and a book called *Venereal Disease: A Doctor Talks to Young Men.*

"That doesn't have to happen, Owen."

"Sometimes girls don't even know who the father is."

"That doesn't have to happen either, Owen. Married people don't have babies if they don't want to have them. Some girls want to have a baby. A baby makes them happy."

Staver turned his cigarette in three fingers.

"Immorality is wrong. Everybody knows that. Doctors and psychiatrists say it's wrong. It always makes people unhappy. It hurts families and causes divorce."

"Not if you're not married, Owen."

"Women sure help to make life interesting." Frank opened another can of beer.

"Lots of people aren't immoral."

"Brother Anderson told you that, didn't he, Owen?" Holding the cigarette in his left hand, Staver reached out with the willow switch and killed a fly on the table. He flipped it away.

"Yes, he did, but he didn't have to. The Church has thousands of missionaries, and they're not immoral. A missionary can't go on a mission if he's immoral. The Church won't let him. And if he's immoral on his mission, he's excommunicated and sent home."

"But who knows about it if a missionary sleeps with some girl, Owen?"

"He'd go to his mission president and confess. He can't be happy if he's immoral and his missionary companion and his mission president would know something was wrong."

"Hey, kid, did any of those missionaries ever take a picture of the Holy Ghost with a camera so he could show people?" Frank drank from a new can of beer.

"No, they didn't"

Frank lowered the can and wiped his mouth with the back of his hand.

"Too bad. I'd sure like to have one to show some ladies I know. Something like that could change a person's whole way of living. That's all they'd need."

"The Holy Ghost is a spirit. He doesn't have a body you can see. You can't take a picture of him.

"Don't get mad, Owen." Staver smiled.

"I'm not mad."

"You sound a little mad."

I stopped turning my Eagle Scout ring on my finger. I stood up. I wanted to make the Scout sign and ask Staver what that meant and why he'd changed, what made him change. During the Second World War some Japanese soldiers were going to behead a captured American pilot with a Samurai sword, but he made the Scout sign and the officer stopped them because he'd been an Eagle Scout. But I knew that Staver would only laugh.

"It's nine o'clock. I've got to go." I looked over at Randy.

"Well, we want you summer hands to get all the sleep you need. See you in the morning, Owen."

"Sleep's good for you. I used to get a lot. Go right to sleep. You don't want to lay awake over there in the dark all alone."

Tobe followed me down the steps. Suddenly, behind me, they all laughed, like somebody had just told a joke. I kept walking.

Old people weren't immoral. Children weren't. Lots of boys at Provo High weren't immoral. They were Priests. They blessed the sacrament every Sunday and they were going on missions. They were clean, really clean. You could feel it. And they went with girls that weren't immoral. Their parents weren't immoral. All the bishops, stake presidents, and seminary teachers weren't immoral. They went to the temple and they wore temple garments, which protected them. And in testimony meeting when they stood up and bore their testimonies you knew they weren't immoral.

I knew that Staver liked to argue with me about the Church, but he didn't really bother me. He couldn't change something that was true.

I stood in front of the cabin. I looked down where the old lane cut left into the trees to the old bridge.

"Come on, Tobe." I didn't want to be around the bunkhouse.

I walked down to the old bridge. I walked out onto the planks; I was very quiet. The river made no sound in the wide deep silver pool under the moon. At the head of the pool on the right side was a big swirl. It was the big trout. He swirled again. He was feeding. I watched. He kept feeding.

I stood watching the ripples move across and vanish in the silver water.

I sat down and unlaced my keds. I undressed except for my shorts; I took off my T-shirt. I lowered myself down into the water from the end of the planks and went underwater. I swam underwater along the edge toward the top of the hole. I came up very slowly and quietly, just my head. I treaded water. I liked being in the water with the big fish. I knew he was there. I wanted him to jump so I could see him up close. I wanted him to swim by and touch me. I went underwater and held my hands out feeling but trying not to move. I came up. I waited. But the big fish didn't swirl again or jump.

I was tired. I swam back to the bridge and got out. I sat down, pulled my legs in tight, and rested my forehead on my knees. I closed my eyes and listened. The big trout had a perfect body, smooth, clean, and rounded. Brother Anderson had us bring a picture of ourselves to seminary. He said to look at it and then turn it over and write "clean" or "unclean" on the back. I wrote "clean," but I thought a lot about it afterwards and what it meant. I hadn't had to do that before.

I felt my forehead against my knees.

When I became fifteen, nights in my bedroom after my shower I turned off the lights and took off my towel to see what my body was like in the dark full-length mirror. I turned, moved my arms and legs, walked up and down, saluted, boxed, lay down, curled in a ball, put out my hands like wings to fly, stood at attention, tried to stand on my head. And once, suddenly, I spoke my father's name into the dark mirror, repeated it quietly, his first name only, and then his whole name, all three words, many times, watching the mirror, which my father had stood before thousands of times and looked into.

I'd read a poem in my English class that said the whole Earth was a great tomb. And all the people who had ever died were there in the Earth, those who had died of diseases, accidents, wars, been murdered, died in great floods, earthquakes, and hurricanes. And the Earth was a great round tomb circling the sun in the universe.

* * *

Saturday I worked most of the day mowing and raking the lawn, cleaning up the yard, and weeding, and in the evening

Randy and I drove the jeep into Silverton. Randy told me to drive at least sixty, but I wouldn't. The Fourth of July decorations were up along Silver Street. Large posters in the windows told what would happen. We parked the jeep and Randy stopped to read the first poster we passed.

"That's going to be a lot of fun. Staver says so."

"The Fourth of July is a nice holiday in Provo."

We went into the Silverton Cafe for our hamburger and malt, but Alice wasn't working. The counter was full, so we sat in a booth. Randy finished in a hurry, went to the cash register and paid, and went outside to stand on the sidewalk.

I finished and walked over to the cash register. The waitress, who had dyed red hair, took my money.

"You two boys work out at the Johnson place don't ya?"

"Yes, we do."

"Staver and Alice sure have a good time together, don't they? That's where she is now. Of course Staver got wounded in the war so he deserves a good time. That scar he got must be an awful thing, just awful."

"Yes it would be."

"People still talk about it. Well, see ya. Have a good time tonight, understand?"

"Yes, thank you."

We went into Thurman's store to pick up a keg of nails that Staver had ordered. Mr. Thurman asked us how we were. He said that I looked like I'd put on some more weight. Randy looked for girls before we went to the movie, which was *High Noon* with Gary Cooper, but he didn't find any alone, and all the girls in the movie had dates. Randy bought a dollar's worth of candy.

Sunday morning Mrs. Cummings went into Silverton with us to go to her church, but Monday she was sick and Staver drove her into Silverton to see her doctor, who sent her into Las Vegas to see a specialist.

After supper I did all the dishes.

"Thank you, son. I don't feel too strong right now." She sat in her rocking chair, but she didn't rock. She wiped her neck with a handkerchief. "Erma Spencer called to see how I was. I don't know how she found out. And then Vera called because Erma told her. People don't have to worry about me. We saw Cliff Hinckley in town for a minute and his girl Donna. He looks good for a man in prison as long as he was."

"What did the doctor tell you to do?"

"Oh, not much, son. But then what can he say. They're still trying to decide if an operation will help any or not. They can't perform miracles no matter how hard they try. Only the Good Lord can do that." Mrs. Cummings nodded toward the pictures on the wall. "I'm not afraid of dying. I've had my life. I'd just like to see Dale home and married to some good woman first. But who knows what he'll want after being in that place. Staver's going to help him find a job." Mrs. Cummings sat looking out through the screen door. "Maybe we didn't love that boy enough, but I sure tried, and so did his father when he was alive. We all got to love a lot more than we do. It's a lot of work sometimes when people don't want to be loved."

Just as I finished the dishes my grandmother called. When I told her I'd gained five pounds the first month, she said that they wouldn't recognize me when I got back, I'd be changed so much. Bishop Matthews had received my Duty to God Award, and she was still deciding on the new paint, wallpaper, carpet, and curtains for my room.

When my mother talked to me she said that Uncle Mark had sold a big apartment house to a doctor from California. She said Becky had gotten my letter.

The sun was just setting when I walked under the trees to the cabin. I looked up. Something had killed one of the white chickens the night before. I'd found feathers under a tree but not the body. I opened the cabin screen and walked in. Randy sat at the table dealing cards. He put down the deck and picked up one of the four hands he'd dealt. He discarded two cards and dealt himself two more. He put that hand down and picked up the next hand on the left.

I sat down on my bunk.

"You ought to really watch Staver when he's playing cards. He's really good."

"What chance have you got against him if he's so good?"

"Same chance as anybody else." Randy discarded three cards from the second hand. "He don't cheat. He don't win all the time either. Frank wins sometimes. I win pots too, and I'm getting better. I'm better than Stan right now. Staver says I'll be ready to play in that big game in Silverton in two months. He's teaching me everything he knows. You ought to really try to get along with him. He's okay."

Randy picked up the third hand. He tipped the front of his hat up with his finger and leaned back in the chair.

I was going to go to the bunkhouse to watch a war movie while Randy played poker. Staver had invited me. I'd learned a lot the first month. Frank and Staver didn't really bother me like they used to. Randy played poker nearly every night, even Sunday, but he hadn't started drinking or smoking. He was saving up his money for the big poker game in Silverton, but I hoped I could talk him out of that. I didn't want him to lose all the money he'd saved. That wouldn't be a very good ending for his summer.

"Well, let's go." Randy picked up all the cards from the table.

"I need to brush my teeth first."

Stan, Frank, and Staver were sitting at the table when Randy opened the bunkhouse screen.

"Well, come on in, Owen. Glad to have you."

The TV was on and a news flash said that two American advisors had been killed in Vietnam.

"Hello, kid." Frank looked up from lighting a cigarette. "You decide you want to play a little poker? Have a seat."

"Frank, Owen didn't come over to play poker. He's going to watch television. There's a good war movie on. Get him a root beer, Randy. Get him two root beers. We're glad to have him."

Staver wore a blue cowboy shirt with pearl buttons. They all wore their hats except Stan. Staver closed his eyes against the smoke from his cigarette.

The movie was just starting. I pulled a chair out from the table and sat down. Randy put four root beers on the table and handed me one.

Staver dealt.

"Hey, Bronco Bill, you sign up for the bronc riding at the rodeo next Saturday when you were in town?"

"Now, Frank, don't start kidding Owen about riding. That could have happened to anybody."

They laughed. Staver won the hand.

"The next one's mine." Randy threw his cards on the table.

"You're learning, lover boy, you're learning." Frank reached over and patted Randy on the shoulder. "Hey, kid, have you got a telephone in your bedroom back home to talk to girls?"

"No, I haven't."

"Wouldn't that be nice? Ol' Randy here's got one."

The movie was about World War Two. The four men, who were all friends, had been drafted together and were in France fighting the Germans in the same platoon, and one of them had just been killed. Every time they stopped marching they dug new foxholes and slept in them at night.

A commercial came on. I drank my root beer. Above the end of the can I saw the gun rack. The oiled barrels gleamed. For shelves Staver had nailed dynamite boxes above his loading table. They were full of boxes of primers, bullets, empty shells, and cans of powder. At the back of the table were boxes of ammunition.

"Do you think that was the way it was, Owen?"

The movie had started again. I turned. "What?"

Staver picked up his cards and nodded toward the TV. "Is that the way it was?"

"I guess. I don't know."

"What about it, Frank? Was it like that when you were over there fighting those Germans in World War Two?"

Frank looked at the television and then back at his cards.

"A little maybe, but those guys are all too clean. They fight all day and don't even get their hands dirty. Living in trenches and foxholes makes ya awful dirty."

Staver and Frank talked about how dirty soldiers got fighting. They went for weeks without taking a bath; they wore the same clothes, and their bodies stank. Sometimes they had to stand in foxholes for three or four days in water up to their knees from the rain. They couldn't get out because they would get shot. So they stood in their own excrement and urine, and their feet started to rot, and they got infections.

When the sun came out and made it hot, the flies got thick. Frank told how a herd of French milk cows got killed by artillery in front of his company and how that stink was different from the stink of dead human bodies. American soldiers went insane after two weeks because of the smell and had to be tied up in their foxholes, or they shot themselves, or they jumped out of their trenches screaming, and the Germans shot them.

"They never tell you about the smell, Owen." Staver reached out and killed a fly with his switch.

The air from the closest rotating fan hit me.

"If everybody lived better there wouldn't be any wars. But we all have our free agency."

Randy asked for three cards.

"Tell us how free agency works, Owen. It sounds interesting."

"It means that every person can choose between right and wrong. You have to have free agency or you can't progress."

"Why do we want to progress, Owen?"

"So we can become perfect."

Randy put two blue chips on the pile in the center of the table. He held his cards up high in front of his face.

"Don't you want to be perfect, Stan? Wouldn't that be nice?"

"I guess."

"How about you, Frank?"

"At a couple of things." Frank started to laugh and then cough. He had to spit in the can by his chair.

"Do you want to be perfect, Randy?"

"Sure."

"Why does a person want to be perfect, Owen?"

"Because you take your personality with you into the next life, and if you were righteous enough you can become a god."

"What if you don't want to take it with you and don't care about being a god?"

"You have to take it with you."

"Why?"

"Because you're eternal."

"Did Brother Anderson tell you that in seminary?"

"Yes, he did."

"Good for him. Did the Angel Moroni come to him like he did to Joseph Smith and tell him all about progression so he could tell you, Owen?"

"No, he didn't, but Brother Anderson knows that the gospel is true because of the Holy Ghost. He bore his testimony to us all the time."

Staver held up his finger and Randy dealt him one card.

"Don't get mad, Owen. We're just having a discussion. I just want to know some of these things. Couldn't an angel tell him something if it wanted to? I mean that's possible isn't it? Not the Angel Moroni, but just any angel?"

"Yes, it is."

"That's a good thing to know."

Staver picked up the two cards and put them in his hand.

"Owen, did you get those minnows trapped and planted in that dead hole?"

"Yes, I did."

"That's a nice thing to do, but it's against the law in Nevada to trap or transport a game fish, so be careful next time so you don't get picked up. Of course they're just minnows and it's the same river, but you don't want to get picked up. And you don't want to get in the habit of breaking the law either."

Staver moved five blue chips out to the center of the table.

"I won't get in the habit."

"Good. We don't want you to learn any bad habits this summer."

I looked at Staver. I knew why he hadn't told me earlier about breaking the law. He wanted me to do it. But I hadn't broken the law on purpose. I knew that I could explain to a game warden and he would understand and not arrest me. He would know that I was helping to get the trout started in the dead holes. But I still wished I hadn't broken the law. I didn't like to do that.

I watched the movie. Two of the four soldiers who were friends had been killed. The two that were still alive helped to liberate a concentration camp. The pictures of the concentration camp were real. They hadn't been made in Hollywood. The pictures showed the barracks, the crematoriums, the stacks of naked, thin dead bodies, the gas chambers, and the separate rooms piled high with shoes, human hair, clothes, and children's toys. The starving inmates in striped suits stood at the open gates afraid to go out because they didn't know they were free.

The next day the third friend was killed when he tried to help a wounded German soldier. At the end of the war the one friend who was left alive was shown receiving the Medal of Honor. The three friends who had been killed were in the upper half of the screen; they turned to smile and wave goodbye as they climbed a hill carrying their packs and rifles.

"Hey, Owen, it looks like your movie's over."

"Yes, it is."

"You know, Owen, if this Vietnam thing keeps going, maybe you'll get to be in the army and fight in a war. You'd really be able to find out what it was like then."

"Maybe."

"That would be a real experience for you. You'd be able to progress a lot then."

I looked at Staver. Two inches of his scar always showed above his T-shirt. The scar was always the same puffy white.

I wanted to ask him if he ever thought about the Korean and Chinese men he'd killed, and about his friends who had been killed, and about Brent. I wanted to ask him if that didn't make him feel bad and make him want to be as good as he could and make people happy and love people. He could marry Alice and have a family and live on the ranch and be happy. He didn't have to drink, be immoral, fight, gamble, and kill things all the time. He could repent if he really wanted to. The Holy Ghost would help teach him what was right. He could start going back to church and be a different person. I wanted to ask him what he thought Brent would think about him now and what Brent would want him to do, and if he talked to Brent before he died and what Brent told him.

But I didn't say anything. I knew that they would only laugh. I stood up and walked over to the screen door. I thanked Staver for the root beer and the movie.

"Hey, kid, you going so soon?" Frank put his beer can down. "Hey, did I tell you you could buy skunks in Silverton that don't stink? A guy comes into the Volcano Casino that's got some. They operate on them so they don't stink. You could take one home with you to Provo when you go." I opened the door and walked out. "Hey, kid, what color pajamas you going to wear tonight?"

They all laughed.

I turned in the yard and walked up past Black Prince in the corral and over to the barn. When I started to climb the ladder, Tobe whined.

I turned and looked down. "It's okay, Tobe."

I climbed to the top and stood on the little platform, my hands on the railing. I looked at the dark high mountains and above the mountains at the stars and the moon. The platform had a railing. I held onto that. I looked out over the whole ranch and down the valley. Book of Mormon prophets like Abinadi, King Benjamin, Samuel, and Alma preached from towers and from the tops of city walls for the people to believe in Jesus Christ. They preached against breaking the commandments, which always brought war. The Book of Mormon was a history of wars. The prophets spoke by the power of the Holy Ghost. They preached great sermons. Thousands and thousands of people were converted and baptized and received the Holy Ghost and took the sacrament for the first time, and the cities that wouldn't repent were destroyed in great storms or earthquakes, or in wars.

I turned and looked east toward Provo. When I got home I could go to school, to church, and practice the piano and read and study in my room all I wanted, and I could date girls. I would graduate from high school, go on my mission, graduate from college and medical school, get married in the temple and live in Provo. I knew everything I was going to do. I wanted to be a bishop, maybe even a stake president.

Below me at the front of the barn Black Prince neighed, the sound shrill and high, carrying on the night air. Across the first pasture the dark body of a coyote hung on the fence. It had been poisoned yesterday.

I hadn't heard a coyote yet.

I took off my glasses and cleaned them.

9

Helen drove Mr. Johnson out to the ranch from Las Vegas Saturday morning. Mr. Johnson had some papers for Staver to sign. I stayed at the house the whole morning to cut the lawn, clean up the yard, and help Mrs. Cummings. I carried the folding table and the kitchen chairs out for the lunch in the shade on the lawn.

Mr. Johnson didn't come into the house. He sat in the shade in Mrs. Cummings' rocking chair from the porch, a small portable green oxygen tank with a green plastic mask by his chair. Helen had introduced me to him after she helped him out of the car and he sat down. As she took me over to him he sat looking off across the fields toward the mountains.

"Dad, this is Owen, the summer hand that I told you reminded me of Brent. He's got Brent's eyes. It looks like you put on a little weight, Owen."

He turned slowly toward us, and he shook my hand.

"It's nice to meet you, son." He put his other hand on mine. His hands were thin and felt light. He nodded his head. "Yes, you're right, sweetheart. He reminds you a little of Brent doesn't he?"

"It's nice to meet you, Mr. Johnson."

"I've got to go back in and help Mrs. Cummings with the lunch, Dad. She's not feeling too well today."

"You go right ahead, sweetheart. I'm okay." Mr. Johnson let go of my hands on the sides of the chair. His hair was white. "Well, son, how do you like working on a hay ranch?" I put down the tablecloth that Mrs. Cummings had sent out with me. "It's harder work than you thought, I'll bet."

"I like it very much, sir."

"Mrs. Cummings said you were doing fine. And Staver's a good foreman. The boys all like him. He teaches them a lot."

Mr. Johnson started to cough and held a red bandana handkerchief against his mouth and bent forward in his chair, the cough deep and watery. He was very thin and wore dressy cowboy clothes.

He stopped coughing and wiped his mouth with the handkerchief. He shook his head. "That emphysema's mean stuff, son." He sat back in his chair and looked out across the fields again. "It's a fine ranch. Plenty of hay, water, and summer grazing. We got a few rattlesnakes to go along with it, but then you got to expect that. They do some good."

Mr. Johnson wiped his mouth again. He kept the handkerchief in his hand.

"My boy Brent loved it. He had a nice girl named Carol. They were going to get married and live here and raise a family." Mr. Johnson turned and pointed up to the house. "That's his room up there, just the same as the day he left it."

Mr. Johnson lowered his hand back to the chair. He shook his head.

"But my boy got drafted and got killed in the war, and his mother died, and I got sick. You never know what's going to happen to you, son. Brent's mother used to say that you just live life a day at a time and accept whatever the Lord sends. I guess that's about it. You do what good you can. Now she's with Brent and I'm still here with Helen."

"It really is a beautiful ranch, Mr. Johnson."

"Well, Staver gets all the credit for that now. He's done everything out here for over ten years now. He was Brent's best friend. They were in Korea together. They always talked about Staver buying a ranch here on the river somewhere close."

Mr. Johnson looked up at me. I wanted to tell about Staver, about the kind of person he really was and all the things he did, but I didn't want to hurt Mr. Johnson or make him upset, and I didn't know how to start or what to say first. I wanted to tell Mr. Johnson not to sell Staver the ranch. I couldn't understand why Helen didn't want to keep it.

"So you turned sixteen. That's a fine age for a boy. I remember when Brent turned sixteen. He was a little heavier than you but not any taller. His mother and me gave him a pair of handmade boots." He smiled. "Brent liked those boots. That was the year Staver gave Brent the saddle. Worked all summer to pay for it. Those two boys had a lot of love for each other. Brent being killed hurt Staver a lot. Did you hear my boy won the Medal of Honor?"

"Yes, I did." I wanted to ask Mr. Johnson if Brent ever gave Staver anything, but I didn't think I should.

Mr. Johnson started to cough again. When he stopped, he reached down and turned on the oxygen tank and held the green plastic mask over his mouth and nose. I asked him if there was anything I could do. He shook his head and lay back in the rocking chair. I went in the kitchen and told Helen, and she went out to him.

"That poor man." Mrs. Cummings shook her head. She handed me a bowl of potato salad to take outside. "He's got to suffer like that till he goes. He's been a good man all of his life too. And he and Helen are doing everything they can to see that Staver gets this ranch. But whether Staver does or not, he's got to settle down. All that chasing around is nonsense for a man his age, and it won't get him anywhere in the long run."

Mrs. Cummings sliced cold chicken onto the plate with the ham and roast beef.

"Doesn't Helen look nice. She's such a nice person. She's going to get married this fall and have a happy life. I've met her young man. His name is Steven and he's an engineer." Mrs. Cummings straightened the last slice of cold chicken on the plate. "If Staver gets this ranch he can't change a thing until Mr. Johnson's gone. Of course, he won't last too long now, poor man." Mrs. Cummings straightened up and handed me the plate. "There. It looks like we're about ready."

She wiped her hands on her white apron and then brushed back her hair.

"Oh, we used to have the loveliest picnics and reunions and holidays when I was a girl. I had so many uncles and aunts and cousins. My grandmother Butcher had the loveliest backyard with grass and trees. It seemed like half of Manti was family, and we were always visiting. There was always plenty of help if anybody got sick or there was any sadness of any kind. My grandmother had a big thick book of genealogy she'd done herself, and we used to look in there to find out who we were. It was like the long families in the Bible."

Helen came back in.

"How is your father?"

"He's better."

"Poor man."

Helen wore a blue dress, and her hair shone when she moved. She wore sandals. I watched her when she moved. I liked her being tall.

Randy, Stan, Frank, and Staver drove up in the blue pickup as I walked out the door with the potato salad and the cold sliced meat. Staver had driven into the yard from Silverton just as I was getting up for work at five-thirty. I had stood at the cabin door and watched him walk into the bunkhouse. I didn't know how he could be out all night and not sleep and still work. He did that quite often, but he didn't seem tired during the day.

As we were finishing lunch, Helen got up and went to the car and brought back a big round wrapped box and gave it to me and wished me a belated happy birthday. It was a grey Stetson. I put it on and Frank whistled. After lunch I thanked Helen again for the hat.

"You're welcome. You're beginning to look like a cowboy." She smiled. "Brent had a hat like that. I bought it for him."

"You're a kind person."

"You can wear it when you come to visit us in September. The summer is going very quickly. They always do."

"Yes, I guess they do."

"Here. Let me straighten your hat for you. There. That's how it should look."

"Thank you."

"The missionaries came by again, Owen. They want to start the discussions."

"Are you going to start?"

"I don't know. I like having them in the house. It's a nice feeling. I need to talk it over with Steve and see if he's interested. He had a college roommate who was a Mormon who wasn't a very good person."

"I'm sorry."

"Well, I guess nobody's perfect are they?" She turned and looked down the lane toward the river trees and the road. "My mother always drove Brent and me into Silverton to church every Sunday when we were children. Mrs. Cummings was our Sunday School teacher one year. I remember she said that one of the most difficult things to do was accept the Lord's love and sacrifice. Brent always liked to go to her class." Helen reached up and pushed the hair back from her face. "Brent was such a loving kid." She shook her head. "I could never imagine what it must have been like for him in Korea."

"Didn't he write and tell you?"

"No, not really. That wasn't something he would do."

"Did Staver tell you?"

"No. Staver was in the hospital for nearly a year after he was wounded, which was the day after Brent was killed."

Helen turned and looked out across the fields.

"Brent crawled out into the minefield five times to bring back men who had been wounded, and then a sniper killed him. It was during a battle."

Helen kept looking out across the fields, and then she turned back and looked at me.

"Well, we'll see what happens with the missionaries, Owen."

Helen offered to drive Mrs. Cummings to Carson City to visit Dale Sunday if she wanted to stay overnight in Las Vegas, so she left with the Johnsons. A friend of Helen's was coming to Silverton Sunday night and would bring Mrs. Cummings back. I told her that I would clean up everything and do the dishes.

Afterward I worked with Stan herding cattle to new pastures with the jeep. We all quit at six, and Randy and I got ready and went into Silverton. I wore my new cowboy outfit and my new Stetson. Frank and Staver were coming in later. Randy drove fast, but I didn't say anything to him. It wouldn't do any good.

Randy and I had a hamburger and a malt at the Silverton Cafe, and when we stood at the end of the counter paying our checks, Alice asked me if my hat was new.

"Helen Johnson gave it to me for my birthday."

Alice handed me back my change.

"She's a nice person. Too bad we can't all be a little nicer."

"I think you're nice."

She smiled. "Why thank you, Owen." She gave Randy his change. "We'll see you on the Fourth. You come and eat with us at the picnic. And we want you to come to Frank's birthday party and sit at our table. That's in two weeks."

"We'll be there," Randy said. "Don't worry about that."

"You boys have a good time now. Happy birthday, Owen."

"Thank you."

The movie was *Apache*, but we didn't see any high school girls without dates. Randy said that all he wanted to do was just talk to one girl for five minutes. After the movie he looked for Staver in all of the casinos and saloons, stood at the open doors.

The new Stetson made me feel tall. I watched myself in the store windows. I felt very tall and like I could do anything. Walking down the street under the red neon lights, I tried to walk natural. I kept taking off my hat to smooth my hair. I felt like I could do very important things. We went back to the Volcano Casino twice, but we didn't see Staver.

I drove the jeep back. I stopped at the Indian battleground at the mouth of the valley. I pulled up so that the lights shone on the bronze plaque set in the rock monument. Randy got out too. It was the biggest battle ever fought by Indians in Nevada. I turned to look out across the sagebrush flat. The wild animals and the vultures would have eaten the scalped dead bodies. In the Book of Mormon the Lamanites killed all the Nephites in the last great battles, and even the women and children fought in the Nephite armies. And because they were so full of hate and so evil, the Lord wouldn't help them win. And the Holy Ghost withdrew from them.

The last day of class after we'd finished the Book of Mormon and got our tests back, Brother Anderson turned to the chalkboard and listed all of the great wars in history down to the Korean war. He put the chalk in the tray and turned to look at us.

"One atomic bomb contains more destructive power than all the other kinds of explosives man has ever used in all of his wars. The great theme of the book you have studied this year is that breaking the commandments leads to violence, war, and final destruction."

Randy walked back to the jeep and got in. I turned and looked at the monument again.

"Come on. Let's go. You going to stand there all night admiring that thing? We'll never get there the way you drive."

The bronze plaque had twelve bullet holes in it. I turned and walked back to the pickup. No cool breeze blew down the valley.

I fixed sandwiches for Randy and Stan and me Sunday afternoon. Frank and Staver weren't back yet. Mrs. Cummings got back late from Las Vegas, and I helped her up the porch steps. I asked her how Dale was; she said he was about the same. She was too tired to talk. She had to sit down in her rocking chair to rest before she went up the stairs. Her breathing was very heavy.

Tuesday, the Fourth of July, we had to irrigate until noon. Frank and Staver left before we did. Stan was going in with us. Randy and I were just finishing dressing when Stan came running up on the cabin porch and jerked open the screen door.

"Okay, we got a fire. Staver just phoned."

"What?"

"We got a fire down on Porcupine Creek. Put your work clothes back on. I'll be back in three minutes. Wear a shirt with long sleeves."

"Nuts." Randy sat back down on his bunk.

"I thought that you wanted to fight a fire."

"I *want* to go to Silverton. I've been looking forward to that, not to fighting some stupid fire."

Randy had shaved.

We met Stan at the bunkhouse. He asked us if we had our gloves. He told me to drive the pickup. Mrs. Cummings stood on the back porch with an apple and a sandwich for each of us.

"You put these in your pocket. You don't know when you'll get to eat again. And you boys be careful. You watch out for them, Stan."

"I'll watch out for 'em."

We stopped at the fire shed by the gate and loaded all the fire-fighting tools into the back of the pickup. We got back in and I took off the brake and shifted.

I turned to Stan. "How long will it take to put it out?"

I shifted to high.

"Hard to say. A few hours maybe, maybe a week. Depends on the wind and how much of a start she's got. Depends on how steep the country is and what equipment you get into it. If we don't get a wind we're okay. If we do, we just sit back and watch her burn. But I wouldn't worry about getting to that picnic today if I was you."

"Nuts." Randy pulled his hat down over his eyes.

"Slow down a little, kid. We want to get there alive."

"I'm sorry." I lifted my foot a little off the gas pedal.

Stan lit a cigarette.

Magpies and ravens flew away from the dead rabbits on the road.

"A fire starts to run and it's too dangerous to fight. You lose men that way. The Forest Service brings in planes to bomb it with that fire-retardant stuff, but that don't help much if she's really moving. They had a fire over in Horse Canyon on the other side of this mountain thirty years ago and killed the whole crew, a hundred men. The outfit they sent in after them just found the shovel blades and ax heads with little piles of white ashes next to 'em. That's how they knew what those white ashes were."

Stan shook his head and took his cigarette out of his mouth.

"Some of the boys on that rescue crew got rich picking up the gold that melted out of those ledges. It just trickled down and got hard, and those boys picked up pure nuggets of it. Of course it didn't make 'em millionaires because there ain't that much gold up there to begin with. But what there was that fire smelted out. With that wind the fire in against those ledges burning those heavy pines was just like a regular furnace."

"I never heard of anything like that before." I turned to look at Stan, then at Randy. Randy didn't say anything.

"I held five of those nuggets in that hand." Stan raised his right hand and held it there. "That fire was so hot it heated up the ground water. Little town of Summit out there got its water from springs from Horse Canyon and they didn't have to heat water for baths for a week. Had to let their drinking water cool. A rancher named Day got steam out of his pipes the first two days. Of course his place was up high. They had a big story in the Las Vegas paper about that. Hottest fire they ever had. One whole side of that mountain burned for a month. Some of those folks thought it was the end of the world. But it was just some coal ledges burning. Took a big rain storm to put it out. Rained solid for ten days."

Stan looked out through the windshield. He closed his eyes to pull deep on his cigarette and let the smoke out. I turned to look at him, but he kept his eyes closed. I'd read about coal mines catching on fire and burning for years. But I'd never read about the fires making the ground water hot. I decided that it could happen.

Randy kept putting his head out the window to look down the road.

Nobody worked in the fields; the fire sheds stood open and empty. The dust haze along the road thickened. We passed Porcupine Campground. Campers stood at the gates looking down the road. They waved.

Stan put out his cigarette in the ash tray. "Down about a mile now." He sat back. "Fighting a big fire is nothing but hard dirty work. You're going to see that soon enough. I've seen kids just sit down and bawl they were so tired. And I've seen 'em wet their pants and run away when the fire got close to the line."

Randy kept sticking his head out the window, like he could see farther that way. I kept licking my lips.

The road left the river and came up over a hill.

"There she is." Stan leaned forward. "She's on the flats. That's good." He sat back. "Easier to get at."

Randy pulled his head in and put his hat back on. "Brother."

"She's burning pretty good. They call in the National Guard for big fires."

To the left a high column of black smoke rose above the brush, sudden great red-orange bursts of flame leaping up into the smoke, then dying back. A blue haze spread all down the valley one side to the other, and ashes fell against the windshield and on the hood. Watching the flames, I hunched forward to grip the steering wheel tighter. The flames vanished as I drove down the hill. I breathed in smoke.

"Better park here, kid, while you got the room."

We had passed several parked pickups. I pulled in behind a green cattle truck.

"Leave the keys in it. They might have to move it in a hurry if the wind shifts. Get a hardhat and one of those tools out of the back, and a full canteen. If they want the other stuff they'll come after it."

A green Forest Service pickup passed us.

Randy and I each took a double-bitted axe from the pile of shovels, mattocks, and axes. We put on the yellow hardhats and left our straw cowboy hats in the cab. Walking down the road I liked carrying the axe and wearing the hardhat. I wanted the fire to be dangerous. I felt complete and ready. We walked through a blue smoky haze.

A jackrabbit ran toward us then veered off to the side under a red pickup. Stan nodded toward the pickup; it was Staver's. Randy went over to look in. Another Forest Service pickup passed us. The driver hollered at Stan and he hollered back. The dust turned the air yellower.

"That was old Sid in that truck." Stan nodded back toward Staver's pickup. "They probably got Staver running a crew. They always get him on a fire if they can because he can do anything—drive a cat, run a crew, dynamite. You boys will get paid extra for this. The government pays you good."

We climbed the bank to a big sagebrush flat. Forty or fifty men stood by a Forest Service truck. They all wore yellow hardhats and held tools. The smoke and flames rose behind them across the flat in one big column.

"Looks like they're getting ready." We followed Stan.

Staver stood at the front of the green pickup with two Forest Service men, who wore brown shirts with patches. They had a map spread out on the hood, and one of the Forest Service men pointed toward the fire and then looked at the map again.

Frank stood at the edge of the group of firefighters. He spoke to Stan as we walked up and then turned to me.

"You look a little pale, kid. You all right?"

"Yes, I'm all right."

"You're not going to throw up are you?"

"No, I'm not."

"Good."

"How'd it get started? Some camper's kid?" Stan lit a cigarette and held the match for Frank.

"Ya, playing with firecrackers. They got him. His old man's going to have to pay for all this. I'll bet he works that kid over with a club when he gets him back to camp." Frank laughed and turned to spit.

Randy and I turned to watch the fire, which burned across the flat in the high oak brush. Big red-black flames kept shooting into the black smoke, but there was no sound because we were too far away. I kept brushing the ashes off my shirt. I reached up and pushed my hardhat on tighter.

"Gee, I wish I had an axe instead of this mattock."

I turned. A boy about as old as I was stood next to me. He held up the mattock for me to see.

"One of the guys killed a rattlesnake with his axe when we first got here from down at the campground."

"Are you on vacation?"

"Ya. The Forest Service came down to get men to fight the fire. You have to be eighteen, but my dad let me come anyway. That guy jumped about six feet in the air when he first saw the rattlesnake. It crawled right toward him. We saw a badger and about six jackrabbits running away from the fire."

"Who said that you had to be eighteen?"

"The Forest Service man over there." He pointed.

"Are you sure?"

"Sure I'm sure."

I told Randy.

"So what? You going to leave and let the whole mountain burn down? All they want right now is bodies. Do you think they're going to ask you how old you are?"

"No."

"Maybe you'd better go back to the ranch, kid, and get dressed in that new cowboy outfit and go to the Fourth of July picnic." Frank grinned at me. "I'll tell Staver. He'll understand."

"I want to help put out the fire, but I don't want to break the law."

"Good. You don't have anything to worry about."

"It's not a law; it's probably just a regulation. You worry too much, cousin."

"Maybe the kid likes to worry, Randy. Lots of things to worry about."

I didn't say anything. I knew that it could just be a regulation and not a law. But I still didn't want to do anything wrong. I'd broken the law when I drove to Silverton without a license and when I trapped the minnows, and this made three times. I'd never broken any laws before. But what I'd done seemed more important than the law. I wanted to be able to make the right decisions all the time.

"Okay, line up in a column of two's and let's move."

I turned. Staver stood in back of the green Forest Service pickup and talked through the bullhorn. He told us how to cut the brush and throw it ahead of us into the path of the fire. They couldn't use a caterpillar or pumper trucks where we were going because Porcupine Creek had cut too many deep channels down through the lava on the flat. A plane was coming to drop fire retardant. We had to cut a firebreak to keep the fire from getting any higher. They had chainsaws to cut the heavy stuff after we cut out the brush. The fire was up to twenty acres now.

"And if I tell you to get out, get out. Don't stop to ask questions or you're going to get fried. And you new guys try not to kill yourselves with those mattocks and axes. They're sharp. If you haven't got a canteen pick up one here in the back of the truck, and keep those hardhats on. All right, move out."

Frank and Stan went up with Staver. I walked behind Randy. We hiked up through the thick brush. I couldn't see the fire, just the smoke above the high brush. I wanted a drink. A man dropped off every twenty feet.

I cut the wrist-thick oak brush and dragged it out to throw it ahead of me. I couldn't see Randy through the brush and haze. The man above me cursed. A chainsaw started. The brush tangled when I tried to drag it free, and branches scratched my face and knocked off my hardhat. I stopped to drink twice from my army canteen.

"Hey, Owen, it looks like you know how to use that axe."

I turned. Frank and Staver stood behind me.

"I had an Explorer leader who taught us how."

"Good." Staver carried a walkie-talkie. He wasn't dirty.

"Haven't seen any skunks have you, kid?"

"No, I haven't."

"You sure want to be careful of skunks when you're fighting a fire. One might run into you."

"I'll be careful."

"Well, a man with your experience shouldn't have too much trouble." Frank started to laugh.

I watched them vanish into the brush and smoke. They didn't bother me. I kept cutting. The work was hard and hot, but I liked to swing the axe and hit the same spot until I cut through the oak trunk as big as my arm. I didn't look up. I expected the flames and terrible heat to suddenly come sweeping up out of the smoke. A big plane flew over, the noise mixing with the chainsaws, and came back low, dropping retardants. Somebody had said that they used a converted B-24. A rabbit ran past me. I sweated.

I saw the rattlesnake just as I raised my axe to swing. I didn't hear him. His head was pulled back but he wasn't all coiled yet. I brought the axe down in one swing, just aiming for the snake, not the head. The blade caught him in the middle. It cut him in two pieces. I hit him three more times without thinking. I stopped. My whole body trembled. The blood spread on the leaf mold, the snake's belly yellow-white. I reached down and picked up my hardhat and put it back on.

"Well, it looks like you got one, kid." I turned. Stan stood behind me. "He didn't nail you did he?"

"No."

"Good. Keep your eyes open. You don't want one of those babies to nail you. They don't like fire. When Staver cut the top off that den with a caterpillar like I was telling you, that burning gasoline really fixed 'em. Those old snakes didn't like that one bit. You should have seen that." Stan shook his head. "Well, got to go. Got some new batteries for Staver's walkie-talkie."

"He went down that way."

"Yeh, I know where he is. See ya, kid."

Down through the smoke I saw the fire, and the heat came in big pulses. The fire crept along through the dry grass and leaves until it came to a clump of brush. It fed up into the brush and then suddenly the whole clump burned in a bright burst of flame, the flames shooting thirty feet into the air, then gradually dying. The fire was fifty yards below me. The whole line was bursts of flame in smoky air, and everything was dim, even the flames, and it was growing darker.

I kept cutting the brush and watching for snakes.

"Okay, pull back behind the firebreak!" Staver came down the line. "Put out any fire that gets across!"

The brush piles we'd made went up in big bursts of flame. The fire cracked and whooshed, and the heat flared hot against us where we stood. I saw Randy and six other men. Burning leaves and pieces of burning brush fell on our side of the break, but we got them all put out. It kept getting darker. I looked at my watch; it was eight o'clock.

Stan walked up and stood next to me.

"That's how it is, kid, when you get a real fire, like those piles of brush, only maybe ten times worse. You get flames a hundred feet high. With a wind it moves faster than a man can run. Not even a coyote can stay ahead of that kind of fire. You have to see it before you can believe it. I've seen grown men run out of the line screaming. You couldn't stop 'em with a gun."

The plane flew over, but you still couldn't see whether it was a B-24 or not. Stan looked up. I watched the dying flames. I knelt down on one knee and leaned on my axe. I was tired. My hands were black. I pulled up the leg of my Levis; my leg was black above my socks. And I felt how dirty my whole body was under my clothes, but I didn't care.

The smoke thinned a little, and above and below me men gathered in groups to talk and smoke. They drank from their canteens.

"Hey, Stan told me you killed a rattler. How big was he?"

Randy walked toward me and I stood up.

"The kid's a killer."

Frank and Staver walked up to Randy and stopped. Frank bent forward and took one more step closer to me. He shook his head and took the cigarette out of his mouth with his thumb, forefinger, and index finger so that the end was cupped in his palm. He straightened up.

"It looks like I was wrong. I was just plain wrong or that fire dried him all out. Stan, I thought you said that that rattler gave old Careful here a bad scare."

"Owen's a good summer hand," Staver said.

I unscrewed the lid of my canteen and took a drink. I didn't look at them.

"Watch it with that water, kid. You don't want any accidents now." They all laughed. "See any skunks?"

I screwed the lid back on.

"I'll be careful."

We stayed another three hours on the line, until all of the little fires were out. We shoveled dirt on them. The Forest Service sent up sandwiches and different kinds of pop in cans. They kept ten men all night to sit on the fire, but we left at midnight.

Mrs. Cummings came out on the back porch when we drove in. She told us to get cleaned up and come over to the kitchen for something to eat.

"You boys leave those dirty clothes out on the porch. Don't you take them in that cabin. You undress right there."

I wanted to go down to the river and just sink and lie on the bottom, but I was too tired. Standing in the shower, my head down, I watched the dirt wash down off my body. I shampooed my hair three times. I'd burned my right wrist between the top of my glove and my cuff. I didn't remember doing that. I looked in the mirror at my face, but it wasn't burned. I put Clearasil on my pimples. Frank had told me that pimples were the meanness coming out.

"But what you want to be careful of, kid, is boils. They're a lot worse." He'd laughed and turned to spit. "You've never had boils before have you kid?"

"No, I haven't."

"Well, give yourself a little time." He'd started to laugh again.

Mrs. Cummings put ointment on the burn on my wrist when I went over to eat. It was a second-degree burn. A letter from Becky lay by my plate. I sat down. I'd never been so tired in my whole life, but I was hungry. I ate a steak. My arms and legs felt loose and heavy. I didn't want to have to move any part of my body ever again.

"Son, you better go over and go to bed. You're going to fall asleep right there in that chair if you don't."

"Owen's a good man."

"It's too bad you all had your Fourth of July ruined."

I picked up Becky's letter and stood up. I wanted to lie down and not move, ever. Mrs. Cummings held the door open for me. I thanked her. I walked out on the porch and down the steps. Tobe licked my hand. I walked toward the cabin. It felt good to be so tired and know I could lie down and go to sleep. My body was bigger than it had ever been in my whole life. Fighting brush fires didn't scare me.

10

The rest of the week we irrigated. Twice I saw Staver across the fields standing beside his pickup watching me with his binoculars. He gave Randy and me another boxing lesson, and he played pass with Randy on the front lawn. Sunday a National Guard unit from Las Vegas came up to build a bridge across the river. Stan said they did it every summer. The captain knew Staver.

Monday morning after breakfast we were standing under the clothes line hung with white sheets, and Staver told me to clean out the tractor shed and the repair shop and then to help the man who was going to come to slaughter a black yearling beef up at the corral west of the barn. Randy waved when he drove out with Frank and Staver.

"See you, cousin. Don't work too hard washing those floors."

"I won't."

"Don't put too much air in those tires, kid, and watch out for skunks." Frank struck a match to light a cigarette.

"I'll be very careful."

Staver drove slowly out under the white sheets so he didn't raise any dust. The sheets hung like a long white flag across the yard. I turned and walked to the cabin to brush my teeth. Tobe walked ahead of me.

After I cleaned up the tractor shed, I washed Brent's pickup, and then I sat in it. I put my hands on the steering wheel. I turned the key in the ignition, but there was no sound. In the jockeybox was the registration with Brent's signature. When I vacuumed under the front seat, I found two paper cups and two straws, one with lipstick, and a penny. I held the penny in the palm of my hand, and then I put it back. Sitting in the seat, I reached up and touched the faded high-school graduation tassel hanging from the rearview mirror. I put my hands back on the steering wheel. I looked at my hands and then out through the windshield. I thought I'd like to have double-dated with Brent in the pickup. I wondered if he'd given Staver a big present like the saddle Staver gave him.

I rolled up the windows, got out, and closed the door.

I was just pulling down the door on the last bay when I heard a truck behind me. I turned around. The sign on the white van said "Silverton Fresh Meats—Custom Slaughtering."

The driver stuck his head out the window. He wore a straw hat and had big heavy round shoulders.

"You the one that's going to help me, boy?"

"Yes, sir."

"Where's the animal?"

"In the corral up at the barn."

"I'll drive on up there then. Jump in." I got in. "I'm Ralph." He shook my hand.

At the barn Ralph turned around and backed the truck in through the big double door and we got out.

"I like to work in the shade. Get a half a bucket of corn and go down and open the door and rattle it. He'll come in if he's been grain fed. Dump a little out for him. Staver said it was a yearling. They come pretty easy."

Black with a white face, the yearling was standing just in front of the door when I opened it. I rattled the corn in the bucket and poured some just inside the door. The yearling came right up and started eating the corn. I dumped a little more, and it followed me.

"Dump it all right there. That's close enough."

I dumped the corn.

"He looks just a little thin for Mr. Johnson, but I guess he's all right. Have to be." Ralph wore a big white rubber apron.

The hoist was on the end of the truck. On the floor at the side of the truck were three tubs made from halves of fifty-gallon barrels with handles welded on. Two wooden boxes were turned upside down. A meat saw, knives, another rubber apron, a big pan, and a rifle lay on a folding aluminum table by the barrels.

"Here, you better put this on." Ralph handed me the rubber apron. It'll keep you from getting too splashed up. Better roll your sleeves all the way up."

I looked at the yearling. He lifted his head and licked his nose with his long blue tongue.

"You ever killed a beef before, boy?"

"No."

"Well, you just follow orders and it'll all work out fine. Nothin' to it. Staver always sends one of you summer hands out to help. It's a good experience. Let's you see where meat comes from. I'd let you shoot him, but you have to do it just right to knock him down the first time. I've seen some men have to shoot a beef two and three times to knock it down."

Ralph told me what to do after he shot the yearling.

He picked up the rifle and worked a shell into the chamber. He aimed, held the rifle three feet from the yearling's head. He shot, and the yearling fell down on its side. Ralph put the rifle down on the table and picked up a knife. He stuck it up to the handle in the throat and cut across. Then he cut the skin on the hocks, and I helped him pull the hoist bar down and fit the hooks in. He worked very fast.

I stepped back when Ralph lifted the beef off the ground with the electric winch, but the head swung around and the half-spurting blood splashed across the bottoms of my Levis and my boots. I pulled the tub under the head; blood splashed up on my hands.

Ralph used a different knife to cut down through the stomach. I handed him the meat saw to cut through the rib cage. He showed me how to hold the cut ribs apart. My arms were bloody past the elbows. I held my breath against the smell. Ralph cut the lungs loose and the diaphragm, and I pulled, guiding the warm steaming entrails down into the tub.

I pulled the hide down while Ralph cut it loose. He sawed off the head so that the skin and head were together and put them in one of the tubs. He'd cut off the front legs at the knee. I held the carcass while Ralph sawed it in half. The ribs looked like the ribs of a huge man.

We pushed the two halves back on the track into the refrigerated truck and closed the door. Ralph told me to take the heart and liver out of the tub and put them in the pan. I did that, holding my breath against the warm sweet smell. I had to cut them loose with a knife after I found them. I had to use both hands to hold the liver. I set the warm heart on top of the liver.

"Mrs. Cummings gets the liver. I like heart."

Ralph had a hose on the truck, and we washed and wiped all of his equipment clean. Then we washed our hands with a special soap he had. I helped him lift the tubs up on the back of the truck. Ralph thanked me for my help and shook my hand. I watched him drive down through the yard and stop at the house. I looked down at the dried blood on my boots and the cuffs of my Levis. I rolled down my sleeves.

After lunch Staver sent Randy to the cabin to tell me to come down to the barn.

"What for?"

"I don't know."

Stan and Frank stood just inside the barn. Staver was squatted down drawing circles in the dirt with a willow.

"Check the corral, Owen." Staver nodded toward the west corral. He didn't look up.

I walked to the corner of the barn. A black yearling stood in the corral.

"What do you see, Owen?"

"A beef."

"What color?"

"Black."

"Is it all black?"

"Yes." My heart began to beat hard. I turned and walked back.

"Did I tell you to kill the black yearling?"

"Yes."

"Was the one you killed all black?"

"Except for a white face."

"Was it all black?"

"No."

"You killed the wrong animal, Owen. That one you killed needed to be fattened up for another three months. This one's ready now. Mr. Johnson likes his meat just right. He takes half a beef; he gives a lot of it to his old friends in Las Vegas. It costs you money when you kill a beef before it's prime, Owen. Do you think we could put this on Owen's bill, Frank?"

"Sure. But it's a good thing that prize young bull wasn't in the corral." Frank spit. "It's a good thing."

"But that bull's brown, Frank."

"Well, you can't be too careful. Ol' Owen here's a killer."

They all laughed.

"Maybe that Angel Moroni was in the barn this morning and told him which one to kill."

"Could that be it, Owen?"

I looked at Staver and didn't say anything. The white puffed tip of the scar showed above his T-shirt. I was afraid they could hear my heart pounding.

"Well, you better go get started on that tool room, Owen. You did a nice job on the tractor shed. It looks real nice."

Walking away from the barn, I heard the pickup leave. I didn't turn around. I felt dumb. I wanted to walk over and hit one of the trees with my fist I felt so dumb. I couldn't believe that I hadn't looked in the corral. I should have looked. I wanted to be able to wrap my arms around my chest and squeeze out all of the dumb, heavy complicated feeling.

I walked into the tool room.

I got the broom and started to sweep the cement floor. I moved everything to sweep under it. I worked hard and fast so I wouldn't think about the beef or feel anything. I felt so dumb. If only I'd checked it wouldn't have happened. I didn't have to make mistakes if I was careful.

I heard a dynamite explosion and stopped sweeping, but there was only one. On the work bench were two dynamite boxes full of used parts. I wiped off all the tools with an oiled cloth and hung them on the wall hooks against their white silhouettes. I liked the feeling of the heavy metal tools. I didn't know the names of some of the tools, but it made me feel strong to hold them. I'd always wished that my father had left me a big box of tools, and things he'd built. I wanted to touch and look at things my father had built and know that he had built them.

At four o'clock I saw through the window a rancher in a yellow pickup pulling a horse trailer drive up and park by the corral. Staver and Frank drove in behind him. They all got out and stood talking. I went out and pulled the hose in and started washing down the cement floor.

"Hey, kid."

I looked up. Frank stood in the doorway.

"Yes."

"Come on over to the corral. We need some help."

I turned off the hose and followed Frank. It was hot. Black Prince wasn't in the corral, and the door from the barn out into the corral was closed. Staver and the rancher stood by the back of the trailer, and Staver introduced me.

"Open that corral gate will you, Owen."

Frank went into the barn. I pushed open the gate. Frank opened the top half of the door leading from the barn to the corral. The rancher backed the mare out down the ramp.

"Okay, baby, okay, take it easy."

The mare kept tossing her head. She lifted her front feet off the ground.

"Take her in, Rex." Staver turned and walked into the barn.

The rancher led the mare through the gate. He unclipped the halter rope, and walked out. I closed the gate.

"This will be her first colt."

"Oh."

The mare stood still watching the barn. The bottom half of the door swung open, and Frank came out. Staver led Black Prince out on a halter rope. Frank closed the door. Black Prince kept jerking his head. Staver unclipped the halter rope.

"Okay, boy."

Frank and Staver walked over to the fence and climbed up. The rancher stood by me. Frank lit a cigarette and held the match for Staver. Black Prince neighed, the sound high and fierce like a scream. He reared up; his head came above the fence. I turned.

"Stay around, Owen."

"No thanks."

"Come on. You might have a ranch some day and want to breed horses."

I kept walking away.

"Hey, Owen."

I kept walking.

"They're animals," I said.

"What did you say, Owen?"

"They're animals!" I shouted it.

"Okay, Boy Scout. You go back and get things all cleaned up."

"Hey, V-i-r-g-i-n-i-a."

I kept walking, listening to Frank and Staver laughing; the rancher wasn't laughing. I walked into the tool room and turned the hose on full force to wash out the dirt.

Reproduction wasn't obscene; it was wonderful. I'd studied insect and animal reproduction in my biology classes. I'd seen films. I'd read *An Introduction to Conception and Birth* and *Life's Chain.* Adam and Eve had to reproduce, which was what sex was for mainly. Brother Anderson had pictures of his eight children in his office. Everybody in the whole world had to be conceived. Reproduction was a commandment. It wasn't a joke.

I turned off the hose and got the broom to sweep the water out to make the floor clean.

Randy was in the cabin when I got there to clean up before supper. He turned from combing his hair and looking at his pictures on the wall. More than a third of the wall was covered with *Playboy* centerfolds now.

"Hey, you should have been with us today. We dynamited another hole on the river. We got one brown that weighed about six pounds."

"Where?"

"Oh, up about a half a mile above the bridge. Why? What's wrong with you?"

"Nothing." I breathed deep.

"You can catch some more minnows and take them up there. You just can't believe that scar of Staver's. It's that wide and about that long. It's really something. He talks a lot about the war, but he never says anything about when he got wounded. I'd like to ask him if he was conscious and what it felt like."

Randy stood in front of the mirror to put on his hat.

I went in the bathroom to wash my hands. I watched the water flow over my hands. Staver could have looked down where the blood was coming out. You could stay conscious when you were wounded. He would have held his chest and stomach with both hands, the blood coming out between his fingers, the whole front of his uniform covered with blood. Riding my bike one evening I almost got hit by a car. An hour later I rode back to the intersection and stopped under the street lamp. I could have lain on the black asphalt with a big cut in my head. My blood could have run down the side of my face, my neck, and onto my white tennis shirt. I could have heard a girl scream and seen people running toward me from the lighted houses before I went unconscious. All the next day I kept reaching up to touch the side of my head. I wanted everybody to feel sorry for me.

"Hey, what happened to you over at the corral today?"

I walked out of the bathroom drying my hands on the towel.

"Why?"

"Oh, Staver and Frank were talking about it and laughing. Staver asked me when you were going to join the race."

"What race?"

"The human race." Randy smiled.

"Very funny. I just don't happen to believe that breeding horses has to be a spectator sport."

"Relax, cousin. You'll live longer. It's very educational."

"Is it?" I walked back in the bathroom to hang up the towel.

Randy laughed. "Sure. Ever heard of the birds and the bees?"

I came out of the bathroom. "Yes, I have. Let's go to supper."

Mrs. Cummings asked Staver to say the blessing. I bowed my head, but I watched him say the words. And I wanted to ask him when I passed him the hot rolls if he remembered that his mother had taught him to pray. Or if he ever thought about how his mother fed him, kept him clean and warm, hugged him and kissed him, and how she took him to church. She gave him Christmas and birthday presents. She took care of him when he was sick and when he got hurt and cried. Didn't he remember how his mother loved him and expected him to be a good person all of his life, and so why wasn't he? What was more important than that?

"You know how to dance, kid? Hey, kid, you dreaming?"

I looked at Frank. "What?"

"You know how to dance?"

"Yes."

"Good. The girls at my birthday parties always like to dance with the summer hands. Lover boy here is all ready to go." Frank reached over and put his hand on Randy's shoulder.

We had apple pie with vanilla ice cream for dessert.

I was just starting to help Mrs. Cummings clear the table when Uncle Mark phoned. Randy was outside. Stan, Frank, and Staver stood by the kitchen porch lighting cigarettes. After Uncle Mark talked to Randy, he talked to me.

"Well, it sounds like you two aren't dead yet."

"No," I said.

"You don't sound absolutely overjoyed. Randy sounds better than you do. Nothing wrong out there is there? You're having a good time aren't you? You're learning a lot."

"I like the ranch."

"Just stick with it. It's already the middle of July. You won't regret it, I can promise you that. I'm having a very good summer. Randy tells me Staver's teaching you two how to box."

"Yes, he is."

"Good. Your mother and grandmother are okay. I was over there Saturday. Your grandmother still can't make up her mind about that bedroom of yours, but I suppose she will eventually. Must be like sleeping in a museum."

"Thanks, Uncle Mark."

I hung up the phone. I wanted to tell Uncle Mark about Frank and Staver and the influence they were having on Randy. But I didn't know what to say. There wasn't anything I could describe. Randy wasn't drinking beer or smoking, and he wasn't gambling for money. He was going to go to Silverton to play in the big poker game, but that was still six weeks away. Something might happen so that he wouldn't go. Randy was working hard and learning a lot. I knew that I had to try harder to be a better influence on him.

After I finished helping Mrs. Cummings I got my swimming stuff and the minnow trap. Tobe ahead of me, I walked down to the old bridge and cut off on the trail leading along the bank. I liked to be under the trees by the river. The sun rested on the top of the west mountains, turning the whole valley and the east mountains a rose color.

Up the trail Tobe stopped, crouched, started to bark, jumping and circling. I walked forward. A rattlesnake lay coiled in the middle of the path. It struck and Tobe jumped back, half the long body coming out then coiling again. It struck again. I wasn't scared. I set the minnow trap down and picked up four rocks. The snake lay coiled, its head pulled back into the coils. I threw the rocks as hard as I could and hit it with the third rock and broke its back. It tried to crawl off, but I smashed its head with a big rock.

I knelt down to pet Tobe. "Good boy, Tobe. Good boy."

I knew that I might have stepped on the rattlesnake if Tobe hadn't been ahead of me. But I wasn't really scared. I got a stick and threw the snake off the path into the brush.

I found the dead hole and set the minnow trap above it. I stood and watched for ten minutes, but not one trout rose to feed on the insects. The entrails and the small dead trout lay on the bottom at the end of the hole. The big flat rock where they'd cleaned the trout was black with dried blood.

I turned and walked back down the trail to the swimming hole, put on my suit, and climbed the big cottonwood. I stood on the limb holding onto a branch. I looked back past the house to the bunkhouse, the windows and door yellow with light. I'd invited Randy to come, but he wouldn't.

I looked down at my arms and my chest and stomach. I'd gained eight pounds. I could see new muscles without even pulling tight. Frank and Staver treated me and Randy just like they treated all the summer hands. But I kept wishing all the time that Brent hadn't been killed in the Korean War. It would have been a perfect place to work for the summer then.

I watched down through the leaves the dark river below. Tipping forward, I dived. I dived three times. I didn't feel like swimming. I took off my suit and wrapped my towel around me and sat on the ledge holding my legs, my head on my knees, feeling tight and round. When I read the article about boys wearing supporters all the time so they wouldn't masturbate, I went down to Sears, but it embarrassed me to buy that many supporters. I decided to buy them through the catalog, but I still had to fill out the order form and give it to the girl. And then I thought about my grandmother washing them and putting them in my drawer clean every week, and so I didn't buy them. I wanted that tight safe feeling all the time.

Sitting there on the ledge, my head on my knees, I thought about what Uncle Mark had said about my room being a museum. I'd never thought about it that way. I guess it was a museum for my grandmother, a little bit. She liked to be in my room.

The next morning I drove Mrs. Cummings in to Silverton to buy groceries. She held the package for Dale on her lap. Cliff Hinckley had been to see her after supper the night before. She wiped her neck with the white handkerchief.

"Ten years of that boy's life gone, but maybe he can settle down now and get some happiness out of life. He's got a girl he was in high school with. She's divorced and has a little girl, so she should have some sense and want to make a good home. His mother's a good woman, and his father was a good man, except he was mean when he was drunk. He used to whip those poor children so you could hear them screaming all across the block. He was always sorry afterward and tried to love 'em to make up for it. I guess drinking was something he couldn't help. Well, he's at peace now."

Mrs. Cummings turned to look out the pickup window.

"I always prayed that I'd be here when Dale got out of prison so I could help him."

I looked at Mrs. Cummings.

"You're going to have your operation aren't you, so you'll be better?"

"Well maybe, son. I guess there's no use worrying about that till the time comes."

"You'll be just fine, Mrs. Cummings."

"Yes, I'm sure I will be. You may as well laugh as cry in this old life. I know that."

I turned and drove down Silver Street past the World Hotel and the Volcano Casino. That afternoon we all worked on setting forms for a new headgate and a hundred-foot section of concrete ditch. All Randy could talk about was his car. Uncle Mark had told him that he'd sold a big motel, so Randy was sure about the Triumph. Frank kept asking him questions about what a Triumph was like and how fast it would go.

"Did your dad give you a new car when you were in high school, Frank?" Staver didn't look up. We were building the forms for the headgate.

"Nope." Frank stood up and tipped back his hat. "He just let me borrow the pickup when I needed it, which was just fine." Frank took the cigarette out of his mouth and spit into the canal. "Just fine. It was fast."

Frank told a story about one of his girl friends, the words obscene, as if he couldn't talk without obscene words, as if they were the only words he knew. Brother Anderson had a clinical psychologist come to seminary who talked about obscene words. He said that people used obscene words because they were afraid to use the dictionary words, which were too honest. They couldn't stand being honest. The psychologist said that one of the first ways you controlled your life was with right words. Right words protected you because they were accurate and you couldn't hide from what they meant. Using right words was one of the ways you were honest. I copied down the list of right words from the chalkboard.

"You going to get a new car too, Owen, now that you've got your license?" Staver stood up from working on the forms. He lit a cigarette, blinking against the smoke.

"No, I'm not. I'm saving my money to go on a mission and to go to medical school."

I stood up from nailing the form and wiped my forehead with the back of my glove. The sun glared off the canal. I really didn't want a new car. Some boys at Provo High dropped out of school so they could work and have a car, or they got part-time jobs and couldn't study. Their girl friends wanted them to have cars. I'd read an article that said boys who owned cars smoked and drank more than boys who didn't, and they were more immoral and got married earlier, and divorced earlier. They got in more accidents and got hurt and killed more. My grandmother said that I could use her car after I got my license. I liked to think about taking Becky for a date and being alone in the car with just her.

"Is the Mormon church the only true church, Owen?" Staver stood up holding his hammer. "It's something I've been thinking about."

"Yes, it is, but everyone who ever lived will receive an opportunity to hear the gospel and either accept it or reject it."

"What about all those people who are dead already?"

"The gospel will be preached to them in paradise before they're resurrected. In our temples we do work for the dead."

"That's very nice."

"Yes, it is."

Staver took off his hat and smoothed his hair with his hand, and put his hat back on. He exhaled smoke and put the cigarette back in his mouth.

Last year I'd been baptized for the dead. Our whole seminary class went to the Salt Lake Temple to do that. And the next day in class Brother Anderson told us to remember our own baptisms and what we'd promised. When we took the sacrament we renewed our covenants. I liked to prepare and pass the sacrament. Everybody was quiet and bowed their heads. I'd always looked forward to being sixteen so I could be a Priest and bless the sacrament. I wanted to be clean for that. Kneeling at the sacrament table, the silver trays on the white linen tablecloths, I would hear my voice blessing the sacrament. I had already memorized the sacrament prayers so I wouldn't have to read them from the small card all the other Priests used.

"I'd join if they'd let me have seven wives." Frank leaned on his shovel. "That'd be paradise for me."

"What do you want seven for, Frank?"

"One for every day of the week."

They all laughed. Randy and Stan, who were working on the forms farther down the ditch, both straightened up. Randy shook his head.

"The Church excommunicates any member who practices polygamy now," I said.

"Too bad." Frank turned and spit in the canal. "It sure was a good idea."

I reached over and got my shovel to dig more dirt away from the forms. I wanted to be able to stand up on the canal bank like one of the prophets out of the Book of Mormon and preach to Frank and Staver until they believed the Church was true and wanted to be baptized. I would be able to baptize people when I became a Priest.

"Do ya think that Angel Moroni might come down and say polygamy was all right again, kid?"

"No, I don't."

"Too bad." Frank leaned toward me. "Turn around, kid. That a boil you got coming on your neck?"

"No, it isn't."

"Just askin'. You want to be careful about those boils."

"I'm careful."

"Good. You know what causes 'em don't you?"

"Yes, I do."

Frank laughed.

We worked late because Staver wanted the headgate and all the ditch formed up and ready to start pouring the cement the next morning. When we quit, Staver stood by the pickup and shot jackrabbits coming down out of the sagebrush to feed in the hay fields. Randy shot five. The rabbits blew apart when the slug hit them, and Randy yelled each time. Staver offered me the rifle, but I told him no.

"Better get in practice, Owen. As soon as we get the hay cut we'll be shooting rabbits every night for a week."

"That's good shootin'." Stan lit a cigarette, breathed in deep and let the smoke out slowly and looked up at the sky. "Of course killing jackrabbits ain't always as safe as you might think." Stan looked at his cigarette in his hand. "I worked on a ranch over by Gold Creek after the war, and a couple of times kids got blowed up out hunting jacks with deer rifles. At first the sheriff figured the kids had got hold of some dynamite or been fooling around with somethin' they stole out of that explosives plant the army built and then closed down when the war ended. But then one of the kids lived long enough to tell the sheriff it was a jackrabbit that exploded. They were shooting those things at thirty or forty feet they were so thick that year."

"I remember reading all about it in the papers, Stan." Frank tipped his hat up and squatted down. "It was even in *Life* magazine. They had pictures."

"Well, of course, they got the army out there to protect people and a bunch of scientists to find out what was wrong. They finally figured out it was that explosives plant where they made a lot of secret stuff during the war, not just regular dynamite powder. They mixed it all wet and then let the waste water go out in a big canal and spread out in the sagebrush and evaporate. They figured that was safe, but those chemicals got in the soil so a-course the grass was full of it. And after two or three years of eating that grass, those jacks was full of it too. Those army scientists figured each one of those jacks was about like two sticks of dynamite running around on four legs."

Stan field-stripped his cigarette. He didn't look up.

"A-course the army fenced off the whole place, and then they brought in some of their light tanks to hunt those rabbits with. It was too dangerous for a man with a rifle. It was just like a war, explosions going off all the time. The jackrabbits wasn't the worst though. They got a coyote inside that fence, and when they shot him it blew up one of those light tanks that was too close. A-course, he'd been eatin' those rabbits."

"I wished I'd saved that *Life* magazine. You boys would be interested in seeing that."

"Well, they got most of those jacks with the tanks, but they finally ended up having to poison everything out there—birds, rabbits, mice, rats, everything. One of those officers stepped on a big grasshopper and it blew his foot right off. It was an awful mess out there till they got things straightened out."

"Stan, I drove out there to Gold Creek to see that place. A lot of people did. It was in all the newspapers and on the radio all the time, but people just couldn't believe it. What year was that, Stan?"

"Ninteen forty-eight."

"That's right. Just after the war."

"Let's go," Staver said. Randy put the rifle back in the cab.

Holding onto the rack, I stood up riding in. I watched the jackrabbits slipping into the dark hay fields. I'd read about insecticides and herbicides and other chemicals building up in body tissue, but I'd never read anything about explosives doing that. When I got back to Provo I was going to go to BYU library and see if there really was the *Life* magazine Frank was talking about.

After supper I pulled my minnow trap out and planted the dead hole.

We worked hard the rest of the week pouring cement and irrigating, and Saturday Randy and I drove the jeep into Silverton to go to Frank's birthday party. At nine o'clock we turned off Silver Street and down an alley to the back door of the Volcano Casino. A small red erupting neon volcano hung above the door. We got out.

"There's Staver's pickup."

I looked at my watch. "We've got to leave early so we can get up and go to church in the morning."

"Don't sweat it, cousin. We'll get there."

"They just want us to have a piece of cake and leave."

"Don't sweat it. Relax. Try to have a little fun."

Randy opened the red door. I pulled it closed behind us. We stood there trying to see in the darkness. The only light came from a big red neon circle on the ceiling and the miniature volcanoes on each table with a lit candle inside. Pale red under the light, people sat at tables around the dance floor or danced to a three-piece band, the laughing and talking mixing in with the music. On the walls were painted erupting volcanoes and huge flows of lava moving toward towns and cities. All the cigarette smoke made it harder to see.

"There they are." Randy pointed.

Stan, Frank, and Staver sat with Alice and two other women near a big lit aquarium. Frank held up his hand. I followed Randy between the round tables. Even the men dancing wore cowboy hats. The cooled smokey air was heavy and damp.

"Well, we're glad to see you men." Staver tapped his cigarette on the ashtray. "Frank thought you'd forgotten all about his party."

"Sure did."

"Here, meet these ladies. You know Alice. This is Linda, and this is Jennifer. These are the two summer hands from Provo, Utah, we've been telling you all about. This is Randy, and this is Owen. He's the one we were telling you about, Linda. Remember?"

"Sure I remember."

"Hello, boys. It's good to see you," Alice smiled.

Linda and Jennifer both said hello. We said hello. On the table were ashtrays, cans of beer, and beer and liquor glasses.

"Sit down, men. There's a couple of chairs." Staver pointed to the next table.

We got the chairs.

"Here, you sit next to Linda, Randy, and, Owen, you sit by Jennifer. Frank and Stan won't be jealous."

"No sir we won't. Will we, Stan?"

"You boys look nice tonight," Alice said.

"Thank you."

They moved closer together to make room. Linda and Jennifer were pretty, their dresses low in front. Linda was blonde, and she kept licking her lips. They were very friendly. Staver wore a blue silk shirt and a brown Stetson.

"Randy here is getting to be a pretty good poker player." Staver drank from his can of beer.

"What do you do, Owen?" Linda leaned forward to look around Frank.

"He's an Explorer." Randy took some nuts out of a dish and leaned his head back and dropped them into his mouth.

"What do you explore?"

"I'm an Explorer Scout," I said.

"That's nice, Owen." Alice smiled at me. "I have a nephew who's in the Explorers. He likes it. He's sixteen."

"Owen here just turned sixteen, didn't you, Owen?"

"That's a nice age to be."

Three couples came up together to the table to wish Frank a happy birthday. Staver introduced Randy and me, and they left.

People leaned over their tables to light their cigarettes from the candles in the volcanoes; their faces were dark under the neon light.

"Don't Randy and Owen need something to drink?" Linda put her arm through Frank's. "They probably need something."

"Sure," Staver said. "Sorry, men." He called a waitress over. "What do you men want? It's all on me tonight, so get whatever you want."

"I'll have an orange."

"One orange."

"What about you, Randy? Do you want an orange too? It's a private party, Randy." Linda reached over and put her left hand on Randy's arm.

"I'll have a can of beer and a glass."

Staver sat up a little straighter and looked at Randy.

"Okay, one orange and one beer, with glasses. Is Lucky okay, Randy?"

"Yes."

"You can have whatever you want."

"That's fine."

Staver nodded to the waitress.

I looked at Randy, but he was talking to Linda. I knew that he'd drunk beer before, and he was just doing it now to show off. The waitress came back and put two cans and glasses on the table. Randy opened his can and poured the beer slowly into the tipped glass so that it wouldn't foam. His lips were distorted through the glass when he drank. Randy only took a sip. He put the glass down and held it with both hands. He didn't look at me.

"How is it, Randy?"

"It's good."

Linda took a cigarette from a pack by her hand on the table.

"How about a light, Randy?"

She held a folder of matches out to him.

"Sure."

Randy took the matches and lit her cigarette.

"Thanks." Linda lifted up her head and took the cigarette out of her mouth. She watched a couple at the table on the other side of the aquarium. With her thumb and forefinger she picked a piece of tobacco off the end of her tongue. "Looks like Cliff is having a good time."

"It sure does," Frank said.

"They've been sitting there holding hands or dancing all night."

"Cliff hasn't drunk anything but about two beers."

"He promised Donna he wouldn't start drinking again. He was really drunk the night he shot the deputy."

"I think Cliff's going to make it," Alice said. "Donna's good for him."

I watched Cliff. He put his arm around the woman's shoulders and pulled her close to him. Their chairs were close together, touching.

I took off my glasses and cleaned them with my handkerchief.

"Hey, Randy, you want to dance with Linda? Frank won't mind will you, Frank?"

I turned and looked at Randy.

"Go ahead, Randy. Enjoy yourself." Frank reached over and put his hand on Randy's shoulder.

Linda looked at Randy and smiled. She put her cigarette in the ash tray. Randy stood up. He pulled Linda's chair back when she stood up. Two men reached up to touch her hand as she passed their tables. She reached back and took Randy's hand. Randy wore his hat. Above the dancers the cigarette smoke was pale red under the neon light.

"Excuse me." Jennifer stood up. "I've got to go powder my nose."

Stan reached over and pulled Jennifer's chair out.

"Hurry back," Frank said.

"I will."

"Why don't you dance with Alice, Owen?" Staver's blue silk cowboy shirt glistened.

Alice turned to Staver. "Maybe he doesn't want to dance. Don't push him."

Her dress was dark blue. "Yes, I'd like to dance if you would."

"Do you really want to, Owen? You don't have to."

"Yes, I would."

I pulled Alice's chair out and let her go first. Everybody said hello to her as she passed between the tables. She stopped in front of me, and I took her hand and put my other hand on her back. The music was slow. Randy and Linda were dancing close together, and Linda had her head on his shoulder. Alice told me that I was a good dancer. I knew Staver and Frank were watching us, but I wasn't nervous. It was nice dancing with Alice. She asked me about living in Provo. When I told her about my father, she said that she was sorry he had died when I was so little. And I wanted to ask her why she went with a man like Staver.

"I've heard that Provo is a nice town. You're lucky to live in a nice religious town like that. I have an aunt who moved to Salt Lake City from Reno. She and her husband joined the Mormon Church. They really enjoy it."

I told her that I was going on a mission, and she said that was a nice thing for a boy to do. She knew what a mission was. I told her I was going to be a doctor. I really liked dancing with Alice. I didn't want her to be Staver's girl.

Cliff and his girl friend danced by us.

"It's *really* nice to see you home again, Cliff."

"Thanks. It's really nice to be here."

"He looks good, Donna."

"He's going to look a lot better."

"This is Owen. He's one of Staver's summer hands this year."

Cliff reached out and shook my hand.

"Hi, Owen."

"Hello."

They nodded and smiled and danced away. Alice watched them as we danced.

"Those two will be okay. They've got enough sense to get married and make it work."

She kept watching them.

When we got back to the table, Randy was telling Linda about his girls.

"Come on, lover boy, tell her about that little blonde that has all the money. The one that's got a car of her own and a swimming pool." Frank leaned over the table toward Randy. "The one who likes all the parties."

"What about you, Owen? Do you have girls?" Linda turned to me.

"No, I don't."

"That's too bad."

"The kid don't shave yet, Linda."

Linda reached up and touched Randy's cheek with the backs of her fingers.

"You shave don't you, Randy?"

"Sure, every day. I'd like another one of these." Randy raised his glass and drank the last of his yellow beer.

"Here, have part of mine." Linda poured most of her beer into Randy's glass.

"Thanks."

Randy lifted the glass and took a long drink, and then he put the glass down and held it with both hands.

"Ever party much in Las Vegas, Randy?" Linda put a cigarette in her mouth and held it for Randy to light it.

"No, but I'd sure like to."

Randy blew out the match and held it while the smoke curled up from it. I turned my ring on my finger.

Suddenly people in the room started to shout and clap. The band played a fanfare. A waitress walked toward our table carrying the big cake Mrs. Cummings had made. It had lit candles on it. Everybody stood up and started to sing happy birthday. Frank stood up and waved to everybody and blew out all the candles at once, and they all cheered and sang happy birthday and asked him how old he was, but he didn't answer. He shook hands with all those people crowded around the table. Linda kissed him and everybody cheered. Alice and Jennifer cut the cake and handed out pieces on napkins.

"Here. You get two pieces, Cliff." Alice handed Cliff an extra piece.

"Thanks."

"You're welcome."

After everybody had a piece of cake, the band started playing again for people to dance. Randy danced four dances with Linda. Some of the people were getting drunk. Linda was almost drunk and so was Jennifer. Alice wasn't. Linda asked Randy if he wore that funny Mormon underwear. She had a cousin who had joined the Church and got married in the temple, and she had to. I stood up. I told Randy it was time to go, but he didn't want to. Nobody else was driving back to the ranch until Sunday evening, not even Stan, so Randy had to come. I had the keys to the pickup.

"Sorry, old buddy," Frank said.

He lit a cigarette for Linda, the match flaring against her white face. She tilted her head up to take the cigarette out of her mouth and breathe out the smoke. Frank blew out the match and put it in the ashtray.

"See you, Owen. Be sure to wear those pretty blue pajamas and say your prayers."

Linda drank from her glass and laughed.

"You boys be careful driving back." Alice smiled. "It's been nice to have you."

"Be sure and watch out for those skunks, kid."

"I will. Thanks for the invitation."

"You're welcome, kid."

Randy stood up. "Thanks for a really nice time."

"See you, Randy. Enjoy church tomorrow."

I walked past the erupting volcanoes on the walls. The cigarette smoke was thicker so that everything was hazy red. I waited for Randy at the door and closed it behind us.

I drove out of Silverton. I kept breathing deep to clean the cigarette smoke out of my lungs.

"So, are you going to phone my dad and tell him I drank a couple of beers?"

"No. You can drink beer if that's what you want to do."

No ravens or magpies flew up from the dead jackrabbits lying on the dark road.

"Look, I drank my first can of beer when I was fourteen. My dad knows all about it. I told him. Do you think I can't go on a mission just because I drink about one beer a month? What's wrong with that? I don't get drunk. A can of beer is better for you than a Coke as long as you don't get drunk. I know a lot of guys at school who drink beer, and they still plan to go on missions. Lots of guys do that. As long as you haven't done anything really wrong for a year before you go, your bishop doesn't care. And you can get married in the temple when you get back."

"Bishops care."

A jackrabbit ran across the road through the headlights.

"But you can still go. It isn't that big a deal. You make it sound worse than murder or something."

"But your body is a temple."

"Oh, don't hit me with that stuff."

"Either it is or it isn't."

"You take everything too serious. You act a little nuts sometimes."

"Maybe."

"You better watch it."

Randy leaned his head back against the door and the seat. He pulled his hat down over his eyes.

Hypnotized by the pickup headlights, a jackrabbit stood in the middle of the road. I slowed down to drive around it, but it jumped in toward the pickup. I felt the left back wheel go over it, a soft bump. I kept looking straight out through the windshield.

I saw my hands on the steering wheel.

I wanted to practice Mozart on the piano. A Mozart sonata, I didn't care which one. I wanted to sit down and practice each phrase until it was perfect. I wanted to practice and practice by myself alone in our quiet house in the quiet front room with the two-foot-thick brick walls until I played the whole piece perfectly. And then I would play it over and over and over. I needed to do something like that.

The headlights hit the first white no-trespassing sign. In the headlights the skeletons were grey.

11

We started cutting hay the Wednesday after Frank's party. When we drove the tractors out of the yard, the knives raised on the hinges and bolted to the crossbars, Mrs. Cummings was hanging up clothes. I'd heard the washer at breakfast. I thought that maybe she hadn't been able to do all her washing Monday because she wasn't feeling well, but I didn't ask her. She waved at us, and I waved back. We each carried an extra knife with us.

Stan rode on the back of my tractor in the first field I cut; Staver rode with Randy. Stan said that there were no ledges of lava left in the hay fields, only in the pastures. Staver had dynamited them all out, so I didn't have to worry about that. In the pastures the ledges looked like the backs of prehistoric monsters breaking up through the earth. I stood on them when we irrigated to see if the water was spreading evenly.

I watched the shining knife, the cut hay falling back over it, and Stan leaned forward to tell me stories of ranchers, their sons, and hired hands who fell into the mower and were killed cutting hay. They left blood trails across the cut hay where they tried to crawl back toward their pickups. Sometimes they tried to crawl through the high hay, got lost and bled to death there.

Stan bent forward to speak into my ear. Three pheasants flew out ahead of us. The extra knife leaned shining against the fence.

"I worked on a ranch once over in Copper County next to a place owned by a man named Stimpson. Used to buy his liquor by the case. Always had a bottle with him. He lived alone. It was two days before they found him in that high hay. Somebody saw his tractor parked on the road. After it cut him up it just kept going, went out through two open gates and down the road till it ran out of gas."

"What? I don't believe—"

"Watch where you're going, kid. You got to watch it all the time. The rancher I worked for, a man named Rhodes, saw the magpies staggering around in the cut half of the field. They couldn't get off the ground because they'd been working on Stimpson. The mortician, his name was Lund, said he didn't even need to embalm him. Said he was a hundred proof almost."

"What?"

"Straight ahead, kid; always look straight ahead. Watch that knife. I knew a heavy drinker like that named Williams. His house burned down one night with him and his wife in it, and they didn't find but only pieces of him, mostly bones. They figured he must have exploded. Alcohol is as bad as gasoline around a fire. It gets hot and builds up a terrible pressure they say. It was an awful mess. They found his wife in her bed all right, but his bed was all blown apart. He blew the whole wall out on his side. Sheriff said it was worse than a stick of dynamite." Stan patted my shoulder. "You're doing a good job, kid, nice and straight, just the way Staver likes it."

"You—"

"Watch where you're going. Can't be turning around every minute. It's the truth. I wouldn't string you along."

I couldn't turn to see Stan's face. I knew that the human body could explode because we'd talked about that one day in my chemistry class. But it was very rare, and conditions had to be just right. Mr. Horton, our chemistry teacher, hadn't said anything about alcohol content in the body tissues. I wanted to ask Stan if his stories were true so I would know. They all seemed at least partly true. But I couldn't ask him. It wouldn't be right to ask him. I didn't want to hurt his feelings, but I didn't like not knowing if they were true or not.

The knife hit something, the soft bump coming up through the knife into the tractor.

"What was that?" I couldn't look back. Already the fields shimmered in the hot sun.

"You probably hit a rabbit or maybe a pheasant. Could have been a duck. I've killed ducks out in these fields. They build their nests out here to get away from the weasels and skunks. Skunks are the worst things to hit, but a badger's about as bad. I cut one's head right off in this field a couple of years ago. He must have been looking up. If you get any pheasants, ducks, or quail, you be sure and bring 'em in. Mrs. Cummings will cook 'em up. You don't want to waste good meat."

I watched the uncut hay ahead of the blade. A jackrabbit ran out across the cut field. We came around.

"You got a jack, kid, but they're no good to eat."

The ears and top of the head stuck up through the layer of cut hay. I turned and looked straight ahead.

"Stop up here by the pickup, kid, and I'll get off. You can drive this thing alone without my help. Staver'll be watching ya though, so keep your mind on what you're doing. He don't want this hay messed up. About three years ago some kid from Los Angeles ruined about five acres before Staver got to him. Cut it all too short. Couldn't even rake it so we just turned it into pasture till it was all fed off. Staver was so mad I thought he was going to kill that kid."

I stopped and let Stan off.

"Good luck, kid."

"Thanks."

I shifted and drove forward into the hay. The heat above the glaring fields blurred the river trees and the mountains, the heat rising in great shimmering waves. The hay fell green across the blade. Twice I saw the red pickup parked on low hills, but I didn't turn to look that way. Once I was changing the knife. Cutting the hay you could feel when your knife was getting dull, the hay not cutting clean but dragging against the knife.

Washing still hung on the line when we went in for lunch; usually Mrs. Cummings had it taken in before noon. Randy walked in the kitchen door behind Stan, Frank, and Staver. I stopped on the porch and turned. The pajamas weren't mine. I was the only one who wore pajamas. I looked at the clothes and bedding. And then I remembered what Mrs. Cummings had said about washing Brent's clothes once a year. They were the clothes he'd worn before he got drafted. Seeing them made me feel funny. Brent wore those clothes. I turned and opened the screen door.

I apologized to Mrs. Cummings for being late for the blessing and sat down. The fans blew away the steam rising from the bowls of vegetables. I looked around the table. It was as if Brent should be there. Bowing my head I saw through the laundry room door a basket of dry clothes on the floor. On top were folded pairs of Levis.

After lunch I changed the knife again and cut hay alone, the tractor's rhythm and noise coming up though the iron seat into my body, me riding high, seeing over the fields. I watched the cut hay fall back over the sharp knife, a continuous stream of hay. I liked the smell. I wanted to bale the hay and help build the line of big rectangular stacks higher and higher. Two rabbits ran out from in front of me and across the flat cut hay; a rooster pheasant flew up into the shimmering heat. I thought about Brent's clothes. I saw Staver's red pickup parked on a hill, but I didn't see Staver. He wasn't looking at me with his binoculars. I finished the first field and drove through the gate to the next. I liked to cut hay, driving the tractor and working the knife.

The soft bump came up through the knife. Not looking back I stopped and took the tractor out of gear. I turned in the seat. The jackrabbit jumped up through the flat hay; he jumped up again. But he didn't go forward, fell over on his side, his front legs cut off. I got down from the tractor. The rabbit jumped up again and fell back. I opened the tool box and got the heavy long-handled crescent wrench. I had to step on the rabbit to hold him. I hit him on the head with the wrench until he stopped moving. Blood was on the wrench, my shoe, and on the grass by his head. One of the cut-off paws lay by the head.

Behind me a pickup drove into the field and across the hay to where I stood. I knew it was Staver. I turned around.

"You sick?"

"No. I cut this rabbit's front feet off with the mower, and so I had to kill it. I didn't want it to suffer."

"Well, it looks like you did a good job. You planning on getting a shovel and digging a grave to bury it, Owen, or are you just going to say a prayer?"

I didn't answer.

"Come on, Killer, let's get back to work. You're wasting Mr. Johnson's time. They don't give medals for killing rabbits."

I turned the long heavy wrench in my hand. I felt very strong. The wrench fit so well in my hand. I knew that I wanted to hit Staver on the side of the head with the wrench. I didn't want to really hurt him, but I did want to hit him. It seemed like such a simple easy thing to do, to see Staver fall. But I knew it was wrong even to think about doing that. A flock of blackbirds flew up out of the hay ahead of the tractor and lit on the barbed-wire fence. I walked over and put the wrench back in the tool box. I climbed up on the tractor and put it in gear. When I came around again Staver was gone.

I passed the dead rabbit. The blood on my boots had turned black. The next time I came around two magpies flew up from the dead rabbit. I looked up, but I saw no vultures circling. One rabbit wasn't enough food for a vulture. The four magpies didn't fly away when I came around the next time. I knew that the hay had to be cut, but tractors needed sirens on them to scare all the birds and animals away. There should be a state law requiring it. Every time I came around I watched the magpies. I knew that all forms of life would be resurrected. Brother Anderson had spent a whole week on the resurrection.

One night I dreamed that it was the morning of the resurrection. My grandmother, mother, and I drove in the slow heavy traffic to the Provo cemetery. We got out. Everybody was talking and laughing and crying, saying hello, shaking hands and hugging each other, many of the resurrected people dressed in their temple robes.

I started to run. I kept shouting, "Dad! Dad! Dad!" I saw him and my grandfather through the crowd under the dark pines, and I ran faster, shouting. And I woke up hearing my own voice shouting. I closed my eyes, didn't move, tried to go back to sleep to start the dream again, but I couldn't. I'd never got to touch him or hear him.

The next day in seminary, Friday, was the last lesson on the resurrection. The bell rang, but Brother Anderson kept talking.

"And all the Mayans, Aztecs, Egyptians, Greeks, Romans, Babylonians, Vikings, Vandals, Lamanites, Nephites, will be resurrected. So will all the murdered Jews in their mass graves and in their pits of ashes. The Lord will reign as King of Kings, the earth will be celestialized. There will be no hate, no violence, no torture, no murder, no war, and no death." He stopped. "Can you even begin to want a world full of love, peace, and knowledge?" He stopped again. Nobody said anything. "No, I guess you're not old enough to want that yet. You're excused." I wanted to go up and ask Brother Anderson what he meant, but I didn't.

The whole flock of blackbirds flew from the fence wire when I came around the field again. They flew in a black line through the heat haze above the fields. I took off my hat and wiped my face and head with my blue bandana handkerchief. I looked up at the white sun. The rhythm came up through the tractor into the metal seat and into my body. Ahead, the whole field blurred in the watery heat. In the corner of the field a yellow poison sign was tacked to the fence post. When an animal or bird took the bait, an explosion would drive the cyanide up into its mouth.

We worked late. At supper Mrs. Cummings told us that two Mormon missionaries had been by to see her, and she had fed them an early supper.

"They're nice clean boys and always welcome at my table. We all need a lot more preaching than we get."

I looked at Brent's ironed shirts hanging on the hall door handle.

After supper I wiped the dishes and went to the bunkhouse for another boxing lesson. Staver could still hit me whenever he wanted. I was getting stronger every week, but I wasn't any faster. I could hit Randy. Randy went to play poker, and I showered and walked around to the front porch to talk to Mrs. Cummings. She'd told me to come. She liked to talk to me, and sometimes she asked me to play the piano for her. I sat on the steps with Tobe next to me and rubbed my hands.

"Your hands hurt, son?" Mrs. Cummings sat in her rocker petting her two cats. On the lawn the darkness met the light from the porch, each fading into the other so there was no sharp line.

"No. They just feel big."

"Well, they are getting bigger, and so are you. Your mother and grandmother will be surprised. Boys grow fast when they get your age. You can't keep shoes and clothes on a boy they grow so fast. A mother prays a lot for a boy your age. Mothers don't have to pray so much for their girls. Sometimes you just get to wishing that the Good Lord would come."

I watched the darkness on the lawn under the trees.

"Son, there's something I wish you'd do for me before you go. Take those socks in that basket in the hall and those ironed shirts up to Brent's room. I wanted to get it all done again before Mr. Johnson came back and went up there to sit. I been up there cleaning that room whenever I had an hour this past week that I felt well enough. I got the curtains to put back up and the bed to make, but I'll get it done. I'm just worn right out tonight."

I stood up.

"Oh you don't have to go right now. Just before you leave."

"I'd be glad to."

"Well, the basket's there in the hall. Brent's room is the last door on the left at the top of the stairs. Hang up the ironed shirts in the closet and put the socks in the second drawer with the other things. There's a place for them there. Put them in neat. Mr. Johnson likes everything nice. That'll save me doing it."

I turned and walked up the steps and into the house. I crossed through the front room and into the hall, where the light burned. I lifted the ironed shirts off the door handle, laid them across the basket, and picked it up. I looked down. The arms of the long-sleeved shirts had slipped down across my wrists and hands.

I turned on the stairway light with my elbow, which also turned on the upstairs light. I climbed the stairs and walked down the hall. I pressed the basket against the door so I had one hand to open it. I turned the handle, took hold of the basket again and pushed the door open. I didn't turn on the light. Enough light came in through the windows and the open door. I walked across and put the basket on the chair by the bed and hung the shirts in the closet on the metal rod in front of the suit and the pairs of pants. I spaced the shirts evenly. I looked down at the shoes and cowboy boots all in trees on the floor. They were all shined.

As I turned I saw myself in the full-length mirror on the back of the closet door. I stopped, and then I turned. Both curtainless windows were open, so the room wasn't stuffy, but there was no breeze yet. Across from the unmade bed and under the window was a desk and a chair, a reading lamp on the desk. A guitar and a banjo stood in the corner. One whole side of the room was book shelves. Above the desk was a corkboard with colored photographs. I looked at them. They were of Brent and his friends. Staver was in a lot of them.

On the wall by the corkboard was a framed newspaper article and a picture showing a general presenting Mrs. Johnson with Brent's Medal of Honor. Mr. Johnson and Helen stood on either side of her. In the corner of the picture was a picture of Brent in uniform. Next to Brent's article was a framed article about Staver receiving the Silver Star and Purple Heart. Staver had wiped out two machine gun nests before he was wounded. It said that Sergeant Brent Johnson, a life-long friend of Staver's, and a recipient of the Medal of Honor, had been killed the day before Staver was wounded. Staver's picture was like Brent's. They looked like pictures they'd had taken after basic training to send home. They were both smiling.

I turned and walked over to the dresser and opened the second drawer. I arranged the rolled socks in rows in the space on the right side next to the T-shirts. On the other side of the drawer next to the shorts was a stack of supporters. I held the last pair of socks in my hand. I looked at the supporters. It was like I could turn around and Brent would be standing there in the dimness, and I could ask him a lot of questions about myself and he would answer me because he'd had the same experiences and feelings. I put the last pair of rolled socks in place. I closed the drawer slowly. I turned around. The room was full of shadows. I picked up the basket on the bed and walked back out into the hall. Mrs. Cummings' door was open, but the other two doors were closed.

I opened the screen door and walked out on the porch. I stood looking out across the lawn. I didn't sit down. I stood above Mrs. Cummings.

She shook her head. "That's a lonely room. I cry every year when I wash and iron that boy's clothes. But terrible things happen to people. That's something you have to expect in this life. We all get humbled one way or the other. I'm glad that Helen took all of her things with her when they moved to Las Vegas." The white cat jumped out of her lap and walked down the porch steps and onto the lawn. Once it stopped to listen and then ran across the lawn and vanished into the deep darkness under the trees.

"Now where's that fool cat going again? A coyote'll be certain to get her if she's not very careful."

I wanted to ask Mrs. Cummings if there were colored slides or home movies of Brent or if his voice was on tape, but I didn't. My Grandmother had all the slides that my father had sent home from his mission and a tape recording of his missionary homecoming. When I was little she showed the slides to me and played the tape every year on my father's birthday. My grandmother regretted that she didn't have movies of my father, but she had never owned a movie camera.

I carried the pictures of my father and the sound of his voice with me into my sleep and my dreams. Some days I ran all the way home from second and third and fourth grades because I thought that my father would be waiting for me on the porch or in the house. And when he wasn't there I went down into the basement to stand in front of the locked door to the room where my grandmother kept all of his things in boxes on shelves and hanging in the cedar closet, his Eagle Scout badge and his Duty to God Award pinned on the left pocket of his Explorer shirt.

Off across the lawn in the high dark trees an owl hooted.

On Thursday morning Staver sent me down to the Spencers' place to cut the weeds along the road to prevent fires. Friday evening we all went down to the Bensons' to cut hay. Staver had rigged the tractors with extra lights so we could work after dark. Mrs. Benson had sandwiches and cold punch for us. Mr. Benson was asleep. He still had to take sleeping pills every night because of the pain in his broken legs.

"The casts are very heavy for him." Mrs. Benson poured Stan another glass of punch.

"Thank you, ma'am." Stan leaned against the bed of the pickup. "I worked for a rancher once named Peacock. A horse rolled on him too, but it broke his back and both his arms and legs. It took five doctors all day to put the casts on him. They just made one big cast from his chin to his toes. His arms and legs was all spread out like he was flying. His wife had them build a hook in the neck. She had a hoist put on the back of their pickup, and she used to lift him that way. He was a big man. She put a mattress down in the back for him so he could ride out to the fields, and then she'd hoist him up to have a look at what was going on and to tell us hired help what to do. She put his bed in the barn so she could back right in. After a month that cast got to stinking, and she used to hoist him up in the evening when there was a breeze to air him out. Once she forgot and left him hanging out all night."

"Must have been awful." Frank picked up his glass of punch.

"The poor man." Mrs. Benson poured Staver more punch.

"He said he really didn't mind, ma'am. It was about as comfortable as sleeping laying down. Mrs. Peacock used to take him into town on Saturday nights and hoist him up so he could talk to his friends walking by. Sometimes they'd unhook him and carry him in and set him against the bar, and he'd drink his beer through this plastic straw about two feet long they got for him."

Nobody laughed or even smiled. I knew that we weren't supposed to, but I didn't know why.

"Well, I'm glad my Bill didn't get hurt that bad. Here now. Have a slice of this chocolate cake." Mrs. Benson started to cut the cake she'd brought out. "We certainly appreciate all you do for us."

After we finished and Mrs. Benson went in to check on Mr. Benson, I walked over to my tractor. I put my foot on the top of the power take-off, grabbed the edge of the seat and stepped up. In the darkness caused by the bowled seat I saw, gradually, a coiled dead rattlesnake. My breath stopped, but I didn't scream or throw myself backward.

"Hey, Careful, what's wrong?" It was Frank.

I looked up. They all stood watching me.

"Nothing."

"Well, let's move out then." Staver pulled on one glove.

I lifted the rattlesnake out of the seat by the tail and threw it on the trash pile by the barn.

"Good grief, kid, that thing must have crawled up there and died." Frank walked over and looked at the seat. "Must have been too hot. You're lucky."

"I guess I am."

I moved into the seat, started the engine, and drove back out to the field. I turned on my lights.

We didn't get back until eleven. It was too late for Randy to play poker, so he went to bed. Later, still awake in the dark, I heard Staver riding by on Black Prince, going fast, hoof sounds hard and quick. I raised up on my elbows, but I couldn't see him through the screen door. He was gone. I listened, then slowly lowered myself back on the bunk.

I turned my head. On the night table was a new letter from Becky. I had five letters from her now, which I kept tied together. I liked to reread her letters. My mother had written me that my grandmother had bought the paint, wallpaper, curtain material, and carpet for my room, but it was very difficult for her to have the man start redecorating. I knew that my room was very special for my grandmother because it had been my father's room. But she didn't have to redecorate it if she didn't want to. It was all right. I decided I would write and tell her that. I turned on my back and stared up at the ceiling. We needed a new spiral of flypaper. I closed my eyes.

Thursday I drove Mrs. Cummings into Silverton to take in a box for Dale, see the doctor, and buy groceries. While she was in Bob's I went over to Thurman's to get a box of lag bolts Staver wanted and some candy and car magazines for Randy. Mrs. Cummings said that as long as she had the basket to hang onto and push she was just fine. Two of her friends who were widows were in Bob's, and she wanted to talk to them.

"Well, young man, it's good to see you again. How are things out at the ranch?"

"Fine."

Mr. Thurman was behind the counter when I walked in.

"You've put on some more weight. You're looking good. I guess you're learning a lot out there."

"Yes, I am."

"Well, your summer's half over. You'll be going home one of these days. What can I do for you?"

I told Mr. Thurman I wanted lag bolts, and he pointed down the aisle where they were. Spools of rope lay on the floor below the shelves of bolts. I squatted down and picked up the end of a coil of thick rope. I held it with both hands. I'd never seen hemp rope that thick before. In the Explorers last year we'd built a rope bridge over the Provo River. I liked the feel of the thick rope. It was as thick as the piece of swing rope hanging down from the limb above the swimming hole. I looked down at the big bale.

I turned and walked up the aisle.

"How much would seventy-five feet of that heaviest hemp rope cost, Mr. Thurman?"

"What does Staver want with that much rope? Is he going to start hanging trespassers now?"

"It's for me. There used to be a rope swing on the river where we swim. I'd like to put it up again."

"That big hole down below the house?"

"Yes."

"I remember that swing. Didn't some boy get hurt or killed on it? Wasn't he drunk?"

"I don't know."

"Well, you want to be careful."

"I will be."

I bought seventy-five feet of rope and a big ball of heavy nylon cord to pull the rope up into the big cottonwood. It was expensive, but it really made me happy to think about replacing the swing. Maybe Randy would spend more time down on the river if there was a swing. I put the rope and cord in the back of the pickup under some gunnysacks. I didn't tell Mrs. Cummings what I was going to do.

We stopped at the post office, and I took in a package for Dale. Mrs. Cummings was wiping her face and neck with one of her men's white handkerchiefs when I got back in the pickup.

"Thank you, son. Now let's go see that doctor and find out what he's got to say."

I sat in the waiting room until Mrs. Cummings came out, and then we went to get her new prescription filled. The houses and buildings glared in the sun. I drove up Silver Street and out of town and started climbing up through the lava ledges.

I turned and looked at Mrs. Cummings. Her face looked yellowish. She was breathing heavy.

"Did the doctor say when you were going to have your operation, Mrs. Cummings?"

"No, son, he didn't say much about that. He's got to phone the specialist again in Las Vegas and talk about the Xrays."

"The new medicine will make you feel better."

"Well, a little maybe, son."

Mrs. Cummings wiped her neck and looked out her window.

"Dale's got friends even if I'm not here when he gets out of prison. If Staver gets the ranch Dale will have a place there until he can find other work. Staver's already promised me that, and that's a blessing. You can't expect the Lord to give you everything you want." She shook her head. "Dale wrote me and said that the man in his cell with him committed murder, but Dale says he's fine to him. You just don't know sometimes."

"You'll be here when Dale comes home, Mrs. Cummings."

She nodded her head. "Thank you, son, thank you. You're a kind boy."

Driving back I watched the big thunderheads building over the northwest mountains. They hung in the sky; they didn't seem to move. I thought that we would drive into a rainstorm, but we didn't. The clouds were too far away, and they didn't move. When I drove down off the rise and into the valley, I couldn't see them. Mrs. Cummings said she liked to ride with me because I was careful. She said that a lot of people got hurt going too fast.

A car was parked at the house when we got back. A man and his son who were staying at Lava Campground wanted permission to fish on the ranch. I told him that Staver was the foreman and he didn't let people fish. Other campers had asked.

"You don't think he'd make an exception? I'd like my boy here to catch one nice trout on his trip anyway. He hasn't been able to catch anything bigger than about a half a pound down below. It's pretty heavily fished. I'd be glad to pay."

"No. I'm sorry."

"Well, thanks anyway. It's a very nice looking ranch."

We watched them drive out. They stopped on the bridge to look at the river, then went on.

"Staver's harder on people than he needs to be sometimes. It's almost like he enjoyed it."

Mrs. Cummings climbed two more steps and stopped and wiped her face.

"Those chickens know how hot it is." All the chickens sat in the shade in the dust. "And it's still going to get hotter, before it ever starts to cool off any."

After I finished unloading the groceries and putting them away, I put Randy's magazines and candy on the table in the cabin and went back out to rake hay into windrows. I worked for three hours before supper. When I walked into the cabin, Randy stood before the dresser mirror in his shorts and T-shirt combing his hair. He'd added two more *Playboy* fold-outs to the wall. I asked him one night if he had pictures like that on his own bedroom wall and he laughed.

"My dad would kill me."

Randy patted his hair.

"Hey, you should have been with us. Staver shot a little two-point buck still in the velvet. We're going to take it into Silverton to a cold storage locker. It's for a venison steak fry some of his friends are having in about two weeks. You should have seen that buck go down. He didn't know what hit him."

"Killing deer out of season is against the law in Nevada just like it is in Utah."

"Ah, come on. They're like cows. They feed in the fields all year long." Randy buttoned his cuffs. "What are you going to do, write a letter to the fish and game department?"

"No, I'm not."

Randy put on his Levis and tightened his belt through his turquoise buckle. It was new. He'd just ordered a pair of hand-tooled boots through the mail from a western store in Las Vegas.

"What are you going to do in Silverton?"

"Nothing. Just deliver the deer, eat a steak at the cafe, talk to Alice, and come back. What'd you think, that Staver and Frank were going to take me on a big drunk or something worse?"

"No."

"Stop worrying about me, will you, cousin? I'm just fine. I like it here. I'm not going to foul up and lose that car. I know these guys now." He looked down at his belt. "You worry too much about things. That's one of your problems."

"Is it?"

Staver honked, and Randy picked up his Stetson from his bunk.

"Yeh. One of 'em. Don't wait up."

Staver leaned forward over the steering wheel to light a cigarette. Frank got out and Randy got in next to Staver, and

Frank got back in and closed the door. The shovel and the two pitchforks glinted in the rack.

"Have a nice evening, Owen. Go over and watch some TV with Stan. He likes company."

"Thank you."

I watched the pickup until it vanished into the river trees. Staver didn't have his lights on yet. I knew that Randy would like the swing and probably not go to the bunkhouse so much to play poker.

After supper I wiped the dishes and went back to the cabin. I brushed my teeth, put on my keds, got my swimming stuff and lifted the coil of heavy rope and the nylon cord out of the back of the pickup. I looked over at the bunkhouse; Stan was watching television. I turned and walked across the yard, Tobe ahead of me. Stars were coming out. I walked down the path and under the quiet trees and into the coolness near the river. I came out on the ledge.

I stopped and looked up at the piece of swing rope hanging down from the high limb. My heart beat hard against my chest. I set the ball of nylon cord on the log by the fire rocks and ran the heavy rope in big loops on the ledge. I looked up at the limb again. I wiped the palms of my hands on my Levis and tied the nylon cord to the rope. I unwound the cord in loose loops, then tied the free end to my belt. I looked up. Tobe whined.

"It's okay, boy."

On the cleats the climbing was easy. I didn't have any of the weight of the rope on the nylon cord. When I got up in the leaves I had to untie the cord from my waist and reach it under the limbs. Below, the river was silver where the moonlight filtered down through the trees. Tobe sat looking up at me. When the trunk sloped out over the river, I had to lie down to reach the cord under the limbs. I held the free end in my teeth when I walked; I had to use both hands to hold onto the branches and limbs. I got to where they dived from.

I had to sit down and straddle the limb to move. I lifted my legs over the branches. The limb swayed. I moved slowly. My feet felt heavy, like they were full of blood. I had to hang on tight to the limb with my legs when I slipped the nylon cord under the branches. It took both hands. I kept looking out at the old rope to see how far it was. I could move only three or four inches at a time. The limb kept getting smaller and swaying more. I pulled up to my hands and then put my hands farther out. I kept doing that.

Lying down on the limb, with one hand I tied the cord back on my belt. My legs and arms tight around the swaying limb, I pulled farther, my cheek pressed tight into the bark. I reached out. My hand touched the old rope. I pulled farther up. Holding on with my legs and left hand, I got my knife out of the sheath with my right hand, and then using both hands under the limb I opened it. I cut the old rope and watched it fall and hit the river. I put my knife away. I untied the nylon cord from my belt and tied it around the limb and pulled my new rope up. Nothing happened. It wasn't hard to do.

I stretched forward to run the rope around the limb to tie it, and I saw the intials "BHJ" above where the old rope had worn a groove in the bark. I lay there for a minute on the limb looking at the initials, and then I tied the rope to the limb with a bowline. I untied the nylon cord, pulled it up and stuffed it in my pocket, and then I looked at Brent's initials. I knew that I was the only person other than Brent who had ever seen them. There wasn't a date. I reached out and touched them, but I didn't carve any initials. Slowly I began to push back down the limb.

Tobe barked and jumped up on me when I got down. I looked up at the heavy yellow-white rope hanging straight down to where it bellied in the water. Watching the rope I changed to my swimming suit, dived off the ledge, and pulled the rope in. I tied a knot where the rope hit the water and cut it off there. Holding the end I climbed up to the top of the ledge at the bottom end of the hole. I turned. I had a clear swing the full length of the hole. I knew it was where they had swung from before.

I stood there, my body tall, holding, then ran across the flat space, grabbed higher on the rope as I left the ledge, swung out over the hole, lifted high above the water, rising beautiful up into the darkness. And I let go at the top of the swing, rose higher, held, flying, the feeling like electricity coming up through my groin and into my whole body, and fell then toward the silver river, going under, down, down.

I swung out like that many times, let go, flew, dropped, and I closed my eyes to swing and fall because I wanted to feel that. And I didn't let go of the rope, but held on until I was still, hung above the river, and then slipped silently down into the water. I got out and took a bath and dressed, stood on the ledge looking at the rope, and then undressed again and put on my suit, and swung again, ran harder across the ledge to go higher and higher into the darkness, hold before falling, which was a feeling I'd never had before. When I did get out and get dressed, I walked up to the old river bridge hole. And the big trout jumped three times, his whole shining body coming up out of the silver river.

12

Raking hay into windrows was dusty. I didn't wear my shirt or T-shirt because I had a good tan now, but I tied a red bandana handkerchief around my neck because I liked feeling it. And I liked to rake the hay and see the long windrows we would bale for stacking. I heard helicopters and looked up. Three Army helicopters flew over me and vanished into the heat haze, a vulture circling high above where they had been. I stopped the tractor and got a drink from the water bag. I looked down toward the big cottonwood. I knew that Randy would like the swing. I planned to tell him about it just before supper so he'd want to go try it and not play poker.

At three, after I finished raking the last field above the house, I went to the barn to paint. Staver wanted all the interior doors and trim repainted red. Because I was out of the sun I could take off my hat. I worked hard; I wanted to finish all the trim on the doors before supper. I got down off my six-foot ladder and pulled it to the middle of the last door; a leg caught, and the paint can on top tipped. I grabbed for it, but I bumped the ladder. The brush on top of the can hit me on the ear and the paint spilled down over my shoulder. I felt it heavy on my shirt and dripping off my hand. I looked down. It spread all down over the front of my shirt and Levis. I felt it soaking through. It spread out around my feet on the cement floor in a big pool. I stood there holding my arms away from my body. I couldn't believe it. I'd just opened a new can. The paint was sole deep.

"Well, Owen, it looks like you might have had another accident."

I looked up at Staver standing silhouetted in the main doorway. I hadn't heard the pickup. He turned.

"Hey, Randy. You better come on over here. Owen's had another accident, and he's going to need some help getting cleaned up. You better come too, Frank."

"What happened, Owen?"

Randy and Frank walked into the barn and stood by Staver.

"What happened, Careful?"

"I just asked Owen what happened."

"I tried to move the ladder with the paint can on top, the leg caught, and when I grabbed for the paint, I bumped the ladder."

"You what, Owen?" Staver shook his head.

"Looks like the kid might have killed a beef right here in the barn just to stay in practice."

"I'll pay for the gallon of paint."

"We'll just put it on your bill, Owen. Bring him the hose, Randy, and then stand back because you don't know what Owen will do next. You'd better bring him a scoop shovel too. He's got a lot of paint here. You're lucky it's waterbase, Owen, or you'd be here all night cleaning up this mess. We'll tell Mrs. Cummings to save your supper." Staver smiled.

"See you, kid."

Frank and Staver left, and Randy brought me the hose and the shovel.

"You sure have a lot of accidents, cousin. Have fun."

"Sure."

Randy left to go to supper and I just stood there looking down at myself and the floor. I'd tried hard not to do anything else wrong. I was really careful. Doing things wrong made me feel heavy. I couldn't forget the other things I'd done wrong. They were there in my mind like a picture, and the dumb feeling was in my whole body and I couldn't get it out, and never would be able to.

I started to scoop up the red paint and put it in the can. My whole body was sticky. I stopped and took off my shirt and T-shirt. My chest and stomach were all red from the paint. I wiped myself off with a feed sack. I scooped up all the paint I could and then washed the rest out with the hose, and I squirted myself off and went to the cabin to shower and change.

I was just walking across the yard toward the house to eat supper when a yellow pickup drove up the lane and stopped by the back porch. Alice got out. Everybody came out of the kitchen. Alice wore a white skirt over a pink bathing suit, and she wore leather sandals.

Staver came down the steps first.

"Well, hello," Alice said. "You ready to go swimming?"

"Be right back, honey. Don't go away."

"Oh, I'm not likely to do that."

Staver walked to the bunkhouse.

"You look good, Owen. The summer's agreeing with you, isn't it."

Frank laughed. "It sure is." He told Alice about the paint.

"That's too bad, Owen."

"We all make mistakes, son." Mrs. Cummings stood on the porch looking down at all of us.

Staver walked back across the yard. He wore his Stetson, a white T-shirt, a blue swimming suit, and his cowboy boots, his arms and legs white. The tip of the scar showed above the neck of the T-shirt. He opened the passenger door on the pickup and took out an ice chest, a portable radio, and two pillows and a blanket.

"This all?"

"That's it. No food. You've already had your supper. Here, I'll take the blanket and the pillow." She turned back toward us. "It's nice to see you all. Come on, let's go. I drove out here to go swimming."

"Is that all?"

"Don't get funny."

We stood and watched them, Alice in front of Staver on the path, until they vanished into the trees. Randy, Stan, and Frank walked across the yard to the bunkhouse, but I stood there. The big cottonwood was dark above the other trees in the twilight. They would see the swing. I turned and walked into the kitchen to eat. After supper I went to brush my teeth, and then I went back to the house to do the dishes for Mrs. Cummings. I made her sit in her rocking chair and rest.

"This is awfully nice of you, son. Getting supper just about wears me out anymore."

I put the glasses in the hot soapy water.

"I'm beginning to think Staver is going to keep on playing the fool till it's too late."

I turned. Mrs. Cummings was looking out the door. She wiped her throat with the dishtowel she held in her hand.

"He has a girl for a few months and then lets her go. Some of them are quite nice girls, too. They act hard, but women want to get married and have a place they can call their own and have children. That's natural. I've known some hard ones in my day, some nothing but common whores, but even they wanted something better."

I rinsed off the last glass.

"Now you take Alice. He's been seeing her longer than any of the rest. Why doesn't he marry her? She'd make him a better wife than most. She runs that cafe and does a good job. A man can't play the fool all his life and not be one. Staver's got to forget the past and go on. What happened to him ain't no worse than what happens to a lot of people."

I lowered the stack of dishes into the water.

"Friends are all well and good, and I've had lots of wonderful friends, but that's not family. Why, growing up in Manti I had family on every street. Both my mother and father came from big families. We used to have the grandest family reunions every summer. My Grandmother Butcher had genealogy charts showing how our family went all the way back to Father Adam. Of course we all do when you stop to think about it, but Grandma Butcher had all the charts."

Mrs. Cummings rocked forward three times to get up from her chair.

"Here, son. I can wipe those dishes. I feel a little better now. I'll just stack them here and you can put them away. You'd better change that water, son."

I changed the water and washed the silverware.

"You go on your mission, son, and preach the gospel. Preach repentance. You get old, and the thing you wish is that you'd done better. You just have to ask the good Lord to forgive you and try to love more. That's all you can do. You have to keep trying to do right even when you know you can't always.

Mrs. Cummings turned and looked up at the pictures on the wall above the table.

"What would there be to hope for without the Lord to forgive us?"

"I want to go to the West German Mission. That's where my father was."

"That will be nice for you, son."

My grandmother had pictures of my father on his mission all dressed in white standing in the Rhine River baptizing people dressed in white, and then on Sunday confirming them and passing them the sacrament for the first time.

After we finished the dishes, Mrs. Cummings said she was going to go to bed. I told her I hoped she would feel better in the morning, but she said she didn't worry much about that anymore.

I walked down the kitchen steps and across the yard. Another chicken had been killed. I passed the bunkhouse. Randy had nearly two hundred dollars saved for the big poker game in Silverton, all in twenty-dollar bills. He'd paid a hundred dollars for the new cowboy boots he'd sent to Las Vegas for. He had started to grow a mustache. I walked up past the corral. Black Prince watched me. I climbed the ladder up the front of the barn, climbed out on the roof and sat down. Legs pulled up, arms on my knees, I watched the big cottonwood. I felt my Eagle Scout ring on my finger. Resting my forehead on my knees, I closed my eyes. I tried not to think about anything.

Saturday morning at breakfast Staver told me how much Alice enjoyed the swing.

"She's going to give you a kiss, Owen. She said she hadn't been on a swing like that since she was a kid. I couldn't get her off it." Staver's teeth were very white.

"What swing?" Randy stopped putting pancakes on his plate.

"Owen put up a new rope swing."

Mrs. Cummings walked over from the stove with more pancakes.

"You stay out of those trees, son. There's enough ways to get yourself hurt or killed around here without falling fifty feet out of a tree in the middle of the night. You got your life to live."

"It's your cooking, Mrs. Cummings." Staver took two pancakes. "Thanks. Owen's a lot stronger than he used to be."

"He's welcome to eat all he wants; he knows that."

I cut the lawn, cleaned up the yard, and pulled weeds in the garden, and then I went to cut hay at the bottom end of the ranch. When we came in at noon, Helen and Mr. Johnson drove in behind us. Nobody had expected them. Mr. Johnson was feeling better, so they had come to take flowers to the cemetery and for Mr. Johnson to talk to Staver. After lunch when they got ready to go, Mrs. Cummings sent me out with a gallon thermos of cold lemonade for them to take.

"They might enjoy something cool to drink out at that cemetery."

I handed the thermos through the window to Helen. Mr. Johnson sat in the back seat with his window down.

"Staver tells me you do the yard work, son. It looks nice. Brent used to keep it nice like that."

I told Mr. Johnson about Brent's initial on the limb where the swing was.

"Yes, son, that was Brent."

Mr. Johnson sat straight up. He turned to look down toward the river. He shook his head.

"He'd be running this ranch and have a boy of his own swimming down there."

"Now, Dad, don't get worked up."

The portable green oxygen tank with the tube and the mask lay next to him on the seat. A bucket with flowers in water sat on the floor.

"I won't, honey. It's just nice to think about Brent hanging up that swing. He would have been the one to do it. All the boys used to have a good time down swimming. That Rawlins boy was killed in Korea too just before Brent was. That war ruined a lot of lives."

Mr. Johnson reached his hand out the window to shake my hand.

"Thanks, son. I'm glad you told me."

"Thanks, Owen." Helen looked up at me. She reached up and put her hand on mine, which was on the window. "Be good. You look great, Owen, heavier and stronger. You look even more like Brent." She smiled. "Remember, you're going to stay at the house overnight on your way home. You've only got a little more than a month left, so don't forget."

"I won't."

"Goodbye." Her lips glistened.

"Goodbye."

She shifted and the Buick started down the lane and then stopped. Helen stuck her head out the window.

"The missionaries are still coming by. It looks like Steve and I might start the discussions. Wish us luck."

"Good luck."

"Thanks."

The Buick picked up speed, Tobe running ahead of it. The windows closed. I wanted to tell Helen not to let her father sell the ranch to Staver, but to get married, join the Church, and come and live on the ranch and be happy. It was really her ranch.

I turned and went up to the equipment shed to get a can of oil for my tractor. Randy, Frank and Staver were there changing the big rear tire on Randy's tractor. Frank straightened up.

"Hey, Moroni, did you come after another gallon of red paint or did ya come to fill these tires with air?"

"I need some oil for my tractor."

"Don't forget about that kiss you got coming. You and Randy go into Silverton tonight for a show, you be sure and go by the cafe."

"He's never kissed a girl."

Randy and Staver stood tightening the lug nuts on the tractor wheel. They turned to look at me.

"Is old Randy right, kid? Ain't you never even kissed a girl?"

"No, I haven't."

"Why not? It ain't against the law in Utah is it?"

"No."

"Then come on, kid. You got to kiss and hug 'em a little to get started."

"You don't have to do that."

I liked to hold girls when I danced with them at the ward parties. I liked girls to wear dresses with their arms bare. And I wanted to kiss girls. My lips would feel funny, and I would keep licking them, and I would feel a pain in my chest. I talked to girls so I could hear their soft voices. I liked to see girls' bodies move. But I knew that you didn't have to kiss a girl to enjoy being with her. She could be your friend. I really liked Becky.

"But, kid, you want all those kisses you can get. You're supposed to enjoy them girls. That's what they're for ain't they? Randy here enjoys 'em. Brigham Young liked 'em a lot. You really have to respect a man like that."

"Polygamy was a commandment of the Lord."

"Sure it was. That Angel Moroni come down and told him what he had to do?"

"No, he didn't."

"How do you know, kid? He was telling lots of other people what to do wasn't he?"

"Maybe you'd better ask Brother Anderson about that, Owen."

I turned and looked at Staver. "I don't have to." I got the can of oil from the open case.

"Well, you boys just keep working hard so you can earn your bonuses. Old Randy here's going to earn his I think. It sure looks like it."

I walked back to the house to turn off the sprinkler I had going on the front lawn. While I was coiling the hose, Mrs. Cummings came out on the back porch and told me how nice it looked. She told me to come in the kitchen and get a cool glass of lemonade before I went back to raking hay. I stood looking at the lawn. In Provo in the evenings I rode my bike to see the lawns I'd cut. They looked smoother, greener, and more even then.

When I went in the kitchen, the glass of lemonade was on the table.

"Sit down for a few minutes, son. It's hot."

I pulled out a chair. Mrs. Cummings sat in her rocking chair with one of the fans blowing on her.

"That breeze at night is a blessing. I lay and wait for it."

I drank the cold lemonade.

"I saw my Fred again last night, son, just as plain as day standing right there in my bedroom. He just smiled like he always does. He never talks. I said, 'Fred,' but he didn't speak a word. My mother came to me one night last week all dressed in white. They're all there, all my brothers and sisters, because I'm the last one left. My little girl's there too. She was such a pretty little girl. They're all there."

Mrs. Cummings nodded her head, and then she turned and looked up at the pictures on the wall.

"The good Lord is the one we got to thank. He died for all of us. Oh, how he must have suffered on that cross. Those poor hands and feet. You know all about the Lord being crucified don't you, son, and rising on the third day."

"Yes, ma'am."

"There's a lot of boys don't know about that. You're lucky. Have another glass of lemonade, son. It's real hot today, and getting hotter."

I finished my lemonade, thanked Mrs. Cummings, and went out to get in the jeep. Stan drove up in the green pickup and stopped.

"Going down to finish cutting that last field?"

"Yes."

"Well, it'll be cooler in the movie house in Silverton tonight. Frank and Staver are going in. If you watch out you might see Staver in a fight one of these Saturday nights. He got in one last year about this time. Turned that kid every way but loose. People were standing on tables and chairs to watch it. Some blond kid from Las Vegas with a couple a beers in him. He had guts though. He kept coming back till he couldn't pick himself up off the floor anymore. There's always some kid around wanting to take Staver."

"Some day somebody will be better than Staver."

"You're right about that, kid, but not for a while yet. Well, we'll see ya later. I got to get back to work."

I turned on the key, shifted, let out the clutch, and followed Stan down across the bridge until he turned left. Driving with one hand I took my new leather gloves out of my back pocket and put them on. I liked the new feel. I'd worn out two pair. The backs of the white no-trespassing signs glinted in the sun. A newly-killed redtail hawk hung by its feet from the barbed wire, its wings half-spread. I turned. Killing redtails was against the federal law. Three magpies flew up from a dead rabbit in the middle of the road.

I parked by the tractor, put the oil in, and started cutting hay. A rooster pheasant flew out in front of the tractor. I watched the hay fall across the knife. I hadn't killed anything during the morning. We were going to start baling Monday, and then start hauling and stacking. I wanted to stack hay the whole last month on the ranch. I wanted to do that hard work, feel my body doing it every day, and know I could do it, my muscles getting stronger and harder all the time under the smooth tanned skin.

I didn't think I would be chosen last now when we divided up to play games in gym. I really liked to feel things. I liked to work and ride Blade and swing and dive and swim because I could feel it. I'd never been able to feel things so much before. Frank kidded me about going swimming all the time in the evening. He said I must be meeting a girl at night, and he told stories about boys swimming with girls and nobody wearing swimming suits. He laughed until he started coughing, and kept spitting and coughing.

I watched the cut hay falling smooth across the knife. I changed the knife every time it started to get dull. I liked the knife sharp so it would cut the hay clean.

At four o'clock black clouds came over the west mountains. On every turn going back down the field I glanced up at the clouds. Lightning flashed off against Lava Peak. A breeze started to pick up.

I was making a turn by the gate when I heard the honking. Staver's red pickup came down the road fast kicking up a big dust cloud. I stopped the tractor. The pickup pulled up and stopped, and Stan jumped out and came running out into the field, the breeze blowing the dust away from the road.

"We got a fire, kid, and Staver needs this outfit to cut firebreaks. Get that knife up and let's go."

"You want to drive?"

"What for? You can handle this thing, can't you?"

"Yes, I can." I jumped down and raised the knife and locked it in place with the crossbar. Stan climbed up and grabbed onto the back of the seat, and I started across the field.

"What?" I had to shout.

"The Spencer place." Stan spoke into my ear.

"Lightning?"

"Probably a cigarette. It's headed toward the house in those fields of weeds. Staver's going to cut firebreaks if you can get this thing there in time. So step on it."

All the Spencers' fields stood shoulder-high in dry brown weeds, the ditches so filled in you couldn't irrigate, so nobody leased the land. When I'd gone to cut the weeds along the river road, Mrs. Cummings had told me that Mrs. Spencer had arthritis and Mr. Spencer had Parkinson's disease and heart trouble. They were going to sell their ranch and move to Reno to live close to their daughter and the doctors. They'd sold all their equipment or let it rust in the fields.

Stan leaned forward to tell me that the Forest Service wasn't at the Spencer place yet. Most of the ranch crews had already quit for the weekend to go into Silverton or Las Vegas.

We came to an open spot in the river trees. I saw the smoke. The breeze blew our dust away. My heart pounded hard. I tightened my hands on the steering wheel.

"She'll really be moving with this wind starting to kick up."

The fire had started at the south end of the Spencers' place near the campground. I came around the turn.

"Here it is, kid."

I turned down the Spencers' lane. The house and barn and the other outbuildings stood close together, the weeds coming right down to the house from the back. Clouds of black smoke rose behind the barn. Mrs. Spencer stood in the yard alone, her hands wrapped in her apron, crying.

"Down to the barn, kid."

I passed Staver's pickup and two cars. I drove out around the barn. Staver had Frank and Randy and five other men mashing down the weeds with shovels, pitchforks, and boards. Acres of high weeds spread out from the barn, and a hundred yards out a spreading column of red flames rose above the weeds, the black smoke blowing ahead of the flames.

I stopped, Staver already running toward the tractor. I climbed down and unlocked the knife and lowered it. The wind bent the tops of the weeds now. The flames leaped higher, whole bursts of flame going up, pushed by the gusts of wind.

"Tell Frank to pull those guys out of there, Stan." Staver climbed up on the tractor. "They're wasting their time. Spread them out to kill any fires that get started behind the break. Wet some gunnysacks. Those pumper trucks better get here fast because this is only going to slow it down."

"Okay."

"How about it, Killer, you want to unclog the knife for me?"

I looked up at Staver. He was happy.

"Got an extra pair of pants with you, kid? You might need 'em." Frank had come up.

I didn't look at him. I climbed up on the back of the tractor and held onto the seat.

Staver swung the tractor around, lowering the knife in one smooth movement as he turned. He started in close to the barn, cut the first swath in a half circle, going fast but keeping the knife level. He rode the knife, turning just at the last minute, raising the knife, dropping it again. The smoke hit us, the smell of fire, the air full of the black windblown ashes.

Staver drove around an old rusted cultivator.

I watched the flames.

I looked down. The thick high weeds cut, but they piled up behind the knife. The tractor smashed them down when we came back, dragging some, leaving them in piles, the dust blowing away, mixing with the smoke.

I watched the flames.

"The knife!" Staver was turned toward me shouting. "The knife."

"What?"

"Unclog the knife!"

I looked down. We were stopped. I jumped down and grapped the pliers out of the tool box. It was old rusted baling wire. Staver kept the tractor running, the vibration coming through the wire into the pliers and into my hand. I pulled at the wire, broke it, got another hold, broke that.

"Come on, come on!"

I didn't look up. I signaled Staver to open the knife. The knife moving in jerks, I pulled the wire free, shoved the pliers into my back pocket and jumped back onto the tractor, Staver already cutting again.

I watched the high red flames, held tight onto the seat, but stood straight to watch the approaching flames. The wind beat the fire, pushing it through the high weeds toward us, most of the black smoke staying high.

We cut another swath, and then another. We had the weeds cut back from the barn maybe thirty feet. I jumped down again to unclog willows from the knife, Staver yelling at me to hurry, cursing not me but the fire.

We cut another swath, and I felt the heat now. We drove through smoke. I heard the fire now, the beginning burning roar, and above it the sound of Staver's voice cursing the fire, the curses becoming laughter.

I breathed only smoke, saw only smoke and the flashes of red flame. I bowed into Staver's back, clung to the seat, knew that he would turn out this time, not go closer, because the heat made it impossible to go closer and the one whole side was flame.

But he turned in again for another swath, and I wanted to scream, hug Staver, my voice rising above his cursing because of the fear and the pain of the heat and the flames burning my body.

The water hit then, the cool water, which at first I thought was fire, thought that my whole body was burning. But when I opened my eyes it was water, a heavy cool spray of water. We turned out then, and I saw the pumper truck at the side of us, Frank on the hose, spraying us till we got out, then hitting the fire where it came to the cut weeds. And the flames lowered, moving slower where the water hit.

Staver drove to the barn and stopped and got down.

"You all right, Owen?" He looked up at me.

"Yes." I kept coughing. I got down, leaned against the back tractor wheel coughing.

"You're not bawling are you?"

"No, I'm not." I kept coughing, and I waited for Staver to say something about my screaming, but he didn't. And I knew that I hadn't screamed. He didn't cough.

"It looks like you got singed a little bit. You lost your hat."

A green Forest Service pickup drove by us. Another pumper drove out to the fire. The flames had singed the hair on the right side of my head. I brushed it with my hand. The back of my hand was red. I didn't have my gloves on. I felt the right side of my face, which was sore.

"There's a first aid kit in the pickup. Better put something on that."

I looked at Staver. He wasn't burned. He wasn't wet. I'd protected him.

"I'm okay."

Frank walked up. I looked down the field. Randy was on the pumper truck hose. All the flames were out, but a lot of places still smoked.

"Owen's Levis are wet from the hose, Frank. I don't want you to get the wrong idea about him."

"I don't want to do that." Frank laughed.

"Owen's a real fire-eater."

I pulled my gloves on. "What do you want me to do?"

Staver told me to mow the weeds for a hundred yards out beyond the house and outbuildings on all sides. After that I hooked up an old dump rake the Spencers still had. Randy operated it to rake the weeds into piles and, afterwards, a pumper truck standing by, we burned them. The piles burst into great orange-black sheets of flame, the heat beating against me as I stood back. It took us until ten o'clock that night to put out all of the burning fence posts, and the logs and trees along the river. The river and the road had stopped the fire on the sides, and the campground on the downstream end. I saw burned rabbits, pheasants, porcupines, and rattlesnakes. People who had come up from the Porcupine Campground still stood in the yard looking when we got ready to leave. Mrs. Spencer thanked each of us. Mr. Spencer was too sick to come out of the house.

"You did a fine job on that tractor, son." Mrs. Spencer shook my hand. You two saved the barn. You're a brave young man."

"He's a hero." Frank lit a cigarette and held the match for Stan and Staver.

Stan blew out smoke. He told a story about a rancher named Myers he'd worked for who lost his barn, corrals, all of his outbuildings, his house, two pickups, a cattle truck, a car, all of his machinery, two hundred tons of hay, and a hundred head of black angus and twenty Arabian horses in a fire.

"Lost everything in less than twenty minutes. Wiped him out." Stan turned to look out toward the road. "He went bankrupt. The angus and the Arabians were all prize breeding stock. First man that I worked for that I ever saw bawl. There must have been fifty people standing there, mostly neighbors and folks who'd come to help. His wife and kids were there. You could smell that burned meat for twenty miles downwind. They just dragged everything out to the gully for the vultures. Every vulture in the county had food for two weeks."

"The poor man." Mrs. Spencer shook her head.

"That was that drought year wasn't it, Stan?" Frank took his cigarette out of his mouth.

"That was the one."

It was too late to go into Silverton to the movie.

Because Stan went in the pickup, I drove the tractor back alone. Driving under the dark trees, I took off my right glove and reached up to touch the side of my face and neck. They hurt a little bit. I wanted to curl up tight when I thought that I might have screamed. When I drove into the yard, Randy was over at the bunkhouse. In the shower I looked at my arm. After I put on my pajamas and said my prayers, I stood in the dark before the mirror. I reached up to touch the side of my face and neck. I touched my right arm with my left hand. I looked at myself. I hadn't screamed. A pickup drove out of the yard. I knew that it was Frank and Staver going to Silverton. I dabbed the Clearasil on the pimples on both sides of my face. I felt good.

13

On July twenty-fourth, which was a Monday, we started baling hay. In Utah it was Pioneer Day, the day President Brigham Young and the pioneers entered Salt Lake Valley in 1847. I didn't mention it to anybody, but when I was helping Mrs. Cummings with the supper dishes, she talked about the big celebrations they always had in Manti. She said that a lot of families had their reunions on Pioneer Day. That evening after Staver gave us another boxing lesson, I went swimming, and then I walked up through the fields with Tobe. I liked the smell, and I liked to see the hundreds of bales in the moonlight. I had a letter from Becky in my shirt pocket. Frank had handed it to me. He smelled the letter first.

"Mighty nice, mighty nice. She's getting anxious to see you, kid. Wish I was you."

Tobe walked back toward me across the dark field, his tongue hanging out from chasing jackrabbits. In the middle of the field I pulled three bales together and lay down.

Looking up I tried only to see, not to smell or hear, just see. I wanted my whole body to be an eye to see the hundred billion galaxies, the billion billion stars.

Space and the worlds had no end; life was eternal, and at night in my bedroom, the lights out, I tried to imagine no beginning and no end so that everything had always existed. A person lived forever, learning forever, and created worlds of his own if he knew enough, became a god. I wanted to study mathematics, physics, chemistry, zoology, botany, and geology, so that I would know all the laws. When I was ten, we had a lesson in Primary on becoming gods, and when I told my grandmother about it, she said that my father would be a god. She picked up his picture from the top of the piano to hold it, and then she went down to the basement to the room where she kept his things and brought up his box of Primary awards to show me.

Lying on the bales I watched the moon come up. I tried to see it move; I lay perfectly still. No clouds were in the sky. I walked across the field and climbed the big rectangular stack to lie on top and watch the sky. I fell asleep listening to a female great horned owl hooting from a tree and woke to curses and the sounds of a running horse. I stood up. I knew it was Staver. I watched him ride to the end of the field and go through the gate, running Black Prince as hard as he would go, his black coat gleaming, then vanishing into the moon shadows and the darkness, the sounds dying.

Staver didn't come back. When I got to the house, all the lights were out in the bunkhouse and Randy was asleep. Magazines lay around him on his bunk, the covers shiny. Standing by the dresser unbuttoning my shirt, I looked across Randy to the stacks of magazines against the wall. At home in my room I had a stack of *Boy's Life.* I'd kept every issue.

We went down to the Bensons' three evenings to bale hay. Saturday morning when I drove Mrs. Cummings into Silverton to buy groceries, I had to pick up a case of dynamite and a roll of fuse at Thurman's. Driving back I kept glancing up at the rearview mirror. My whole body tightened when I hit a bump, my buttocks squeezing together. I knew that the dynamite was safe because I studied about it in chemistry, but I kept imagining the explosion coming through the cab of the pickup and blowing off my arms and legs. I drove slowly.

Saturday evening Randy and I drove back into Silverton. But Randy didn't really care about buying a malt and hamburger or going to a movie anymore. He wanted to see girls. I told him we weren't going to pick up any.

"I just want to talk. What do you think I want to do? Didn't you ever just talk to girls? That's what Playboy clubs are for, so men can talk to girls. They have Playboy clubs all over the world just so men can talk to girls. That's what they're for. Salt Lake City needs one."

Randy had started getting a phone call from Lana nearly every night in the bunkhouse, or he called her. She always talked to Stan, Frank, and Staver. I hadn't talked to Becky on the phone all summer.

Single women sat at the bars drinking when we looked in through the open doors of the casinos. Women walked down the street alone, but not high-school girls. I watched to see if any of the women walked up the steps and into the World Hotel, but they didn't. The windows above the ground floor were blinded and unlit. Even during the day the big white globes over the front door were always lit.

I wanted to know if prostitutes ever went back to their hometowns to visit, and I wanted to hear them talking to their brothers, sisters, fathers, and their mothers. I wanted to hear the words they used and what they said. I wondered if they ever looked at pictures of themselves as babies or little girls, or if they looked into mirror very often, or if they liked to buy new clothes to wear, or liked clean clothes, or if they took a lot of showers.

Frank told stories about prostitutes in Holland after the Second World War who sat in special windows to get men to come into the houses of prostitution.

"It's true, kid." He smiled. "Just like those dummies in Sears or J. C. Penneys windows, except they're alive. They sure are alive. Have you got a Sears and J. C. Penneys in Provo, kid?"

"Yes, we do."

"Provo's a civilized town, Frank."

"I guess it is."

I knew from my reading that prostitutes had high rates of drug addiction, alcoholism, venereal disease, and suicide. If a woman had children who were starving, I thought she might become a prostitute to get money to buy food. I couldn't think of any other reason. Every morning she would take the money she'd earned and buy food. She would earn only enough money every night to buy food the next day for her children.

Brother Anderson told us that every young person had one great sexual passion to spend and that it could be wasted. He sat on his desk. "You should have that with the person you marry, your husband or your wife. That is the person you will be with for the rest of your life. That passion changes you both. It melts something in you, changes its nature, and brings you closer together as no other thing can. And you want to have those memories, keep them, always be reminded of them, and your first child comes from that great new passion. If you are promiscuous you waste it."

Everybody in the room was quiet.

On August first, the week after we started to bale hay, everybody but Frank started loading and stacking. Frank was still baling. Stan drove the tractor to pull the hayrack and the loader behind it. We wore heavy canvas hay chaps. Staver showed us how to lift the bales by the two strands of binder twine and drop them onto the loader, which pulled them up a chute and dropped them on the rack.

Staver leaned back against the front fender of the red pick-up, which he'd driven onto the field.

"Think you can load and stack hay every day for the next month, Owen?"

"Yes."

"It's hard work, and we go twelve hours a day sometimes."

"I can do it."

"Good."

I knew that I was stronger than I'd ever been before in my life. I'd gained twelve pounds in two months, and I had muscles in my whole body that I didn't have to tighten in the shower to see. And sometimes my body felt like everything was joined. Out working alone in the fields or down at the river swimming, swinging, or diving, I felt that way sometimes. In the morning when I first woke up I felt it too, like I'd been feeling it all night even asleep, and my body wasn't just parts always, but whole, everything joined. It was a feeling I liked and wanted all the time. And I knew now, after two months working on the ranch, that I could stack hay.

"Okay, Stan, roll it. Let's move. Owen here is very anxious to get to work. You ready, Randy?"

"Sure."

"A month of throwing bales will put you in good shape for wrestling."

"We'll take state."

"Lana will be proud of you."

We started. Staver rode on the rack to stack the bales as they came off the conveyor after Randy and I put them on. We had to load the bales in front of the tractor and on the sides out two rows, which meant that we worked on five rows of bales, and you just watched for the next bale and didn't have time to look up.

I kept up the first hour. I didn't ever look at the sky; I concentrated on the next bale I had to load. I didn't talk. I kept hoping for light bales, lighter than eighty-five or ninety pounds. Randy got all the bales in front of the tractor. I could just get the ones on the side and stay up. Staver jumped off the moving rack to help.

I didn't want him to, but I needed the help. I didn't say anything. I kept being afraid I couldn't lift the next bale, or that when I lifted it I would suddenly lose my strength and it would pull me down with it, and I would be lying on top of it. I didn't feel the burning sun. I kept thinking that I was tearing a hole in my stomach and every bale I lifted the hole got bigger. Staver had warned us about rattlesnakes under the bales. Frank said that sometimes skunks burrowed under the bales to hide during the day. I didn't care.

The rack stopped. I looked up. It was loaded.

"Hey, Owen. Take five."

I sat down on a bale. I didn't look up; I closed my eyes. I listened. They unhooked the full rack, and Stan drove the tractor to the end of the field and got another one. They unhooked the loader from the full rack and hooked it to the empty rack. I opened my eyes. I hadn't even taken off my gloves.

"You going to vomit, Owen?"

I looked up at Staver. He wasn't even tired. He was smiling. I stood up. "No, I'm not."

"Give easy-money here a drink, Randy." Staver's big belt buckle glinted when he turned.

Randy handed me the water bag.

After I drank I took off my hat, leaned forward and poured the cool water over my head.

"You going to get sick again, Owen?"

"No, I'm not."

"Good. Let's go back to work then."

By lunch time we'd loaded three racks. Loading the last one I kept stumbling. Staver kept jumping off the rack to help.

At lunch Mrs. Cummings put her hand on my forehead.

"You all right, son?"

"Yes."

Staver looked at me. He was passing the steaks to Randy.

"Maybe you better rest this afternoon, Owen."

"No."

After I finished eating, I went out on the lawn and lay down till we left. I didn't eat any of the chocolate pie with whipped cream we had for dessert.

Staver gave me the job of helping Stan unload the three racks. We didn't have to carry the bales or lift them, just drop them onto the loader that carried them to the top of the stack. It was easier. Staver and Randy built the stack.

"Don't kill yourself, kid. Take it a little easy. You'll be okay in a couple of days. Staver ain't hollering yet."

I didn't want to eat supper that night, just shower and go to bed, but Mrs. Cummings made me come in and eat. She said I had to eat. I didn't wipe the dishes; I didn't go down swimming. I slept ten hours. Tuesday morning I knew I'd be okay. I was stiff, all my muscles sore, especially my fingers, but I knew I'd be okay. I lay feeling all my sore muscles and trying to open and close my stiff fingers.

At breakfast Staver asked me how I felt.

"I feel fine."

"You look good."

"I feel fine."

"He does look good." Mrs. Cummings put three more pancakes on my plate.

Staver took Frank off baling to have him work on my side of the rack. We worked until noon, and I felt a lot better. When we came back from lunch we started right where we had left off. Frank started on my outside again so I didn't have so far to carry the bales.

I picked up my third bale. I could just barely lift it off the ground. I had to set it back down. I lifted it again and staggered toward the rack and had to let it drop.

"Hey, what's the matter, Muscles? I thought you said you felt better today."

Frank whistled, and Stan stopped the tractor. Frank walked over to me.

"You're not sick are you, Muscles?"

Randy walked around the front of the tractor. Stan got down.

"No, I'm not. I don't get sick anymore."

"What's wrong with him, Frank?" Staver stood at the end of the rack. He didn't climb down.

"He says it's just too heavy. He can't lift it."

"Is he sick?"

"He says no."

"Have him try it again."

"Try it again, Muscles. Maybe you were just tired."

I still couldn't lift the bale more than a foot off of the ground.

"He can't do it."

"Better look at it, Frank. Maybe it's one of those extra heavy bales. Maybe you'll have to help him get it on."

Frank pushed the bale on its side with his foot. He knelt down by it.

"Yup, one of those extra heavy bales all right, kid."

From the side of the bale, Frank pulled a long thick bar of lead and laid it on the ground. He pulled out two more.

"Well, I guess that was the problem, kid. Must've got baled with the hay. Must've been laying out here for years. The baler picks up all kinds of stuff."

Frank stood up. He turned toward Staver. "He got some lead bars tied up in this one. I guess that made it too heavy for him."

Randy laughed.

"Can he lift it now or does he need some help?"

"Can you lift it, Muscles?"

"I better do it for him." Frank picked up the bale and carried it over and put it on the loader.

"I worked for a guy once up in Montana." Stan stood by the tractor. "We baled a field of wild grass hay down by the Yellowstone River that had never been cut before, and two grown men couldn't move one of those bales. We opened it up, and it was full of gold nuggets. Some of those nuggets was as big as your fist. That river had flooded there the year before and dropped those nuggets, and nobody knew it. Of course that's all great gold country up there in Montana. That rancher's name was Roberts now that I think about it."

Stan turned and spit.

"We spent that whole afternoon breaking those bales open and loading gold nuggets in the back of the pickup. We just threw 'em in. Roberts drove it right to the bank in Billings. Pure gold nuggets. After about three months he sold out and moved to California. Never did hear what became of him down there. There sure was a lot of people looking for gold on their places along the river after that and praying for floods. Of course all that old Yellowstone ever dropped was mostly mud and gravel, but that time it was gold. That field of grass hay had never been cut."

"Been looking for a ranch like that myself," Frank said. "What about you, Randy? Would you like a ranch like that?"

"I sure would."

"The girls would sure like you then. They like boys with plenty of money."

The three lead bars lying on the field glinted in the sun. I looked at the next bale. I wanted to walk over and pick it up and throw it the thirty feet onto the rack. Just have a suddenly incredible surge of adrenalin so I could do that. Not say anything, but just do that. I'd read of men who lifted cars off people, lifted big logs, and slabs of concrete because of surges of adrenalin. I just didn't want any more tricks played on me. I was tired of it.

We started loading again, and Frank kept asking me if the bale I was picking up was too heavy, and I'd say that I didn't need any help.

"Just don't want you to work too hard, Careful, and get sick."

"I won't get sick."

I watched Staver, but he never got tired.

At four o'clock we had all three racks full, and we started stacking. I liked dropping the bales on the loader and helping to build the stack, seeing it get higher and higher. I liked the compact rectangular bales and the rectangular stacks. I always watched the stacks when I drove down the road. Wherever I worked on the ranch I could always see at least one stack. At night they cast a shadow from the moon when I climbed them with Tobe to watch the stars and see the ranch and listen for owls and coyotes.

During our breaks Stan told stories about hay loads tipping over, racks breaking through canal bridges, and whole hay fields catching fire. He'd worked for a rancher named Meecham, who accidentally set a load of hay on fire with a cigarette. It was before they baled hay. The hay was piled loose on the hayrack with pitchforks, and horses pulled the racks. Meecham's team of horses ran away and pulled the burning rack of hay around and around the big field with Meecham cursing and screaming and trying to stop them, the three hired hands running after the rack too. The burning hay from the moving wagon dropped on the cut hay on the ground to set it on fire so that the whole field was burning, the stack too, the horses and wagon appearing and disappearing through the smoke and the flames. And the horses ran through the open gate into the next cut field and the next, setting them all afire, and the other stacks.

"Old Meecham lost fifty acres of hay all told and three stacks. It was the biggest hay fire I ever did see. People came from all over the county just to see the burned fields and the dead horses. Meecham ran all the way back to the house and got his rifle and shot those two horses. He couldn't catch up to 'em, so he had to shoot 'em or they'd have burned the whole ranch down. They just laid there still harnessed to the wagon. He was so mad he never did take the harnesses off. It was a bad winter, and the coyotes came down out of the hills and ate the horses harnesses and all. Didn't make any difference to them. It was fifty degrees below."

"I knew Meecham's foreman." Frank lit his cigarette, blew out the match, and then rolled the head between his thumb and forefinger. "He told me all about that fire. It must have been a big one."

"It was."

I looked at Stan and Frank. I knew that sometimes there were big hay fires, but I was thinking about the gold nuggets the rancher found in his field next to the Yellowstone River in Montana. I'd read about rivers depositing silt and gravel when they flooded and sometimes depositing gold in pockets, but I didn't think the Yellowstone would drop gold nuggets across a whole field like that.

On Friday in the early evening just before we quit loading to go in, Randy lifted a bale off a rattlesnake. He hollered, dropped the bale, and jumped back. I threw my bale on the loader and then turned. The snake coiled. Staver jumped down off the rack carrying a pitchfork. Frank walked over and got a pitchfork from the red pickup. Stan turned off the tractor and got down. He stood by me and Randy.

"We don't want any noise. You want to hear that snake."

Staver held the pitchfork out to the snake. It struck three times at the tines, the buzzing hard and loud.

"He's mean. He's mad, too. Hey, Frank, you want him?"

"Sure."

Staver lifted the coiled rattlesnake with his pitchfork and tossed it to Frank. The snake hit Frank's held-out pitchfork, fell between the tines, and coiled again.

Laughing, hollering, cursing, they tossed the rattlesnake back and forth on the pitchforks, trying to drop it at each other's feet, and sometimes they tossed the buzzing angry snake toward us so we had to step back.

The snake kept uncoiling and trying to crawl off. Staver and Frank stopped finally, stood lighting new cigarettes and laughing.

Staver kept turning to watch the crawling snake. When it was about twenty feet away, Staver, still carrying his pitchfork, his cigarette in his mouth, ran, leaped into the air, and, before the snake could coil, came down on its head with the heels of his boots. The brown and yellow body looped around his ankles. He stepped away from the snake and took the cigarette out of his mouth.

"The next one's yours, Killer."

"Thanks."

"What did I tell you?" Stan said. "What'd I tell you he'd do before the summer was over? He always does it."

I picked up a bale of hay by the two tight loops of binder twine and carried it to the rack and dropped it on.

Thunder rolled down the mountains and into the valley. To the northwest the line of thunderheads lay against the mountains. I had watched them earlier. I turned my face, hoping to feel a cooling breeze and smell the damp smell of rain it carried, but there was no breeze, the thunderheads turning from white to grey and darker on the bottoms.

That evening Randy went into Silverton with Frank and Staver. He didn't tell me he was going. I saw him through the kitchen window as I was wiping dishes. My grandmother phoned. When my mother talked to me she said that the Church had called Brother Anderson as a mission president to Germany and that I would get to go to his farewell because he and his family weren't leaving for six weeks. I hung up the phone. Brother Anderson told us in seminary one day that every missionary in the Church should be flown to Germany to see the concentration camps before they started to preach the gospel of Jesus Christ, because that was the kind of evil they were preaching against all over the world.

The next morning, which was Saturday, I had to wake Randy up three times. He told me that he hadn't gotten in from Silverton until two.

"You've got to work all day stacking hay," I said.

"No real problem, cousin."

"Where did you go last night?"

"Went to Linda's birthday party. You remember Linda. She was at Frank's birthday party. She's his girl. She wanted me to come special. She didn't think you'd enjoy it." Randy folded his arms across his chest.

"I might have."

"Did you like Frank's party?"

"No, I didn't."

"So that's why she didn't invite you. But it was very nice, very nice." Randy put his hands under his head and looked across at the calendar and his pictures. "She said she'd find me a girl if I had more time left." Randy turned his head to look over at me. "You wouldn't like riding with Staver anyway. He drives too fast for you."

"You'd better get up, or you're going to be late." I walked out on the porch and petted Tobe. The ranch was still shaded by the east mountains, the sunlight hitting the other side of the valley.

I'd tried all summer to help Randy stop playing poker and stop spending so much time with Frank and Staver. That hadn't worked, but at least he hadn't started smoking or drinking, except for the two cans of beer at Frank's birthday party. And he didn't swear or tell obscene stories. Even if he lost some of his money in the big poker game in Silverton, he'd still get his car because he'd stayed the whole three months on the ranch, and he'd get his bonus, too. I was glad Randy had earned his car; it meant a lot to him to have a new car for his senior year, even a Volkswagen. I knew that Randy was basically a good person.

We stacked hay all morning, but when we came in for lunch Mrs. Cummings was sick, and so Staver had me drive her into Silverton because the doctor wanted to see her. After she came out of the doctor's we went to Bob's. She gave me a list, and I bought the few groceries she needed while she sat on a bench at the front of the store. Bob shook his head when he handed me the meat.

"I don't know how she keeps going. She was supposed to have died ten years ago. I guess she's not quite ready yet."

"I guess not."

"She's probably trying to hang on until Dale gets out, but that's quite a while yet."

I didn't say anything.

We stopped at the drugstore, and I went in and got Mrs. Cummings' new prescription and bought another tube of Clearasil. Mrs. Cummings didn't talk during the drive either way. She just sat and watched out through the windshield. She didn't wipe the sweat off her neck and face. I didn't ask her if she was going to have her operation. She fixed us sandwiches for supper and went up to her room to lie down. Randy didn't want to go into Silverton to see a movie and buy a hamburger and a malt. He said it was kid's stuff. Staver didn't go anywhere because the doctor said that Mrs. Cummings would have to be taken to Las Vegas to the hospital if she didn't feel better. Randy went over to the bunkhouse to play poker.

I sat on the cabin porch. Tobe put his head on my lap, and I petted him. Mrs. Cummings didn't turn on her light. I decided that she had gone to bed. The doctor had told her to get a lot of rest. I knew that Mrs. Cummings could die, but I didn't think she would. It gave me a funny heavy feeling when I thought about it, so I tried not to.

I walked down to the river and went swimming and swung on the swing, and walked down to the old bridge to watch the big trout. And then I walked out across the field and climbed up on top of the haystack we'd worked on that day. I lay down and put my hands under my head. I watched the stars and listened for coyotes and owls. Tobe put his head on my chest.

The first thing I was going to do when I got home in three weeks was buy a new bicycle. I really liked to think about going home. I'd learned a lot on the ranch, and I'd gained almost fifteen pounds. I'd be a junior that fall and next year a senior. I'd go to B.Y.U. for one year and then go on my mission. I'd come back and finish college, get married, go to medical school, do a residency, and then start a practice in Provo and raise my family there.

I'd decided to spend about two hundred dollars for a new bicycle. An Avanti would cost six hundred, but I could get a Schwinn for two hundred. Becky had a bicycle, and we planned to go riding together when I got home. We'd written each other about that. Lying there on the haystack, I named the constellations, saying the names out loud to myself. I'd wash and polish and vacuum the car every time I took Becky on a date. She would be there to see me bless the sacrament for the first time and to see me receive my Duty to God Award.

Sunday morning Mrs. Cummings felt better and fixed breakfast, but she didn't go to church because she had to rest. Randy didn't go either. He said he was too tired.

"I guess I can miss once in a summer without being excommunicated." I told him that he needed to take the sacrament, but he turned over and pulled the pillow down tight over his ears. He didn't even go in to breakfast.

When I got back I helped Mrs. Cummings set the table for dinner, and I did all the dishes afterward while she sat in her rocking chair with the fans on her and her eyes closed. When she opened them I asked her how she was, and she smiled.

"Son, I know people a lot worse off than I am. My friend Nora's been sick for twenty years, sick every day, and I've never known her to complain once. Always doing for somebody else as much as she could. When it comes right down to it, we all want a little longer. I just worry about Dale that's all. He's my only worry now."

"You'll live a long time, Mrs. Cummings."

She smiled. "You're a good boy, son. It's been a real pleasure having you this summer. I like somebody I can talk to. You can't always talk to a boy your age. They know too much already. And you're learning how to work hard. We've had boys come out here looking for work and praying they won't find any."

Monday we started loading and stacking hay again. Tuesday the Forest Service called us on a fire in Dry Canyon, but we had it out in two hours. They called us out again Wednesday for one in Saw Mill, but it was small too. We had two thunderstorms high in the mountains with a lot of lightning, but Stan said it didn't look like Randy and I would get to fight a real fire before we went home, though August was the hottest month and a good month for fires. I knew what to do on a fire now, which was a feeling I liked. I'd learned to do a lot of things I'd never done before. When we boxed, Staver didn't hit me as easily as he used to, and I could hit Randy almost as often as he hit me. I was learning to keep my arms and gloves up, stay crouched, and move. When I got home people would be surprised how strong I was, and they wouldn't know that I could box.

Frank lit a cigarette, "You're going to be able to take care of yourself, kid."

Already the north fields, which we had cut first, were green with the start of the third crop of hay. Every evening hundreds of jackrabbits came down out of the sagebrush to feed on the new hay. Stan told stories of rabbits so thick they climbed trees to eat the leaves, jumped through windows to eat potted plants, devoured a whole lawn overnight, roots and all, so that the rancher woke up the next morning to his wife standing on the front porch screaming, her house plants vanished, the lawn dirt, the trees leafless.

Nobody laughed, and I knew suddenly, sitting there listening, watching Stan and the others, that the stories weren't entirely true. Maybe parts of them were, but not all of them, and they weren't supposed to be, but everybody had to figure that out for himself and nobody could tell him, which was part of the fun. It made me feel very good to understand what Stan was doing. I wanted to shout that I understood, but I didn't because that wouldn't have been right. I thought back on all the stories Stan had told all summer and tried to decide how true each story was.

Thursday at supper Staver said we were going to start shooting rabbits that night.

"Those rabbits are nothing but a pest." Mrs. Cummings put the pie on the table. "They'll run you right out of the ranching business if you don't stop them."

We met at the bunkhouse porch. Staver brought out the scope-sighted Browning .22 automatics, and Frank carried out a carton of shells each for me and Randy. Randy and I loaded the long tube magazines before we climbed up into the back of the pickup Stan drove. I'd told Staver I'd drive, but he said to think of shooting rabbits as part of the job and it'd be easier.

Randy kept putting his rifle to his shoulder and aiming at things.

"You want to bet on who gets the most?"

"No, I don't."

"Just asking."

Staver parked his pickup, turned off the lights, and he and Frank rode with us through the first field. Stan drove across the wooden bridge and turned right, driving slowly. Two rabbits raised from feeding to stand facing the headlights. I raised the Browning and put the scope on the left rabbit, centered the crosshairs on his shoulders. I slowly squeezed the trigger, and the rabbit dropped. I heard Randy shoot twice. His rabbit dropped.

"Should have had you boys in Korea with me." Staver wore a new straw cowboy hat.

Stan drove very slowly so we could aim. Three more rabbits stood at the edge of the lights. I raised my Browning.

"Don't get anxious, Killer. Get close enough."

"I'm not anxious."

"Good."

I swallowed against the excitement. I shot two of the three rabbits. They dropped and didn't move. Randy shot the third rabbit.

"You boys are going to do all right."

At the end of the first sweep around the field, Frank and Staver got out. Stan turned farther into the field for the second sweep, the lights casting long black shadows from the lava ledges on the hillside.

I tried not to get excited. I didn't want killing rabbits to make me happy. I tried to shoot them through the head so that they flipped over dead without pain. If I hit a rabbit in the stomach, he hunched down or hopped slowly away, and I had to shoot him again if I could before we passed. We saw more and more rabbits as it got later, sometimes five or six standing staring into the lights at one time. I kept shooting, shot one rabbit then moved the scope over to another one, clenching my jaws so I didn't shout or scream, stopping only to feed shells into the magazine, my hands full of shells, trembling.

The barrel burned my hand. Randy kept hollering. Hit, a rabbit sometimes did a sommersault, ran in tight circles, or lay kicking one leg. We shot rabbits until midnight, and I lost count of the number of rabbits I killed.

Friday morning Staver sent me and Randy with the pickup to drive through the fields and collect the dead and dying rabbits and then go burn them.

"Use the forks," he said. He lit a cigarette. He turned his head to the side, closed one eye against the smoke. "You'll need about ten gallons of gas."

Two vultures and dozens of feeding magpies and ravens jumped up ahead of the pickup as we drove across the field. I lifted the dead rabbits and dropped them into the back of the pickup. I hit the wounded rabbits on the head with the back of the pitchfork. I didn't stab them. I felt it all the way up through the handle when I hit them. Some of the wounded female rabbits had given birth. We had killed more than three hundred.

We dumped them into a brushless lava gully, soaking each layer with gasoline. Randy threw the match. We stepped back farther from the exploding yellow flames, the whole end of the gully full of fire, the rabbits' bodies hidden by the flames.

"What's wrong with you?" Randy leaned on his pitchfork. "Like Stan says, five or six jackrabbits eat as much as a sheep. They're pests. So what's wrong."

"Nothing." I kept thinking about how I'd felt shooting the rabbits. I couldn't stop thinking about that.

"You sure act like it."

The flames warmed my face, neck, and hands.

After we got back to the yard from the burning rabbits, we washed the hundreds of spent .22 shells, the balls of grey fur, and the blood out of the back of the pickup. Vultures, magpies, and ravens flew out of the gully when we drove up with a load the second and third mornings. Randy stood and watched them fly off.

"I guess they like a cooked meal too when they can get one."

14

August fifteenth was the day my father had died, and on Sunday my grandmother had phoned to remind me. On that day every year she always played my father's missionary homecoming tape for me, read to me from his letters and journals, showed me his missionary slides, and went through her photograph albums with me. In the morning and the evening she put flowers on his grave. In the evening under the high black spruces the red flowers grew darker than the other flowers. My grandmother always told me that I was like my father.

Loading and stacking hay, I thought about him. Twice I took his picture out of my wallet to look at it. It was his missionary picture. My grandmother had my father's obituary, but I'd ridden my bicycle up to the *Herald* office and read in their archives the paper printed on the day he died. I wanted to see all the other things that happened on that day. After supper, when I was drying the dishes, I told Mrs. Cummings what day it was. She had been gone for two days to visit Dale in prison and had just gotten back the night before. She rinsed off a plate and put it on the drain rack, and then she turned and looked at me.

"You think about your father a lot don't you?"

I picked up the plate. "Yes."

"He wants you to live a good full life, son. You'll see him again. You don't have to worry about that. Have you got his picture?"

I took out my wallet and handed Mrs. Cummings the picture. She wiped off her hands on her apron to take it.

"It was his missionary picture."

"Well, he was a fine clean-looking young man. He's proud of you, and he wants you to be happy. That's the way to please him, son. Be happy. Too many people spend their lives doing nothing but making themselves miserable."

Mrs. Cummings handed me back the picture.

When I got outside, Randy and Staver were playing tackle on the front lawn. I stood and watched. Staver passed the ball to Randy and then Randy tried to get by him, but Staver tackled him. Every time Randy received the ball Staver tackled him, but he never tackled Staver.

That night, lying in my bunk, my hands under my head, I decided to make the last two weeks on the ranch the best two weeks of the whole summer. I was going to work even harder and be more careful not to do anything wrong. I wanted it to be a perfect two weeks. And I was going to try harder to get Randy not to go to the big poker game in Silverton. I was going to talk to him again. He didn't have to go. It wasn't something he needed to do. He would feel bad if he lost a lot of money. He would still get his car because he'd stayed on the ranch all summer, but he would have to explain to Uncle Mark what had happened to his money. I could tell him that.

I lay and thought about going home to Provo, which was a good feeling. School started the Wednesday before Labor Day, so we would miss the first three days. I didn't like to miss any school. I always looked forward to school starting. I liked to take new classes. It made me happy to study chemistry, physics, mathematics, biology, history, and English. I wanted all the knowledge I could get. Across the room, Randy's pictures covered the whole half of the wall around his *Playboy* calendar. I looked up at the ceiling.

Brother Anderson had told us how a boy who became a fornicator changed. He had to worry all the time about people knowing, about if he had a venereal disease, and if the girl was pregnant, and if he would have to get married and drop out of school and get a job. He thought about all of his friends differently and about his mother and father and brothers and sisters, and the girl when he saw her in class or in the halls. Fornication changed his body, his spirit, how he felt about everything. He couldn't be happy again until he went to his bishop to confess and start repenting. He wasn't worthy to take the sacrament or bless it or even sit at the sacrament table or to hold the Aaronic Priesthood or receive the Holy Ghost.

I looked at Randy's pictures again and then back up at the ceiling. The new clean spiral of flypaper glinted as it moved in the air from the fans. My mother had written in her last letter that my *Boy's Life* and my *Explorer* subscriptions had expired. I wrote her not to resubscribe to *Boy's Life.* It didn't interest me anymore.

Tuesday Randy and I irrigated the fields that the hay had been hauled out of. Twice during the morning I saw Staver standing by his red pickup watching us with his binoculars. Stan brought us our lunches because we couldn't leave the stream we had going. Stan said that Helen and Mr. Johnson were back at the house and that Helen had said to tell us she was sorry she'd missed us and she expected us to stay overnight in Las Vegas on our way home.

After Stan drove out, we sat in the jeep to eat. I'd parked it in the shade.

"I hope she takes us to see all the big casinos at night. I really want to see them at night all lit up."

Randy ate his piece of chocolate cake first. He had slid down so that his head rested on the back of the seat.

"Two more weeks and I get my car. I bet I can talk my dad into a Triumph. He'll buy it for me; he's made a lot of money this summer. Won't those Provo High women like old Randy boy then."

Across the fields I watched the low dust cloud coming toward us above the willows. The blue pickup came around the end of the willows.

"Stan's coming back."

Randy raised his head. He was trying to find a western station on the radio.

"What does he want?"

Stan started to honk.

I put my sandwich back in the sack.

"It's probably a fire."

"Nuts."

Stan pulled up, but didn't get out.

"We got a fire on Spanish Flats, and it looks like a big one. Come on. They're taking everybody down the whole valley for this one. You summer hands are going to see what a real fire is like this time."

Randy sank down in the seat and took a sandwich out of the baggie.

"I'll just stay here. I've done all the fire fighting I want to do for one summer. It's about as exciting as cutting hay."

"Come on, let's go. Leave that jeep and bring your lunch. You might not get fed again till breakfast. And not then unless you're lucky. Staver's already got the tools out of the fire shed."

Randy groaned.

Two miles before we got to Spanish Flats, which was on Battle Mountain, I saw the great cloud of smoke. The fire was moving up the side of the mountain in the dense high oak and maple brush toward big groves of pines on the north slopes of the ravines.

"She's big, not the biggest, but big. She's going to be a bugger to fight if she gets up the side of that mountain very far."

I saw the flames now rising up into the smoke, huge sheets of red flame going up, a moving line of fire across the base of the mountain for two miles. And below the line of flame everything was black and smoking, with patches of low flame. A B-24 flew low dropping the red flame retardant.

We passed two parked semi-trucks dropping their ramps to unload the yellow Caterpillars. The heavy dust made the heat worse.

"Just wonderful," Randy said.

"They'll be using all the big stuff they can bring in on this one." Stan lit a cigarette. "If we get a wind half the state of Nevada is going to go. They'll have Staver up on one of those cats or knocking holes in those ledges with dynamite to get those cats up where they can do some good. The only way they can stop a fire like this is drop everything in front of it."

Pickups lined the road on both sides.

"Better park while I still got a chance."

Stan parked and left the keys in. We got out and hiked half a mile down the road to where the Forest Service was putting more crews together.

"You two watch out now. I've seen a wind push fire through brush like this at thirty miles an hour. And that's a lot faster than you can run uphill or down. Not even an elk can outrun a fire like that, and I've seen whole herds try. Just so much cooked meat. If your crew boss says get out, don't argue. Just get out."

"Hello, Stan. Looks like you got a couple of live ones for us. You boys been on fire before haven't you?"

"Yes, sir."

"Pick up your stuff out of the back of that pickup and go over there where they're putting those crews together." The Forest Service official took off his hardhat and wiped his forehead with his arm. "It's hot enough without a fire, Stan."

"It's always hot enough around here without a fire. It's even hot in the winter. See you boys. You watch yourselves."

"We will."

"It's good to have somebody on a crew that knows what they're doing, Stan."

"Well, those boys do. Pretty good workers, too."

We got our canteens, hardhats, and axes at the pickup and walked up to the large group of firefighters being assigned to crews. I watched Stan get a hardhat and then cut back down toward the road, so I knew he had a special job.

Our crew was mostly University of Nevada freshmen on a summer geology field trip in the valley studying volcanoes. They were all laughing and joking. The crew chief was the foreman from the Stimpson ranch.

"What's that noise?"

One of the University of Nevada students stood by me.

"Dynamite explosions. They're knocking holes in the lava ledges to get the caterpillars through."

"Gee."

I took off my glasses to clean them.

"You nearsighted?"

"Yes, I am."

"So am I."

I put my glasses back on and tied my bandana handkerchief around my neck.

"What's that for?"

"To keep the sparks off my neck."

"Wish I had one."

He turned to look back toward the fire. He had a lot of pimples.

Our crew chief explained what we were going to be doing, told us about axe safety, and what to do if he hollered for us to get out.

"Okay, let's move it."

We formed a line and hiked up a ridge for twenty minutes and then formed a line just below the top of the ridge. We cut the heavy brush and threw it down the slope into the path of the fire. We were at the east end of the line, the highest point. The fire moved across the flats, slowed down by the patches of sagebrush. The oak and maple brush went up in big puffs of flame. Two cats worked ahead of the fire making a firebreak. We were cutting another firebreak if the fire got past the first one. The B-24 flew over low dropping flame retardant ahead of the fire, the roaring pounding against the mountain. Dynamite explosions boomed across the ridge. There was no wind, but now the rising smoke had become so thick I couldn't see Randy twenty feet above me. I heard a lot of chainsaws going.

The crew boss came down the ridge with two of the geology students who were sick from the heat. They'd drunk all their water the first hour. I only stopped to sharpen my axe with my file. I wasn't tired. Ashes fell on my hands and arms, the air hot and thick, but I saw no flames. Gradually everything was growing darker. I looked at my watch.

Somebody screamed. He screamed again, below me.

"I cut my leg! I cut my leg! Somebody help me! Please help me!"

I got down to him as fast as I could through the brush and smoke. It was one of the college students. He sat in the dry leaves holding his leg above his sock, his Levis pulled up. The blood seeped up between his fingers. His hardhat had fallen off.

"Help me. I'm bleeding to death."

"Okay, take it easy, or you might." I laid my axe against a log. I wasn't scared.

"Put on a tourniquet."

"That's a good way to lose your foot."

I knelt down. "Okay, let me see." I tried to pull his hands away. "Let me see or I can't help you." He relaxed and I pulled his hands back and the blood spurted up. "Here, hold this thumb here and press hard." I put his thumb just above the middle of the four-inch cut.

It was arterial bleeding. I had my first-aid merit badge and my certificate, but I'd never given anybody first aid before. I wasn't scared.

"It's not stopping."

"Push harder."

I untied the red bandana handkerchief from around my neck and folded it into a compress over the cut.

"Press on that."

"I can't. I feel sick. I'm going to throw up."

"Press on it."

I put his hands around his leg so that he pressed on the compress with both his thumbs.

"I'm going to throw up."

"Go ahead, but keep pressing on that hard."

When he turned his head to vomit he tipped forward and let go of the compress to stop his fall with his hands. The blood spurted up onto my hands as I put the compress back and pressed hard to stop the bleeding. I hollered for Randy and sent him to get the crew chief and the first-aid man. They came, and the first-aid man took over. I helped him put on a heavy compress bandage.

"Thanks. You did a good job."

The geology student, whose name was Scott, said that he could walk, so the first-aider said he'd help him down off the ridge. Scott thanked me, and I picked up my axe and walked back to where I'd been working on the line. Randy held my canteen while I washed the blood off my hands. I had to rub them hard to get it off. I watched it wash away, the water pink-red. I'd never had another person's blood on my hands before.

"I'm glad you were down there and not me." Randy screwed the lid back on my canteen.

"It wasn't that bad."

"I'm still glad."

Later the crew chief came by.

"You work for Staver on the Johnson place don't you?"

"Yes."

"I thought you were one of the summer hands. Well, you knew what you were doing with that first aid. That college kid would've been in real trouble without somebody who knew what to do, with enough sense to do it."

"Thank you."

"If I see Staver I'll tell him he's got a good man."

"Thank you."

I started back cutting oak brush, and I kept thinking about what I'd done and how it had made me feel good helping somebody and maybe saving his life. I kept thinking about it to make the feeling come back. I wanted to tell somebody what I'd done. It got dark. The evening breeze off the mountain cleared out the smoke and pushed the fire back on itself so that it didn't move forward so much. The dynamite explosions and chainsaws had stopped when it got dark, and the B-24 dropping the fire retardant had stopped coming.

We quit working at ten o'clock and hiked back down the ridge. The Forest Service had two camps set up, one on each side of the fire. They furnished us with tents and sleeping bags. I washed my face and hands before supper, but there were no showers. I didn't see either Frank or Staver. Stan was in our camp. He said they'd have the fire out in a day or two unless there was a wind. He'd been down on the road directing traffic all day.

We fought the fire all day Wednesday and Thursday and got it under control so that the Forest Service let the ranch crews off Battle Mountain Thursday night. I had to shower for half an hour to get clean. Mrs. Cummings had a special supper for us. She'd been resting while we were gone, and she felt a little better.

Staver handed me the plate of steaks. The pearl buttons on his clean yellow cowboy shirt shone.

"Did you know that Owen here is a hero, Mrs. Cummings?"

"A what?"

"A hero. A college kid cut his leg with an axe and Owen saved his life."

"I just stopped the bleeding." I looked at Staver. He smiled.

"That makes you a hero. In Korea medics got medals for doing that."

"Pass the gravy will ya, Hero."

Mrs. Cummings sat in her rocking chair. "It's nice to be able to help people when they need it."

After supper I dried the dishes for Mrs. Cummings, and she told me Helen Johnson had said Tuesday morning when she was there with her father that the Mormon missionaries were going to start the discussions.

"She said that they were very nice young men. One of them was from Provo, but he didn't know you."

Mrs. Cummings said Cliff had come by that morning to talk to her again about Dale and tell her he had found a good job in Las Vegas driving heavy equipment for a construction company. He was going to get married in September. Mrs. Cummings was happy about that. She said it showed Cliff had good sense because now he would have something to live for. She said Staver should take a lesson from Cliff.

When I got to the cabin Randy sat at the table practicing shuffling and dealing cards. He'd learned four or five different ways to shuffle cards. I was surprised to see him still at the cabin. His boots had come from Las Vegas and he had them on, but he wasn't going to wear them outside until he went to Silverton for the big poker game. Staver had given him some special boot wax to polish them with.

"Well, how are you, cousin?"

"I'm tired. I'm going to go to bed."

"Hey, I'm ready for those guys. I'll bet I at least break even. Staver says I play a good game of poker. I'm as good as Frank." Randy took out his wallet and tossed it on the table. "Look in there. Go ahead, count it."

I picked up his wallet and opened it.

"Count it."

I ran my finger across the twenty-dollar bills.

"Fifteen twenties. Staver says that's plenty."

"What if you lose it all? What if they get you drunk on beer?"

"I won't lose it, and they don't try to get people drunk. You still got to learn to stop worrying, cousin."

"Maybe. What will you tell your father if you lose it? He expects you to save some of your money for your mission."

"I won't have to tell him anything. I'm going to come out at least even. I might even win a few bucks."

Randy left for the bunkhouse, and I put on my pajamas, knelt down and said my prayers, and then got in my bunk. I was very tired, but I felt good. I liked to be tired. It was a good feeling. Tobe lay against the screen. I kept thinking about Randy and what I could do. I'd prayed for him. His mustache was dark and heavy now.

We hauled and stacked hay all day Friday, and after supper Randy was waiting for me in the cabin. He said he wanted to go swimming, which surprised me.

"You haven't been swimming for a month. Aren't you going to play poker tonight?"

"No. Frank's gone into Silverton for something. I want to use the swing."

"Can't three of you play poker? You have before."

"I want to go swimming. You're always trying to get me to go swimming."

"Okay." I got my swimming stuff.

"Do you still wear that thing and your suit?"

"Yes, I do."

"Maybe Frank's right."

"Right about what?"

"About you being afraid some girls might see ya."

We walked off the porch and down the path to the trees, Tobe ahead of me.

"I'm not afraid of girls."

"Oh, I forgot. You're being modest. Modest, modest, modest. It's a nice word. Modest, modest, modest, modest."

"I like to be dressed."

We walked out through the trees to the ledge. All the time Randy was undressing he kept saying "modest." Running across the ledge to dive in he kept saying it until he hit the water.

I changed and dived in. I closed my eyes, just felt the water touching me. I stayed under as long as I could then rose slowly, felt my head in the air. I opened my eyes.

Staver walked out of the trees carrying two gunnysacks and three pitchforks. Tobe stood up. Staver laid the pitchforks on the ledge, and he knelt down and took two heavy rocks, two pieces of nylon cord, and two half sticks of dynamite with fuses out of one of the sacks. Randy climbed out and knelt down by Staver and tied one of the rocks to a half stick of dynamite.

"What are you going to do?"

"Take off my clothes, Owen. Is that okay?" Staver took two matches out of his Levis pocket and put them in his mouth.

He stood up and pulled off his cowboy boots and his socks and started unbuttoning his yellow shirt.

"Randy, did you forget to tell Owen we were going to get some fish tonight?"

"I guess I did."

"You can't. You can't do that here." I hurried and climbed out. "You can't. This is where we swim. It's against the law."

Staver pulled his T-shirt off and then his shorts.

"Is it, Owen?" He turned to look at me.

The scar went from the bottom of his throat down his chest, down his stomach where his navel had been, and stopped in his groin. It was pointed on both ends and three inches wide in the middle, with the double row of stitch marks on each side. It was whiter than his skin and puffy so that it raised above his other skin. The scar glinted. No hair grew on it. The scar was two feet long and it looked like it might just suddenly break open again.

Staver turned away.

"Here, Randy."

He handed Randy one of the matches out of his mouth and then picked up the other half stick of dynamite with the rock tied to it.

"Take the middle; I'll take the top."

"You'll kill everything." I tried not to look at the scar.

"Pick up all the clothes, Owen, and bring them back. We don't want them to get wet."

"Don't do it." I picked up the clothes.

Staver struck his match, lit the short fuse, and lobbed the dynamite tied to the rock into the deep water at the top of the hole. Randy lobbed his into the middle.

"Come on, Owen. We have to get back a little bit."

I followed Staver.

"Come here, Tobe."

"Put the clothes down, Owen."

I put the clothes down.

"You . . ."

The water erupted, cascaded up white, the explosion muffled, the water coming down on us like heavy rain. And then the middle of the hole came up the same way, the second explosion pushing me more, my head bowing under the falling water.

"Okay, let's go. Don't want any of them big German browns to get away."

I followed them out of the trees. Randy picked up a pitchfork. Staver picked up the other two and handed one to me.

"I don't want to help. It's against the law." The scar was incredible.

"The fish are for the Bensons, Owen. I should have told you. They're going to have a family reunion and want a big fish fry in the evening. Old man Benson used to be quite a fisherman. They have a fish fry every year, but he can't get out and fish this year. They just took those casts off his legs. I think he'll appreciate a few fish, don't you?"

"Hey, they're getting past me! Hurry up! I need help!"

Randy stood in the water up to his waist at the end of the pool. He pulled a big trout off the tines of his pitchfork and threw it up on the wet ledge.

"If they get past us down into that next hole, we won't be able to get them, Owen. You don't want them to go to waste now do you? They're dead. The river is too wide for two of us to cover with Frank not here."

"Hurry up! They're comin'! They're comin'!"

Staver stood facing me.

I took the pitchfork. I walked to the end of the hole and lowered myself down and pushed out toward Randy. Staver was on my other side.

"Get 'em! There's a big one! Get 'im! Don't let 'im get away! He's comin' right to you!"

I was breathing fast. My body felt like it could split open. Staver, who was on my other side, lunged at a trout with his pitchfork.

A big German brown drifted gold up out of the deep water toward me. I watched him turn in the current. He moved his tail slowly. I raised the pitchfork and jabbed the tines through him and lifted him out of the water wiggling, the feeling coming down through the handle into my hands and arms. I tried to toss him onto the ledge, but he wouldn't come off the tines, and I had to lower the pitchfork and pull him off with my hand.

His gills opened and closed; he bled from the tine holes, the blood slipping down his wet slick sides. He weighed three or four pounds and was orange and gold, with black and red spots, some ringed in white. He opened and closed his mouth. I had never held a trout in my bare hands before.

"Come on, don't stand there all day looking at that thing. They're getting past you."

I threw the big trout up on the ledge. Tobe watched me.

Sometimes two and three trout drifted down toward me at one time. I stabbed them, lifted them, pulled them off the tines and threw them bleeding up on the pile. Randy kept yelling, sometimes swearing and laughing.

"Get that one! Get that one!"

"Let the little ones go!"

"I am! I am!" Randy shouted. "This is a big one!"

"Get all of 'em!"

We waded up to our chests looking for big trout caught in the bottom rocks. We dived under looking for the golden trout lying in the rocks on the bottom. I came up to throw off a big trout. A dead water snake drifted by me on its back showing its white stomach. Randy threw a small trout up on the pile.

We stood looking down into the water. A magpie screeched from the trees. I shivered.

"Looks like that's got 'em all. Come on. Let's get these cleaned and down to the Benson's place."

We climbed out, and with our pitchforks we scooped the pile of trout onto the grass. We got our sheath knives and knelt down. Staver showed me how to cut the gills so that after I'd slit the trout open I could pull the gills and entrails all out at once. We threw them into the swift water below the hole for the mink.

I watched Staver. He cleaned the biggest trout. The blood ran down his hands and forearms and dropped onto his legs above his knees. Heavy drops of blood splattered his white stomach and chest. Drops splattered on his scar and ran down it in little short streaks till there was no more blood and they stopped. After we finished cleaning the trout we washed them off and put them into one of the gunnysacks. The trout felt heavy and cold, and I put each one in carefully. Both sacks were about a third full.

Randy and Staver got the soap out of the red coffee can and took a bath to wash to blood off. They dried themselves with their T-shirts. Except for his hands, neck, and face, Staver's whole body was white. It was hard and smooth as if it were made out of white metal, except for the puffy scar.

After they got dressed, they each picked up one of the heavy gunnysacks of trout.

"You bring the pitchforks. Okay, Owen?" Staver lifted his sack a little higher and looked down at it. "The whole Benson family will be grateful. You were a big help, Killer."

"Thanks."

Standing there, holding my hands and arms away from my body, my knife in my hand, I watched them walk out between the trees carrying the two heavy sacks. The grass and ledge were shiny and smeared with blood where we'd piled the trout and where we'd cleaned them. I looked down at the blood on me. I knew that Randy and Staver had planned everything, but that didn't help how I felt. It was like my whole body was so heavy that it kept pulling me toward the ground. Nothing seemed simple or easy.

I looked down at my knife. I knelt down on the ledge and washed my knife off, dried it on my towel, and put it back in the sheath. I got a can and washed the blood off the grass and ledge, and then I got my soap and took off my suit and washed it with the soap to get the blood off. I lowered myself into the water and washed the blood off me.

After I got dressed I stood and watched the hole for a long time, but I knew that no trout would rise to feed on the night insects. I would put some trout minnows in the hole, but it would take a long time for them to grow. I felt bad.

Tobe touched my hand with his nose.

"Let's go, Tobe."

I took the three pitchforks from against the big cottonwood and walked up the path. Mrs. Cummings' bedroom light was on. I walked past the house and the trees. Stan was watching TV. I leaned the three pitchforks against the cabin. I looked at my watch. It was ten after nine. I knew that Randy wouldn't be in until at least midnight. I petted Tobe and then went in the cabin and lay down on my bunk. For a long time I lay with my hands under my head staring up at the ceiling. And then I got up and went down and put the minnow trap in the river.

Saturday we irrigated all day, and in the evening Randy wanted to go into Silverton to the movie.

"I thought you said that movies were for kids. You were there last night."

"I know. I changed my mind."

Staver had gone in earlier, but he wouldn't take Randy with him. He told Randy that he and Frank had to make some arrangements for the poker game the next Saturday.

When we drove into Silverton and up Silver Street, Randy kept turning on the seat to look up all the streets on both sides.

"I wonder where Staver is?"

After the movie we walked past the Volcano Casino twice because Randy wanted to find Staver. Randy looked in all the casinos. The blinds were pulled on all the upstairs windows of the World Hotel.

"Why do you want to see Staver so badly?"

"I'd just like to see him. I like Staver. I like to be with him. I'm interested in that game. Is there any law against that?"

"No, there isn't."

"I wish I was twenty-one."

I watched myself in the big glass doors and the big front windows as we walked along Silver Street. The neon sign over the Volcano Casino spouted red lava. In the window I was all red. I held up my hands to look at them.

"What are you doing?" Randy turned from the open door.

"Looking at the reflection of my hands."

"Brother."

We left Silverton at midnight, and then the next morning I drove back to go to church. Randy wouldn't go, and Mrs. Cummings didn't go because she was sick again. The skeletons hanging on the fence looked like the skeletons of small children. I hadn't heard a coyote all summer.

15

We irrigated all day Monday, and we were going to irrigate all week. We'd loaded and stacked all of the hay. It was the hottest it had been all summer. Thunderstorms had built up every afternoon for two weeks, but it didn't rain on us. Monday I received a letter from my mother, and she said my grandmother hadn't been able to bring herself to redecorate my bedroom. But she'd redecorated and refurnished the spare bedroom if I wanted to move in there. My mother said that she hoped I wasn't disappointed. She said I could still have my old bedroom if I wanted it. I would decide when I got home. I kept thinking what that would be like.

Monday night when I went to bed I lay for a long time and thought about it being the last week. I got excited thinking about going home to Provo, seeing everybody (everybody surprised at how much I'd grown), starting school, starting piano lessons again, buying my new Schwinn, seeing Becky and dating her in a car, being ordained a Priest, and receiving my Duty to God Award. I got so excited I felt like I was going to float off the bed. And I kept thinking about it just so I could feel that way.

Across the dark room Randy's *Playboy* pictures covered the whole wall now. I'd kept talking to Randy about not going to Silverton for the poker game, but he wouldn't listen. I was sure he would lose some of his money; I couldn't do anything about it. Even if I sat beside him at the table, I couldn't stop him from losing his money or drinking beer, so I wasn't going to go, although Frank kept inviting me. I turned my head to look at my wallet on the nightstand. I had three hundred dollars in my wallet. I'd saved my last two checks and cashed them. Sunday evening when we left, I was going to pay my bill. I didn't know how much it would be, but I would pay Staver for everything I'd broken or for things I'd done wrong that had cost Mr. Johnson money. I'd make Staver take the money. I didn't want to owe anybody anything. I fell asleep thinking about that.

All week Frank still kept inviting me to come with Randy and them to the poker game. He said that I didn't have to play; I could just watch if I wanted to.

"No thanks."

"We'll have some girls there afterward for a little going-away party. You're looking forward to that ain't you, lover boy?" Frank turned to Randy. "Look at that mustache."

"Sure."

"Maybe Owen doesn't like a good time." Staver lit his cigarette from the match Frank held.

"I like to enjoy myself." I knew that they didn't want me to come. They hadn't wanted me at Linda's birthday party.

"Stan's going to go. He wouldn't miss it." Staver lifted his head toward Stan and blew out the cigarette smoke. "Would you, Stan?"

"Not this one. I never miss the big poker game."

"Think of it as part of your bonus, kid." Frank laughed until he started to cough and had to turn away to spit.

Saturday I spent most of the day mowing the lawn and weeding Mrs. Cummings' flowers and her vegetable garden. I did the best job I could so it all looked nice. Saturday night Randy took a long time to get ready. I sat at the table turning the pages of an old *National Geographic* from the stack of magazines. Randy combed his hair twice after he put on his T-shirt, which he wore tight, tucked down inside his shorts. Standing in front of the full-length mirror, he tucked in his cowboy shirt and buckled his belt. He sat down and pulled on his new boots, which he'd spent a half an hour polishing again.

"You know what your problem is, cousin?"

"No. What is my problem?" I didn't look up.

"You earned too many merit badges."

"Is that my problem?" I turned another page and looked up.

"Sure." Randy smoothed his hair with his hand. "Hey, we'll double-date in my new car this fall. I'll introduce you to some girls. I know lots of girls, and Lana can line you up too."

"Thanks, but I can get my own dates."

"Sure you can. Becky's a really nice girl."

Randy held both sides of his Stetson and set it on his head, and then he turned and looked at me.

"Cousin, I'm not going to get drunk, and I'm not going to lose all my money. Why should I lose it?"

"You might lose it."

"No, I won't lose it. I've been practicing all summer. I'm as good as some of the guys who will be playing. I just want to play in this one real game. It's the last poker game I'll ever play in. I'm going on a mission." Randy bent his knees a little to see in the mirror to straighten his Stetson. "Why don't you come tonight if you're so worried about me losing everything?"

I looked down at the cover of the *National Geographic*, which was a photograph of stars. The whole issue was about stars and the universe.

"Because I don't want to have to sit there for four or five hours and listen to that kind of language and breathe in the cigarette smoke, and I don't want to watch all of that drinking and gambling. And nobody really wants me to come anyway now, even if they do invite me."

"Well, you sure wouldn't enjoy yourself sitting there watching us play."

I saw Staver drive up in the red pickup. He honked. Randy was going to ride with Staver, and Stan and Frank were driving the blue pickup.

Randy took his wallet out of his pocket and checked his money, and then he walked over to the pictures on the wall. He tipped up his Stetson and kissed one of the girls.

"Wish me luck, baby. Old Randy's playing big time tonight." Randy turned toward me as he straightened his Stetson. "See you, cousin."

I stood up from the table and walked to the screen door.

"Hey, cowboy, you got those fancy Las Vegas boots on?" Frank stuck his head out of the window of the blue pickup.

"You bet."

"Good for you. They're sure fancy."

Randy got in the truck with Staver and closed the door. Staver struck a match and cupped his hands to light his cigarette, his whole face orange. He said something to Randy as he put the match in the ashtray, and they both laughed. Staver shifted, and Randy waved to me as Staver pulled out.

Stan drove by, Frank waving at me.

"See you, Explorer Boy Scout!"

Frank stuck his whole arm out the window to wave, his face at the window. The two pickups went faster down the lane and across the bridge, the two sets of red taillights vanishing into the river trees and the darkness. Tobe didn't chase them. He followed me across the yard to the front of the house. Mrs. Cummings sat rocking on the porch petting her white cat. Mrs. Cummings looked down at where I stood on the sidewalk.

"You didn't go, son?"

"No."

"You could have seen the movie."

"Yes, I could have."

"Randy will lose his money. Most of the summer boys do."

"I hope he doesn't lose all of it."

"Well, those who won't hear have to feel I guess. That never changes." Mrs. Cummings petted the white cat. "I wonder where that fool grey cat is. I haven't seen him all day."

I had found the grey cat down by the canal dead. Some animal had torn it to pieces, but I hadn't told Mrs. Cummings.

"Won't you sit down, son?"

"No, thank you."

"You're all excited about going home tomorrow?"

"Yes, ma'am."

"That's a nice feeling to be going home." She petted the cat. "I won't be going to church in the morning. I'm too tired."

"You'll feel better as soon as you have your operation."

Mrs. Cummings kept petting the cat and looking out toward the dark trees.

I talked with Mrs. Cummings and then left and walked up past the corral and Black Prince, who turned to watch me, and I climbed the ladder to the top of the barn. I walked out to the middle of the roof and sat facing down the valley, my arms folded across the tops of my knees. Tomorrow evening we would leave for home, and after that I wouldn't have to worry about Randy anymore. I watched the valley, but saw no lights. I thought about going home, closed my eyes, rested my forehead on my arms to imagine again how it would be and have that feeling. A great horned owl hooted. I listened, but I couldn't see him. I wouldn't be around Frank and Staver anymore.

At nine o'clock I went back to the cabin. I stood in front. The bunkhouse was dark. Mrs. Cummings' light was out in the house. Only the porch lights burned. I turned and looked down toward the river. The big cottonwood rose up above the other trees. I hadn't been swimming since I'd helped Staver when he dynamited the hole. I'd put minnows in the hole, but I didn't go swimming.

Mrs. Cummings' white chickens roosted on all the lower limbs of the yard trees. I petted Tobe and turned slowly and walked up the steps into the cabin. I was going to put on my pajamas and lie on my bunk and read and wait for Randy.

* * *

Laughter and the noise of the pickups by the cabin porch woke me. A pickup door shut. I raised up on my elbows. I'd fallen asleep with the night lamp on. I still wore my glasses.

"See you, Randy," Staver said. They laughed.

"Hey, lover boy, you forgot your hat. That's twice. Better hang on to that hat. You don't want to always be in such a rush."

Frank and Staver laughed again.

"We'll see you, lover boy. You need to rest up and get your strength back."

They laughed, and the pickups pulled down to the bunkhouse. I sat up. I waited. I heard Randy walk slowly up the steps. Tobe got up from lying by the screen door. I stood up facing the screen door. I saw Randy walk slowly across the porch and stop at the screen door. He lifted his hand and pulled the door open and walked in slowly. His shirt was pulled out all the way around. He held his Stetson, and his hair was all messed up. I knew without even asking him that he'd been drinking beer and lost all his money playing poker.

"We went to Las Vegas."

Randy sat down on his bunk facing the other wall. I stood by my bunk.

"I guess I'd better take a shower."

I didn't say anything. I sat down on the edge of my bunk facing my wall. I just wanted to go home. I heard Randy's boots drop on the floor.

"Ooooh, I lost it all."

Randy's bunk creaked. I waited, but he didn't say anything else.

I turned to look at Randy. He lay on his side curled up, holding his head with his hands. He'd taken off his shirt and Levis. He was already asleep; I listened to his breathing. I looked at Randy. The label and the heavy seams showed on his T-shirt. It was on inside out. So were his shorts. I stood up and walked around to the end of Randy's bunk and looked at him. The label on his undershirt said "Fruit of the Loom." When I raised my eyes I was looking at Randy's *Playboy* calendar and his pictures. I closed my eyes. I knew where Staver had taken Randy and why he'd gotten him to drink beer.

I opened my eyes. I was still looking at the pictures. Staver had been planning all summer to take Randy to Las Vegas to a house of prostitution. Staver did that every summer. And now Randy was changed; his whole life was changed; his body was changed, the way he felt, everything. I should have gone with him. Staver wouldn't have been able to do it if I'd gone with him. I should have helped Randy more all summer. It was partly my fault. I felt very heavy and like I was sick.

Laughter came from the bunkhouse. I turned. My heart beat hard against my chest; I breathed deep. My hands tingled. I walked to the screen door. They laughed again. Tobe stood up, and I pushed the screen door open and walked out onto the porch. They kept laughing. I walked down the four steps. The laughter became louder. I began to walk toward the bunkhouse, and then I walked faster, and then I ran.

I ran up the steps and across the porch. I yanked open the screen door. They sat at the table drinking beer and smoking. Frank leaned forward on his elbows. Staver turned in his chair to look at me and then drank from his beer can and lowered it.

"Owen, you're up a little early for Sunday School."

"Virginia's got on her nice blue pajamas too and no shoes. Must have been in a hurry."

Trembling, fists clenched, I walked up to Staver. Stan and Frank stood up, one on each side of me.

"Why did you have to do it?" I shouted down at Staver. "Why did you?"

Stan and Frank grabbed my arms from behind.

"Now, now, kid. Don't get all excited." Frank leaned close, breathed his beery-tobacco breath into my face, laughing.

"You're kind of upset tonight aren't you, Owen?" Staver's voice was a little slurred.

"Why did you do it?" I shouted down at Staver.

"Do what, Owen?" Staver stood up slowly and pushed back his chair. Staver picked up the willow switch from the table. He tapped his palm with it.

"What you did to Randy!" I could only shout, and my whole body trembled.

"Ah, Careful. Old lover boy was just collecting some of that bonus he had coming. Summer hands always like to do that." Frank laughed.

Staver squinted against the smoke from the cigarette.

"You know what they say about leading a horse to water, Owen."

I lunged at Staver, pulling Stan and Frank with me. All I wanted to do was hit Staver in the mouth with my fist.

"What do you think, Frank, about Owen here? What would your daddy have done if you shouted at him like that?" Staver kept tapping his palm with the switch.

"Why, he would have whipped me raw. That's how he taught me to be polite."

"That's right. Explorers should always be polite."

Frank laughed. "Come on, Careful. Bend a little."

Frank twisted my arm to make me bend, but Stan didn't.

"Maybe we better pull down these pretty blue pajamas first."

"No!" I shouted, "no!" and tried to turn.

I felt Frank's fingers under the band of my shorts and against my back.

Losing all control, I jerked my right arm as hard as I could, hitting Stan with my shoulder at the same time. He slipped and fell, and I brought my fist around hard against Frank's right temple. He stumbled back holding his head and cursing. Fists raised, I turned back toward Staver.

"You been asking for it all summer, Owen." Staver smiled. Slowly he raised his hands, his hands not fists yet.

If I could just hit Staver once, I didn't care how many times he hit me. Just once right in the mouth, as hard as I could for what he'd done to Randy. He was a little drunk; it might slow him down. My whole body tightened and hardened to hit him. I felt very strong. I wasn't scared. I knew I wasn't scared. I took my glasses off and put them on the table.

"Come on, Owen, come on."

"No," Stan said behind me, "don't do it. You don't have to."

Crouching a little, I moved toward Staver. I held my fists and forearms up to protect my face.

Frank kept cursing.

Staver jabbed me with his left hand on the shoulder and chest, but not hard.

"Come on, Killer. You've learned a lot this summer." He kept smiling.

I jabbed at Staver but didn't touch him. I saw the tip of his scar. I pulled back my right hand a little to hit him as hard as I could, and he jabbed me on the right side of my mouth, but not hard. I didn't see him move. He just hit me. I shook my head. I raised my hands, and he hit me again in the same place. I tasted blood. I kept moving toward him around the table. He jabbed me in the chest and stomach. I dropped my hands a little, and he jabbed me hard on the right side of the mouth again. My head snapped back, and I went down on one knee.

I shook my head. I wiped my mouth with my pajama sleeve. I stood up and raised my hands. I moved toward Staver.

I felt him hit me on the mouth again. I didn't see his hand. I went down on both knees. I held onto a chair. I shook my head.

"You keep asking for it, Killer."

I rubbed my pajama sleeve across my mouth. I saw the blood. I tasted it. I saw Staver's boots. I pulled myself up with the chair. I saw Staver, his white T-shirt. I raised my fists and moved toward Staver.

"One more time, Owen."

Staver hit me on the mouth again in the same place hard. My head snapped back again, my knees buckled. I grabbed a chair with both hands as I went down. I knelt there shaking my head and holding onto the chair. I couldn't stand up.

"That's enough, kid." It was Stan. He helped me up.

"I'm okay. I'm okay." I shook my head.

I touched my mouth with my fingers. I looked at the blood.

"Now get out of here."

I looked at Staver. He stood lighting a cigarette. Frank sat in a chair rubbing the side of his head. I picked up my glasses from the table and put them on.

"Get. You're not hurt very much, Killer."

"Come on, kid, you'd better go."

"I'm okay." I could walk. I pulled my arm loose from Stan.

On the wall the pale naked woman climbing the stairs, her candle before her, looked down at me. My whole body trembled now.

"Get."

Trembling I turned and walked to the screen door, pushed it open, and walked across the porch. I tried to keep my body tight against the trembling and the rage. I walked down the steps.

Behind me Staver laughed, and the television went on. I stopped. I stood by the red pickup. The window was rolled down. The .22-250 hanging in the rack glinted in the moonlight.

Staver laughed again above the sound of the television.

Trembling, I opened the pickup door, my whole body inside on fire with rage. Slowly I reached up and took down the rifle. Watching my hands, trembling, I slowly pulled back the bolt. The top shell gleamed in the magazine. I pushed the bolt slowly forward, bringing the shell into the chamber, and slowly clicked the bolt into place. I felt my trembling finger move inside the trigger guard.

"Son, son."

I turned. Mrs. Cummings stood under the trees in her long white nightgown, her white hair down over her shoulders.

"What's wrong son? I heard something."

I looked down at the rifle. Mrs. Cummings couldn't see it because of the pickup.

"Are you all right, son?"

The rifle was heavy.

"You'd better get your rest. You're going home today."

I kept trembling.

"Well, good night then, son."

"Good night."

I watched Mrs. Cummings turn and walk across the yard to the porch, go slowly up the steps and into the house. No lights were on.

I looked down at the rifle in my hands. Trembling, feeling like I would fall down, I pulled the bolt back and pushed the shell back down into the magazine with my thumb. I pushed the bolt forward and put on the safety. I set the rifle back in the rack and closed the pickup door. Above the sound of the television Staver laughed. My whole body kept trembling.

I walked to the cabin. I sat down on my bunk. I put my arms around me and pulled hard to stop the trembling. I lay down on my side holding myself tight, my knees pulled up. I knew that I would have shot Staver if Mrs. Cummings hadn't called to me. My whole body felt different, like it was full of a knowledge I'd never had before, but I didn't know what it was yet. I didn't know what to say if I prayed. I kept thinking about how I would explain and what I would ask for. I closed my eyes and kept holding on tight. Every time I saw Staver lying face-down on the floor, the blood spreading out around him on the linoleum, I pulled tighter. And then I pushed myself off the bunk and knelt down, but I couldn't say any words.

When I woke up it was nine o'clock. I lay curled on my side on the bunk. I saw my dusty feet. I turned to look at Randy. He had pulled his sheet up over his head. I got up and looked at the corner of my mouth in the mirror and touched it. I held up my arm to see the blood on my pajama sleeve. I took a shower. After I'd dried myself with the towel, I stood very still, but my body still felt different, like the trembling and heaviness were deep inside and wouldn't go away. I raised my hands to look at them. I put on my glasses to look at my hands. I kept turning them over to look at them trying to understand what the new knowledge was inside my body.

Randy still had the sheet pulled up over his head when I left for church. As I drove out of the yard the sun hit Brent's window through the trees, making it a mirror.

I waited to take the sacrament. The sacrament song was "I Stand All Amazed." I couldn't sing. Every time I tried, tears would come to my eyes. I repeated under my breath the prayer on the bread with the Priest. I didn't hate Staver. I watched the deacon come down the aisle a row at a time. He started the bread tray down our row. I watched my hands. I took a white piece of bread without any crust. I chewed it very slowly tasting it, keeping it in my mouth until it melted. I repeated the prayer on the water. I looked at the water in the little paper cup as I brought it up to my mouth. I held the water in my mouth, just letting a little go down my throat at a time, feeling it. Afterward as I sat listening to the testimonies, I still felt the trembling deep inside like a hum, and the heaviness.

Driving back to the ranch, I saw a rattlesnake crossing the road, but I didn't try to run over it. I knew that I had changed, but I still didn't have a word for what had happened.

Randy got up to eat dinner. He took a shower, and when he came out of the bathroom he'd shaved off his mustache, which left a white line on his lip. He didn't say anything about what had happened in Las Vegas, and I didn't tell him about the bunkhouse. He didn't ask me about my mouth. I wanted to tell him that I was sorry I hadn't gone with him and that what had happened was partly my fault.

Stan was the only one from the bunkhouse who ate dinner. Mrs. Cummings asked me how I hurt my mouth.

"I bumped into something."

Stan looked down at his plate.

"You'll have to be more careful, son."

"Yes, I guess I will."

"Randy, you look better without that mustache. It made you look different."

"I guess it did."

I helped Mrs. Cummings with the dishes, and she talked about how happy my grandmother and mother would be to see me. "They'll be surprised how much you've grown."

After I finished drying the dishes I went to the cabin and got our dirty sheets and towels and put them by the washer. Mrs. Cummings gave me the clean laundry she'd done for me and Randy so we wouldn't be taking dirty clothes home.

"You like things clean, don't you, son?"

"Yes."

I looked up at the pictures above the table. In every picture Jesus wore a white robe that was whiter than anything else in the picture.

Randy and I packed and put our bags out on the porch. We wore our cowboy clothes. Randy helped me straighten up the cabin. He'd taken down all of his *Playboy* pictures and the calendar and put them in the trash. We still had time before we left, so I walked down to the old bridge. Tobe went with me. I stood by a tree watching the water. A big hatch of mayflies was on, and the big trout was feeding. He didn't jump or swirl, but just sucked the larvae, concentric circles moving out from where he fed. I knew that it was the big trout.

Walking back up the lane, I saw Randy sitting in a chair facing the late afternoon sun. I walked across the yard and up on the cabin porch. His eyes were closed, his face held up to the sun. He was trying to tan the white line under his nose where he'd shaved off his mustache. I walked into the cabin.

Stan pulled up in the blue pickup, got out, and put our bags in. I turned at the door to look back before I closed it. The spiral of flypaper hung down by the light cord over the table, flies stuck on it. I hadn't taken it down. I closed the door.

Randy put the chair back up on the porch, and, Tobe ahead of us, we walked over to the house to say goodbye to Mrs. Cummings. She came out on the porch carrying a shoe box. Holding onto the railing, she walked slowly down the steps. Her white cat sat on the other railing.

"Here's some cookies for you boys to eat. I phoned Helen, and she's going to fix you a nice lunch to take with you tomorrow. It's been nice having you boys this summer. You're good boys. I guess you've said goodbye to Frank and Staver."

"Yes, last night."

Sitting in the pickup, Stan reached up to his shirt pocket for his cigarettes.

She hugged Randy and then turned and hugged me, and held my hands.

"Thank you for all your help, Mrs. Cummings."

"It was a pleasure, son. All a pleasure, and thank you." She looked down. "They're good hands, son. Always see that they do the Lord's will."

"I'll try. I hope you feel better."

"I've got the Lord, son, so nothing's going to happen that he can't help me with. Nothing ever has."

I kissed Mrs. Cummings on the cheek. I wanted to tell her I loved her.

"Thank you, son." She squeezed my hands and let them go. "Your folks will see a real change in you when you get home."

Stan started the engine. Randy was already in the pickup.

Tobe put his paws up on me, and I knelt down and hugged him.

"Good boy, Tobe. Good dog."

I looked up. Across the yard Staver walked out of the bunkhouse. He was reaching out to strike a match on the post to light his cigarette when he saw me looking at him. He lowered his arm. He didn't strike the match. He watched me.

Turning, I got in the pickup and closed the door. I waved to Mrs. Cummings as we pulled away.

"Goodbye, goodbye, son. Say hello to Helen and Mrs. Johnson. God bless you."

I waved. Tobe stood by Mrs. Cummings. He didn't run ahead of the pickup. In the big side-view mirror I saw Staver still standing on the bunkhouse porch. He lit his cigarette. We drove down into the river trees and across the bridge. When we came out on the road I watched the big cottonwood against the evening sky. The white no-trespassing signs flashed in the grey darkness, the hanging bodies dark on the fences. I hadn't heard one coyote all summer. Stan turned on his headlights. It got dark earlier now. A jackrabbit ran across the road. The doors on all the fire sheds were closed. Randy slid down in his seat and pulled his Stetson down over his eyes. The campgrounds were full of Labor Day campers. Kids waved to us as we passed. I waved back. In the corner of a pasture four jackrabbits stood watching us. Across the sagebrush flat was the Indian battle monument, a dark rectangle now. I still had the heavy feeling; I still couldn't find the words for what I knew.

We drove into Silverton. I watched as we passed Bob's Grocery, the World Hotel, Thurman's, and the Volcano Casino. Stan drove through Silverton. I turned, and Randy sat up.

"Staver said to drive you two on into Vegas." Stan reached in his shirt pocket. "He gave me your checks. You got your bonuses."

"I can sure use that extra hundred bucks."

Randy took out his wallet. He folded the check and put it in the empty bill pocket and put his wallet back. He opened the box of cookies and took three. Stan reached over and took a handful.

I held my check. It didn't have a bill attached charging me for all of my mistakes. No money had been deducted. Feeling the check in my hand I watched the desert. We passed a National Guard convoy.

The Johnson house stood on a hill above Las Vegas. Helen came out but had to go back when the phone rang. Mr. Johnson was already asleep. Randy walked around to the back to look at the swimming pool.

"You didn't deserve that last night, kid," Stan said. "We just had too much to drink. You did a good job this summer. Staver don't have any complaint coming."

"It's okay," I said.

"Well, I guess things like that happen sometimes."

"Yes, I guess they do," I said. I held out my hand, and Stan shook it.

After Stan left we had supper and then sat on the deck looking down at all the lights of Las Vegas.

"What do you think, Randy?" Helen asked.

"Well, it's sure different than Provo."

"I suppose it is. Sorry we don't have time for a big tour."

"That's okay."

Helen turned to me.

"How's Mrs. Cummings?"

"Not very well."

"She's not going to have the operation."

I looked out across Las Vegas toward the unlit hills.

"She's very brave about everything, Owen."

"Yes, she is."

Randy stayed on the deck, and Helen and I went inside to look at photo albums of the ranch. She had a whole album of pictures of Brent.

"I was twelve when he was killed in Korea." She smiled and reached up to push back her hair. "My mother kept all of his letters. I read them sometimes. I loved him, admired him so much. I hated to see him go in the army. I didn't see how he could do it."

"I guess it was easier for him being drafted with Staver?"

Helen looked down at the pictures in the album. She didn't say anything, and then she looked up.

"Staver was drafted and Brent volunteered for the draft to be with him."

"Brent volunteered?"

"Yes. He wanted to be with Staver. He never told Dad because he didn't want to upset him. I was the only one he told. Staver knew of course. Nobody in Silverton knew; the induction center was in Las Vegas. Brent didn't want people to know. Staver was his friend."

"He died because of Staver."

"Well, he went to Korea because Staver was his best friend. But that was the way Brent was. They had been friends all their lives. I don't think Staver's ever really been able to accept what Brent did. It was too much."

Helen stood up from the sofa and walked over to a small table under a large picture of Brent hanging on the wall. I'd seen the picture from the other end of the room when we went out on the deck to eat supper.

"This is Brent's Medal of Honor."

I stood up and walked over.

The open blue velvet box lay under a glass case with the citation. I read the citation.

"It's a beautiful medal."

Helen smiled.

"Yes it is, Owen. But you have to let go, don't you. You can't live in the past."

"I guess you can't."

"Staver's loan went through. Maybe he will marry Alice and raise a family on the ranch."

"I hope he does."

"I do too."

"It's a beautiful ranch."

"Yes, it is. I've always loved it." Helen turned and walked over to the window to look down at Las Vegas. "Steve and I have started the missionary discussions, Owen."

"I'm glad."

Helen didn't turn around.

"I have always believed I would see Brent again, and our mother. That's one of the beautiful things the Church teaches, isn't it."

"Yes."

I watched Helen. She turned and looked at me.

"You're probably tired. I hope that you and Randy don't mind sharing a bedroom. We only have one extra room."

"That's fine."

"What did you do to your mouth?"

"Nothing very much."

"I'll get you some salve for it."

Randy was already in bed when I was ready.

"Do you mind if I say my prayers?"

"No, go ahead. I'll turn off the light." Randy turned off the night lamp.

"Do you want to kneel down with me?"

"Sure, why not."

I prayed for both of us.

Afterward Randy didn't say anything. He got in bed and faced the wall. I said good night, and he said good night.

I lay down. I listened to Randy breathing. I thought about Brent dying because of Staver and of what Staver must feel. I kept thinking about that, and about Helen wanting Staver to have the ranch.

In the morning we had breakfast and then went in to say hello to Mr. Johnson in his bedroom, and then we went swimming in the pool. Helen's fiance Steve came over, and Helen introduced us. After lunch Helen went in the house, and Randy walked out on the deck to sit in the sun and look at Las Vegas, so Steve and I were alone.

"Helen thinks that you're a fine person, Owen."

"Thank you. I guess I look a little like Brent."

"Yes, but it's more than that, and she's a good judge of character. If you hadn't come out this summer, we wouldn't be listening to the missionaries."

"Helen told me that you were."

"Helen thinks a family needs a religion. I know a lot of Mormons here in Las Vegas. Many of them are fine people and have very fine families."

"But not all of them."

"No, not all of them."

"That wouldn't be human would it?"

"No, I guess not."

After lunch Steve stayed with Mr. Johnson, and Helen drove us down to the bus station. Randy walked over to the magazine stand, but he didn't pick any up.

"Have you got your ticket, Owen?"

"Yes. Uncle Mark bought us round-trip tickets."

Helen opened her purse and handed me a small blue velvet jeweler's box.

"It's a present. I gave them to Brent his last Christmas when he was on furlough. He never got to wear them. I'd like you to have them."

I opened the box.

"Thank you." It was a set of gold cuff links.

"I saved up a whole year to buy them."

"Thank you." I didn't know what else to say.

I kissed her on the cheek, and she smiled.

"I like your cowboy outfit."

"I guess I'm sort of a cowboy now."

"I guess you are. You've changed."

She looked at me.

"I'll write you about Mrs. Cummings."

"Thank you."

"I'll send you a wedding invitation, too."

"I'll look forward to it."

"We're going to be married at Christmas."

"That's a nice time."

I closed the blue velvet box, unzipped the bag I was carrying, and put it in.

"Thank you again. I'll keep them all my life."

"You're welcome, Owen."

Helen stood and waved to us as the bus backed out, and I waved back until she disappeared. We sat in front behind the driver. Randy talked across the aisle to a girl from Mesquite, and then he moved over to sit with her. I knew what she would say if I asked her about Mr. Wayne, the big rancher from Mesquite who talked to me all the way from Mesquite to Las Vegas, so I didn't ask her.

After Mesquite we crossed the Utah border. There were speed limit signs, but the desert didn't change. Ravens and magpies fed on dead rabbits along the road. In St. George Randy phoned Lana to tell her what time he would be at her house. They were going to go look at new Volkswagens and sports cars.

In Nephi a woman who had been sitting next to me got off and left her *Life* magazine on the seat. I picked it up and turned the pages. There was a section on famous war photographs. One full page was of a young German soldier holding a rifle and looking down from a guard tower at the people in a concentration camp. I looked at him. The rifle didn't have a scope sight. I closed the *Life* and put it down. I looked at my hands, and then I looked at Randy and the other people in the bus whose faces I could see. I knew that I wasn't any different from them, and I knew that was part of what I'd learned. But there was something else, something even more important, that I didn't have a word for yet. But I would. It was a word like "prayer," or "faith," or "love." I looked out the window. The bus passed the Utah County sign.

It was evening when we drove to the top of the Ironton Hill, and I saw the trees of Provo. We passed the Provo Cemetery, and I turned to watch it out of sight, the headstones white under the black spruces.

The bus turned off Third South on First East and then turned on First South to go into the station. My heart beat hard. I saw my mother and grandmother waving. I waved. I walked down the steps behind Randy.

"Oh, son, son." I hugged my mother, and she kissed me and kept holding me at arm's length to look at me, and then she kissed me again. "I can't believe it. I just can't believe it. You must have gained twenty pounds. You're taller. You look wonderful." She kept laughing, her eyes full of tears, but not crying. "Hasn't he grown, Mother? And he's so tanned."

My grandmother hugged me and then stood holding my hands.

"It's so nice to have you home again safe, Owen. We missed you every day. What did you do to your mouth, son?"

"Nothing. It's fine."

"Look at you. I'll have to change all the clothes I bought for a size larger. And I'll have to make an appointment for you with the dermatologist."

"I don't think it will help."

Uncle Mark shook my hand.

"Well, Cowboy, it looks like you two survived. I didn't hear any complaints from Staver. You both did a good job. And you look like you might be able to try out for the wrestling team, Owen. You'll have to talk to the coach, Randy."

"Sure."

Uncle Mark held Randy out a set of car keys. "Here you are, son. It's parked over there. Uncle Mark nodded his head. "Congratulations."

"Dad, the red Triumph?"

"Yes, the Triumph. It's been a very good summer for real estate, so you got something a little nicer."

"Dad, Dad, that's great, that's great!" Randy hugged Uncle Mark. Thanks a million. Gee, Mom, a real Triumph!" He hugged Aunt Susan and his two little sisters.

He ran over to his car and got in. Everybody told him how nice it was.

"Yours is over there by the wall, Owen."

"My what?"

"Your welcome-home present."

A new bicycle stood by the station wall.

"It's an Avanti," I said.

"That's what you've always wanted, isn't it?"

"Yes."

"Well, it's yours. Think of it as a late birthday present."

My mother touched my arm. "It's a wonderful gift, son."

"Yes, it is, Mom."

I walked over to the Avanti.

"Do you like the color?" Uncle Mark stood behind me.

It was red.

"Yes, I do. Thank you very much."

I put my hands on the handlebars and pushed up the kickstand. The whole bicycle gleamed.

Randy came over and told me how great my bicycle was, and then he said goodbye to everybody and drove off to see Lana.

Uncle Mark watched him.

"We won't see Randy until midnight probably. Well, that's what it's for I guess. We didn't even have time to tell him about the supper."

He turned to me.

"Like it?"

"I don't deserve it, Uncle Mark."

"Sure you do. You and Randy worked hard and had a good summer. Enjoy it."

Everybody congratulated me. I shook Uncle Mark's hand.

"Your grandmother has a nice welcome-home supper fixed for everybody, son." Mom put her hand on my grandmother's arm.

"You better go for a ride on that thing first and try it out." Uncle Mark smiled. "Haven't you got a girl here in the ward you can go show it to?"

"Yes."

"What's her name?"

"Becky Stewart."

"Well, go show it to Becky Stewart. He's got time before we eat, hasn't he?"

"Yes."

"Well, go. That's what the salesman said the name meant. Go."

"Thanks, Uncle Mark." I shook his hand again.

"My pleasure. You earned it."

"Take my hat home will you, Mom?" I kissed her and my grandmother.

I pushed off and then turned to wave. Everybody waved. The Avanti was light. It was beautiful. I went out on University Avenue, shifted, went faster, thinking about seeing Becky. The Avanti was smooth, perfect. I went faster, feeling the coolness, the smooth beautiful perfect Avanti, and my hair lifting. I wondered what Becky would say when she saw me. I looked up. The setting sun made all the mountains red, the clouds red, the red reflected in the store windows, red touching the streets. I shifted again, went faster, feeling the Avanti, and how much stronger I was.